To
J. McNEILL

The Shadow of that hyddeous strength
Sax myle and more it is of length.

SIR DAVID LINDSAY: from *Ane Dialog*
(describing the Tower of Babel)

Contents

Preface

I have called this a fairy-tale in the hope that no one who dislikes fantasy may be misled by the first two chapters into reading further, and then complain of his disappointment. If you ask why – intending to write about magicians, devils, pantomime animals and planetary angels – I nevertheless begin with such hum-drum scenes and persons, I reply that I am following the traditional fairy-tale. We do not always notice its method, because the cottages, castles, woodcutters and petty kings with which a fairy-tale opens have become for us as remote as the witches and ogres to which it proceeds. But they were not remote at all to the men who made and first enjoyed the stories. They were, indeed, more realistic and commonplace than Bracton College is to me: for many German peasants had actually met cruel stepmothers, whereas I have never, in any university, come across a college like Bracton. This is a 'tall story' about devilry, though it has behind it a serious 'point' which I have tried to make in my *Abolition of Man*. In the story, the outer rim of that devilry had to be shown touching the life of some ordinary and respectable profession. I selected my own profession, not, of course, because I think fellows of colleges more likely to be thus corrupted than anyone else, but because my own is the only profession I know well enough to write about. A very small university is imagined because that has certain conveniences for fiction. Edgestow has no resemblance, save for its smallness, to Durham – a university with which the only connection I have had was entirely pleasant.

I believe that one of the central ideas of this tale came into my head from conversations I had with a scientific colleague, some time before I met a rather similar suggestion in the works of Mr Olaf Stapledon. If I am mistaken in this, Mr Stapledon is so rich in invention that he can well afford to lend, and I admire his invention (though not his philosophy) so much that I should feel no shame to borrow.

Those who would like to learn further about Numinor and the True West must (alas!) await the publication of much that still exists only in the MSS of my friend, Professor J. R. R. Tolkien.

The period of this story is vaguely 'after the war'. It concludes the Trilogy of which *Out of the Silent Planet* was the first part, and *Perelandra* the second, but can be read on its own.

C. S. Lewis

Magdalen College,
    Oxford.
Christmas Eve, 1943.

1

Sale of College Property

'Matrimony was ordained, thirdly,' said Jane Studdock to herself, 'for the mutual society, help, and comfort that the one ought to have of the other.' She had not been to church since her schooldays until she went there six months ago to be married, and the words of the service had stuck in her mind.

Through the open door she could see the tiny kitchen of the flat and hear the loud, ungentle tick tick of the clock. She had just left the kitchen and knew how tidy it was. The breakfast things were washed up, the tea towels were hanging above the stove, and the floor was mopped. The beds were made and the rooms 'done'. She had just returned from the only shopping she need do that day, and it was still a minute before eleven. Except for getting her own lunch and tea, there was nothing that had to be done till six o'clock, even supposing that Mark was really coming home for dinner. But there was a College Meeting today. Almost certainly Mark would ring up about teatime to say that the meeting was taking longer than he had expected and that he would have to dine in College. The hours before her were as empty as the flat. The sun shone and the clock ticked.

'Mutual society, help, and comfort,' said Jane bitterly. In reality marriage had proved to be the door out of a world of work and comradeship and laughter and innumerable things to do, into something like solitary confinement. For some years before their marriage she had never seen so little of Mark as she had done in the last six months. Even when he was at home he hardly ever talked. He was always either sleepy or intellectually preoccupied.

While they had been friends, and later when they were lovers, life itself had seemed too short for all they had to say to each other. But now ... why had he married her? Was he still in love? If so, 'being in love' must mean totally different things to men and women. Was it the crude truth that all the endless talks which had seemed to her, before they were married, the very medium of love itself, had never been to him more than a preliminary?

'Here I am, starting to waste another morning, mooning,' said Jane to herself sharply. 'I *must* do some work.' By work she meant her doctorate thesis on Donne. She had always intended to continue her own career as a scholar after she was married: that was one of the reasons why they were to have no children, at any rate for a long time yet. Jane was not perhaps a very original thinker and her plan had been to lay great stress on Donne's 'triumphant vindication of the body'. She still believed that if she got out all her notebooks and editions and really sat down to the job, she could force herself back into her lost enthusiasm for the subject. But before she did so – perhaps in order to put off the moment of beginning – she turned over a newspaper which was lying on the table and glanced at a picture on the back page.

The moment she saw the picture, she remembered her dream. She remembered not only the dream but the measureless time after she had crept out of bed and sat waiting for the first hint of morning, afraid to put on the light for fear Mark should wake up and fuss, yet feeling offended by the sound of his regular breathing. He was an excellent sleeper. Only one thing ever seemed able to keep him awake after he had gone to bed, and even that did not keep him awake for long.

The terror of this dream, like the terror of most dreams, evaporates in the telling, but it must be set down for the sake of what came afterwards.

She had begun by dreaming simply of a face. It was a foreign-looking face, bearded and rather yellow, with a hooked nose. Its expression was frightening because it was frightened. The mouth sagged open and the eyes stared as she had seen other men's eyes stare for a second or two when some sudden shock had occurred. But this face seemed to be meeting a shock that lasted for hours. Then gradually she became aware of more. The face belonged to a man who was sitting hunched up in one corner of a little square room with white-washed walls – waiting, she thought, for those who had him in their power, to come in and do something horrible to him. At last the door was opened and a rather good-looking man with a pointed grey beard came in. The prisoner seemed to recognise him as an old acquaintance, and they sat down together and began to talk. In all the dreams which Jane had hitherto dreamed, one either understood what the dream-people were saying or else one did not hear it. But in this dream – and that helped to make its extraordinary realism – the conversation was in French and Jane understood bits of it, but by no means all, just as she would have done in real life. The visitor was telling the prisoner something which he apparently intended him to regard as good news. And the prisoner at first looked up with a gleam of hope in his eye and said, '*Tiens ... ah ... ça marche*'; but then he wavered and changed his mind. The visitor continued in a low, fluent voice to press his point. He was a good-looking man in his rather cold way, but he wore pince-nez and these kept on catching the light so as to make his eyes invisible. This, combined with the almost unnatural perfection of his teeth, somehow gave Jane a disagreeable impression. And this was increased by the growing distress, and finally the terror, of the prisoner. She could not make out what it was that the visitor was proposing to him, but she did discover that the prisoner was under sentence of death. Whatever the visitor was offering him was something that frightened him more than that. At this point the dream abandoned all pretence to realism and became ordinary nightmare. The visitor, adjusting his pince-nez and still smiling his cold smile, seized the prisoner's head between his two hands. He gave it a sharp turn – just as Jane had last summer seen men give a sharp turn to the helmet on a diver's head. The visitor unscrewed the prisoner's head and took it away. Then all became confused. The Head was still the centre of the dream but it was quite a different head now – a head with a flowing white beard all covered with earth. It belonged to an old man whom some people were digging up in a kind of churchyard – a sort of ancient British, druidical kind of man, in a long mantle. Jane didn't mind this much at first because she thought it was a corpse. Then suddenly she noticed that this ancient thing was coming to life. 'Look out!' she cried in her dream. 'He's alive. Stop! Stop! You're waking him.' But they did not stop. The old, buried man sat up and began talking in something that sounded vaguely like Spanish. And this for some reason frightened Jane so badly that she woke up.

That was the dream – no worse, if also no better, than many another nightmare. But it was not the mere memory of a nightmare that made the sitting room of the flat swim before Jane's eyes and caused her to sit down quickly for fear she should fall. The trouble was elsewhere. There, on the back page of the newspaper, was the Head she had seen in the nightmare: the first head (if there had been two of them) – the head of the Prisoner. With extreme reluctance, she took up the paper. EXECUTION OF ALCASAN was the headline, and beneath it SCIENTIST BLUEBEARD GOES TO GUILLOTINE. She remembered having vaguely followed the case. Alcasan was a distinguished radiologist in a neighbouring country – an Arab by descent, they said – who had cut short an otherwise brilliant career by poisoning his wife. So that was the origin of her dream. She must have looked at this photo in the paper – the man certainly had a very unpleasant face – before going to bed. But no: that couldn't be it. It was this morning's paper. But, of course, there must have been some earlier picture which she had seen and forgotten – probably weeks ago when the trial began. It was silly to have let it give her such a turn. And now for Donne. Let's see, where were we? The ambiguous passage at the end of *Love's Alchymie*,

> *Hope not for minde in women; at their best*
> *Sweetnesse and wit, they are but Mummy possest.*

4

'Hope not for mind in women.' Did any man really *want* mind in women? But that wasn't the point. 'I *must* get back my power of concentrating,' said Jane; and then, 'was there a previous picture of Alcasan? Supposing …'

Five minutes later she swept all her books away, went to the mirror, put on her hat, and went out. She was not quite sure where she was going. Anywhere, to be out of that room, that flat, that whole house.

◆ ○ ◆

Mark, himself, meanwhile, was walking down to Bracton College, and thinking of a very different matter. He did not notice at all the morning beauty of the little street that led him from the sandy hillside suburb where he and Jane lived down into the central and academic part of Edgestow.

Though I am Oxford-bred and very fond of Cambridge, I think that Edgestow is more beautiful than either. For one thing it is so small. No maker of cars or sausages or marmalades has yet come to industrialise the country town which is the setting of the University, and the University itself is tiny. Apart from Bracton and from the nineteenth-century women's college beyond the railway, there are only two colleges: Northumberland which stands below Bracton on the river Wynd, and Duke's opposite the Abbey. Bracton takes no undergraduates. It was founded in 1300 for the support of ten learned men whose duties were to pray for the soul of Henry de Bracton and to study the laws of England. The number of Fellows has gradually increased to forty, of whom only six (apart from the Bacon Professor) now study Law and of whom none, perhaps, prays for the soul of Bracton. Mark Studdock was himself a Sociologist and had been elected to a fellowship in that subject five years ago. He was beginning to find his feet. If he had felt any doubt on that point (which he did not) it would have been laid to rest when he found himself meeting Curry just outside the Post Office and seen how natural Curry found it that they should walk to College together and discuss the agenda for the meeting. Curry was the Sub-Warden of Bracton.

'Yes,' said Curry, 'it will take the hell of a time. Probably go on after dinner. We shall have all the obstructionists wasting time as hard as they can. But luckily that's the worst they can do.'

You would never have guessed from the tone of Studdock's reply what intense pleasure he derived from Curry's use of the pronoun 'we'. So very recently he had been an outsider, watching the proceedings of what he then called 'Curry and his gang' with awe and with little understanding, and making at College meetings short, nervous speeches which never influenced the course of events. Now he was inside and 'Curry and his gang' had become 'we' or 'the Progressive Element in College'. It had all happened quite suddenly and was still sweet in the mouth.

'You think it'll go through, then?' said Studdock.

'Sure to,' said Curry. 'We've got the Warden, and the Bursar, and all the chemical and bio-chemical people for a start. I've tackled Pelham and Ted and they're sound. I've made Sancho believe that he sees the point and that he's in favour of it. Bill the Blizzard will probably do something pretty devastating but he's bound to side with us if it comes to a vote. Besides, I haven't yet told you. Dick's going to be there. He came up in time for dinner last night and got busy at once.'

Studdock's mind darted hither and thither in search of some safe way to conceal the fact that he did not know who Dick was. In the nick of time he remembered a very obscure colleague whose Christian name was Richard.

'Telford?' said Studdock in a puzzled voice. He knew very well that Telford could not be the Dick that Curry meant and therefore threw a slightly whimsical and ironical tone into his question.

'Good Lord! Telford!!' said Curry with a laugh. 'No. I mean Lord Feverstone – Dick Devine as he used to be.'

'I *was* a little baffled by the idea of Telford,' said Studdock, joining in the laugh. 'I'm glad Feverstone is coming. I've never met him, you know.'

'Oh, but you must,' said Curry. 'Look here, come and dine in my rooms tonight. I've asked him.'

'I should like to very much,' said Studdock quite truly. And then, after a pause, 'By the way, I suppose Feverstone's own position is quite secure?'

'How do you mean?' asked Curry.

'Well, there was some talk, if you remember, as to whether someone who was away quite so much could go on holding a fellowship.'

'Oh, you mean Glossop and all that ramp. Nothing will come of that. Didn't you think it absolute blah?'

'As between ourselves, yes. But I confess if I were put up to explain *in public* exactly why a man who is nearly always in London should go on being a Fellow of Bracton, I shouldn't find it altogether easy. The real reasons are the sort that Watson would call imponderables.'

'I don't agree. I shouldn't have the least objection to explaining the real reasons in public. Isn't it important for a college like this to have influential connections with the outer world? It's not in the least impossible that Dick will be in the next Cabinet. Even already Dick in London has been a damn sight more use to the College than Glossop and half a dozen others of that sort have been by sitting here all their lives.'

'Yes. Of course, that's the real point. It would be a little difficult to put in that form at a College meeting, though!'

'There's one thing,' said Curry in a slightly less intimate tone, 'that perhaps you ought to know about Dick.'

'What's that?'

'He got you your fellowship.'

Mark was silent. He did not like things which reminded him that he had once been not only outside the Progressive Element but even outside the College. He did not always like Curry either. His pleasure in being with him was not that sort of pleasure.

'Yes,' said Curry. 'Denniston was your chief rival. Between ourselves, a good many people liked his papers better than yours. It was Dick who insisted all through that you were the sort of man we really wanted. He went around to Duke's and ferreted out all about you. He took the line that the one thing to consider is the type of man we need, and be damned to paper qualifications. And I must say he turned out to be right.'

'Very kind of you,' said Studdock, with a little mock bow. He was surprised at the turn the conversation had taken. It was an old rule at Bracton, as presumably in most colleges, that one never mentioned in the presence of a man the circumstances of his own election, and Studdock had not realised till now that this also was one of the traditions the Progressive Element was prepared to scrap. It had also never occurred to him that his own election had depended on anything but the excellence of his work in the fellowship examination: still less that it had been so narrow a thing. He was so accustomed to his position by now that this thought gave him the same curious sensation which a man has when he discovers that his father once very nearly married a different woman.

'Yes,' continued Curry, pursuing another train of thought. 'One sees now that Denniston would never have done. Most emphatically not. A brilliant man at that time, of course, but he seems to have gone quite off the rails since then with all his Distributivism and what not. They tell me he's likely to end up in a monastery.'

'He's no fool, all the same,' said Studdock.

'I'm glad you're going to meet Dick,' said Curry. 'We haven't time now, but there's one thing about him I wanted to discuss with you.'

Studdock looked enquiringly at him.

'James and I and one or two others,' said Curry in a somewhat lower voice, 'have been thinking he ought to be the new Warden. But here we are.'

'It's not yet twelve,' said Studdock. 'What about popping into the Bristol for a drink?'

Into the Bristol they accordingly went. It would not have been easy to preserve the atmosphere in which the Progressive Element operated without a good many of these little courtesies. This weighed harder on Studdock than on Curry who was unmarried and had a Sub-Warden's stipend. But the Bristol was a very pleasant place. Studdock brought a double whiskey for his companion and half a pint of beer for himself.

The only time I was a guest at Bracton I persuaded my host to let me into the Wood and leave me there alone for an hour. He apologised for locking me in.

Very few people were allowed into Bragdon Wood. The gate was by Inigo Jones and was the only entry: a high wall enclosed the Wood, which was perhaps a quarter of a mile broad and a mile from east to west. If you came in from the street and went through the College to reach it, the sense of gradual penetration into a holy of holies was very strong. First you went through the Newton quadrangle which is dry and gravelly; florid, but beautiful, Gregorian buildings look down upon it. Next you must enter a cool tunnel-like passage, nearly dark at midday unless either the door into Hall should be open on your right or the buttery hatch on your left, giving you a glimpse of indoor daylight falling on panels, and a whiff of the smell of fresh bread. When you emerged from this tunnel you would find yourself in the medieval College: in the cloister of the much smaller quadrangle called Republic. The grass here looks very green after the aridity of Newton and the very stone of the buttresses that rise from it gives the impression of being soft and alive. Chapel is not far off: the hoarse, heavy noise of the works of a great and old clock comes to you from somewhere overhead. You went along this cloister, past slabs and urns and busts that commemorate dead Bractonians, and then down shallow steps into the full daylight of the quadrangle called Lady Alice. The buildings to your left and right were seventeenth-century work: humble, almost domestic in character, with dormer windows, mossy and grey-tiled. You were in a sweet, Protestant world. You found yourself, perhaps, thinking of Bunyan or of Walton's *Lives*. There were no buildings straight ahead on the fourth side of Lady Alice: only a row of elms and a wall: and here first one became aware of the sound of running water and the cooing of wood pigeons. The street was so far off by now that there were no other noises. In the wall there was a door. It led you into a covered gallery pierced with narrow windows on either side. Looking out through these, you discovered that you were crossing a bridge and the dark brown dimpled Wynd was flowing under you. Now you were very near your goal. A wicket at the far end of the bridge brought you out on the Fellows' bowling green, and across that you saw the high wall of the Wood, and through the Inigo Jones gate you caught a glimpse of sunlit green and deep shadows.

I suppose the mere fact of being walled in gave the Wood part of its peculiar quality, for when a thing is enclosed, the mind does not willingly regard it as common. As I went forward over the quiet turf I had the sense of being received. The trees were just so wide apart that one saw uninterrupted foliage in the distance but the place where one stood seemed always to be a clearing; surrounded by a world of shadows, one walked in mild sunshine. Except for the sheep whose nibbling kept the grass so short and who sometimes raised their long, foolish faces to stare at me, I was quite alone; and it felt more like the loneliness of a very large room in a deserted house than like any ordinary solitude out of doors. I remember thinking, 'This is the sort of place which, as a child, one would have been rather afraid of or else would have liked very much indeed.' A moment later I thought, 'But when alone – really alone – everyone is a child: or no one?' Youth and age touch only the surface of our lives.

Half a mile is a short walk. Yet it seemed a long time before I came to the centre of the Wood. I knew it was the centre, for there was the thing I had chiefly come to see. It was a well: a well with steps going down to it and the remains of an ancient pavement about it. It was very imperfect now. I did not step on it, but I lay down in the grass and touched it with my fingers. For this was the heart of Bracton or Bragdon Wood: out of this all the legends had come and on this, I suspected, the very existence of the College had originally depended. The archaeologists were agreed that the masonry was very late British-Roman work, done on the eve of the Anglo-Saxon invasion. How Bragdon the wood was connected with Bracton the lawyer was a mystery, but I fancy myself that the Bracton family had availed themselves of an accidental similarity in the names to believe, or make believe, that they had something to do with it. Certainly, if all that was told were true, or even half of it, the Wood was older than the Bractons. I suppose no one now would attach much importance to Strabo's *Balachthon* though it had led a sixteenth-century Warden of the College to say that 'We know not by ancientest report of any Britain without Bragdon.' But the medieval song takes us back to the fourteenth century.

In Bragdon bricht this ende dai
Herde ich Merlin ther he lai
Singende woo and welawai.

It is good enough evidence that the well with the British-Roman pavment was already 'Merlin's Well', though the name is not found till Queen Elizabeth's reign when good Warden Shovel surrounded the Wood with a wall 'for the taking away of all profane and heathenish superstitions and the deterring of the vulgar sort from all wakes, may games, dancings, mummings, and baking of Morgan's bread, heretofore used about the fountain called in vanity Merlin's Well, and utterly to be renounced and abominated as a gallimaufrey of papistry, gentilism, lewdness and dunsicall folly'. Not that the College had by this action renounced its own interest in the place. Old Dr Shovel, who lived to be nearly a hundred, can scarcely have been cold in his grave when one of Cromwell's Major Generals, conceiving it his business to destroy 'the groves and the high places', sent a few troopers with power to impress the country people for this pious work. The scheme came to nothing in the end; but there had been a bicker between the College and the troopers in the heart of Bragdon, and the fabulously learned and saintly Richard Crowe had been killed by a musket-ball on the very steps of the Well. He would be a brave man who would accuse Crowe either of popery or 'gentilism'; yet the story is that his last words had been, 'Marry, Sirs, if Merlin who was the Devil's son was a true King's man as ever ate bread, is it not a shame that you, being but the sons of bitches, must be rebels and regicides?' And always, through all changes, every Warden of Bracton, on the day of his election, had drunk a ceremonial draught of water from Merlin's Well in the great cup which, both for its antiquity and beauty, was the greatest of the Bracton treasures.

All of this I thought of, lying beside Merlin's Well, beside the well which must certainly date from Merlin's time if there had ever been a real Merlin: lying where Sir Kenelm Digby had lain all one summer night and seen a certain strange appearance: where Collins the poet had lain, and where George the Third had cried: where the brilliant and much-loved Nathaniel Fox had composed the famous poem three weeks before he was killed in France. The air was so still and the billows of foliage so heavy above me, that I fell asleep. I was wakened by my friend hallooing to me from a long way off.

◆ ○ ◆

The most controversial business before the College Meeting was the question of selling Bragdon Wood. The purchaser was the NICE, the National Institute of Co-ordinated Experiments. They wanted a site for the building which would worthily house this remarkable organisation. The NICE was the first-fruits of that constructive fusion between the state and the laboratory on which so many thoughtful people base their hopes of a better world. It was to be free from almost all the tiresome restraints – 'red tape' was the word its supporters used – which have hitherto hampered research in this country. It was also largely free from the restraints of economy, for, as it was argued, a nation which can spend so many millions a day on a war can surely afford a few millions a month on productive research in peacetime. The building proposed for it was one which would make a quite noticeable addition to the skyline of New York, the staff was to be enormous, and their salaries princely. Persistent pressure and endless diplomacy on the part of the Senate of Edgestow had lured the new Institute away from Oxford, from Cambridge, from London. It had thought of all these in turn as possible scenes for its labours. At times the Progressive Element in Edgestow had almost despaired. But success was now practically certain. If the NICE could get the necessary land, it would come to Edgestow. And once it came, then, as everyone felt, things would at last begin to move. Curry had even expressed a doubt whether, eventually, Oxford and Cambridge could survive as major universities at all.

Three years ago, if Mark Studdock had come to a College Meeting at which such a question was to be decided, he would have expected to hear the claims of sentiment against progress and beauty against utility openly debated. Today, as he took his seat in the Soler, the long upper room on the south of Lady Alice, he expected no such matter. He knew now that that was not the way things are done.

The Progressive Element managed its business really very well. Most of the Fellows did not know when they came into the Soler that there was any question of selling the Wood. They saw, of course, from their agenda paper that item Fifteen was 'Sale of College land', but as that appeared at almost every College Meeting, they were not very interested. On the other hand, they did see that item One was 'Questions about Bragdon Wood'. These were not concerned with the proposed sale. Curry, who rose as Sub-Warden to introduce them, had a few letters to read to the College. The first was from a society concerned for the preservation of ancient monuments. I think myself that this society had been ill-advised to make two complaints in one letter. It would have been wiser if they had confined themselves to drawing the College's attention to the disrepair of the wall round the Wood. When they went on to urge the desirability of building some protection over the Well itself, and even to point out that they had urged this before, the College began to be restive. And when, as a kind of afterthought, they expressed a wish that the College could be a little more accommodating to serious antiquaries who wanted to examine the Well, the College became definitely ill-tempered. I would not like to accuse a man in Curry's position of misreading a letter; but his reading of this letter was certainly not such as to gloss over any defects in the tone of the original composition. Before he sat down, nearly every one in the room desired strongly to make the outer world understand that Bragdon Wood was the private property of Bracton College and that the outer world had better mind its own business. Then he rose again to read another letter. This was from a society of Spiritualists who wanted leave to investigate the 'reported phenomena' in the Wood – a letter 'connected', as Curry said, 'with the next which, with the Warden's permission, I will now read to you.' This was from a firm who had heard of the Spiritualists' proposal and wanted permission to make a film, not exactly of the phenomena, but of the Spiritualists looking for the phenomena. Curry was directed to write short refusals to all three letters.

Then came a new voice from quite a different part of the Soler. Lord Feverstone had risen. He fully agreed with the action which the College had taken about these impertinent letters from various busybodies outside. But was it not, after all, a fact, that the wall of the Wood *was* in a very unsatisfactory condition? A good many Fellows – Studdock was not one of them – imagined they were watching a revolt on Feverstone's part against 'Curry and his gang' and became intensely interested. Almost at once the Bursar, James Busby, was on his feet. He welcomed Lord Feverstone's question. In his Bursarial capacity he had recently taken expert advice about the wall of the Wood. 'Unsatisfactory' was, he feared, much too mild a word to describe its condition. Nothing but a complete new wall would really meet the situation. With great difficulty the probable cost of this was elicited from him; and when the College heard the figure it gasped. Lord Feverstone inquired icily whether the Bursar was seriously proposing that the College should undertake such an expense. Busby (a very large ex-clergyman with a bushy black beard) replied with some temper that he had proposed nothing: if he *were* to make a suggestion, it would be that the question could not be treated in isolation from some important financial considerations which it would become his duty to lay before them later in the day. There was a pause at this ominous statement, until gradually, one by one, the 'outsiders' and 'obstructionists', the men not included in the Progressive Element, began coming into the debate. Most of these found it hard to believe that nothing short of a complete new wall would be any use. The Progressive Element let them talk for nearly ten minutes. Then it looked once again as if Lord Feverstone were actually leading the outsiders. He wanted to know whether it was possible that the Bursar and the Preservation Committee could really find no alternative between building a new wall and allowing Bragdon Wood to degenerate into a common. He pressed for an answer. Some of the outsiders even began to feel that he was being too rude to the Bursar. At last the Bursar answered in a low voice that he *had* in a purely theoretical way got some facts about possible alternatives. A barbed wire fence – but the rest was drowned in a roar of disapproval, during which old Canon Jewel was heard to say that he would sooner have every tree in the Wood felled to the ground than see it caged in barbed wire. Finally, the matter was postponed for consideration at the next meeting.

The next item was one of those which the majority of the Fellows could not understand. It involved the recapitulation (by Curry) of a long correspondence between the College and the Senate of the University about the proposed incorporation of the NICE in the University of Edgestow. The words 'committed to' kept recurring in the debate that followed. 'We appear,' said Watson, 'to have pledged ourselves as a college to the fullest possible support of the new Institute.' 'We appear,' said Feverstone, 'to have tied ourselves up hand and foot and given the University *carte blanche*.' What all this actually amounted to never became clear to any of the outsiders. They remembered fighting hard at a previous meeting against the NICE and all its works, and being defeated; but every effort to find out what their defeat had meant, though answered with great lucidity by Curry, served only to entangle them further in the impenetrable mazes of the university constitution and the still darker mystery of the relations between

University and College. The result of the discussion was to leave them under the impression that the honour of the College was not involved in the establishment of the NICE at Edgestow.

During this item the thoughts of more than one Fellow had turned to lunch, and attention had wandered. But when Curry rose at five minutes to one to introduce item Three, there was a sharp revival of interest. It was called, 'Rectification of an anomaly of the Stipends of Junior Fellows.' I would not like to say what the most junior Fellows of Bracton were getting at this time, but I believe it hardly covered the expenses of their residence in College, which was compulsory. Studdock who had only recently emerged from this class felt great sympathy with them. He understood the look in their faces. The Rectification, if it went through, would mean to them clothes and holidays and meat for lunch and a chance to buy a half, instead of a fifth, of the books they needed. All their eyes were fixed on the Bursar when he rose to reply to Curry's proposals. He hoped that no one would imagine he approved the anomaly which had, in 1910, excluded the lowest class of the Fellows from the new clauses in the eighteenth paragraph of Statute 17. He felt sure that every one present would *wish* it to be rectified; but it was his duty, as Bursar, to point out that this was the second proposal involving very heavy expenditure which had come before them that morning. He could only say of this, as he had said of the previous proposal, that it could not be isolated from the whole problem of the present financial position of the College, which he hoped to lay before them during the course of the afternoon. A great deal more was said, but the Bursar remained unanswered, the matter was postponed, and when, at quarter to two, the Fellows came surging out of the Soler for lunch, hungry and headachy and ravenous for tobacco, every junior had it fixed in his mind that a new wall for the Wood and a rise in his own stipend were strictly exclusive alternatives. 'That darn Wood has been in our way all morning,' said one. 'We're not out of it yet,' answered another.

In this frame of mind, the College returned to the Soler after lunch to consider its finances. Busby, the Bursar, was naturally the principal speaker. It is very hot in the Soler on a sunny afternoon; and the smooth flow of the Bursar's exposition, and even the flashing of his level, white teeth above his beard (he had remarkably fine teeth) had a sort of hypnotic power. Fellows of colleges do not always find money matters easy to understand: if they did, they would probably not have been the sort of men who became Fellows of colleges. They gathered that the situation was bad, very bad, indeed. Some of the youngest and most inexperienced members ceased to wonder whether they would get a new wall or a rise of stipend and began to wonder instead whether the College would continue to function at all. The times, as the Bursar so truly said, were extraordinarily difficult. Older members had heard of such times very often before from dozens of previous Bursars and were less disturbed. I am not suggesting for a moment that the Bursar of Bracton was in any way misrepresenting the position. It is very seldom that the affairs of a large corporation, indefinitely committed to the advancement of learning, can be described as being, in a quite unambiguous sense, satisfactory. His delivery was excellent. Each sentence was a model of lucidity: and if his hearers found the gist of his whole statement less clear than the parts, that may have been their own fault. Some minor retrenchments and reinvestments which he suggested were unanimously approved and the College adjourned for tea in a chastened mood. Studdock rang up Jane and told her he would not be home for dinner.

It was not till six o'clock that all the converging lines of thought and feeling aroused by the earlier business came together upon the question of selling Bragdon Wood. It was not called, 'the sale of Bragdon Wood'. The Bursar called it the 'sale of the area coloured pink on the plan which, with the Warden's permission, I will now pass round the table'. He pointed out quite frankly that this involved the loss of *part* of the Wood. In fact, the proposed NICE site still left to the College a strip about sixteen feet broad along the far half of the south side but there was no deception for the Fellows had the plan to look at with their own eyes. It was a small scale plan and not perhaps perfectly accurate – only meant to give one a general idea. In answer to questions he admitted that unfortunately – or perhaps fortunately – the Well itself was in the area which the NICE wanted. The rights of the College to access would, of course, be guaranteed; and the Well and its pavement would be preserved by the Institute in a manner to satisfy all the archaeologists in the world. He refrained from offering any advice and merely mentioned the quite astonishing figure which the NICE was offering. After that, the meeting became lively. The advantages of the sale discovered themselves one by one like ripe fruit dropping into the hand. It solved the problem of the wall; it solved the problem of protecting ancient monuments; it solved the financial problem; it looked like solving the problem of the junior Fellows' stipends. It appeared further that the NICE regarded this as the only possible site in Edgestow; if by any chance Bracton would not sell, the whole scheme miscarried and the Institute would undoubtedly go to Cambridge. It was even drawn out of the Bursar by much questioning that he knew of a Cambridge college very anxious to sell.

The few real 'Die-hards' present, to whom Bragdon Wood was almost a basic assumption of life, could hardly bring themselves to realise what was happening. When they found their voices, they struck a discordant note amid the general buzz of cheerful comment. They were manoeuvered into the position of appearing as the party who passionately desired to see Bragdon surrounded with barbed wire. When at last old Jewel, blind and shaky and almost weeping, rose to his feet, his voice was hardly audible. Men turned round to gaze at, and some to admire, the clear-cut, half-childish face and the white hair which had become more conspicuous as the long room grew darker. But only those close to him could hear what he said. At this moment Lord Feverstone sprang to his feet, folded his arms, and looking straight at the old man said in a very loud, clear voice:

'If Canon Jewel wishes us *not* to hear his views, I suggest that his end could be better attained by silence.'

Jewel had been already an old man in the days before the first war when old men were treated with kindness, and he had never succeeded in getting used to the modern world. For a moment as he stood with his head thrust forward, people thought he was going to reply. Then quite suddenly he spread out his hands with a gesture of helplessness, shrunk back, and began laboriously to resume his chair.

The motion was carried.

◆ ○ ◆

After leaving the flat that morning Jane also had gone down to Edgestow and bought a hat. She had before now expressed some contempt for the kind of woman who buys hats, as a man buys drinks, for a stimulant and a consolation. It did not occur to her that she was doing so herself on this occasion. She liked her clothes to be rather severe and in colours that were really good on serious aesthetic grounds – clothes which would make it plain to everyone that she was an intelligent adult and not a woman of the chocolate-box variety – and because of this preference, she did not know that she was interested in clothes at all. She was therefore a little annoyed when Mrs Dimble met her coming out of Sparrow's and said, 'Hullo dear! Been buying a hat? Come home to lunch and let's see it. Cecil has the car just round the corner.'

Cecil Dimble, a Fellow of Northumberland, had been Jane's tutor for her last year as a student and Mrs Dimble (one tended to call her Mother Dimble) had been a kind of unofficial aunt to all the girls of her year. A liking for the female pupils of one's husband is not, perhaps, so common as might be wished among dons' wives; but Mrs Dimble appeared to like all Dr Dimble's pupils of both sexes and the Dimbles' house, away on the far side of the river, was a kind of noisy *salon* all the term. She had been particularly fond of Jane with that kind of affection which a humorous, easy natured and childless woman sometimes feels for a girl whom she thinks pretty and rather absurd. For the last year or so Jane had been somewhat losing sight of the Dimbles and felt rather guilty about it. She accepted the invitation to lunch.

They drove over the bridge to the north of Bracton and then south along the bank of the Wynd, past the cottages, then left and eastward at the Norman church and down the straight road with the poplars on one side and the wall of Bragdon Wood on the other, and so finally to the Dimbles' front door.

'How lovely it's looking,' said Jane quite sincerely as she got out of the car. The Dimbles' garden was famous.

'You'd better take a good look at it then,' said Dr Dimble.

'What do you mean?' asked Jane.

'Haven't you told her?' said Dr Dimble to his wife.

'I haven't screwed myself up to it yet,' said Mrs Dimble. 'Besides, poor dear, her husband is one of the villains of the piece. Anyway, I expect she knows.'

'I've no idea what you're talking about,' said Jane.

'Your own College is being so tiresome, dear. They're turning us out. They won't renew the lease.'

'Oh, Mrs Dimble!' exclaimed Jane. 'And I didn't even know this was Bracton property.'

'There you are!' said Mrs Dimble. 'One half of the world doesn't know how the other half lives. Here have I been imagining that you were using all your influence with Mr Studdock to try to save us, whereas in reality –'

'Mark never talks to me about College business.'

'Good husbands never do,' said Dr Dimble. 'At least, only about the business of other people's colleges. That's why Margaret knows all about Bracton and nothing about Northumberland. Is no one coming in to have lunch?'

Dimble guessed that Bracton was going to sell the Wood and everything else it owned on that side of the river. The whole region seemed to him now even more of a paradise than when he first came to live there twenty-five years ago, and he felt much too strongly on the subject to wish to talk about it before the wife of one of the Bracton men.

'You'll have to wait for lunch till I've seen Jane's new hat,' said Mother Dimble, and forthwith hurried Jane upstairs. Then

followed some minutes of conversation which was strictly feminine in the old-fashionèd sense. Jane, while preserving a certain
sense of superiority, found it indefinably comforting; and though
Mrs Dimble had really the wrong point of view about such things,
there was no denying that the one small alteration which she suggested did go to the root of the matter. When the hat was being put
away again Mrs Dimble suddenly said,

'There's nothing wrong, is there?'

'Wrong?' said Jane. 'Why? What should there be?'

'You're not looking yourself.'

'Oh, I'm all right,' said Jane aloud. Mentally she added, 'She's
dying to know whether I'm going to have a baby. That sort of
woman always is.'

'Do you hate being kissed?' said Mrs Dimble unexpectedly.

'Do I hate being kissed?' thought Jane to herself. 'That indeed is
the question. Do I hate being kissed? Hope not for mind in women
– ' She had intended to reply, 'Of course not,' but inexplicably, and
to her great annoyance, found herself crying instead. And then, for
a moment, Mrs Dimble became simply a grown-up as grown-ups
had been when one was a very small child: large, warm, soft objects
to whom one ran with bruised knees or broken toys. When she
thought of her childhood, Jane usually remembered those occasions on which the voluminous embrace of Nurse or Mother had
been unwelcome and resisted as an insult to one's maturity; now,
for the moment, she was back in those forgotten, yet infrequent,
times when fear or misery induced a willing surrender and surrender brought comfort. Not to detest being petted and pawed was
contrary to her whole theory of life; yet, before they went downstairs, she had told Mrs Dimble that she was not going to have a
baby, but was a bit depressed from being very much alone, and
from a nightmare.

During lunch Dr Dimble talked about the Arthurian legend.
'It's really wonderful,' he said, 'how the whole thing hangs together, even in a late version like Malory's. You've noticed how there
are two sets of characters? There's Guinevere and Launcelot and all

those people in the centre: all very courtly and nothing particular-ly British about them. But then in the background – on the other side of Arthur, so to speak – there are all those *dark* people like Morgan and Morgawse, who are very British indeed and usually more or less hostile though they are his own relatives. Mixed up with magic. You remember that wonderful phrase, how Queen Morgan "set all the country on fire with ladies that were enchantresses". Merlin too, of course, is British, though not hos-tile. Doesn't it look very like a picture of Britain as it must have been on the eve of the invasion?'

'How do you mean, Dr Dimble?' said Jane.

'Well, wouldn't there have been one section of society that was almost purely Roman? People wearing togas and talking a Celticised Latin – something that would sound to us rather like Spanish: and fully Christian. But further up country, in the out-of-the way places, cut off by the forests, there would have been little courts ruled by real old British under-kings, talking something like Welsh, and practising a certain amount of the druidical religion.'

'And what would Arthur himself have been?' said Jane. It was silly that her heart should have missed a beat at the words 'rather like Spanish'.

'That's just the point,' said Dr Dimble. 'One can imagine a man of the old British line, but also a Christian and a fully-trained gen-eral with Roman technique, trying to pull this whole society together and almost succeeding. There'd be jealousy from his own British family, and the Romanised section – the Launcelots and Lionels – would look down on the Britons. That'd be why Kay is always represented as a boor: he is part of the native strain. And always that under-tow, that tug back to druidism.'

'And where would Merlin be?'

'Yes … He's the really interesting figure. Did the whole thing fail because he died so soon? Has it ever struck you what an odd creation Merlin is? He's not evil; yet he's a magician. He is obvi-ously a druid; yet he knows all about the Grail. He's "the devil's son"; but then Layamon goes out of his way to tell you that the kind of being who fathered Merlin needn't have been bad after all. You remember, "There dwell in the sky many kinds of wights. Some of them are good, and some work evil."'

'It *is* rather puzzling. I hadn't thought of it before.'

'I often wonder,' said Dr Dimble, 'whether Merlin doesn't represent the last trace of something the later tradition has quite forgotten about – something that became impossible when the only people in touch with the supernatural were either white or black, either priests or sorcerers.'

'What a horrid idea,' said Mrs Dimble, who had noticed that Jane seemed to be preoccupied. 'Anyway, Merlin happened a long time ago if he happened at all and he's safely dead and buried under Bragdon Wood as every one of us knows.'

'Buried but *not* dead, according to the story,' corrected Dr Dimble.

'Ugh!' said Jane involuntarily, but Dr Dimble was musing aloud.

'I wonder what they *will find* if they start digging up that place for the foundations of their NICE,' he said.

'First mud and then water,' said Mrs Dimble. 'That's why they can't really build it there.'

'So you'd think,' said her husband. 'And if so, why should they want to come here at all? A little cockney like Jules is not likely to be influenced by any poetic fancy about Merlin's mantle having fallen on him!'

'Merlin's mantle indeed!' said Mrs Dimble.

'Yes,' said the Doctor, 'it's a rum idea. I daresay some of his set would like to recover the mantle well enough. Whether they'll be big enough to fill it is another matter! I don't think they'd like it if the old man himself came back to life along with it.'

'That child's going to faint,' said Mrs Dimble, suddenly jumping up.

'Hullo! What's the matter?' said Dr Dimble, looking with amazement at Jane's face. 'Is the room too hot for you?'

'Oh, it's too ridiculous,' said Jane.

'Let's come into the drawing room,' said Dr Dimble. 'Here. Lean on my arm.'

A little later, in the drawing room, seated beside a window that opened onto the lawn, now strewn with bright yellow leaves, Jane attempted to excuse her absurd behaviour by telling the story of her dream. 'I suppose I've given myself away dreadfully,' she said. 'You can both start psycho-analysing me now.'

From Dr Dimble's face, Jane might have indeed conjectured that her dream had shocked him exceedingly. 'Extraordinary thing . . . most extraordinary,' he kept muttering. '*Two* heads. And one of them Alcasan's. Now is that a false scent ...?'

'Don't, Cecil,' said Mrs Dimble.

'Do you think I ought to be analysed?' said Jane.

'Analysed?' said Dr Dimble, glancing at her as if he had not quite understood. 'Oh, I see. You mean going to Brizeacre or someone of that sort?' Jane realised that her question had recalled him from some quite different train of thought and even – disconcertingly – that the problem of her own health had been shouldered aside. The telling of her dream had raised some other problem, though what this was she could not even imagine.

Dr Dimble looked out of the window. 'There is my dullest pupil just ringing the bell,' he said. 'I must go to the study, and listen to an essay on Swift beginning, "Swift was born." Must try to keep my mind on it, too, which won't be easy.' He rose and stood for a moment with his hand on Jane's shoulder. 'Look here,' he said, 'I'm not going to give any advice. But if you do decide to go to anyone about that dream, I wish you would *first* consider going to someone whose address Margery or I will give you.'

'You don't believe in Mr Brizeacre?' said Jane.

'I can't explain,' said Dr Dimble. 'Not now. It's all so complicated. Try not to bother about it. But if you *do*, just let us know first. Good-bye.'

Almost immediately after his departure some other visitors arrived, so that there was no opportunity of further private conversation between Jane and her hostess. She left the Dimbles about half an hour later and walked home, not along the road with the poplars but by the footpath across the common, past the donkeys and the geese, with the towers and spires of Edgestow to her left and the old windmill on the horizon to her right.

Dinner with the Sub-Warden

'THIS IS A BLOW!' said Curry standing in front of the fireplace in his magnificent rooms which overlooked Newton. They were the best set in College.

'Something from NO?' said James Busby. He and Lord Feverstone and Mark were all drinking sherry before dining with Curry. NO, which stood for Non-Olet, was the nickname of Charles Place, the Warden of Bracton. His election to this post, some fifteen years before, had been one of the earliest triumphs of the Progressive Element. By dint of saying that the College needed 'new blood' and must be shaken out of its 'academic grooves', they had succeeded in bringing in an elderly civil servant who had certainly never been contaminated by academic weaknesses since he left his rather obscure Cambridge college in the previous century, but who had written a monumental report on National Sanitation. The subject had, if anything, rather recommended him to the Progressive Element. They regarded it as a slap in the face for the *dilettanti* and Die-hards, who replied by christening their new Warden Non-Olet. But gradually even Place's supporters had adopted the name. For Place had not answered their expectations, having turned out to be a dyspeptic with a taste for philately, whose voice was so seldom heard that some of the junior Fellows did not know what it sounded like.

'Yes, blast him,' said Curry, 'wishes to see me on a most important matter as soon as I can conveniently call on him after dinner.'

'That means,' said the Bursar, 'that Jewel and Co. have been getting at him and want to find some way of going back on the whole business.'

'I don't give a damn for that,' said Curry. 'How can you go back on a Resolution? It isn't that. But it's enough to muck up the whole evening.'

'Only *your* evening,' said Feverstone. 'Don't forget to leave out that very special brandy of yours before you go.'

'Jewel! Good God!' said Busby, burying his left hand in his beard.

'I was rather sorry for old Jewel,' said Mark. His motives for saying this were very mixed. To do him justice, it must be said that the quite unexpected and apparently unnecessary brutality of Feverstone's behaviour to the old man had disgusted him. And then, too, the whole idea of his debt to Feverstone in the matter of his own fellowship had been rankling all day. Who was this man Feverstone? But paradoxically, even while he felt that the time had come for asserting his own independence and showing that his agreement with all the methods of the Progressive Element must not be taken for granted, he also felt that a little independence would raise him to a higher position within that Element itself. If the idea 'Feverstone will think all the more of you for showing your teeth' had occurred to him in so many words, he would probably have rejected it as servile; but it didn't.

'Sorry for Jewel?' said Curry wheeling round. 'You wouldn't say that if you knew what he was like in his prime.'

'I agree with you,' said Feverstone to Mark, 'but then I take the Clausewitz view. Total war is the most humane in the long run. I shut him up instantaneously. Now that he's got over the shock, he's quite enjoying himself because I've fully confirmed everything he's been saying about the Younger Generation for the last forty years. What was the alternative? To let him drivel on until he'd worked himself into a coughing fit or a heart attack, and give him in addition the disappointment of finding that he was treated civilly.'

'That's a point of view, certainly,' said Mark.

'Damn it all,' continued Feverstone, 'no man likes to have his stock in trade taken away. What would poor Curry, here, do if the

Die-hards one day all refused to do any Die-harding? Othello's occupation would be gone.'

'Dinner is served, Sir,' said Curry's 'Shooter' – for that is what they call a College servant at Bracton.

'That's all rot, Dick,' said Curry as they sat down. 'There's nothing I should like better than to see the end of all these Die-hards and obstructionists and be able to get on with the job. You don't suppose I *like* having to spend all my time merely getting the road clear?' Mark noticed that his host was a little nettled at Lord Feverstone's banter. The latter had an extremely virile and infectious laugh. Mark felt he was beginning to like him.

'The job being …?' said Feverstone, not exactly glancing, much less winking, at Mark, but making him feel that he was somehow being included in the fun.

'Well, some of us have got work of our own to do,' replied Curry, dropping his voice to give it a more serious tone, almost as some people drop their voices to speak of medical or religious matters.

'I never knew you were *that* sort of person,' said Feverstone.

'That's the worst of the whole system,' said Curry. 'In a place like this you've either got to be content to see everything go to pieces – I mean, become stagnant – or else to sacrifice your own career as a scholar to all these infernal college politics. One of these days I *shall* chuck that side of it and get down to my book. The stuff's all there, you know, Feverstone. One long vacation clear and I really believe I could put it into shape.'

Mark, who had never seen Curry baited before, was beginning to enjoy himself.

'I see,' said Feverstone. 'In order to keep the place going as a learned society, all the best brains in it have to give up doing anything about learning.'

'Exactly!' said Curry. 'That's just –' and then stopped, uncertain whether he was being taken quite seriously. Feverstone burst into laughter. The Bursar who had up till now been busily engaged in eating, wiped his beard carefully and spoke seriously.

'All that's very well in theory,' he said, 'but I think Curry's quite right. Supposing he resigned his office as Sub-Warden and retired into his cave. He might give us a thundering good book on economics – '

'Economics?' said Feverstone lifting his eyebrows.

'I happen to be a military historian, James,' said Curry. He was often somewhat annoyed at the difficulty which his colleagues seemed to find in remembering what particular branch of learning he had been elected to pursue.

'I mean military history, of course,' said Busby. 'As I say, he might give us a thundering good book on military history. But it would be superseded in twenty years. Whereas the work he is actually doing for the College will benefit it for centuries. This whole business, now, of bringing the NICE to Edgestow. What about a thing like that, Feverstone? I'm not speaking merely of the financial side of it, though as Bursar I naturally rate that pretty high. But think of the new life, the awakening of new vision, the stirring of dormant impulses. What would any book on economics –'

'Military history,' said Feverstone gently, but this time Busby did not hear him.

'What would any book on economics be, compared with a thing like that?' he continued. 'I look upon it as the greatest triumph of practical idealism that this century has yet seen.'

The good wine was beginning to do its good office. We have all known the kind of clergyman who tends to forget his clerical collar after the third glass; but Busby's habit was the reverse. It was after the third glass that he began to remember his collar. As wine and candlelight loosened his tongue, the parson still latent within him after thirty years' apostasy began to wake into a strange galvanic life.

'As you chaps know,' he said, 'I make no claim to orthodoxy. But if religion is understood in the deepest sense, I have no hesitation in saying that Curry, by bringing the NICE to Edgestow, has done more for it in one year than Jewel has done in his whole life.'

'Well,' said Curry modestly, 'that's rather the sort of thing one had hoped. I mightn't put it exactly as you do, James – '

'No, no,' said the Bursar, 'of course not. We all have our different languages; but we all really mean the same thing.'

'Has anyone discovered,' asked Feverstone, 'what, precisely, the NICE is, or what it intends to do?'

Curry looked at him with a slightly startled expression. 'That comes oddly from you, Dick,' he said. 'I thought you were in on it, yourself.'

'Isn't it a little naïf,' said Feverstone, 'to suppose that being in on a thing involves any distinct knowledge of its official programme?'

'Oh well, if you mean *details*,' said Curry, and then stopped.

'Surely, Feverstone,' said Busby, 'you're making a great mystery about nothing. I should have thought the objects of the NICE were pretty clear. It's the first attempt to take applied science seriously from the national point of view. The difference in scale between it and anything we've had before amounts to a difference in kind. The buildings alone, the apparatus alone –! Think what it has done already for industry. Think how it is going to mobilise all the talent of the country; and not only scientific talent in the narrower sense. Fifteen departmental directors at fifteen thousand a year each! Its own legal staff! Its own police, I'm told! Its own permanent staff of architects, surveyors, engineers! The thing's stupendous!'

'Careers for our sons,' said Feverstone. 'I see.'

'What do you mean by that, Lord Feverstone?' said Busby putting down his glass.

'Lord!' said Feverstone, his eyes laughing, 'what a brick to drop. I'd quite forgotten you had a family, James.'

'I agree with James,' said Curry, who had been waiting somewhat impatiently to speak. 'The NICE marks the beginning of a new era – the *really* scientific era. Up to now, everything has been haphazard. This is going to put science itself on a scientific basis. There are to be forty interlocking committees sitting every day and they've got a wonderful gadget – I was shown the model last time I was in town – by which the findings of each committee print themselves off in their own little compartment on the Analytical Notice-Board every half hour. Then, that report slides itself into the right position where it's connected up by little arrows with all the relevant parts of the other reports. A glance at the Board shows you the policy of the whole Institute actually taking shape under your own eyes. There'll be a staff of at least twenty experts at the top of the building working this Notice-Board in a room rather like the Tube control rooms. It's a marvellous gadget. The different kinds of business all come out in the Board in different coloured lights. It must have cost half a million. They call it a Pragmatometer.'

'And there,' said Busby, 'you see again what the Institute is already doing for the country. Pragmatometry is going to be a big thing. Hundreds of people are going in for it. Why this Analytical Notice-Board will probably be out of date before the building is finished!'

'Yes, by Jove,' said Feverstone, 'and NO himself told me this morning that the sanitation of the Institute was going to be something quite out of the ordinary.'

'So it is,' said Busby sturdily. 'I don't see why one should think that unimportant.'

'And what do you think about it, Studdock?' said Feverstone.

'I think,' said Mark, 'that James touched on the most important point when he said that it would have its own legal staff and its own police. I don't give a fig for Pragmatometers and sanitation *de luxe*. The real thing is that this time we're going to get science applied to social problems and backed by the whole force of the state, just as war has been backed by the whole force of the state in the past. One hopes, of course, that it'll find out more than the old free-lance science did; but what's certain is that it can *do* more.'

'Damn,' said Curry, looking at his watch. 'I'll have to go and talk to NO now. If you people would like any brandy when you've finished your wine, it's in that cupboard. You'll find balloon glasses on the shelf above. I'll be back as soon as I can. You're not going, James, are you?'

'Yes,' said the Bursar. 'I'm going to bed early. Don't let me break up the party for you two. I've been on my legs nearly all day, you know. A man's a fool to hold any office in this College. Continual anxiety. Crushing responsibility. And then you get people suggesting that all the little research-beetles who never poke their noses outside their libraries and laboratories are the real workers! I'd like to see Glossop or any of that lot face the sort of day's work I've had today. Curry, my lad, you'd have had an easier life if you'd stuck to economics.'

'I've told you before,' began Curry, but the Bursar, now risen, was bending over Lord Feverstone and telling him a funny story.

As soon as the two men had got out of the room, Lord Feverstone looked steadily at Mark for some seconds with an enigmatic expression. Then he chuckled. Then the chuckle developed into a laugh. He threw his lean, muscular body well back into his chair and laughed louder and louder. He was very infectious in his laughter and Mark found himself laughing too – quite sincerely and even helplessly, like a child. 'Pragmatometers – palatial lavatories – practical idealism,' gasped Feverstone. It was a moment of extraordinary liberation for Mark. All sorts of things about Curry and Busby which he had not previously noticed, or else, noticing, had slurred over in his reverence for the Progressive Element, came back to his mind. He wondered how he could have been so blind to the funny side of them.

'It really is rather devastating,' said Feverstone when he had partially recovered, 'that the people one has to use for getting things done should talk such drivel the moment you ask them about the things themselves.'

'And yet they *are*, in a sense, the brains of Bracton,' said Mark.

'Good Lord no! Glossop and Bill the Blizzard, and even old Jewel, have ten times their intelligence.'

'I didn't know you took that view.'

'I think Glossop, etc., are quite mistaken. I think their idea of culture and knowledge and what not is unrealistic. I don't think it fits the world we're living in. It's a mere fantasy. But it is quite a clear idea and they follow it out consistently. They know what they want. But our two poor friends, though they can be persuaded to take the right train, or even to drive it, haven't a ghost of a notion where it's going to, or why. They'll sweat blood to bring the NICE to Edgestow: that's why they're indispensable. But what the point of the NICE is, what the point of anything is – ask them another. Pragmatometry! Fifteen sub-directors!'

'Well, perhaps I'm in the same boat myself.'

'Not at all. You saw the point at once. I knew you would. I've read everything you've written since you were in for your fellowship. That's what I wanted to talk to you about.'

Mark was silent. The giddy sensation of being suddenly whirled up from one plane of secrecy to another, coupled with the growing effect of Curry's excellent port, prevented him from speaking.

'I want you to come into the Institute,' said Feverstone.

'You mean – to leave Bracton?'

'That makes no odds. Anyway, I don't suppose there's anything you want here. We'd make Curry Warden when NO retires and –'

'They were talking of making you Warden.'

'God!' said Feverstone and stared. Mark realised that from Feverstone's point of view this was like the suggestion that he should become Headmaster of a small idiots' school, and thanked his stars that his own remark had not been uttered in a tone that made it obviously serious. Then they both laughed again.

'You,' said Feverstone, 'would be absolutely wasted as Warden. That's the job for Curry. He'll do it very well. You want a man who loves business and wire-pulling for their own sake and doesn't really ask what it's all about. If he did, he'd start bringing in his own – well, I suppose he'd call them "ideas". As it is, we've only got to tell him that he thinks so-and-so is a man the College wants, and he *will* think it. And then he'll never rest till so-and-so gets a fellowship. That's what we want the College for: a drag net, a recruiting office.'

'A recruiting office for the NICE, you mean?'

'Yes, in the first instance. But it's only part of the general show.'

'I'm not sure that I know what you mean.'

'You soon will. The Home Side, and all that, you know! It sounds rather in Busby's style to say that Humanity is at the cross-roads. But it is the main question at the moment: which side one's on – obscurantism or Order. It does really look as if we now had the power to dig ourselves in as a species for a pretty staggering period, to take control of our own destiny. If Science is really given a free hand it can now take over the human race and re-condition it: make man a really efficient animal. If it doesn't – well, we're done.'

'Go on.'

'There are three main problems. First, the interplanetary problem –'

'What on earth do you mean?'

'Well, that doesn't really matter. We can't do anything about that at present. The only man who could help was Weston.'

'He was killed in a blitz, wasn't he?'

'He was murdered.'

'Murdered?'

'I'm pretty sure of it, and I've a shrewd idea who the murderer was.'

'Good God! Can nothing be done?'

'There's no evidence. The murderer is a respectable Cambridge don with weak eyes, a game leg, and a fair beard. He's dined in this College.'

'What was Weston murdered for?'

'For being on our side. The murderer is one of the enemy.'

'You don't mean to say he murdered him for that?'

'Yes,' said Feverstone, bringing his hand down smartly on the table. 'That's just the point. You'll hear people like Curry or James burbling away about the "war" against reaction. It never enters their heads that it might be a real war with real casualties. They think the violent resistance of the other side ended with the persecution of Galileo and all that. But don't believe it. It is just seriously beginning. They know now that we have at last got *real* powers: that the question of what humanity is to be is going to be decided in the next sixty years. They're going to fight every inch. They'll stop at nothing.'

'They can't win,' said Mark.

'We'll hope not,' said Lord Feverstone. 'I think they can't. That is why it is of such immense importance to each of us to choose the right side. If you try to be neutral you become simply a pawn.'

'Oh, I haven't any doubt which is *my* side,' said Mark. 'Hang it all – the preservation of the human race – it's a pretty rock-bottom obligation.'

'Well, personally,' said Feverstone, 'I'm not indulging in any Busbyisms about that. It's a little fantastic to base one's actions on a supposed concern for what's going to happen millions of years hence; and you must remember that the other side would claim to be preserving humanity, too. Both can be explained psycho-analytically if they take that line. The practical point is that you and I don't like being pawns, and we do rather like fighting – specially on the winning side.'

'And what is the first practical step?'

'Yes, that's the real question. As I said, the interplanetary problem must be left on one side for the moment. The second problem is our rivals on this planet. I don't mean only insects and bacteria. There's far too much life of every kind about, animal and vegetable. We haven't really cleared the place yet. First we couldn't; and then we had aesthetic and humanitarian scruples; and we still haven't short-circuited the question of the balance of nature. All that is to be gone into. The third problem is Man himself.'

'Go on. This interests me very much.'

'Man has got to take charge of Man. That means, remember, that some men have got to take charge of the rest – which is another reason for cashing in on it as soon as one can. You and I want to be the people who do the taking charge, not the ones who are taken charge of. Quite.'

'What sort of thing have you in mind?'

'Quite simple and obvious things, at first – sterilisation of the unfit, liquidation of backward races (we don't want any dead weights), selective breeding. Then real education, including pre-natal education. By real education I mean one that has no "take-it-or-leave-it" nonsense. A real education makes the patient what it wants infallibly: whatever he or his parents try to do about it. Of course, it'll have to be mainly psychological at first. But we'll get on to biochemical conditioning in the end and direct manipulation of the brain ...'

'But this is stupendous, Feverstone.'

'It's the real thing at last. A new type of man: and it's people like you who've got to begin to make him.'

'That's my trouble. Don't think it's false modesty, but I haven't yet seen how I can contribute.'

'No, but *we* have. You are what we need: a trained sociologist with a radically realistic outlook, not afraid of responsibility. Also, a sociologist who can write.'

'You don't mean you want me to write up all this?'

'No. We want you to write it *down* – to camouflage it. Only for the present, of course. Once the thing gets going we shan't have to bother about the great heart of the British public. We'll make the great heart what we want it to be. But in the meantime, it *does* make a difference how things are put. For instance, if it were even whispered that the NICE wanted powers to experiment on crimi-nals, you'd have all the old women of both sexes up in arms and yapping about humanity. Call it re-education of the mal-adjusted, and you have them all slobbering with delight that the brutal era of retributive punishment has at last come to an end. Odd thing it is – the word "experiment" is unpopular, but not the word "experi-mental". You musn't experiment on children; but offer the dear lit-tle kiddies free education in an experimental school attached to the NICE and it's all correct!'

'You don't mean that this – er – journalistic side would be my main job?'

'It's nothing to do with journalism. Your readers in the first instance would be Committees of the House of Commons, not the public. But that would only be a side line. As for the job itself – why, it's impossible to say how it might develop. Talking to a man like you, I don't stress the financial side. You'd start at something quite modest: say about fifteen hundred a year.'

'I wasn't thinking about that,' said Mark, flushing with pure excitement.

'Of course,' said Feverstone, 'I ought to warn you, there is the danger. Not yet, perhaps. But when things really begin to hum, it's quite on the cards they may try to bump you off, like poor old Weston.'

'I don't think I was thinking about that either,' said Mark.

'Look here,' said Feverstone. 'Let me run you across tomorrow to see John Wither. He told me to bring you for the week-end if you were interested. You'll meet all the important people there and it'll give you a chance to make up your mind.'

'How does Wither come into it? I thought Jules was the head of the NICE.' Jules was a distinguished novelist and scientific populariser whose name always appeared before the public in connection with the new Institute.

'Jules! Hell's bells!' said Feverstone. 'You don't imagine that little mascot has anything to say to what really goes on? He's all right for selling the Institute to the great British public in the Sunday papers and he draws a whacking salary. He's no use for work. There's nothing inside his head except some nineteenth-century socialist stuff, and blah about the rights of man. He's just about got as far as Darwin!'

'Oh quite,' said Mark. 'I was always rather puzzled at his being in the show at all. Do you know, since you're so kind, I think I'd better accept your offer and go over to Wither's for the week-end. What time would you be starting?'

'About quarter to eleven. They tell me you live out Sandawn way. I could call and pick you up.'

'Thanks very much. Now tell me about Wither.'

'John Wither,' began Feverstone, but suddenly broke off. 'Damn!' he said. 'Here comes Curry. Now we shall have to hear everything NO said and how wonderfully the arch-politician has managed him. Don't run away. I shall need your moral support.'

◆ ○ ◆

The last bus had gone long before Mark left College and he walked home up the hill in brilliant moonlight. Something happened to him the moment he had let himself into the flat which was very unusual. He found himself, on the doormat, embracing a frightened, half-sobbing Jane – even a humble Jane – who was saying, 'Oh Mark, I've been so frightened.'

There was a quality in the very muscles of his wife's body which took him by surprise. A certain indefinable defensiveness had momentarily deserted her. He had known such occasions before, but they were rare. They were already becoming rarer. And they tended, in his experience, to be followed next day by inexplicable quarrels. This puzzled him greatly, but he had never put his bewilderment into words.

It is doubtful whether he could have understood her feelings even if they had been explained to him; and Jane, in any case, could not have explained them. She was in extreme confusion. But the reasons for her unusual behaviour on this particular evening were simple enough. She had got back from the Dimbles at about half-past four, feeling much exhilarated by her walk, and hungry, and quite sure that her experiences on the previous night and at lunch were over and done with. She had had to light up and draw the curtains before she had finished tea, for the days were getting short. While doing so, the thought had come into her mind that her fright at the dream and at the mere mention of a mantle, an old man, an old man buried but not dead, and a language like Spanish, had really been as irrational as a child's fear of the dark. This had led her to remember moments when she had feared the dark as a child. Perhaps, she allowed herself to remember them too long. At any rate, when she sat down to drink her last cup of tea, the evening had somehow deteriorated. It never recovered. First, she found it rather difficult to keep her mind on her book. Then, when she had acknowledged this difficulty, she found it difficult to fix on any book. Then she realised that she was restless. From being restless, she became nervous. Then followed a long time when she was not frightened, but knew that she would be very frightened indeed if she did not keep herself in hand. Then came a curious reluctance to go into the kitchen to get herself some supper, and a difficulty – indeed, an impossibility – of eating anything when she had got it. And now, there was no disguising the fact that she was frightened. In desperation she rang up the Dimbles. 'I think I might go and see the person you suggested, after all,' she said. Mrs Dimble's voice came back, after a curious little pause, giving her the address. Ironwood was the name – Miss Ironwood, apparently. Jane had assumed it would be a man and was rather repelled. Miss Ironwood lived out at St Anne's on the Hill. Jane asked if she should make an appointment. 'No,' said Mrs Dimble, 'they'll be – you needn't make an appointment.' Jane kept the conversation going as long as she could. She had rung up not chiefly to get the address but to hear Mother Dimble's voice. Secretly she had had a wild hope that Mother Dimble would recognise her distress and say at once, 'I'll come straight up to you by car.' Instead, she got the mere information and a hurried 'Good-night.' It seemed to Jane that there was something queer about Mrs Dimble's voice. She felt that by ringing up she had interrupted a conversation about herself – or no – not about herself but about something else more important, with which she was somehow connected. And what had Mrs Dimble meant by, 'They'll be –' 'They'll be expecting you?' Horrible, childish night-nursery visions of *They* 'expecting her' passed before her mind. She saw Miss Ironwood, dressed all in black, sitting with her hands folded on her knees and then some-one leading her into Miss Ironwood's presence and saying, 'She's come,' and leaving her there.

'Damn the Dimbles!' said Jane to herself, and then unsaid it, more in fear than in remorse. And now that the life-line had been used and brought no comfort, the terror, as if insulted by her futile attempt to escape it, rushed back on her with no possibility of disguise, and she could never afterwards remember whether the horrible old man and the mantle had actually appeared to her in a dream or whether she had merely sat there, huddled and wild eyed, hoping, hoping, hoping (even praying, though she believed in no one to pray to) that they would not.

And that is why Mark found such an unexpected Jane on the doormat. It was a pity, he thought, that this should have happened on a night when he was so late and so tired and, to tell the truth, not perfectly sober.

◆ ○ ◆

'Do you feel quite all right this morning?' said Mark.

'Yes, thank you,' said Jane shortly.

Mark was lying in bed and drinking a cup of tea. Jane was seated at the dressing table, partially dressed, and doing her hair. Mark's eyes rested on her with indolent, early-morning pleasure. If he guessed very little of the mal-adjustment between them, this was partly due to our race's incurable habit of 'projection'. We think the lamb gentle because its wool is soft to our hands: men call a woman voluptuous when she arouses voluptuous feelings in them. Jane's body, soft though firm and slim though rounded, was so exactly to Mark's mind that it was all but impossible for him not to attribute to her the same sensations which she excited in him.

'You're quite sure you're all right?' he asked again.

'Quite,' said Jane more shortly still.

Jane thought she was annoyed because her hair was not going up to her liking and because Mark was fussing. She also knew, of course, that she was deeply angry with herself for the collapse which had betrayed her last night, into being what she most detested – the fluttering, tearful 'little woman' of sentimental fiction running for comfort to male arms. But she thought this anger was only in the back of her mind, and had no suspicion that it was pulsing through every vein and producing at that very moment the clumsiness in her fingers which made her hair seem intractable.

'Because,' continued Mark, 'if you felt the least bit uncomfortable, I *could* put off going to see this man Wither.'

Jane said nothing.

'If I did go,' said Mark, 'I'd certainly have to be away for the night, perhaps two.'

Jane closed her lips a little more firmly and still said nothing.

'Supposing I did,' said Mark, 'you wouldn't think of asking Myrtle over to stay?'

'No thank you,' said Jane emphatically, and then, 'I'm quite accustomed to being alone.'

'I know,' said Mark in a rather defensive voice. 'That's the devil of the way things are in College at present. That's one of the chief reasons I'm thinking of another job.'

Jane was still silent.

'Look here, old thing,' said Mark, suddenly sitting up and throwing his legs out of bed. 'There's no good beating about the bush. I don't feel comfortable about going away while you're in your present state – '

'What state?' said Jane, turning round and facing him for the first time.

'Well – I mean – just a bit nervy – as anyone may be temporarily.'

'Because I happened to be having a nightmare when you came home last night – or rather this morning – there's no need to talk as if I was a neurasthenic.' This was not in the least what Jane had intended or expected to say.

'Now there's no good going on like that …' began Mark.

'Like what?' said Jane icily, and then, before he had time to reply, 'If you've decided that I'm going mad you'd better get Brizeacre to come down and certify me. It would be convenient to do it while you're away. They could get me packed off while you are at Mr Wither's without any fuss. I'm going to see about the breakfast now. If you don't shave and dress pretty quickly, you'll not be ready when Lord Feverstone calls.'

The upshot of it was that Mark gave himself a very bad cut while shaving (and saw, at once, a picture of himself talking to the all-important Wither with a great blob of cotton-wool on his upper lip) while Jane decided, from a mixture of motives, to cook Mark an unusually elaborate breakfast – of which she would rather die than eat any herself – and did so with the swift efficiency of an angry woman, only to upset it all over the new stove at the last moment. They were still at the table and both pretending to read newspapers when Lord Feverstone arrived. Most unfortunately Mrs Maggs arrived at the same moment. Mrs Maggs was that element in Jane's economy represented by the phrase 'I have a woman who comes in twice a week.' Twenty years earlier Jane's mother would have addressed such a functionary as 'Maggs' and been addressed by her as 'Mum'. But Jane and her 'woman who came in' called one another Mrs Maggs and Mrs Studdock. They were about the same age and to a bachelor's eye there was no very noticeable difference in the clothes they wore. It was therefore perhaps not inexcusable that when Mark attempted to introduce Feverstone to his wife Feverstone should have shaken Mrs Maggs by the hand; but it did not sweeten the last few minutes before the two men departed.

Jane left the flat under pretence of shopping almost at once. 'I really couldn't stand Mrs Maggs today,' she said to herself. 'She's a terrible talker.' So that was Lord Feverstone – that man with the loud, unnatural laugh and the mouth like a shark, and no manners. Apparently a perfect fool too! What good could it do Mark to go about with a man like that? Jane had distrusted his face. She could always tell – there was something shifty about him. Probably he was making a fool of Mark. Mark was so easily taken in. If only he wasn't at Bracton! It was a horrible college. What did Mark see in people like Mr Curry and the odious old clergyman with the beard? And meanwhile, what of the day that awaited her, and the night, and the next night, and beyond that – for when men say they may be away for two nights, it means that two nights is the minimum, and they hope to be away for a week. A telegram (never a trunk call) puts it all right, as far as they are concerned.

She must do something. She even thought of following Mark's advice and getting Myrtle to come and stay. But Myrtle was her sister-in-law, Mark's twin sister, with much too much of the adoring sister's attitude to the brilliant brother. She would talk about Mark's health and his shirts and socks with a continual undercurrent of unexpressed yet unmistakable astonishment at Jane's good luck in marrying him. No, certainly not Myrtle. Then she thought of going to see Dr Brizeacre as a patient. He was a Bracton man and would therefore probably charge her nothing. But when she came to think of answering, to Brizeacre of all people, the sort of questions which Brizeacre would certainly ask, this turned out to be impossible. She must do something. In the end, somewhat to her own surprise, she found that she had decided to go out to St Anne's and see Miss Ironwood. She thought herself a fool for doing so.

◆ ○ ◆

An observer placed at the right altitude above Edgestow that day might have seen far to the south a moving spot on a main road and later, to the east, much nearer the silver thread of the Wynd, and much more slowly moving, the smoke of a train.

The spot would have been the car which was carrying Mark Studdock towards the Blood Transfusion Office at Belbury, where the nucleus of the NICE had taken up its temporary abode. The very size and style of the car had made a favorable impression on him the moment he saw it. The upholstery was of such quality that one felt it ought to be good to eat. And what fine, male energy (Mark felt sick of women at the moment) revealed itself in the very gestures with which Feverstone settled himself at the wheel and put his elbow on the horn, and clasped his pipe firmly between his teeth! The speed of the car, even in the narrow streets of Edgestow, was impressive, and so were the laconic criticisms of Feverstone on other drivers and pedestrians. Once over the level crossing and beyond Jane's old college (St Elizabeth's), he began to show what his car could do. Their speed became so great that even on a rather

43

empty road the inexcusably bad drivers, the manifestly half-witted pedestrians and men with horses, the hen that they actually ran over and the dogs and hens that Feverstone pronounced 'damned lucky', seemed to follow one another almost without intermission. Telegraph posts raced by, bridges rushed overhead with a roar, villages streamed backward to join the country already devoured, and Mark, drunk with air and at once fascinated and repelled by the insolence of Feverstone's driving sat saying, 'Yes,' and 'Quite,' and 'It was *their* fault,' and stealing side-long glances at his companion. Certainly, he was a change from the fussy importance of Curry and the Bursar! The long, straight nose and the clenched teeth, the hard bony outlines beneath the face, the very way he wore his clothes, all spoke of a big man driving a big car to somewhere where they would find big stuff going on. And he, Mark, was to be in it all. At one or two moments when his heart came into his mouth he wondered whether the quality of Lord Feverstone's driving quite justified its speed. 'You need never take a cross-road like that seriously,' yelled Feverstone as they plunged on after the narrowest of these escapes. 'Quite,' bawled Mark. 'No good making a fetish of them!' 'Drive much yourself?' said Feverstone. 'Used to a good deal,' said Mark.

The smoke which our imaginary observer might have seen to the east of Edgestow would have indicated the train in which Jane Studdock was progressing slowly towards the village of St Anne's. Edgestow itself, for those who had reached it from London, had all the appearance of a terminus; but if you looked about you, you might see presently, in a bay, a little train of two or three coaches and a tank engine – a train that sizzled and exuded steam from beneath the foot-boards and in which most of the passengers seemed to know one another. On some days, instead of the third coach, there might be a horse-box, and on the platform there would be hampers containing dead rabbits or live poultry, and men in brown bowler hats and gaiters, and perhaps a terrier or a sheep-dog that seemed to be used to travelling. In this train, which started at half-past one, Jane jerked and rattled along an embankment whence she looked down through some bare branches and some branches freckled with red and yellow leaves into Bragdon Wood itself and thence through the cutting and over the level crossing at Bragdon Camp and along the edge of Brawl Park (the great house was just visible at one point) and so to the first stop at Duke's Eaton. Here, as at Woolham and Cure Hardy and Fourstones, the train settled back, when it stopped, with a little jerk and something like a sigh. And then there would be a noise of milk cans rolling and coarse boots treading on the platform and after that a pause which seemed to last long, during which the autumn sunlight grew warm on the window pane and smells of wood and field from beyond the tiny station floated in and seemed to claim the railway as part of the land. Passengers got in and out of her carriage at every stop; apple-faced men, and women with elastic-side boots and imitation fruit on their hats, and schoolboys. Jane hardly noticed them: for though she was theoretically an extreme democrat, no social class save her own had yet become a reality to her in any place except the printed page. And in between the stations things flitted past, so isolated from their context that each seemed to promise some unearthly happiness if one could but have descended from the train at that very moment to seize it: a house backed with a group of haystacks and wide brown fields about it, two aged horses standing head to tail, a little orchard with washing hanging on a line, and a rabbit staring at the train, whose two eyes looked like the dots, and his ears like the uprights, of a double exclamation mark. At quarter-past two she came to St Anne's, which was the real terminus of the branch, and the end of everything. The air struck her as cold and tonic when she left the station.

Although the train had been chugging and wheezing up-hill for the latter half of her journey, there was still a climb to be done on foot, for St Anne's is one of those villages perched on a hilltop which are commoner in Ireland than in England, and the station is some way from the village. A winding road between high banks led her up to it. As soon as she had passed the church she turned left, as she had been instructed, at the Saxon Cross. There were no houses on her left – only a row of beech trees and unfenced ploughland falling steeply away, and beyond that the timbered midland plain spreading as far as she could see and blue in the distance. She was on the highest ground in all that region. Presently, she came to a high wall on her right that seemed to run on for a great way: there was a door in it and beside the door an old iron bell-pull. A kind of flatness of spirit was on her. She felt sure she had come on a fool's errand; nevertheless she rang. When the jangling noise had ceased there followed a silence so long, and in that upland place so chilly, that Jane began to wonder whether the house were inhabited. Then, just as she was debating whether to ring again or to turn away, she heard the noise of someone's feet approaching briskly on the inside of the wall.

Meanwhile Lord Feverstone's car had long since arrived at Belbury – a florid Edwardian mansion which had been built for a millionaire who admired Versailles. At the sides, it seemed to have sprouted into a widespread outgrowth of newer cement buildings, which housed the Blood Transfusion Office.

3

Belbury and St Anne's-on-the-Hill

On his way up the wide staircase Mark caught sight of himself and his companion in a mirror. Feverstone looked, as always, master of his clothes, his face, and of the whole situation. The blob of cotton wool on Mark's upper lip had been blown awry during the journey so that it looked like one-half of a fiercely up-turned false moustache and revealed a patch of blackened blood beneath it. A moment later he found himself in a big-windowed room with a blazing fire, being introduced to Mr John Wither, Deputy Director of the NICE.

Wither was a white-haired old man with a courtly manner. His face was clean shaven and very large indeed, with watery blue eyes and something rather vague and chaotic about it. He did not appear to be giving them his whole attention and this impression must, I think, have been due to the eyes, for his actual words and gestures were polite to the point of effusiveness. He said it was a great, a very great pleasure, to welcome Mr Studdock among them. It added to the deep obligations under which Lord Feverstone had already laid him. He hoped they had had an agreeable journey. Mr Wither appeared to be under the impression that they had come by air and, when this was corrected, that they had come from London by train. Then he began enquiring whether Mr Studdock found his quarters perfectly comfortable and had to be reminded that they had only that moment arrived. 'I suppose,' thought Mark, 'the old chap is trying to put me at my ease.' In fact, Mr Wither's conversation was having precisely the opposite effect. Mark wished he would offer him a cigarette. His growing

47

conviction that this man really knew nothing about him and even that all the well-knit schemes and promises of Feverstone were at this moment dissolving into some sort of mist, was extremely uncomfortable. At last he took his courage in both hands and endeavoured to bring Mr Wither to the point by saying that he was still not quite clear in what capacity he would be able to assist the Institute.

'I assure you, Mr Studdock,' said the Deputy Director with an unusually far away look in his eye, 'that you needn't anticipate the slightest – er – the slightest difficulty on that point. There was never any idea of circumscribing your activities and your general influence on policy, much less your relations with your colleagues and what I might call in general the terms of reference under which you would be collaborating with us, without the fullest possible consideration of your own views and, indeed, your own advice. You will find us, Mr Studdock, if I might express myself in that way, a very happy family.'

'Oh, don't misunderstand me, Sir,' said Mark. 'I didn't mean that at all. I only meant that I felt I should like some sort of idea of what exactly I should be doing if I came to you.'

'Well now, when you speak of coming to us,' said the Deputy Director, 'that raises a point on which I hope there is no misunderstanding. I think we all agreed that no question of residence need be raised – I mean, at this stage. We thought, we all thought, that you should be left entirely free to carry on your work wherever you pleased. If you care to live in London or Cambridge –'

'Edgestow,' prompted Lord Feverstone.

'Ah yes, Edgestow,' here the Deputy Director turned round and addressed Feverstone. 'I was just explaining to Mr – er – Studdock, and I feel sure you will fully agree with me, that nothing was further from the mind of the Committee than to dictate in any way, or even to advise, where Mr – where your friend should live. Of course, wherever he lives we should naturally place air transport and road transport at his disposal. I daresay, Lord Feverstone, you have already explained to him that he will find all questions of that sort will adjust themselves without the smallest difficulty.'

'Really, Sir,' said Mark, 'I wasn't thinking about that at all. I haven't – I mean I shouldn't have the smallest objection to living anywhere: I only – '

The Deputy Director interrupted him, if anything so gentle as Wither's voice can be called an interruption. 'But I assure you, Mr – er – I assure you, Sir, that there is not the smallest objection to your residing wherever you may find it convenient. There was never, at any stage, the slightest suggestion – ' But here Mark, almost in desperation, ventured to interrupt himself.

'It is the exact nature of the work,' he said, 'and of my qualifications for it that I wanted to get clear.'

'My dear friend,' said the Deputy Director, 'you need not have the slightest uneasiness in that direction. As I said before, you will find us a very happy family, and may feel perfectly satisfied that no questions as to your entire suitability have been agitating anyone's mind in the least. I should not be offering you a position among us if there were the slightest danger of your not being completely welcome to all, or the least suspicion that your very valuable qualities were not fully appreciated. You are – you are among *friends* here, Mr Studdock. I should be the last person to advise you to connect yourself with any organisation where you ran the risk of being exposed – er – to disagreeable personal contacts.'

Mark did not ask again in so many words what the NICE wanted him to do; partly because he began to be afraid that he was supposed to know this already, and partly because a perfectly direct question would have sounded a crudity in that room – a crudity which might suddenly exclude him from the warm and almost drugged atmosphere of vague, yet heavily important, confidence in which he was gradually being enfolded.

'You are very kind,' he said. 'The only thing I should like to get just a little clearer is the exact – well, the exact scope of the appointment.'

'Well,' said Mr Wither in a voice so low and rich that it was almost a sigh, 'I am very glad you have raised this issue now in a quite informal way. Obviously neither you nor I would wish to commit ourselves, in this room, in any sense which was at all injurious to the powers of the Committee. I quite understand your motives and – er – respect them. We are not, of course, speaking of an Appointment in the quasi-technical sense of the term; it would be improper for both of us (though, you may well remind me, in different ways) to do so – or at least it might lead to certain inconveniences. But I think I can most definitely assure you that nobody wants to force you into any kind of straight waistcoat or bed of Procrustes. We do not really think, among ourselves, in terms of strictly demarcated functions, of course. I take it that men like you and me are – well, to put it frankly, hardly in the habit of using concepts of that type. Everyone in the Institute feels that his own work is not so much a departmental contribution to an end already defined as a moment or grade in the progressive self-definition of an organic whole.'

And Mark said – God forgive him, for he was young and shy and vain and timid, all in one – 'I do think that is so important. The elasticity of your organisation is one of the things that attracts me.' After that, he had no further chance of bringing the Director to the point and whenever the slow, gentle voice ceased he found himself answering it in its own style, and apparently helpless to do otherwise despite the torturing recurrence of the question, 'What are we both talking *about*?' At the very end of the interview there came one moment of clarity. Mr Wither supposed that he, Mark, would find it convenient to join the NICE club: even for the next few days he would be freer as a member than as someone's guest. Mark agreed and then flushed crimson like a small boy on learning that the easiest course was to become a life member at the cost of £200. He had not that amount in the bank. Of course if he had got the new job with its fifteen hundred a year, all would be well. But had he got it? Was there a job at all?

'How silly,' he said aloud, 'I haven't got my cheque book with me.'

A moment later he found himself on the stairs with Feverstone. 'Well?' asked Mark eagerly. Feverstone did not seem to hear him.

'Well?' repeated Mark. 'When shall I know my fate? I mean, have I got the job?'

'Hullo Guy!' bawled Feverstone suddenly to a man in the hall beneath. Next moment he had trotted down to the foot of the stairs, grasped his friend warmly by the hand, and disappeared. Mark, following him more slowly, found himself in the hall, silent, alone, and self-conscious, among the groups and pairs of chattering men, who were all crossing it towards the big folding doors on his left.

◆ ○ ◆

It seemed to last long, this standing, this wondering what to do, this effort to look natural and not to catch the eyes of strangers. The noise and the agreeable smells which came from the folding doors made it obvious that people were going to lunch. Mark hesitated, uncertain of his own status. In the end, he decided that he couldn't stand there looking like a fool any longer, and went in.

He had hoped that there would be several small tables at one of which he could have sat alone. But there was only a single long table, already so nearly filled that, after looking in vain for Feverstone, he had to sit down beside a stranger. 'I suppose one sits where one likes?' he murmured as he did so; but the stranger apparently did not hear. He was a bustling sort of man who was eating very quickly and talking at the same time to his neighbour on the other side.

'That's just it,' he was saying. 'As I told him, it makes no difference to me which way they settle it. I've no objection to the IJP people taking over the whole thing if that's what the DD wants but what I dislike is one man being responsible for it when half the work is being done by someone else. As I said to him, you've now got three HD's all tumbling over one another about some job that could really be done by a clerk. It's becoming ridiculous. Look at what happened this morning.' Conversation on these lines continued throughout the meal.

Although the food and the drinks were excellent, it was a relief to Mark when people began getting up from table. Following the general movement, he recrossed the hall and came into a large room furnished as a lounge where coffee was being served. Here at last he saw Feverstone. Indeed, it would have been difficult not to notice him for he was the centre of a group and laughing prodigiously. Mark wished to approach him, if only to find out whether he were expected to stay the night and, if so, whether a room had been assigned to him. But the knot of men round Feverstone was of that confidential kind which it is difficult to join. He moved towards one of the many tables and began turning over the glossy pages of an illustrated weekly. Every few seconds he looked up to see if there were any chance of getting a word with Feverstone alone. The fifth time he did so, he found himself looking into the face of one of his own colleagues, a Fellow of Bracton called William Hingest. The Progressive Element called him, though not to his face, Bill the Blizzard.

Hingest had not, as Curry anticipated, been present at the College Meeting and was hardly on speaking terms with Lord Feverstone. Mark realised with a certain awe that here was a man *directly* in touch with the NICE – one who started, so to speak, at a point beyond Feverstone. Hingest, who was a physical chemist, was one of the two scientists at Bracton who had a reputation outside England. I hope the reader has not been misled into supposing that the Fellows of Bracton were a specially distinguished body. It was certainly not the intention of the Progressive Element to elect mediocrities to fellowships, but their determination to elect 'sound men' cruelly limited their field of choice and, as Busby had once said, 'You can't have everything.' Bill the Blizzard had an old-fashioned curly moustache in which white had almost, but not completely, triumphed over yellow, a large beak-like nose, and a bald head.

'This is an unexpected pleasure,' said Mark with a hint of formality. He was always a little afraid of Hingest.

'Huh?' grunted Bill. 'Eh? Oh, it's you, Studdock? Didn't know they'd secured your services here.'

'I was sorry not to see you at the College Meeting yesterday,' said Mark.

This was a lie. The Progressive Element always found Hingest's presence an embarrassment. As a scientist – and the only really eminent scientist they had – he was their rightful property; but he was that hateful anomaly, the wrong sort of scientist. Glossop, who was a classic, was his chief friend in College. He had the air (the 'affectation' Curry called it) of not attaching much importance to his own revolutionary discoveries in chemistry and of valuing himself much more on being a Hingest: the family was of almost mythical antiquity, 'never contaminated,' as its nineteenth-century historian had said, 'by traitor, placeman or baronetcy'. He had given particular offence on the occasion of de Broglie's visit to Edgestow. The Frenchman had spent his spare time exclusively in Bill the Blizzard's society, but when an enthusiastic junior Fellow had thrown out a feeler about the rich feast of science which the two *savants* must have shared, Bill the Blizzard had appeared to search his memory for a moment and then replied that he didn't think they had got onto that subject. 'Gassing Almanac de Gotha nonsense, I suppose,' was Curry's comment, though not in Hingest's presence.

'Eh? What's that? College Meeting?' said the Blizzard. 'What were they talking about?'

'About the sale of Bragdon Wood.'

'All nonsense,' muttered the Blizzard.

'I hope you would have agreed with the decision we came to.'

'It made no difference what decision they came to.'

'Oh!' said Mark with some surprise.

'It was all nonsense. The NICE would have had the Wood in any case. They had powers to compel a sale.'

'What an extraordinary thing! I was given to understand they were going to Cambridge if we didn't sell.'

Hingest sniffed loudly.

'Not a word of truth in it. As to its being an extraordinary thing, that depends on what you mean. There's nothing extraordinary in the Fellows of Bracton talking all afternoon about an unreal issue. And there's nothing extraordinary in the fact that the NICE should wish, if possible, to hand over to Bracton the odium of turning the heart of England into a cross between an abortive American hotel and a glorified gas works. The only real puzzzle is why the NICE should want that bit of land.'

'I suppose we shall find out as things go on.'

'You may. I shan't.'

'Oh?' said Mark interrogatively.

'I've had enough of it,' said Hingest, lowering his voice, 'I'm leaving tonight. I don't know what you were doing at Bracton, but if it was any good I'd advise you to go back and stick to it.'

'Really!' said Mark. 'Why do you say that?'

'Doesn't matter for an old fellow like me,' said Hingest, 'but they could play the devil with *you*. Of course it all depends on what a man likes.'

'As a matter of fact,' said Mark, 'I haven't fully made up my mind.' He had been taught to regard Hingest as a warped reactionary. 'I don't even know yet what my job would be if I stayed.'

'What's your subject?'

'Sociology.'

'Huh,' said Hingest. 'In that case I can soon point you out the man you'd be under. A fellow called Steele. Over there by the window, do you see?'

'Perhaps you could introduce me.'

'You're determined to stay then?'

'Well, I suppose I ought at least to see him.'

'All right,' said Hingest. 'No business of mine.' Then he added in a louder voice, 'Steele.'

Steele turned round. He was a tall, unsmiling man with that kind of face which, though long and horse-like, has nevertheless rather thick and pouting lips.

'This is Studdock,' said Hingest, 'the new man for your department.' Then he turned away.

'Oh,' said Steele. Then after a pause, 'Did he say *my* department?'

'That's what he *said*,' replied Mark with an attempt at a smile, 'but perhaps he's got it wrong. I'm supposed to be a sociologist – if that throws any light on it.'

'I'm HD for Sociology all right,' said Steele, 'but this is the first I've heard about you. Who told you you were to be there?'

'Well, as a matter of fact,' said Mark, 'the whole thing is rather vague. I've just had a talk with the Deputy Director but we didn't actually go into any details.'

'How did you manage to see *him*?'

'Lord Feverstone introduced me.'

Steele whistled. 'I say, Cosser,' he called out to a freckle-faced man who was passing by, 'listen to this. Feverstone has just unloaded this chap on our department. Taken him straight to the DD without saying a word to me about it. What do you think of that?'

'Well, I'm damned!' said Cosser, hardly glancing at Mark but looking very hard at Steele.

'I'm sorry,' said Mark, a little more loudly and a little more stiffly than he had yet spoken. 'Don't be alarmed. I seem to have been put in rather a false position. There must have been some mis-understanding. As a matter of fact I am, at the moment, merely having a look round. I'm not at all certain that I intend to stay in any case.'

Neither of the other two took any notice of this last suggestion.

'That's Feverstone all over,' said Cosser to Steele.

Steele turned to Mark. 'I shouldn't advise you to take much notice of what Lord Feverstone says here,' he remarked. 'This isn't his business at all.'

'All I object to,' said Mark, wishing that he could prevent his face from turning red, 'is being put in a false position. I only came over as an experiment. It is a matter of indifference to me whether I take a job in the NICE or not.'

'You see,' said Steele to Cosser, 'there isn't really any room for a man in our show – specially for someone who doesn't know the work. Unless they put him on the UL.'

'That's right,' said Cosser.

'Mr Studdock, I think,' said a new voice at Mark's elbow, a treble voice which seemed disproportionate to the huge hill of a man whom he saw when he turned his head. He recognised the speaker at once. His dark, smooth face and black hair were unmistakable, and so was the foreign accent. This was Professor Filostrato, the great physiologist, whom Mark had sat next to at a dinner about two years before. He was fat to that degree which is comic on the stage, but the effect was not funny in real life. Mark was charmed that such a man should have remembered him.

'I am very glad you have come to join us,' said Filostrato taking hold of Mark's arm and gently piloting him away from Steele and Cosser.

'To tell you the truth,' said Mark, 'I'm not sure that I have. I was brought over by Feverstone but he has disappeared, and Steele – I'd have been in his Department I suppose – doesn't seem to know anything about me.'

'Bah! Steele!' said the Professor. 'That is all a bagatelle. He get too big for his boots. He will be put in his place one of these days. It may be you who will put him. I have read all your work, *si si*. Do not consider him.'

'I have a strong objection to being put in a false position –' began Mark.

'Listen, my friend,' interrupted Filostrato, 'you must put all such ideas out of your head. The first thing to realise is that the NICE is serious. It is nothing less than the existence of the human race that depends on our work: our *real* work, you comprehend? You will find frictions and impertinences among this *canaglia*, this rabble. They are no more to be regarded than your dislike of a brother officer when the battle is at its crisis.'

'As long as I'm given something to do that is worth doing,' said Mark, 'I shouldn't allow anything of that sort to interfere with it.'

'Yes, yes, that is right. The work is more important than you can yet understand. You will see. These Steeles and Feverstones – they are of no consequence. As long as you have the good will of the

Deputy Director, you snap your fingers at them. You need listen to no one but him, you comprehend? Ah – and there is one other. Do not have the Fairy for your enemy. For the rest – you laugh at them.'

'The Fairy?'

'Yes. Her they call the Fairy. Oh my God, a terrible *Inglesaccia!* She is the head of our police, the Institutional Police. *Ecco*, she come. I will present you. Miss Hardcastle, permit that I present to you Mr Studdock.'

Mark found himself writhing from the stoker's or carter's hand-grip of a big woman in a black, short-skirted uniform. Despite a bust that would have done credit to a Victorian barmaid, she was rather thickly built than fat and her iron-grey hair was cropped short. Her face was square, stern and pale, and her voice deep. A smudge of lipstick laid on with violent inattention to the real shape of her mouth was her only concession to fashion and she rolled or chewed a long black cheroot, unlit, between her teeth. As she talked she had a habit of removing this, staring intently at the mixture of lipstick and saliva on its mangled end, and then replacing it more firmly than before. She sat down immediately in a chair close to where Mark was standing, flung her right leg over one of the arms, and fixed him with a gaze of cold intimacy.

◆ ○ ◆

Click – clack, distinct in the silence, where Jane stood waiting, came the tread of the person on the other side of the wall. Then the door opened and Jane found herself facing a tall woman of about her own age. This person looked at her with keen, non-committal eyes.

'Does a Miss Ironwood live here?' said Jane.

'Yes,' said the other girl, neither opening the door any further nor standing aside.

'I want to see her, please,' said Jane.

'Have you an appointment?' said the tall woman.

'Well, not exactly,' said Jane. 'I was directed here by Dr Dimble who knows Miss Ironwood. He said I shouldn't need an appointment.'

'Oh, if you're from Dr Dimble that is another matter,' said the woman. 'Come in. Now wait a moment while I attend to this lock. That's better. Now we're all right. There's not room for two on this path so you must excuse me if I go first.'

The woman led her along a brick path beside a wall on which fruit trees were growing, and then to the left along a mossy path with gooseberry bushes on each side. Then came a little lawn with a see-saw in the middle of it, and beyond that a greenhouse. Here they found themselves in the sort of hamlet that sometimes occurs in the purlieus of a large garden – walking in fact down a little street which had a barn and a stable on one side and, on the other, a second green-house, and a potting shed and a pigstye – inhabited, as the grunts and the not wholly agreeable smell informed her. After that were narrow paths across a vegetable garden that seemed to be on a fairly steep hillside, and then, rose bushes, all stiff and prickly in their winter garb. At one place, they were going along a path made of single planks. This reminded Jane of something. It was a very large garden. It was like – like – yes, now she had it: it was like the garden in *Peter Rabbit*. Or was it like the garden in the *Romance of the Rose*? No, not in the least like really. Or like Klingsor's garden? Or the garden in *Alice*? Or like the garden on the top of some Mesopotamian ziggurat which had probably given rise to the whole legend of Paradise? Or simply like all walled gardens? Freud said we liked gardens because they were symbols of the female body. But that must be a man's point of view. Presumably gardens meant something different in women's dreams. Or did they? Did men and women both feel interested in the female body and even, though it sounded ridiculous, in almost the same way? A sentence rose to her memory. 'The beauty of the female is the root of joy to the female as well as to the male, and it is no accident that the goddess of Love is older and stronger than the god.' Where on earth had she read that? And, incidentally, what frightful nonsense she had been thinking for the last minute or so! She shook off all these ideas about gardens and determined to pull herself together. A curious feeling that she was now on hostile, or at least alien, ground warned her to keep all her wits about her. At that moment, they suddenly emerged from between plantations of rhododendron and laurel, and found themselves at a small side door, flanked by a water butt, in the long wall of a large house. Just as they did so a window clapped shut upstairs.

A minute or two later Jane was sitting waiting in a large sparely furnished room with a shut stove to warm it. Most of the floor was bare, and the walls, above the waist-high wainscotting, were of greyish white plaster, so that the whole effect was faintly austere and conventual. The tall woman's tread died away in the passages and the room became very quiet when it had done so. Occasionally the cawing of rooks could be heard. 'I've let myself in for it now,' thought Jane. 'I shall have to tell this woman that dream and she'll ask all sorts of questions.' She considered herself, in general, a modern person who could talk without embarrassment of anything, but it began to look quite different as she sat in that room. All sorts of secret reservations in her programme of frankness – things which, she now realised, she had set apart as never to be told – came creeping back into consciousness. It was surprising that very few of them were connected with sex. 'In dentists',' said Jane, 'they at least leave illustrated papers in the waiting room.' She got up and opened the one book that lay on the table in the middle of the room. Instantly her eyes lit on the following words: 'The beauty of the female is the root of joy to the female as well as to the male, and it is no accident that the goddess of Love is older and stronger than the god. To desire the desiring of her own beauty is the vanity of Lilith, but to desire the enjoying of her own beauty is the obedience of Eve, and to both it is in the lover that the beloved tastes her own delightfulness. As obedience is the stairway of pleasure, so humility is the – '

At that moment the door was suddenly opened. Jane turned crimson as she shut the book and looked up. The same girl who had first let her in had apparently just opened the door and was still standing in the doorway. Jane now conceived for her that almost passionate admiration which women, more often than is supposed, feel for other women whose beauty is not of their own type. It would be nice, Jane thought, to be like that – so straight, so forthright, so valiant, so fit to be mounted on a horse, and so divinely tall.

'Is – is Miss Ironwood in?' said Jane.

'Are you Mrs Studdock?' said the girl.

'Yes,' said Jane.

'I will bring you to her at once,' said the other. 'We have been expecting you. My name is Camilla – Camilla Denniston.'

Jane followed her. From the narrowness and plainness of the passages, Jane judged that they were still in the back parts of the house, and that, if so, it must be a very large house indeed. They went a long way before Camilla knocked at a door and stood aside for Jane to enter, after saying in a low, clear voice ('like a servant', Jane thought), 'She has come.' And Jane went in; and there was Miss Ironwood dressed all in black and sitting with her hands folded on her knees, just as Jane had seen her when dreaming – if she were dreaming – last night in the flat.

'Sit down, young lady,' said Miss Ironwood.

The hands which were folded on her knees were very big and bony though they did not suggest coarseness, and even when seated Miss Ironwood was extremely tall. Everything about her was big – the nose, the unsmiling lips, and the grey eyes. She was perhaps nearer sixty than fifty. There was an atmosphere in the room which Jane found uncongenial.

'What is your name, young lady?' said Miss Ironwood, taking up a pencil and a notebook.

'Jane Studdock.'

'Are you married?'

'Yes.'

'Does your husband know you have come to us?'

'No.'

'And your age, if you please?'

'Twenty-three.'

'And now,' said Miss Ironwood, 'what have you to tell me?'

Jane took a deep breath. 'I've been having bad dreams and – and feeling depressed lately,' she said.

'What were the dreams?' asked Miss Ironwood.

Jane's narrative – she did not do it very well – took some time. While she was speaking she kept her eyes fixed on Miss Ironwood's large hands and her black skirt and the pencil and the notebook. And that was why she suddenly stopped. For as she proceeded she saw Miss Ironwood's hand cease to write and the fingers wrap themselves round the pencil: immensely strong fingers they seemed. And every moment they tightened, till the knuckles grew white and the veins stood out on the backs of the hands and at last, as if under the influence of some stifled emotion, they broke the pencil in two. It was then that Jane stopped in astonishment and looked up at Miss Ironwood's face. The wide grey eyes were still looking at her with no change of expression.

'Pray continue, young lady,' said Miss Ironwood.

Jane resumed her story. When she had finished Miss Ironwood put a number of questions. After that she became silent for so long that Jane said,

'Is there, do you think, anything very seriously wrong with me?'

'There is nothing wrong with you,' said Miss Ironwood.

'You mean it will go away?'

'I have no means of telling. I should say probably not.'

Disappointment shadowed Jane's face.

'Then – can't anything be done about it? They were horrible dreams – horribly vivid, not like dreams at all.'

'I can quite understand that.'

'Is it something that can't be cured?'

'The reason you cannot be cured is that you are not ill.'

'But there must be something wrong. It's surely not natural to have dreams like that.'

There was a pause. 'I think,' said Miss Ironwood, 'I had better tell you the whole truth.'

'Yes, do,' said Jane in a strained voice. The other's words had frightened her.

'And I will begin by saying this,' continued Miss Ironwood. 'You are a more important person than you imagine.'

Jane said nothing, but thought inwardly, 'She is humouring me. She thinks I am mad.'

'What was your maiden name?' asked Miss Ironwood.

'Tudor,' said Jane. At any other moment she would have said it rather self-consciously, for she was very anxious not to be supposed vain of her ancient ancestry.

'The Warwickshire branch of the family?'

'Yes.'

'Did you ever read a little book – it is only forty pages long – written by an ancestor of yours about the battle of Worcester?'

'No. Father had a copy – the only copy, I think he said. But I never read it. It was lost when the house was broken up after his death.'

'Your father was mistaken in thinking it the only copy. There are at least two others: one is in America, and the other is in this house.'

'Well?'

'Your ancestor gave a full and, on the whole, correct account of the battle, which he says he completed on the same day on which it was fought. But he was not at it. He was in York at the time.'

Jane, who had not really been following this, looked at Miss Ironwood.

'If he was speaking the truth,' said Miss Ironwood, 'and we believe that he was, he dreamed it. Do you understand?'

'Dreamed about the battle?'

'Yes. But dreamed it right. He saw the real battle in his dream.'

'I don't see the connection.'

'Vision – the power of dreaming realities – is sometimes hereditary,' said Miss Ironwood.

Something seemed to be interfering with Jane's breathing. She felt a sense of injury – this was just the sort of thing she hated: something out of the past, something irrational and utterly uncalled for, coming up from its den and interfering with her.

'Can it be proved?' she asked. 'I mean, we have only his word for it.'

'We have your dreams,' said Miss Ironwood. Her voice, always grave, had become stern. A fantastic thought crossed Jane's mind. Could this old woman have some idea that one ought not to call even one's remote ancestors liars?

'My dreams?' she said a little sharply.

'Yes,' said Miss Ironwood.

'What do you mean?'

'My opinion is that you have seen real things in your dreams. You have seen Alcasan as he really sat in the condemned cell, and you have seen a visitor whom he really had.'

'But – but – oh, this is ridiculous,' said Jane. '*That* part was a mere coincidence. The rest was just a nightmare. It was all impossible. He screwed off his head, I tell you. And they – dug up the horrible old man. They made him come to life.'

'There are some confusions there, no doubt. But in my opinion there are realities behind even those episodes.'

'I am afraid I don't believe in that sort of thing,' said Jane coldly.

'Your upbringing makes it natural that you should not,' replied Miss Ironwood. 'Unless, of course, you have discovered for yourself that you have a tendency to dream real things.'

Jane thought of the book on the table which she had apparently remembered before she saw it, and then there was Miss Ironwood's own appearance – that too she had seen before she saw it. But it must be nonsense.

'Can you then do nothing for me?'

'I can tell you the truth,' said Miss Ironwood. 'I have tried to do so.'

'I mean, can you not stop it – cure it?'

'Vision is not a disease.'

'But I don't *want* it,' said Jane passionately. 'I must stop it. I hate this sort of thing.' Miss Ironwood said nothing.

'Don't you even know anyone who could stop it?' said Jane. 'Can't you recommend anyone?'

'If you go to an ordinary psychotherapist,' said Miss Ironwood, 'he will proceed on the assumption that the dreams merely reflect your own sub-conscious. He would try to treat you. I do not know what would be the results of treatment based on that assumption. I am afraid they might be very serious. And – it would certainly not remove the dreams.'

'But what is this all about?' said Jane. 'I want to lead an ordinary life. I want to do my own work. It's unbearable! Why should I be selected for this horrible thing?'

'The answer to that is known only to authorities much higher than myself.'

There was a short silence. Jane made a vague movement and said, rather sulkily, 'Well, if you can do nothing for me, perhaps I'd better be going – ' Then suddenly she added, 'But how can you *know* all this? I mean – what realities are you talking about?'

'I think,' said Miss Ironwood, 'that you yourself have probably more reason to suspect the truth of your dreams than you have yet told me. If not, you soon will have. In the meantime, I will answer your question. We know your dreams to be partly true because they fit in with information we already possess. It was because he saw their importance that Dr Dimble sent you to us.'

'Do you mean he sent me here not to be cured but to give information?' said Jane. The idea fitted in with things she had observed in his manner when she first told him.

'Exactly.'

'I wish I had known that a little earlier,' said Jane coldly, and now definitely getting up to go. 'I'm afraid it has been a misunderstanding. I had imagined Dr Dimble was trying to help me.'

'He was. But he was also trying to do something more important at the same time.'

'I suppose I should be grateful for being considered at all,' said Jane drily, 'and how, exactly, was I to be helped by – by all this sort of thing?' The attempt at icy irony collapsed as she said these last words and red, undisguised anger rushed back into her face. In some ways she was very young.

'Young lady,' said Miss Ironwood, 'You do not at all realise the seriousness of this matter. The things you have seen concern something compared with which the happiness, or even the life, of you and me, *is* of no importance. I must beg you to face the situation. You cannot get rid of your gift. You can try to suppress it, but you will fail, and you will be very badly frightened. On the other hand, you can put it at our disposal. If you do so, you will be much less frightened in the long run and you will be helping to save the human race from a very great disaster. Or thirdly, you may tell someone else about it. If you do that, I warn you that you will almost certainly fall into the hands of other people who are at least as anxious as we to make use of your faculty and who will care no more about your life and happiness than about those of a fly. The people you have seen in your dreams are real people. It is not at all unlikely that they know you have, involuntarily, been spying on them. And, if so, they will not rest till they have got hold of you. I would advise you, even for your own sake, to join our side.'

'You keep on talking of *We* and *Us*. Are you some kind of company?'

'Yes. You may call it a company.'

Jane had been standing for the last few minutes; and she had almost been believing what she heard. Then suddenly, all her repugnance came over her again – all her wounded vanity, her resentment of the meaningless complication in which she seemed to be caught, and her general dislike of the mysterious and the unfamiliar. At that moment, nothing seemed to matter but to get out of that room and away from the grave, patient voice of Miss Ironwood. 'She's made me worse already,' thought Jane, still regarding herself as a patient. Aloud, she said,

'I must go home now. I don't know what you are talking about. I don't want to have anything to do with it.'

◆ ○ ◆

Mark discovered in the end that he was expected to stay, at least for the night, and when he went up to dress for dinner he was feeling more cheerful. This was partly due to a whisky and soda taken with 'Fairy' Hardcastle immediately before and partly to the fact that by a glance at the mirror he saw that he could not remove the objectionable piece of cotton wool from his lip. The bedroom with its bright fire and its private bathroom attached had also something to do with it. Thank goodness, he had allowed Jane to talk him into buying that new dress suit! It looked very well, laid out on the bed; and he saw now that the old one really would not have done. But what had reassured him most of all was his conversation with the Fairy.

It would be misleading to say that he liked her. She had indeed excited in him all the distaste which a young man feels at the proximity of something rankly, even insolently sexed, and at the same time wholly unattractive. And something in her cold eye had told him that she was well aware of this reaction and found it amusing. She had told him a good many smoking-room stories. Often before now Mark had shuddered at the clumsy efforts of the emancipated female to indulge in this kind of humour, but his shudders had always been consoled by a sense of superiority. This time he had the feeling that he was the butt; this woman was exasperating male prudery for her diversion. Later on, she drifted into police reminiscences. In spite of some initial scepticism, Mark was gradually horrified by her assumption that about thirty per cent of our murder trials ended by the hanging of an innocent man. There were details, too, about the execution shed which had not occurred to him before.

All this was disagreeable. But it was made up for by the deliciously esoteric character of the conversation. Several times that day he had been made to feel himself an outsider; that feeling completely disappeared while Miss Hardcastle was talking to him. He had the sense of getting *in*. Miss Hardcastle had apparently lived an exciting life. She had been, at different times, a suffragette, a pacifist, and a British Fascist. She had been manhandled by the police and imprisoned. On the other hand, she had met Prime Ministers, Dictators and famous film stars; all her history was secret history.

She knew from both ends what a police force could do and what it could not, and there were in her opinion very few things it could not do. 'Specially now,' she said. 'Here in the Institute, we're backing the crusade against Red Tape.'

Mark gathered that, for the Fairy, the police side of the Institute was the really important side. It existed to relieve the ordinary executive of what might be called all sanitary cases – a category which ranged from vaccination to charges of unnatural vice – from which, as she pointed out, it was only a step to bringing in all cases of blackmail. As regards crime in general, they had already popularised in the press the idea that the Institute should be allowed to experiment pretty largely in the hope of discovering how far humane, remedial treatment could be substituted for the old notion of 'retributive' or 'vindictive' punishment. That was where a lot of legal Red Tape stood in their way. 'But there are only two papers we don't control,' said the Fairy. 'And we'll smash them. You've got to get the ordinary man into the state in which he says "Sadism" automatically when he hears the word Punishment.' And then one would have *carte blanche*. Mark did not immediately follow this. But the Fairy pointed out that what had hampered every English police force up to date was precisely the idea of deserved punishment. For desert was always finite: you could do so much to the criminal and no more. Remedial treatment, on the other hand, need have no fixed limit; it could go on till it had effected a cure, and those who were carrying it out would decide when *that* was. And if cure were humane and desirable, how much more prevention? Soon anyone who had ever been in the hands of the police at all would come under the control of the NICE; in the end, every citizen. 'And that's where you and I come in, Sonny,' added the Fairy, tapping Mark's chest with her forefinger. 'There's no distinction in the long run between police work and Sociology. You and I've got to work hand in hand.'

This had brought Mark back to his doubts as to whether he were really being given a job and, if so, what it was. The Fairy had warned him that Steele was a dangerous man. 'There are two people you want to be very cautious about,' she said. 'One is Frost and the other is old Wither.' But she had laughed at his fears in general. 'You're in all right, Sonny,' she said. 'Only don't be too particular about what exactly you've got to do. You'll find out as it comes along. Wither doesn't like people who try to pin him down. There's no good saying you've come here to do *this* and you won't do *that*. The game's too fast just at present for that sort of thing. You've got to make yourself useful. And don't believe everything you're told.'

At dinner Mark found himself seated next to Hingest.

'Well,' said Hingest, 'have they finally roped you into it, eh?'

'I rather believe they have,' said Mark.

'Because,' said Hingest, 'if you thought the better of it, I'm motoring back tonight and I could give you a lift.'

'You haven't yet told me why you are leaving us yourself,' said Mark.

'Oh well, it all depends what a man likes. If you enjoy the society of that Italian eunuch and the mad parson and that Hardcastle girl – her grandmother would have boxed her ears if she were alive – of course, there's nothing more to be said.'

'I suppose it's hardly to be judged on purely social grounds – I mean, it's something more than a club.'

'Eh? Judged? Never judged anything in my life, to the best of my knowledge, except at a flower show. It's all a question of taste. I came here because I thought it had something to do with science. Now that I find it's something more like a political conspiracy, I shall go home. I'm too old for that kind of thing, and if I wanted to join a conspiracy, this one wouldn't be my choice.'

'You mean, I suppose, that the element of social planning doesn't appeal to you? I can quite understand that it doesn't fit in with your work as it does with sciences like Sociology, but –'

'There *are* no sciences like Sociology. And if I found chemistry beginning to fit in with a secret police run by a middle-aged virago who doesn't wear corsets and a scheme for taking away his farm and his shop and his children from every Englishman, I'd let chemistry go to the devil and take up gardening again.'

'I think I *do* understand the sentiment that still attaches to the small man, but when you come to study the reality as I have to do –'

'I should want to pull it to bits and put something else in its place. Of course. That's what happens when you study men: you find mare's nests. I happen to believe that you can't study men; you can only get to know them, which is quite a different thing. Because you study them, you want to make the lower orders govern the country and listen to classical music, which is balderdash. You also want to take away from them everything which makes life worth living and not only from them but from everyone except a parcel of prigs and professors.'

'Bill!' said Fairy Hardcastle suddenly, from the far side of the table, in a voice so loud that even he could not ignore it. Hingest fixed his eyes upon her and his face grew a dark red.

'Is it true,' bawled the Fairy, 'that you're going off by car immediately after dinner?'

'Yes, Miss Hardcastle, it is.'

'I was wondering if you could give me a lift.'

'I should be happy to do so,' said Hingest in a voice not intended to deceive, 'if we are going in the same direction.'

'Where are you going?'

'I am going to Edgestow.'

'Will you be passing Brenstock?'

'No. I leave the by-pass at the crossroads just beyond Lord Holywood's front gate and go down what they used to call Potter's Lane.'

'Oh, damn! No good to me. I may as well wait till the morning.'

After this Mark found himself engaged by his left-hand neighbour and did not see Bill the Blizzard again until he met him in the hall after dinner. He was in his overcoat and just ready to go to his car.

He began talking as he opened the door and thus Mark was drawn into accompanying him across the gravel sweep to where his car was parked.

'Take my advice, Studdock,' he said. 'Or at least think it over. I don't believe in Sociology myself, but you've got quite a decent career before you if you stay at Bracton. You'll do yourself no good by getting mixed up with the NICE – and, by God, you'll do nobody else any good either.'

'I suppose there are two views about everything,' said Mark.

'Eh? Two views? There are a dozen views about everything until you know the answer. Then there's never more than one. But it's no affair of mine. Good night.'

'Good night, Hingest,' said Mark. The other started up the car and drove off.

There was a touch of frost in the air. The shoulder of Orion, though Mark did not know even that earnest constellation, flamed at him above the tree-tops. He felt a hesitation about going back into the house. It might mean further talk with interesting and influential people; but it might also mean feeling once more an outsider, hanging about and watching conversations which he could not join. Anyway, he was tired. Strolling along the front of the house he came presently to another and smaller door by which, he judged, one could enter without passing through the hall or the public rooms. He did so, and went upstairs for the night immediately.

◆ ○ ◆

Camilla Denniston showed Jane out – not by the little door in the wall at which she had come in but by the main gate which opened on the same road about a hundred yards further on. Yellow light from a westward gap in the grey sky was pouring a short-lived and chilly brightness over the whole landscape. Jane had been ashamed to show either temper or anxiety before Camilla; as a result both had in reality been diminished when she said goodbye. But a settled distaste for what she called 'all this nonsense' remained. She was not indeed sure that it was nonsense; but she had already resolved to treat it as if it were. She would not get 'mixed up in it'. would not be drawn in. One had to live one's own life. To avoid entanglements and interferences had long been one of her first principles. Even when she had discovered that she was going to marry Mark if he asked her, the thought 'but I must still keep up my own life' had arisen at once and had never for more than a few minutes at a stretch been absent from her mind. Some resentment against love itself, and therefore against Mark, for thus invading her life, remained. She was at least very vividly aware how much a woman gives up in getting married. Mark seemed to her insufficiently aware of this. Though she did not formulate it, this fear of being invaded and entangled was the deepest ground of her determination not to have a child – or not for a long time yet. One had one's own life to live.

Almost as soon as she got back to the flat the telephone went. 'Is that you, Jane?' came a voice. 'It's me, Margaret Dimble. Such a dreadful thing's happened. I'll tell you when I come. I'm too angry to speak at the moment. Have you a spare bed by any chance? What? Mr Studdock's away? Not a bit, if *you* don't mind. I've sent Cecil to sleep in College. You're sure it won't be a nuisance? Thanks most awfully. I'll be round in half an hour.'

The Liquidation of Anachronisms

Almost before Jane had finished putting clean sheets on Mark's bed, Mrs Dimble, with a great many parcels, arrived. 'You're an angel to have me for the night,' she said. 'We'd tried every hotel in Edgestow, I believe. This place is going to become unendurable. The same answer everywhere! All full up with the hangers-on and camp-followers of this detestable NICE. Secretaries here – typists there – commissioners of works – the thing's outrageous. If Cecil hadn't had a room in College I really believe he'd have had to sleep in the waiting room at the station. I only hope that man in College has aired the bed.'

'But what on earth's happened?' asked Jane.

'Turned out, my dear!'

'But it isn't possible, Mrs Dimble. I mean, it can't be legal.'

'That's what Cecil said … Just think of it, Jane. The first thing we saw when we poked our heads out of the window this morning was a lorry on the drive with its back wheels in the middle of the rose bed, unloading a small army of what looked like criminals, with picks and spades. Right in our own garden! There was an odious little man in a peaked cap who talked to Cecil with a cigarette in his mouth, at least it wasn't in his mouth but seccotined onto his upper lip – you know – and guess what he said? He said they'd have no objection to our remaining in possession (of the *house*, mind you, not the garden) till 8 o'clock tomorrow morning. No objection!'

'But surely – surely – it must be some mistake.'

'Of course, Cecil rang up your Bursar. And, of course, your Bursar was out. That took nearly all morning, ringing up again and again, and by that time, the big beech that you used to be so fond of had been cut down, and all the plum trees. If I hadn't been so angry, I'd have sat down and cried my eyes out. That's what I felt like. At last Cecil did get onto your Mr Busby, who was perfectly useless. Said there must be some misunderstanding but it was out of his hands now and we'd better get onto the NICE at Belbury. Of course, it turned out to be quite impossible to get *them*. But by lunch-time we saw that one simply *couldn't* stay there for the night, whatever happened.'

'Why not?'

'My dear, you've no conception what it was like. Great lorries and traction engines roaring past all the time, and a crane on a thing like a railway truck. Why, our own tradesmen couldn't get through it. The milk didn't arrive till eleven o'clock. The meat never arrived at all; they rang up in the afternoon to say their people hadn't been able to reach us by either road. We'd the greatest difficulty in getting into town ourselves. It took us half an hour from our house to the bridge. It was like a nightmare. Flares and noise everywhere and the road practically ruined and a sort of great tin camp already going up on the Common. And the people! Such horrid men. I didn't know we *had* workpeople like that in England. Oh, horrible, horrible!' Mrs Dimble fanned herself with the hat she had just taken off.

'And what are you going to do?' asked Jane.

'Heaven knows!' said Mrs Dimble. 'For the moment, we have shut up the house and Cecil has been at Rumbold, the solicitor's, to see if we can at least have it sealed and left alone until we've got our things out of it. Rumbold doesn't seem to know where he is. He keeps on saying the NICE are in a very peculiar position legally. After that, I'm sure I don't know. As far as I can see, there won't be *any* houses in Edgestow. There's no question of trying to live on the far side of the river any longer, even if they'd let us. What did you say? Oh, indescribable. All the poplars are going down. All those nice little cottages by the church are going down. I found poor Ivy – that's your Mrs Maggs, you know – in tears. Poor things! They do look dreadful when they cry on top of powder. She's being turned out too. Poor little woman; she's had enough troubles in her life without this. I was glad to get away. The men were so horrible. Three big brutes came to the back door asking for hot water and went on so that they frightened Martha out of her wits and Cecil had to go and speak to them. I thought they were going to strike Cecil, really I did. It was most horribly unpleasant. But a sort of special constable sent them away. What? Oh yes, there are dozens of what look like policemen all over the place, and I didn't like the look of *them* either. Swinging some kind of truncheon things, like what you'd see in an American film. Do you know Jane, Cecil and I both thought the same thing: we thought, it's almost as if we'd lost the war. Oh, good girl – tea! That's just what I wanted.'

'You must stay here as long as you like, Mrs Dimble,' said Jane. 'Mark'll just have to sleep in College.'

'Well, really,' said Mother Dimble, 'I feel at the moment that no Fellow of Bracton ought to be allowed to sleep anywhere! But I'd make an exception in favour of Mr Studdock. As a matter of fact, I shan't have to behave like the sword of Siegfried – and, incidentally, a nasty fat stodgy sword I should be! But that side of it is all fixed up. Cecil and I are to go out to the Manor at St Anne's. We have to be there so much at present, you see.'

'Oh,' said Jane, involuntarily prolonging the exclamation as the whole of her own story flowed back on her mind.

'Why, what a selfish pig I've been,' said Mother Dimble. 'Here have I been chattering away about my own troubles and quite forgetting that you've been out there and are full of things to tell me. Did you see Grace? And did you like her?'

'Is "Grace" Miss Ironwood?' asked Jane.

'Yes.'

'I saw her. I don't know if I liked her or not. But I don't want to talk about all that. I can't think about anything except this outrageous business of yours. It's you who are the real martyr, not me.'

'No, my dear,' said Mrs Dimble, 'I'm not a martyr. I'm only an angry old woman with sore feet and a splitting head (but that's beginning to be better) who's trying to talk herself into a good temper. After all, Cecil and I haven't lost our livelihood as poor Ivy Maggs has. It doesn't *really* matter leaving the old house. Do you know, the pleasure of living there was in a way a melancholy pleasure. (I wonder, by the bye, do human beings really *like* being happy?) A little melancholy, yes. All those big upper rooms which we thought we should want because we thought we were going to have lots of children, and then we never had. Perhaps I was getting too fond of mooning about them on long afternoons when Cecil was away. Pitying oneself. I shall be better away from it, I daresay. I might have got like that frightful woman in Ibsen who was always maundering about dolls. It's really worse for Cecil. He did so love having all his pupils about the place. Jane, that's the third time you've yawned. You're dropping asleep and I've talked your head off. It comes of being married thirty years. Husbands were made to be talked to. It helps them to concentrate their minds on what they're reading – like the sound of a weir. There! – you're yawning again.'

Jane found Mother Dimble an embarrassing person to share a room with because she said prayers. It was quite extraordinary, Jane thought, how this put one out. One didn't know where to look, and it was so difficult to talk naturally again for several minutes after Mrs Dimble had risen from her knees.

◆ ○ ◆

'Are you awake now?' said Mrs Dimble's voice, quietly, in the middle of the night.

'Yes,' said Jane. 'I'm sorry. Did I wake you up? Was I shouting?'

'Yes. You were shouting out about someone being hit on the head.'

'I saw them killing a man – a man in a big car driving along a country road. Then he came to a crossroads and turned off to the right past some trees, and there was someone standing in the middle of the road waving a light to stop him. I couldn't hear what they said; I was too far away. They must have persuaded him to get out of the car somehow, and there he was talking to one of them. The light fell full on his face. He wasn't the same old man I saw in my other dream. He hadn't a beard, only a moustache. And he had a very quick, kind of proud, way. He didn't like what the man said to him and presently he put up his fists and knocked him down. Another man behind him tried to hit him on the head with something but the old man was too quick and turned round in time. Then it was rather horrible, but rather fine. There were three of them at him and he was fighting them all. I've read about that kind of thing in books but I never realised how one would feel about it. Of course, they got him in the end. They beat his head about terribly with the things in their hands. They were quite cool about it and stooped down to examine him and make sure he was really dead. The light from the lantern seemed all funny. It looked as if it made long uprights of light – sort of rods – all round the place. But perhaps I was waking up by then. No thanks, I'm all right. It was horrid, of course, but I'm not really frightened – not the way I would have been before. I'm more sorry for the old man.'

'You feel you can go to sleep again?'

'Oh rather! Is your headache better, Mrs Dimble?'

'Quite gone, thank you. Good night.'

◆ ○ ◆

'Without a doubt,' thought Mark, 'this must be the Mad Parson that Bill the Blizzard was talking of.' The Committee at Belbury did not meet till ten-thirty, and ever since breakfast he had been walking with the Reverend Straik in the garden, despite the raw and misty weather of the morning. At the very moment when the man had first buttonholed him, the threadbare clothes and clumsy boots, the frayed clerical collar, the dark, lean, tragic face, gashed and ill-shaved and seamed, and the bitter sincerity of his manner, had struck a discordant note. It was not a type Mark had expected to meet in the NICE.

'Do not imagine,' said Mr Straik, 'that I indulge in any dreams of carrying out our programme without violence. There will be resistance. They will gnaw their tongues and not repent. We are not to be deterred. We face these disorders with a firmness which will lead traducers to say that we have desired them. Let them say so. In a sense we have. It is no part of our witness to preserve that organisation of ordered sin which is called Society. To that organisation the message which we have to deliver is a message of absolute despair.'

'Now that is what I meant,' said Mark, 'when I said that your point of view and mine must, in the long run, be incompatible. The preservation, which involves the thorough planning, of Society is just precisely the end I have in view. I do not think there is or can be any other end. The problem is quite different for you because you look forward to something else, something better than human society, in some other world.'

'With every thought and vibration of my heart, with every drop of my blood,' said Mr Straik, 'I repudiate that damnable doctrine. That is precisely the subterfuge by which the World, the organization and body of Death, has sidetracked and emasculated the teaching of Jesus, and turned into priestcraft and mysticism the plain demand of the Lord for righteousness and judgment here and now. The Kingdom of God is to be realised here – in this world. And it will be. At the name of Jesus every knee shall bow. In that name I dissociate myself completely from all the organised religion that has yet been seen in the world.'

And at the name of Jesus, Mark, who would have lectured on abortion or perversion to an audience of young women without a qualm, felt himself so embarrassed that he knew his cheeks were slightly reddening; and he became so angry with himself and Mr Straik at this discovery that they then proceeded to redden very much indeed. This was exactly the kind of conversation he could not endure; and never since the well remembered misery of scripture lessons at school had he felt so uncomfortable. He muttered something about his ignorance of theology.

'Theology!' said Mr Straik with profound contempt. 'It's not theology I'm talking about, young man, but the Lord Jesus. Theology is talk – eyewash – a smoke screen – a game for rich men. It wasn't in lecture rooms I found the Lord Jesus. It was in the coal pits, and beside the coffin of my daughter. If they think that Theology is a sort of cotton wool which will keep them safe in the great and terrible day, they'll find their mistake. For, mark my words, this thing is going to happen. The Kingdom is going to arrive: in this world: in this country. The powers of science are an instrument. An irresistible instrument, as all of us in the NICE know. And why are they an irresistible instrument?'

'Because science is based on observation,' suggested Mark.

'They are an irresistible instrument,' shouted Straik, 'because they are an instrument in His hand. An instrument of judgment as well as of healing. That is what I couldn't get any of the Churches to see. They are blinded. Blinded by their filthy rags of humanism, their culture and humanitarianism and liberalism, as well as by their sins, or what they think their sins, though they are really the least sinful thing about them. That is why I have come to stand alone: a poor, weak, unworthy man, but the only prophet left. I knew that He was coming in power. And therefore, where we see power, we see the sign of His coming. And that is why I find myself joining with communists and materialists and anyone else who is really ready to expedite the coming. The feeblest of these people here has the tragic sense of life, the ruthlessness, the total commitment, the readiness to sacrifice all merely human values, which I could not find amid all the nauseating cant of the organised religions.'

'You mean, do you,' said Mark, 'that as far as immediate practice is concerned, there are no limits to your co-operation with the programme?'

'Sweep away all idea of co-operation!' said the other. 'Does clay co-operate with the potter? Did Cyrus co-operate with the Lord? These people will be used. I shall be used too. Instruments. Vehicles. But here comes the point that concerns you, young man.

You have no choice whether you will be used or not. There is no turning back once you have set your hand to the plough. No one goes *out* of the NICE Those who try to turn back will perish in the wilderness. But the question is, whether you are content to be one of the instruments which is thrown aside when it has served His turn – one which having executed judgment on others, is reserved for judgment itself – or will you be among those who enter on the inheritance? For it's all true, you know. It is the Saints who are going to inherit the Earth – here in England, perhaps within the next twelve months – the Saints and no one else. Know you not that we shall judge angels?' Then, suddenly lowering his voice, Straik added: 'The *real* resurrection is even now taking place. The real life everlasting. Here in this world. You will see it.'

'I say,' said Mark, 'it's nearly twenty past. Oughtn't we to be going to the Committee?'

Straik turned with him in silence. Partly to avoid further conversation along the same lines, and partly because he really wanted to know the answer, Mark said presently, 'A rather annoying thing has happened. I've lost my wallet. There wasn't much money in it – only about three pounds. But there were letters and things, and it's a nuisance. Ought I to tell someone about it?'

'You could tell the Steward,' said Straik.

◆　○　◆

The Committee sat for about two hours and the Deputy Director was in the chair. His method of conducting business was slow and involved and to Mark, with his Bracton experience to guide him, it soon became obvious that the real work of the NICE must go on somewhere else. This, indeed, was what he had expected, and he was too reasonable to suppose that he should find himself, at this early stage, in the Inner Ring or whatever at Belbury corresponded to the Progressive Element at Bracton. But he hoped he would not be kept marking time on phantom committees for too long. This morning the business mainly concerned the details of the work which had already begun at Edgestow. The NICE had apparently won some sort of victory which gave it the right to pull down the little Norman church at the corner. 'The usual objections were, of course, tabled,' said Wither. Mark, who was not interested in architecture and who did not know the other side of the Wynd nearly so well as his wife, allowed his attention to wander. It was only at the end of the meeting that Wither opened a much more sensational subject. He believed that most of those present had already heard ('Why do chairmen always begin that way?' thought Mark) the very distressing piece of news which it was, nevertheless, his duty now to communicate to them in a semi-official manner. He was referring, of course, to the murder of William Hingest. As far as Mark could discover from the chairman's tortuous and allusive narrative, Bill the Blizzard had been discovered with his head beaten in by some blunt instrument, lying near his car in Potter's Lane at about four o'clock that morning. He had been dead for several hours. Mr Wither ventured to suppose that it would be a melancholy pleasure to the committee to know that the NICE police had been on the scene of the crime before five and that neither the local authorities nor Scotland Yard were making any objections to the fullest collaboration. He felt that if the occasion were more appropriate he would have welcomed a motion for some expression of the gratitude they must all feel to Miss Hardcastle and possibly of congratulations to her on the smooth interaction between her own forces and those of the state. This was a most gratifying feature in the sad story and, he suggested, a good omen for the future. Some decently subdued applause went round the table at this. Mr Wither then proceeded to speak at some length about the dead man. They had all much regretted Mr Hingest's resolution to withdraw from the NICE, while fully appreciating his motives; they had all felt that this official severance would not in the least alter the cordial relations which existed between the deceased and almost all – he thought he could even say all without exception – of his former colleagues in the Institute. The obituary (in Raleigh's fine phrase) was an instrument which the Deputy Director's talents well fitted him to play, and he spoke at great length. He concluded by suggesting that they should all stand in silence for one minute as a token of respect for the memory of William Hingest.

And they did – a world-without-end minute in which odd creakings and breathings became audible, and behind the mask of each glazed and tight-lipped face, shy, irrelevant thoughts of this and that came creeping out as birds and mice creep out again in the clearing of a wood when the picnickers have gone, and everyone silently assured himself that he, at least, was not being morbid and not thinking about death.

Then there was a stir and a bustle and the Committee broke up.

◆ ○ ◆

The whole process of getting up and doing the 'morning jobs' was more cheerful, Jane found, because she had Mrs Dimble with her. Mark often helped; but as he always took the view – and Jane could feel it even if he did not express it in words – that 'anything would do' and that Jane made a lot of unnecessary work and that men could keep house with a tithe of the fuss and trouble which women made about it, Mark's help was one of the commonest causes of quarrels between them. Mrs Dimble, on the other hand, fell in with her ways. It was a bright sunny morning and as they sat down to breakfast in the kitchen Jane was feeling bright herself. During the night her mind had evolved a comfortable theory that the mere fact of having seen Miss Ironwood and 'had it all out' would probably stop the dreams altogether. The episode would be closed. And now – there was all the exciting possibility of Mark's new job to look forward to. She began to see pictures in her mind.

Mrs Dimble was anxious to know what had happened to Jane at St Anne's and when she was going there again. Jane answered evasively on the first question and Mrs Dimble was too polite to press it. As to the second, Jane thought she wouldn't 'bother' Miss Ironwood again, or wouldn't 'bother' any further about the dreams. She said she had been 'silly' but felt sure she'd be all right now. And she glanced at the clock and wondered why Mrs Maggs hadn't yet turned up.

'My dear, I'm afraid you've lost Ivy Maggs,' said Mrs Dimble. 'Didn't I tell you they'd taken her house too? I thought you'd understand she wouldn't be coming to you in future. You see there's nowhere for her to live in Edgestow.'

'Bother!' said Jane, and added, without much interest in the reply, 'What is she doing, do you know?'

'She's gone out to St Anne's.'

'Has she got friends there?'

'She's gone to the Manor, along with Cecil and me.'

'Do you mean she's got a job there?'

'Well, yes. I suppose it is a job.'

Mrs Dimble left at about eleven. She also, it appeared, was going to St Anne's, but was first to meet her husband and lunch with him at Northumberland. Jane walked down to the town with her to do a little shopping and they parted at the bottom of Market Street. It was just after this that Jane met Mr Curry.

'Have you heard the news, Mrs Studdock?' said Curry. His manner was always important and his tone always vaguely confidential, but this morning they seemed more so than usual.

'No. What's wrong?' said Jane. She thought Mr Curry a pompous fool and Mark a fool for being impressed by him. But as soon as Curry began speaking, her face showed all the wonder and consternation he could have wished. Nor were they, this time, feigned. He told her that Mr Hingest had been murdered, sometime during the night, or in the small hours of that morning. The body had been found lying beside his car, in Potter's Lane, badly beaten about the head. He had been driving from Belbury to Edgestow. Curry was at the moment hastening back to college to talk to the Warden about it; he had just been at the police station. One saw that the murder had already become Curry's property. The 'matter' was, in some indefinable sense, 'in his hands', and he was heavy with responsibility. At another time Jane would have found this amusing. She escaped from him as soon as possible and went into Blackie's for a cup of coffee. She felt she must sit down.

The death of Hingest in itself meant nothing to her. She had met him only once and she had accepted from Mark the view that he was a disagreeable old man and rather a snob. But the certainty that she herself in her dream had witnessed a real murder shattered at one blow all the consoling pretences with which she had begun the morning. It came over her with sickening clarity that the affair of her dreams, far from being ended, was only beginning. The bright, narrow little life which she had proposed to live was being irremediably broken into. Windows into huge, dark landscapes were opening on every side and she was powerless to shut them. It would drive her mad, she thought, to face it alone. The other alternative was to go back to Miss Ironwood. But that seemed to be only a way of going deeper into all this darkness. This Manor at St Anne's – this 'kind of company' – was 'mixed up in it'. She didn't want to get drawn in. It was unfair. It wasn't as if she had asked much of life. All she wanted was to be left alone. And the thing was so preposterous! The sort of thing which, according to all the authorities she had hitherto accepted, could not really happen.

◆ ○ ◆

Cosser – the frecklefaced man with the little wisp of black moustache – approached Mark as he was coming away from the Committee.

'You and I have a job to do,' he said. 'Got to get out a report about Cure Hardy.'

Mark was very relieved to hear of a job. But he was a little on his dignity, not having liked Cosser much when he had met him yesterday, and he answered:

'Does that mean I *am* to be in Steele's department after all?'

'That's right,' said Cosser.

'The reason I ask,' said Mark, 'is that neither he nor you seemed particularly keen on having me. I don't want to push myself in, you know. I don't need to stay at the NICE at all if it comes to that.'

'Well, don't start talking about it here,' said Cosser. 'Come upstairs.'

They were talking in the hall and Mark noticed Wither pacing thoughtfully towards them. 'Wouldn't it be as well to speak to *him* and get the whole thing thrashed out?' he suggested. But the Deputy Director, after coming within ten feet of them, had turned in another direction. He was humming to himself under his breath and seemed so deep in thought that Mark felt the moment unsuitable for an interview. Cosser, though he said nothing, apparently thought the same and so Mark followed him up to an office on the third floor.

'It's about the village of Cure Hardy,' said Cosser when they were seated. 'You see, all that land at Bragdon Wood is going to be little better than a swamp once they get to work. Why the hell we wanted to go there I don't know. Anyway, the latest plan is to divert the Wynd: block up the old channel through Edgestow altogether. Look. Here's Shillingbridge, ten miles north of the town. It's to be diverted there and brought down an artificial channel – here, to the east, where the blue line is – and rejoin the old bed down here.'

'The university will hardly agree to that,' said Mark. 'What would Edgestow be without the river?'

'We've got the university by the short hairs,' said Cosser. 'You needn't worry about that. Anyway it's not our job. The point is that the new Wynd must come right through Cure Hardy. Now look at your contours. Cure Hardy is in this narrow little valley. Eh? Oh, you've been there, have you? That makes it all the easier. I don't know these parts myself. Well, the idea is to dam the valley at the southern end and make a big reservoir. You'll need a new water supply for Edgestow now that it's to be the second city in the country.'

'But what happens to Cure Hardy?'

'That's another advantage. We build a new model village (it's to be called Jules Hardy or Wither Hardy) four miles away. Over here, on the railway.'

'I say, you know, there'll be the devil of a stink about this. Cure Hardy is famous. It's a beauty spot. There are the sixteenth-century almshouses, and a Norman church and all that.'

'Exactly. That's where you and I come in. We've got to make a report on Cure Hardy. We'll run out and have a look round tomorrow, but we can write most of the report today. It ought to be pretty easy. If it's a beauty spot, you can bet it's insanitary. That's the first point to stress. Then we've got to get out some facts about the population. I think you'll find it consists almost entirely of the two most undesirable elements – small *rentiers* and agricultural labourers.'

'The small *rentier* is a bad element, I agree,' said Mark. 'I suppose the agricultural labourer is more controversial.'

'The Institute doesn't approve of him. He's a very recalcitrant element in a planned community, and he's always backward. We're not going in for English agriculture. So you see, all we have to do is to verify a few facts. Otherwise the report writes itself.'

Mark was silent for a moment or two.

'That's easy enough,' he said. 'But before I get down to it, I'd just like to be a bit clearer about my own position. Oughtn't I go and see Steele? I don't fancy settling down to work in this department if he doesn't want to have me.'

'I wouldn't do that,' said Cosser.

'Why not?'

'Well, for one thing, Steele can't prevent you if the DD backs you up, as he seems to be doing for the moment. For another, Steele is rather a dangerous man. If you just go quietly on with the job, he may get used to you in the end; but if you go and see him it might lead to a bust-up. There's another thing too.' Cosser paused, picked his nose thoughtfully, and proceeded. 'Between ourselves, I don't think things can go on indefinitely in this department in the way they are at present.'

The excellent training which Mark had had at Bracton enabled him to understand this. Cosser was hoping to get Steele out of the department altogether. He thought he saw the whole situation. Steele was dangerous while he lasted, but he might not last.

'I got the impression yesterday,' said Mark, 'that you and Steele hit it off together rather well.'

'The great thing here,' said Cosser, 'is never to quarrel with anyone. I hate quarrels myself. I can get on with anybody – as long as the work gets done.'

'Of course,' said Mark. 'By the way, if we go to Cure Hardy tomorrow I might as well run in to Edgestow and spend the night at home.'

For Mark a good deal hung on the answer to this. He might find out whether he were actually under orders from Cosser. If Cosser said, 'You can't do that,' he would at least know where he stood. If Cosser said that Mark couldn't be spared, that would be better still. Or Cosser might reply that he'd better consult the DD. That also would have made Mark feel surer of his position. But Cosser merely said 'Oh,' leaving Mark in doubt whether no one needed leave of absence or whether Mark was not sufficiently established as a member of the Institute for his absence to be of any consequence. Then they went to work on their report.

It took them the rest of the day, so that Cosser and he came in to dinner late and without dressing. This gave Mark a most agreeable sensation. And he enjoyed the meal too. Although he was among men he had not met before, he seemed to know everyone within the first five minutes and to be joining naturally in the conversation. He was learning how to talk their shop.

'How nice it is!' said Mark to himself next morning as the car left the main road at Duke's Eaton and began descending the bumpy little lane into the long valley where Cure Hardy lay. Mark was not as a rule very sensitive to beauty, but Jane and his love for Jane had already awakened him a little in this respect. Perhaps the winter morning sunlight affected him all the more because he had never been taught to regard it as specially beautiful and it therefore worked on his senses without interference. The earth and sky had the look of things recently washed. The brown fields looked as if they would be good to eat, and those in grass set off the curves of the little hills as close-clipped hair sets off the body of a horse. The sky looked further away than usual, but also clearer, so that the long slender streaks of cloud (dark slate colour against the pale blue) had edges as clear as if they were cut out of cardboard. Every little copse was black and bristling as a hairbrush, and when the car stopped in Cure Hardy itself the silence that followed the turning off of the engine was filled with the noise of rooks that seemed to be calling, 'Wake! Wake!'

'Bloody awful noise those birds make,' said Cosser. 'Got your map? Now ...' He plunged at once into business.

They walked about that village for two hours and saw with their own eyes all the abuses and anachronisms they came to destroy. They saw the recalcitrant and backward labourer and heard his views on the weather. They met the wastefully supported pauper in the person of an old man shuffling across the courtyard of the almshouses to fill a kettle, and the elderly *rentier* (to make matters worse, she had a fat old dog with her) in earnest conversation with the postman. It made Mark feel as he were on a holiday, for it was only on holidays that he had ever wandered about an English village. For that reason he felt pleasure in it. It did not quite escape him that the face of the backward labourer was rather more interesting than Cosser's and his voice a great deal more pleasing to the ear. The resemblance between the elderly *rentier* and Aunt Gilly (When had he last thought of *her*? Good Lord, that took one back.) did make him understand how it was possible to like that kind of person. All this did not in the least influence his sociological convictions. Even if he had been free from Belbury and wholly unambitious, it could not have done so, for his education had had the curious effect of making things that he read and wrote more real to him than things he saw. Statistics about agricultural labourers were the substance; any real ditcher, ploughman or farmer's boy, was the shadow. Though he had never noticed it himself, he had a great reluctance, in his work, ever to use such words as 'man' or 'woman'. He preferred to write about 'vocational groups', 'elements', 'classes' and 'populations': for, in his own way, he believed as firmly as any mystic in the superior reality of the things that are not seen.

And yet, he could not help rather liking this village. When, at one o'clock, he persuaded Cosser to turn into the Two Bells, he even said so. They had both brought sandwiches with them, but Mark felt he would like a pint of beer. In the Two Bells it was very warm and dark, for the window was small. Two labourers (no doubt recalcitrant and backward) were sitting with earthenware mugs at their elbows, munching very thick sandwiches, and a third was standing up at the counter conducting a conversation with the landlord.

'No beer for me, thanks,' said Cosser, 'and we don't want to muck about here too long. What were you saying?'

'I was saying that on a fine morning there is something rather attractive about a place like this, in spite of all its obvious absurdities.'

'Yes, it *is* a fine morning. Makes a real difference to one's health, a bit of sunlight.'

'I was thinking of the place.'

'You mean *this*?' said Cosser glancing round the room. 'I should have thought it was just the sort of thing we wanted to get rid of. No sunlight, no ventilation. Haven't much use for alcohol myself (read the Miller Report) but if people have got to have their stimulants, I'd like to see them administered in a more hygienic way.'

'I don't know that the stimulant is quite the whole point,' said Mark, looking at his beer. The whole scene was reminding him of drinks and talks long ago – of laughter and arguments in undergraduate days. Somehow one had made friends more easily then. He wondered what had become of all that set – of Carey and Wadsden and Denniston, who had so nearly got his own Fellowship.

'Don't know, I'm sure,' said Cosser, in answer to his last remark. 'Nutrition isn't my subject. You'd want to ask Stock about that.'

'What I'm really thinking about,' said Mark, 'is not this pub, but the whole village. Of course, you're quite right: that sort of thing has to go. But it had its pleasant side. We'll have to be careful that whatever we're building up in its place will really be able to beat it on all levels – not merely in efficiency.'

'Oh, architecture and all that,' said Cosser. 'Well, that's hardly my line, you know. That's more for someone like Wither. Have you nearly finished?'

All at once it came over Mark what a terrible bore this little man was, and in the same moment he felt utterly sick of the NICE. But he reminded himself that one could not expect to be in the interesting set at once; there would be better things later on. Anyway, he had not burnt his boats. Perhaps he would chuck up the whole thing and go back to Bracton in a day or two. But not at once. It would be only sensible to hang on for a bit and see how things shaped.

On their way back Cosser dropped him near Edgestow station, and as he walked home Mark began to think of what he would say to Jane about Belbury. You will quite misunderstand him if you think he was consciously inventing a lie. Almost involuntarily, as the picture of himself entering the flat, and of Jane's questioning face, arose in his mind, there arose also the imagination of his own voice answering her, hitting off the salient features of Belbury in amusing, confident phrases. This imaginary speech of his own gradually drove out of his mind the real experiences he had undergone. Those real experiences of misgivings and of uneasiness, indeed, quickened his desire to cut a good figure in the eyes of his wife. Almost without noticing it, he had decided not to mention the affair of Cure Hardy; Jane cared for old buildings and all that sort of thing. As a result, when Jane, who was at that moment drawing the curtains, heard the door opening and looked round and saw Mark, she saw a rather breezy and buoyant Mark. Yes, he was almost sure he'd got the job. The salary wasn't absolutely fixed, but he'd be going into that tomorrow. It was a very funny place: he'd explain all that later. But he had already got onto the real people there. Wither and Miss Hardcastle were the ones that mattered. 'I *must* tell you about the Hardcastle woman,' he said. 'She's quite incredible.'

Jane had to decide what she would say to Mark much more quickly than he had decided what he would say to her. And she decided to tell him nothing about the dreams or St Anne's. Men hated women who had things wrong with them, specially queer, unusual things. Her resolution was easily kept for Mark, full of his own story, asked her no questions. She was not, perhaps, entirely convinced by what he said. There was a vagueness about all the details. Very early in the conversation she said in a sharp, frightened voice (she had no idea how he disliked that voice), 'Mark, you haven't given up your fellowship at Bracton?' He said, No, of course not, and went on. She listened only with half her mind. She knew he often had rather grandiose ideas, and from something in his face she divined that during his absence he had been drinking much more than he usually did. And so, all evening, the male bird displayed his plumage and the female played her part and asked questions and laughed and feigned more interest than she felt. Both were young, and if neither loved very much, each was still anxious to be admired.

◆ ○ ◆

That evening the Fellows of Bracton sat in Common Room over their wine and dessert. They had given up dressing for dinner, as an economy during the war, and not yet resumed the practice, so that their sports coats and cardigans struck a somewhat discordant note against the dark Jacobean panels, the candle light, and the silver of many different periods. Feverstone and Curry were sitting together. Until that night for about three hundred years this Common Room had been one of the pleasant quiet places of England. It was in Lady Alice, on the ground floor beneath the soler, and the windows at its eastern end looked out on the river and on Bragdon Wood, across a little terrace where the Fellows were in the habit of taking their dessert on summer evenings. At this hour and season these windows were of course shut and curtained. And from beyond them came such noises as had never been heard in that room before – shouts and curses and the sound of lorries heavily drumming past or harshly changing gear, rattling of chains, drumming of mechanical drills, clanging of iron, whistles, thuddings, and an all pervasive vibration. *Saeva sonare verbera, tum stridor ferri tractaeque catenae*, as Glossop, sitting on the far side of the fire, had observed to Jewel. For beyond those windows, scarcely thirty yards away on the other side of the Wynd, the conversion of an ancient woodland into an inferno of mud and noise and steel and concrete was already going on apace. Several members even of the Progressive Element – those who had rooms on this side of College – had already been grumbling about it. Curry himself had been a little surprised by the form which his dream had taken now that it was a reality, but he was doing his best to brazen it out, and though his conversation with Feverstone had to be conducted at the top of their voices, he made no allusion to this inconvenience.

'It's quite definite, then,' he bawled, 'that young Studdock is not coming back?'

'Oh quite,' shouted Feverstone. 'He sent me a message through a high official to tell me to let the College know.'

'When will he send a formal resignation?'

'Haven't an earthly! Like all these youngsters, he's very casual about these things. As a matter of fact, the longer he delays the better.'

'You mean it gives us a chance to look about us?'

'Quite. You see, nothing need come before the College till he writes. One wants to have the whole question of his successor taped *before* that.'

'Obviously. That is most important. Once you present an open question to all these people who don't understand the field and don't know their own minds, you get anything happening.'

'Exactly. That's what we want to avoid. The only way to manage a place like this is to produce your candidate – bring the rabbit out of a hat – two minutes after you've announced the vacancy.'

'We must begin thinking about it at once.'

'Does his successor have to be a sociologist? I mean is the fellowship tied to the subject?'

'Oh, not in the least. It's one of those Paston fellowships. Why? Had you any subject in mind?'

'It's a long time since we had anyone in Politics.'

'Um – yes. There's still a considerable prejudice against Politics as an academic subject. I say, Feverstone, oughtn't we to give this new subject a leg up?'

'What new subject?'

'Pragmatometry.'

'Well now, it's funny you should say that, because the man I was beginning to think of is a Politician who has also been going in a good deal for Pragmatometry. One could call it a fellowship in social Pragmatometry, or something like that.'

'Who is the man?'

'Laird – from Leicester, Cambridge.'

It was automatic for Curry to look very thoughtful, though he had never heard of Laird, and to say, 'Ah, Laird. Just remind me of the details of his academic career.'

'Well,' said Feverstone, 'as you remember, he was in bad health at the time of his finals, and came rather a cropper. The Cambridge examining is so bad nowadays that one hardly counts that. Everyone knew he was one of the most brilliant men of his year. He was President of the Sphinxes and used to edit *The Adult*. David Laird, you know.'

'Yes, to be sure. David Laird. But I say, Dick ...'

'Yes?'

'I'm not quite happy about his bad degree. Of course I don't attach a superstitious value to examination results any more than you do. Still . . . We have made one or two unfortunate elections lately.' Almost involuntarily, as he said this, Curry glanced across the room to where Pelham sat – Pelham with his little button-like mouth and his pudding face. Pelham was a sound man; but even Curry found it difficult to remember anything that Pelham had ever done or said.

'Yes, I know,' said Feverstone, 'but even our worst elections aren't quite so dim as those the College makes when we leave it to itself.'

Perhaps because the intolerable noise had frayed his nerves, Curry felt a momentary doubt about the 'dimness' of these outsiders. He had dined recently at Northumberland and found Telford dining there the same night. The contrast between the alert and witty Telford whom everyone at Northumberland seemed to know, whom everyone listened to, and the 'dim' Telford in Bracton Common Room had perplexed him. Could it be that the silences of all these 'outsiders' in his own College, their monosyllabic replies when he condescended and their blank faces when he assumed his confidential manner, had an explanation which had never occurred to him? The fantastic suggestion that he, Curry, might be a bore, passed through his mind so swiftly that a second later he had forgotten it forever. The much less painful suggestion that these traditionalists and research beetles affected to look down on him was retained. But Feverstone was shouting at him again.

'I'm going to be at Cambridge next week,' he said. 'In fact I'm giving a dinner. I'd as soon it wasn't mentioned here, because, as a matter of fact, the PM may be coming, and one or two big newspaper people and Tony Dew. What? Oh, of course you know Tony. That little dark man from the Bank. Laird is going to be there. He's some kind of cousin of the PM's. I was wondering if you could join us. I know David's very anxious to meet you. He's heard a lot about you from some chap who used to go to your lectures. I can't remember the name.'

'Well, it would be very difficult. It rather depends on when old Bill's funeral is to be. I should have to be here for that of course. Was there anything about the inquest on the six o'clock news?'

'I didn't hear. But of course that raises a second question. Now that Blizzard has gone to blow in a better world, we have *two* vacancies.'

'I can't hear,' yelled Curry. 'Is this noise getting worse? Or am I getting deaf?'

'I say, Sub-Warden,' shouted Brizeacre from beyond Feverstone, 'what the devil are your friends outside doing?'

'Can't they work without shouting?' asked someone else.

'It doesn't sound like work at all to me,' said a third.

'Listen!' said Glossop suddenly. 'That's not work. Listen to the feet. It's more like a game of rugger.'

'It's getting worse every minute,' said Raynor.

Next moment nearly everyone in the room was on his feet. 'What was that?' shouted one. 'They're murdering someone,' said Glossop. 'There's only one way of getting a noise like that out of a man's throat.' 'Where are you going?' asked Curry. 'I'm going to see what's happening,' said Glossop. 'Curry, go and collect all the shooters in College. Someone ring up the police.' 'I shouldn't go out if I were you,' said Feverstone who had remained seated and was pouring himself out another glass of wine. 'It sounds as if the police, or something, was there already.'

'What do you mean?'

'Listen. There!'

'I thought that was their infernal drill.'

'Listen!'

'My God ... you really think it's a machine gun?'

'Look out! Look out!' said a dozen voices at once as a splintering of glass became audible and a shower of stones fell onto the Common Room floor. A moment later several of the Fellows had made a rush for the windows and put up the shutters; and then they were all standing staring at one another, and silent but for the noise of their heavy breathing. Glossop had a cut on the forehead, and on the floor lay the fragments of that famous east window on which Henrietta Maria had once cut her name with a diamond.

5

Elasticity

Next morning Mark went back to Belbury by train. He had promised his wife to clear up a number of points about his salary and place of residence, and the memory of all these promises made a little cloud of uneasiness in his mind, but on the whole he was in good spirits. This return to Belbury – just sauntering in and hanging up his hat and ordering a drink – was a pleasant contrast to his first arrival. The servant who brought the drink knew him. Filostrato nodded to him. Women *would* fuss, but this was clearly the real world. After the drink he strolled upstairs to Cosser's office. He was there for only five minutes, and when he came out, his state of mind had been completely altered.

Steele and Cosser were both there and both looked up with the air of men who have been interrupted by a total stranger. Neither spoke.

'Ah – good morning,' said Mark awkwardly.

Steele finished making a pencil note on some large document which was spread out before him.

'What is it, Mr Studdock?' he said without looking up.

'I came to see Cosser,' said Mark, and then, addressing Cosser, 'I've just been thinking over the last section but one in that report –'

'What report's this?' said Steele to Cosser.

'Oh, I thought,' replied Cosser with a little twisty smile at one corner of his mouth, 'that it would be a good thing to put together a report on Cure Hardy in my spare time, and as there was nothing particular to do yesterday I drew it up. Mr Studdock helped me.'

'Well, never mind about that now,' said Steele. 'You can talk to Mr Cosser about it some other time, Mr Studdock. I'm afraid he's busy at present.'

'Look here,' said Mark, 'I think we'd better understand one another. Am I to take it that this report was simply a private hobby of Cosser's? And if so, I should like to have known that before I spent eight hours' work on it. And whose orders am I under?'

Steele, playing with his pencil, looked at Cosser.

'I asked you a question about my position, Mr Steele,' said Mark.

'I haven't time for this sort of thing,' said Steele. 'If you haven't any work to do, I have. I know nothing about your position.'

Mark though, for a moment, of turning to Cosser; but Cosser's smooth, freckled face and non-committal eyes suddenly filled him with such contempt that he turned on his heel and left the room, slamming the door behind him. He was going to see the Deputy Director.

At the door of Wither's room he hesitated for a moment because he heard voices from within. But he was too angry to wait. He knocked and entered without noticing whether the knock had been answered.

'My dear boy,' said the Deputy Director looking up but not quite fixing his eyes on Mark's face. 'I'm delighted to see you.' As he heard these words Mark noticed that there was a third person in the room. It was a man called Stone whom he had met at dinner the day before yesterday. Stone was standing in front of Wither's table, rolling and unrolling a piece of blotting paper with his fingers. His mouth was open, his eyes fixed on the Deputy Director.

'Delighted to see you,' repeated Wither. 'All the more so because you – er – interrupted me in what I am afraid I must call a rather painful interview. As I was just saying to poor Mr Stone when you came in, nothing is nearer to my heart than the wish that this great Institute should all work together like one family ... the greatest unity of will and purpose, Mr Stone, the fullest mutual confidence ... that is what I expect of my colleagues. But then as you may remind me, Mr – ah – Studdock, even in family life, there are occasionally strains and frictions and misunderstandings. And that is why, my dear boy, I am not at the moment quite at leisure – don't go, Mr Stone. I have a great deal more to say to you.'

'Perhaps I'd better come back later?' said Mark.

'Well, perhaps in all the circumstances ... it is *your* feelings that I am considering, Mr Stone ... perhaps ... the usual method of seeing me, Mr Studdock, is to apply to my secretary and make an appointment. Not, you will understand, that I have the least wish to insist on any formalities or would be other than pleased to see you whenever you looked in. It is the waste of *your* time that I am anxious to avoid.'

'Thank you, Sir,' said Mark. 'I'll go and see your secretary.'

The secretary's office was next door. When one went in, one found not the secretary himself, but a number of subordinates who were cut off from their visitors behind a sort of counter. Mark made an appointment for ten o'clock tomorrow which was the earliest hour they could offer him. As he came out he ran into Fairy Hardcastle.

'Hullo, Studdock,' said the Fairy. 'Hanging round the DD's office? That won't do, you know.'

'I have decided,' said Mark, 'that I must either get my position definitely fixed once and for all or else leave the Institute.'

She looked at him with an ambiguous expression in which amusement seemed to predominate. Then she suddenly slipped her arm through his.

'Look, Sonny,' she said, 'you drop all that, see? It isn't going to do you any good. You come along and have a talk with me.'

'There's really nothing to talk about, Miss Hardcastle,' said Mark. 'I'm quite clear in my mind. Either I get a real job here, or I go back to Bracton. That's simple enough: I don't even particularly mind which, so long as I know.'

To this, the Fairy made no answer, and the steady pressure of her arm compelled Mark, unless he was prepared to struggle, to go with her along the passage. The intimacy and authority of her grip was ludicrously ambiguous and would have fitted almost equally well the relations of policeman and prisoner, mistress and lover, nurse and child. Mark felt that he would look a fool if they met anyone.

She brought him to her own offices which were on the second floor. The outer office was full of what he had already learned to call Waips, the girls of the Women's Auxiliary Institutional Police. The men of the force, though very much more numerous, were not so often met with indoors, but Waips were constantly seen flitting to and fro wherever Miss Hardcastle appeared. Far from sharing the masculine characteristics of their chief they were (as Feverstone once said) 'feminine to the point of imbecility' – small and slight and fluffy and full of giggles. Miss Hardcastle behaved to them as if she were a man, and addressed them in tones of half-breezy, half-ferocious, gallantry. 'Cocktails, Dolly,' she bawled as they entered the outer office. When they reached the inner office she made Mark sit down but remained standing herself with her back to the fire and her legs wide apart. The drinks were brought and Dolly retired closing the door behind her. Mark had grumblingly told his grievance on the way.

'Cut it all out, Studdock,' said Miss Hardcastle. 'And whatever you do, don't go bothering the DD. I told you before that you needn't worry about all those little third floor people provided you've got him on your side. Which you have at present. But you won't have if you keep on going to him with complaints.'

'That might be very good advice, Miss Hardcastle,' said Mark, 'if I were committed to staying here at all. But I'm not. And from what I've seen I don't like the place. I've very nearly made up my mind to go home. Only I thought I'd just have a talk with him first, to make everything clear.'

'Making things clear is the one thing the DD can't stand,' replied Miss Hardcastle. 'That's not how he runs the place. And mind you, he knows what he's about. It works, Sonny. You've no idea yet how well it works. As for leaving … you've not superstitious, are you? I am. I don't think it's lucky to leave the NICE.

You needn't bother your head about all the Steeles and Cossers. That's part of your apprenticeship. You're being put through it at the moment, but if you hold on you'll come out above them. All you've got to do is to sit tight. Not one of them is going to be left when we get going.'

'That's just the sort of line Cosser took about Steele,' said Mark, 'and it didn't seem to do me much good when it came to the point.'

'Do you know, Studdock,' said Miss Hardcastle, 'I've taken a fancy to you. And it's just as well I have. Because if I hadn't, I'd be disposed to resent that last remark.'

'I don't mean to be offensive,' said Mark. 'But – damn it all – look at it from my point of view.'

'No good, Sonny,' said Miss Hardcastle shaking her head. 'You don't know enough facts yet for your point of view to be worth sixpence. You haven't yet realised what you're in on. You're being offered a chance of something far bigger than a seat in the cabinet. And there are only two alternatives, you know. Either to be in the NICE or to be out of it. And I know better than you which is going to be most fun.'

'I *do* understand that,' said Mark. 'But anything is better than being nominally in and having nothing to do. Give me a real place in the Sociological Department and I'll …'

'Rats! That whole Department is going to be scrapped. It had to be there at the beginning for propaganda purposes. But they're all going to be weeded out.'

'But what assurance have I that I'm going to be one of their successors?'

'You aren't. They're not going to have any successors. The real work has nothing to do with all these departments. The kind of sociology we're interested in will be done by my people – the police.'

'Then where do I come in?'

'If you'll trust me,' said the Fairy, putting down her empty glass and producing a cheroot, 'I can put you onto a bit of your real work – what you were really brought here to do – straight away.'

'What's that?'

'Alcasan,' said Miss Hardcastle between her teeth. She had started one of her interminable dry smokes. Then, glancing at Mark
with a hint of contempt, 'You know who I'm talking about, don't
you?'

'You mean the radiologist – the man who was guillotined?'
asked Mark who was completely bewildered. The Fairy nodded.

'He's to be rehabilitated,' she said. 'Gradually. I've got all the
facts in the dossier. You begin with a quiet little article – not questioning his guilt, not at first, but just hinting that of course he *was*
a member of their Quisling government and there was a prejudice
against him. Say you don't doubt the verdict was just, but it's disquieting to realise that it would almost certainly have been the
same even if he'd been innocent. Then you follow it up in a day or
two with an article of quite a different kind. Popular account of the
value of his work. You can mug up the facts – enough for *that* kind
of article – in an afternoon. Then a letter, rather indignant, to the
paper that printed the first article, and going much further. The
execution *was* a miscarriage of justice. By that time – '

'What on earth is the point of all this?'

'I'm telling you, Studdock. Alcasan is to be rehabilitated. Made
into a martyr. An irreparable loss to the human race.'

'But what for?'

'There you go again! You grumble about being given nothing to
do, and as soon as I suggest a bit of real work you expect to have
the whole plan of campaign told you before you do it. It doesn't
make sense. That's not the way to get on here. The great thing is to
do what you're told. If you turn out to be any good you'll soon
understand what's going on. But you've got to begin by doing the
work. You don't seem to realise what we are. We're an army.'

'Anyway,' said Mark, 'I'm not a journalist. I didn't come here to
write newspaper articles. I tried to make that clear to Feverstone at
the very beginning.'

'The sooner you drop all that talk about what you came here to
do, the better you'll get on. I'm speaking for your own good,

Studdock. You *can* write. That's one of the things you're wanted for.'

'Then I've come here under a misunderstanding,' said Mark. The sop to his literary vanity, at that period of his career, by no means compensated for the implication that his Sociology was of no importance. 'I've no notion of spending my life writing newspaper articles,' he said. 'And if I had, I'd want to know a good deal more about the politics of the NICE before I went in for that sort of thing.'

'Haven't you been told that it's strictly non-political?'

'I've been told so many things that I don't know whether I'm on my head or my heels,' said Mark. 'But I don't see how one's going to start a newspaper stunt (which is about what this comes to) without being political. Is it Left or Right papers that are going to print all this rot about Alcasan?'

'Both, Honey, both,' said Miss Hardcastle. 'Don't you understand *anything*? Isn't it absolutely essential to keep a fierce Left and a fierce Right, both on their toes and each terrified of the other? That's how we get things done. Any opposition to the NICE is represented as a Left racket in the Right papers and a Right racket in the Left papers. If it's properly done, you get each side outbidding the other in support of us – to refute the enemy slanders. *Of course* we're non-political. The real power always is.'

'I don't believe you can do that,' said Mark. 'Not with the papers that are read by educated people.'

'That shows you're still in the nursery, Lovey,' said Miss Hardcastle. 'Haven't you yet realised that it's the other way round?'

'How do you mean?'

'Why you fool, it's the educated reader who *can* be gulled. All our difficulty comes with the others. When did you meet a workman who believes the papers? He takes it for granted that they're all propaganda and skips the leading articles. He buys his paper for the football results and the little paragraphs about girls falling out of windows and corpses found in Mayfair flats. He is our problem. We have to recondition him. But the educated public, the people who read the highbrow weeklies, don't need reconditioning. They're all right already. They'll believe anything.'

'As one of the class you mention,' said Mark with a smile, 'I just don't believe it.'

'Good Lord!' said the Fairy. 'Where are your eyes? Look at what the weeklies have got away with! Look at the *Weekly Question*. There's a paper for you. When Basic English came in simply as the invention of a free-thinking Cambridge don, nothing was too good for it; as soon as it was taken up by a Tory Prime Minister it became a menace to the purity of our language. And wasn't the Monarchy an expensive absurdity for ten years? And then, when the Duke of Windsor abdicated, didn't the *Question* go all monarchist and legitimist for about a fortnight? Did they drop a single reader? Don't you see that the educated reader *can't* stop reading the high-brow weeklies whatever they do? He can't. He's been conditioned.'

'Well,' said Mark, 'this is all very interesting, Miss Hardcastle, but it has nothing to do with me. In the first place, I don't want to become a journalist at all, and if I did, I should like to be an honest journalist.'

'Very well,' said Miss Hardcastle. 'All you'll do is help to ruin this country, and perhaps the whole human race. Besides dishing your own career.'

The confidential tone in which she had been speaking up till now had disappeared and there was a threatening finality in her voice. The citizen and the honest man which had been awakened in Mark by the conversation, quailed a little; his other and far stronger self, the self that was anxious at all costs not to be placed among the outsiders, leaped up, fully alarmed.

'I don't mean,' he said, 'that I don't see your point. I was only wondering ...'

'It's all one to me, Studdock,' said Miss Hardcastle seating herself at last at her table. 'If you don't like the job, of course, that's your affair. Go and settle it with the DD. He doesn't *like* people resigning, but of course you can. He'll have something to say to Feverstone for bringing you here. We'd assumed you understood.'

The mention of Feverstone brought sharply before Mark as a reality the plan, which had up till now been slightly unreal, of going back to Edgestow and satisfying himself with the career of a Fellow of Bracton. On what terms would he go back? Would he still be a member of the Inner Circle even at Bracton? To find himself no longer in the confidence of the Progressive Element, to be thrust down among the Telfords and Jewels, seemed to him unendurable. And the salary of a mere don looked a poor thing after the dreams he had been dreaming for the last few days. Married life was already turning out more expensive than he had reckoned. Then came a sharp doubt about that two hundred pounds for membership of the NICE club. But no – that was absurd. They couldn't possibly dun him for that.

'Well obviously,' he said in a vague voice, 'the first thing is to see the DD.'

'Now that you're leaving,' said the Fairy, 'there's one thing I've got to say; I've laid all the cards on the table. If it should ever enter your head that it would be fun to repeat any of this conversation in the outer world, take my advice and don't. It wouldn't be at all healthy for your future career.'

'Oh but of course,' began Mark.

'You'd better run along now,' said Miss Hardcastle. 'Have a nice talk with the DD. Be careful not to annoy the old man. He does so hate resignations.'

Mark made an attempt to prolong the interview but the Fairy did not permit this and in a few seconds he was outside the door.

The rest of that day he passed miserably enough, keeping out of people's way as much as possible lest his lack of occupation should be noticed. He went out before lunch for one of those short, unsatisfactory walks which a man takes in a strange neighbourhood when he has brought with him neither old clothes nor a walking stick. After lunch he explored the grounds. But they were not the sort of grounds that anyone could walk in for pleasure. The

Edwardian millionaire who had built Belbury had enclosed about twenty acres with a low brick wall surmounted by an iron railing, and laid it all out in what his contractor called Ornamental Pleasure Grounds. There were trees dotted about and winding paths covered so thickly with round white pebbles that you could hardly walk on them. There were immense flower beds, some oblong, some lozenge-shaped, and some crescents. There were plantations – slabs would be almost a better word – of that kind of laurel which looks as if it were made of cleverly painted and varnished metal. Massive summer seats of bright green stood at regular intervals along the paths. The whole effect was like that of a municipal cemetery. Yet, unattractive as it was, he sought it again after tea, smoking though the wind blew the lit part down the side of his cigarette and his tongue was already burning. This time he wandered round to the back parts of the house where the newer and lower buildings joined it. Here he was surprised by a stable-like smell and a medley of growls, grunts and whimpers – all the signs, in fact, of a considerable zoo. At first he did not understand, but presently he remembered that an immense programme of vivisection, freed at last from Red Tape and from niggling economy, was one of the plans of the NICE. He had not been particularly interested and had thought vaguely of rats, rabbits, and an occasional dog. The confused noises from within suggested something very different. As he stood there a loud melancholy howl arose and then, as if it had set the key, all manner of trumpetings, bayings, screams, laughter even, which shuddered and protested for a moment and then died away into mutterings and whines. Mark had no scruples about vivisection. What the noise meant to him was the greatness and grandiosity of this whole undertaking from which, apparently, he was likely to be excluded. There were all sorts of things in there: thousands of pounds' worth of living animality, which the Institute could afford to cut up like paper on the mere chance of some interesting discovery. He *must* get the job: he must somehow solve the problem of Steele. But the noise was disagreeable and he moved away.

Mark woke next morning with the feeling that there would certainly be one fence and perhaps two fences for him to get over during the day. The first was his interview with the Deputy Director. Unless he could get a very definite assurance about a post and a salary, he would cut his connection with the Institute. And then, when he reached home, the second fence would be his explanation to Jane of how the whole dream had faded away.

The first real fog of the autumn had descended on Belbury that morning. Mark ate his breakfast by artificial light, and neither post nor newspaper had arrived. It was a Friday and a servant handed him his bill for the portion of a week, which he had already spent in the Institute. He put it in his pocket after a hasty glance with a resolution that this, at any rate, should never be mentioned to Jane. Neither the total nor the items were of the sort that wives easily understand. He himself doubted whether there were not some mistake, but he was still at that age when a man would rather be fleeced to his last penny than dispute a bill. Then he finished his second cup of tea, felt for cigarettes, found none, and ordered a new packet.

The odd half hour which he had waited before keeping his appointment with the Deputy Director passed slowly. No one spoke to him. Everyone else seemed to be hasting away on some important and well-defined purpose. For part of the time he was alone in the lounge and felt that the servants looked at him as if he ought not to be there. He was glad when he was able to go upstairs and knock on Wither's door.

He was admitted at once, but the conversation was not easy to begin because Wither said nothing, and though he looked up as soon as Mark entered, with an expression of dreamy courtesy, he did not look exactly at Mark, nor did he ask him to sit down. The room, as usual, was extremely hot, and Mark, divided between his desire to make it clear that he had fully resolved to be left hanging about no longer and his equally keen desire not to lose the job if there were any real job going, did not perhaps speak very well. At all events, the Deputy Director left him to run down – to pass into disjointed repetitions and thence into complete silence. That silence lasted for some time. Wither sat with his lips pouted and slightly open as though he were humming a tune.

'So I think, Sir, I'd better go,' said Mark at last with vague reference to what he had been saying.

'You are Mr Studdock, I think?' said Wither tentatively after another prolonged silence.

'Yes,' said Mark impatiently. 'I called on you with Lord Feverstone a few days ago. You gave me to understand that you were offering me a position on the sociological side of the NICE. But as I was saying –'

'One moment, Mr Studdock,' interrupted the Deputy Director. 'It is so important to be perfectly clear what we are doing. You are no doubt aware that in certain senses of the words it would be most unfortunate to speak of my offering anyone a post in the Institute. You must not imagine for a moment that I hold any kind of autocratic position, nor, on the other hand, that the relation between my own sphere of influence and the powers – I am speaking of their temporary powers, you understand – of the Permament Committee or those of the Director himself are defined by any hard and fast system of what – er – one might call a constitutional, or even a constitutive, character. For example –'

'Then, Sir, can you tell me whether anyone has offered me a post, and, if so, who?'

'Oh,' said Wither suddenly, changing both his position and his tone, as if a new idea had struck him. 'There has never been the least question of that sort. It was always understood that your co-operation with the Institute would be entirely acceptable – would be of the greatest value.'

'Well, can I – I mean, oughtn't we to discuss the details? I mean the salary for example and – who should I be working under?'

'My dear friend,' said Wither with a smile, 'I do not anticipate that there will be any difficulty about the – er – the financial side of the matter. As for –'

'What would the salary be, Sir?' said Mark.

'Well, there you touch on a point which it is hardly for me to decide. I believe that members in the position which we had envisaged you as occupying usually draw some sum like fifteen hundred a year, allowing for fluctuations calculated on a very liberal basis. You will find that all questions of that sort will adjust themselves with the greatest of ease.'

'But when should I know, Sir? Who ought I go to about it?'

'You mustn't suppose, Mr Studdock, that when I mention fifteen hundred I am at all excluding the possibility of some higher figure. I don't think any of us here would allow a disagreement on that point – '

'I should be perfectly satisfied with fifteen hundred,' said Mark. 'I wasn't thinking of that at all. But – but – ' The Deputy Director's expression became more and more courtly and confidential as Mark stammered, so that when he finally blurted out, 'I suppose there'd be a contract or something of the kind,' he felt he had committed an unutterable vulgarity.

'Well,' said the Deputy Director fixing his eyes on the ceiling and sinking his voice to a whisper as though he too were profoundly embarrassed, 'that is not exactly the sort of procedure … it would, no doubt, be possible …'

'And that isn't the main point, Sir,' said Mark reddening. 'There's the question of my status. Am I to work under Mr Steele?'

'I have here a form,' said Wither opening a drawer, 'which has not, I believe, been ever actually used but which was designed for such agreements. You might care to study it at your leisure and if you are satisfied we could sign it at any time.'

'But about Mr Steele?'

At that moment a secretary entered and placed some letters on the Deputy Director's table.

'Ah! The post at last!' said Wither. 'Perhaps, Mr Studdock, er – you will have letters of your own to attend to. You are, I believe, married?' A smile of fatherly indulgence overspread his face as he said these words.

'I'm sorry to delay you, Sir,' said Mark, 'but about Mr Steele? There is no good my looking at the form of agreement until that question is settled. I should feel compelled to refuse any position which involved working under Mr Steele.'

'That opens up a very interesting question about which I should like to have a quite informal and confidential chat with you on some future occasion,' said Wither. 'For the moment, Mr Studdock, I shall not regard anything you have said as final. If you cared to call on me tomorrow ...' He became absorbed in the letter he had opened, and Mark, feeling that he had achieved enough for one interview, left the room. Apparently, they did really want him at the NICE and were prepared to pay a high price for him. He would fight it out about Steele later; meanwhile, he would study the form of agreement.

He came downstairs again and found the following letter waiting for him.

Bracton College,
Edgestow,
Oct. 20th, 19 –

My dear Mark,

We were all sorry to hear from Dick that you are resigning your fellowship, but feel quite certain you've made the right decision as far as your own career is concerned. Once the NICE is settled in here I shall expect to see almost as much of you as before. If you have not yet sent a formal resignation to NO, I shouldn't be in any hurry to do so. If you wrote early next term, the vacancy would come up at the February meeting, and we should have time to get ready a suitable candidate as your successor. Have you any ideas on the subject yourself? I was talking to James and Dick the other night about David Laird (James hadn't heard of him before). No doubt, you know his work: could you let me have a line about it, and about his more general qualifications? I may see him next week when I'm running over to

Cambridge to dine with the Prime Minister and one or two others, and I think Dick might be induced to ask Laird as well. You'll have heard that we had rather a shindy here the other night. There was apparently some sort of *fracas* between the new workmen and the local inhabitants. The NICE police, who seem to be a nervy lot, made the mistake of firing a few rounds over the head of the crowd. We had the Henrietta Maria window smashed and several stones came into Common Room. Glossop lost his head and wanted to go out and harangue the mob, but I managed to quiet him down. This is in strict confidence. There are lots of people ready to make capital out of it here and to get up a hue and cry against us for selling the wood. In haste – I must run off and make arrangements about Hingest's funeral.

Yours,

G. C. CURRY.

At the first words of this letter a stab of fear ran through Mark. He tried to reassure himself. An explanation of the misunderstanding – which he would write and post immediately – would be bound to put everything right. They couldn't shove a man out of his fellowship simply on a chance word spoken by Lord Feverstone in Common Room. It came back to him with miserable insight that what he was now calling 'a chance word' was exactly what he had learned, in the Progressive Element, to describe as 'settling real business in private', or 'cutting out the Red Tape', but he tried to thrust this out of his mind. It came back to him that poor Conington had actually lost his job in a way very similar to this, but he explained to himself that the circumstances had been quite different. Conington had been an outsider; he was inside, even more inside than Curry himself. But was he? If he were not 'inside' at Belbury (and it began to look as if he were not), was he still in Feverstone's confidence? If he had to go back to Bracton, would he find that he retained even his old status there? *Could* he go to Bracton? Yes, of course. He must write a letter at once explaining that he had not resigned, and would not resign, his fellowship. He sat down at a table in the writing room and took out his pen. Then another thought struck him. A letter to Curry, saying plainly that he meant to stay at Bracton, would be shown to Feverstone. Feverstone would tell Wither. Such a letter could be regarded as a refusal of any post at Belbury. Well – let it be! He would give up this shortlived dream and fall back on his fellowship. But how if that were impossible? The whole thing might have been arranged simply to let him fall between the two stools – kicked out of Belbury because he was retaining the Bracton fellowship and kicked out of Bracton because he was supposed to be taking a job at Belbury – then he and Jane left to sink or swim with not a *sou* between them – perhaps, with Feverstone's influence against him when he tried to get another job. And where *was* Feverstone?

Obviously, he must play his cards very carefully. He rang the bell and ordered a large whisky. At home he would not have drunk till twelve and even then would have drunk only beer. But now – and anyway, he felt curiously chilly. There was no point in catching a cold on top of all his other troubles.

He decided that he must write a very careful and rather elusive letter. His first draught was, he thought, not vague enough: it could be used as a proof that he had abandoned all idea of a job at Belbury. He must make it vaguer. But then, if it were too vague, it would do no good. Oh damn, damn, damn the whole thing. The two hundred pounds entrance fee, the bill for his first week, and snatches of imagined attempts to make Jane see the whole episode in the proper light, kept coming between him and his task. In the end, with the aid of the whisky and of a great many cigarettes, he produced the following letter:

The National Institute for Co-ordinated Experiments, Belbury.

Oct. 21st, 19 –

My dear Curry,

Feverstone must have got me wrong. I never made the slightest suggestion of resigning my fellowship and don't in the least wish to do so. As a matter of fact, I have almost made up my mind not to take a full time job with the NICE and hope to be back in college in a day or two. For one thing, I am rather worried about my wife's health and don't like to commit myself to being much away at present. In the second place, though everyone here has been extremely flattering and all press me to stay, the kind of job they want me for is more on the administrative and publicity side and less scientific than I had expected. So be sure and contradict it if you hear anyone saying I am thinking of leaving Edgestow. I hope you'll enjoy your jaunt to Cambridge: what circles you do move in!

Yours,

Mark G. Studdock

PS Laird wouldn't have done in any case. He got a third, and the only published work he's ventured on has been treated as a joke by serious reviewers. In particular, he has no *critical* faculty at all. You can always depend on him for admiring anything that is thoroughly bogus.

The relief of having finished the letter was only momentary, for almost as soon as he had sealed it the problem of how to pass the rest of this day returned to him. He decided to go and sit in his own room; but when he went up there he found the bed stripped and a vacuum cleaner in the middle of the floor. Apparently, members were not expected to be in their bedrooms at this time of day. He came down and tried the lounge; the servants were tidying it. He looked into the library. It was empty but for two men who were talking with their heads close together. They stopped and looked up as soon as he entered, obviously waiting for him to go. He pretended that he had come to get a book and retired. In the hall he saw Steele himself standing by the notice board and talking to a man with a pointed beard. Neither looked at Mark but as he passed them they became silent. He dawdled across the hall and pretended to examine the barometer. Wherever he went he heard doors opening and shutting, the tread of rapid feet, occasional ringing of telephones; all the signs of a busy institution carrying on a vigorous life from which he was excluded. He opened the front door and looked out; the fog was thick, wet and cold.

There is one sense in which every narrative is false; it dare not attempt, even if it could, to express the actual movement of time. This day was so long to Mark that a faithful account of it would be unreadable. Sometimes he sat upstairs – for at last they finished 'doing' his bedroom – sometimes he went out into the fog, sometimes he hung about the public rooms. Every now and then these would be unaccountably filled up by crowds of talking people and for a few minutes the strain of trying not to look unoccupied, not to seem miserable and embarrassed, would be imposed on him; then suddenly, as if summoned by their next engagement, all these people would hurry away.

Some time after lunch he met Stone in one of the passages. Mark had not thought of him since yesterday morning, but now, looking at the expression on his face and something furtive in his whole manner, he realised that here, at any rate, was someone who felt as uncomfortable as himself. Stone had the look which Mark had often seen before in unpopular boys or new boys at school, in 'outsiders' at Bracton – the look which was for Mark the symbol of all his worst fears, for to be one who must wear that look was, in his scale of values, the greatest evil. His instinct was not to speak to this man Stone. He knew by experience how dangerous it is to be friends with a sinking man or even to be seen with him: you cannot keep him afloat and he may pull you under. But his own craving for companionship was now acute, so that against his better judgment he smiled a sickly smile and said, 'Hullo!'

Stone gave a start as if to be spoken to were almost a frightening experience. 'Good afternoon,' he said nervously and made to pass on.

'Let's come and talk somewhere, if you're not busy,' said Mark.

'I am – that is to say – I'm not quite sure how long I shall be free,' said Stone.

'Tell me about this place,' said Mark. 'It seems to me perfectly bloody, but I haven't yet made up my mind. Come to my room.'

'I don't think that at all. Not at all. Who said I thought that?' answered Stone very quickly. And Mark did not answer because at that moment he saw the Deputy Director approaching them. He was to discover during the next few weeks that no passage and no public room at Belbury was ever safe from the prolonged indoor walks of the Deputy Director. They could not be regarded as a form of espionage for the creak of Wither's boots and the dreary little tune which he was nearly always humming would have defeated any such purpose. One heard him quite a long way off. Often one saw him a long way off as well, for he was a tall man (without his stoop he would have been very tall indeed) and often, even in a crowd, one saw that face at a distance staring vaguely towards one. But this was Mark's first experience of that ubiquity and he felt that the DD could not have appeared at a more unfortunate moment. Very slowly he came towards them, looked in their direction though it was not plain from his face whether he recognised them or not, and passed on. Neither of the young men attempted to resume their conversation.

At tea Mark saw Feverstone and went at once to sit beside him. He knew that the worst thing a man in his position could do was to try to force himself on anyone, but he was now feeling desperate.

'I say, Feverstone,' he began gaily, 'I'm in search of information' – and was relieved to see Feverstone smile in reply.

'Yes,' said Mark. 'I haven't had exactly what you'd call a glowing reception from Steele. But the DD won't hear of my leaving. And the Fairy seems to want me to write newspaper articles. What the hell *am* I supposed to be doing?'

Feverstone laughed long and loud.

'Because,' concluded Mark, 'I'm damned if I can find out. I've tried to tackle the old boy direct –'

'God!' said Feverstone laughing even louder.

'Can one *never* get anything out of him?'

'Not what *you* want,' said Feverstone with a chuckle.

'Well, how the devil is one to find out what's wanted if nobody offers any information?'

'Quite.'

'Oh, and by the way, that reminds me of something else. How on earth did Curry get hold of the idea that I'm resigning my fellowship?'

'Aren't you?'

'I never had the faintest notion of resigning it.'

'Really! I was told distinctly by the Fairy that you weren't coming back.'

'You don't suppose I'd do it through her if I *was* going to resign?'

Feverstone's smile brightened and widened. 'It doesn't make any odds, you know,' he said. 'If the NICE want you to have a nominal job somewhere outside Belbury, you'll have one; and if they don't, you won't. Just like that.'

'Damn the NICE. I'm merely trying to retain the fellowship I already had, which is no concern of theirs. One doesn't want to fall between two stools.'

'One doesn't *want* to.'

'You mean?'

'Take my advice and get into Wither's good books again as soon as you can. I gave you a good start but you seem to have rubbed him up the wrong way. His attitude has changed since this morning. You need to humour him, you know. And just between ourselves, I wouldn't be too thick with the Fairy: it won't do you any good higher up. There are wheels within wheels.'

'In the meantime,' said Mark, 'I've written to Curry to explain that it's all rot about my resignation.'

'No harm if it amuses you,' said Feverstone, still smiling.

'Well, I don't suppose College wants to kick me out simply because Curry misunderstood something Miss Hardcastle said to you.'

'You *can't* be deprived of a fellowship under any statute I know, except for gross immorality.'

'No, of course not. I didn't mean that. I meant not being re-elected when I come up for re-electon next term.'

'Oh. I see.'

'And that's why I must rely on you to get that idea out of Curry's head.'

Feverstone said nothing.

'You will be sure,' urged Mark against his own better judgment, 'to make it quite clear to him that the whole thing was a mis-understanding.'

'Don't you know Curry? He will have got his whole wangling-machine going on the problem of your successor long ago.'

'That's why I am relying on you to stop him.'

'Me?'

'Yes.'

'Why me?'

'Well – damn it all, Feverstone, it was you who first put the idea into his head.'

'Do you know,' said Feverstone, helping himself to a muffin, 'I find your style of conversation rather difficult. You will come up for re-election in a few months. The College may decide to re-elect you; or, of course, it may not. As far as I can make out, you are at present attempting to canvass my vote in advance. To which the proper answer is the one I now give – go to Hell!'

'You know perfectly well that there was no doubt about my re-election until you spoke a word in Curry's ear.'

Feverstone eyed the muffin critically. 'You make me rather tired,' he said. 'If you don't know how to steer your own course in a place like Bracton, why come and pester me? I'm not a bucking nurse. And for your own good, I would advise you, in talking to people here, to adopt a more agreeable manner than you are using now. Otherwise your life may be, in the famous words, "nasty, poor, brutish, and short!" '

'Short?' said Mark. 'Is that a threat? Do you mean my life at Bracton or at the NICE?'

'I shouldn't stress the distinction too much if I were you,' said Feverstone.

'I shall remember that,' said Mark, rising from his chair. As he made to move away, he could not help turning to this smiling man once again and saying, 'It was you who brought me here. I thought you at least were my friend.'

'Incurable romantic!' said Lord Feverstone, deftly extending his mouth to an even wider grin and popping the muffin into it entire.

And thus Mark knew that if he lost the Belbury job he would lose his fellowship at Bracton as well.

◆ ○ ◆

During these days Jane spent as little time as possible in the flat and kept herself awake reading in bed, as long as she could, each night. Sleep had become her enemy. In the day-time she kept on going to Edgestow – nominally in the attempt to find another 'woman who would come in twice a week' instead of Mrs Maggs. On one of these occasions she was delighted to find herself suddenly addressed by Camilla Denniston. Camilla had just stepped out of a car and next moment she introduced a tall dark man as her husband. Jane saw at once that both the Dennistons were the sort of people she liked. She knew that Mr Denniston had once been a friend of Mark's but she had never met him; and her first thought was to wonder, as she had wondered before, why Mark's present friends were so inferior to those he once had. Carey and Wadsden and the Taylors, who had all been members of the set in which she first got to know him, had been nicer than Curry and Busby, not to mention the Feverstone man – and this Mr Denniston was obviously much nicer indeed.

'We were just coming to see you,' said Camilla. 'Look here, we have lunch with us. Let's drive you up to the woods beyond Sandown and all feed together in the car. There's lots to talk about.'

'Or what about your coming to the flat and lunching with me?' said Jane inwardly wondering how she could manage this. 'It's hardly a day for picnicking.'

'That only means extra washing up for you,' said Camilla. 'Had we better go somewhere in town, Frank? – if Mrs Studdock thinks it's too cold and foggy.'

'A restaurant would hardly do, Mrs Studdock,' said Denniston. 'We want to be private.' The 'we' obviously meant 'we three' and established at once a pleasant, business-like unity between them. 'As well,' he continued. 'don't you like a rather foggy day in a wood in autumn? You'll find we shall be perfectly warm sitting in the car.'

Jane said she'd never heard of anyone liking fogs before but she didn't mind trying. All three got in.

'That's why Camilla and I got married,' said Denniston as they drove off. 'We both like Weather. Not this or that kind of weather, but just Weather. It's a useful taste if one lives in England.'

'How ever did you learn to do that, Mr Denniston?' said Jane. 'I don't think I should ever learn to like rain and snow.'

'It's the other way round,' said Denniston. 'Everyone begins as a child by liking Weather. You learn the art of disliking it as you grow up. Haven't you ever noticed it on a snowy day? The grown-ups are all going about with long faces, but look at the children – and the dogs? *They* know what snow's made for.'

'I'm sure I hated wet days as a child,' said Jane.

'That's because the grown-ups kept you in,' said Camilla. 'Any child loves rain if it's allowed to go out and paddle about in it.'

Presently, they left the unfenced road beyond Sandown and went bumping across grass and among trees and finally came to rest in a sort of little grassy bay with a fir thicket on one side and a group of beeches on the other. There were wet cobwebs and a rich autumnal smell all round them. Then all three sat together in the back of the car and there was some unstrapping of baskets, and then sandwiches and a little flask of sherry and finally hot coffee and cigarettes. Jane was beginning to enjoy herself.

'Now!' said Camilla.

'Well,' said Denniston, 'I suppose I'd better begin. You know of course where we've come from, Mrs Studdock?'

'From Miss Ironwood's,' said Jane.

'Well, from the same house. But we don't belong to Grace Ironwood. She and we both belong to someone else.'

'Yes?' said Jane.

'Our little household, or company, or society, or whatever you like to call it is run by a Mr Fisher-King. At least that is the name he has recently taken. You might or might not know his original name if I told it to you. He is a great traveller but now an invalid. He got a wound in his foot, on his last journey, which won't heal.'

'How did he come to change his name?'

'He had a married sister in India, a Mrs Fisher-King. She has just died and left him a large fortune on condition that he took the name. She was a remarkable woman in her way; a friend of the great native Christian mystic whom you may have heard of – the Sura. And that's the point. The Sura had reason to believe, or thought he had reason to believe, that a great danger was hanging over the human race. And just before the end – just before he disappeared – he became convinced that it would actually come to a head in this island. And after he'd gone – '

'Is he dead?' asked Jane.

'That we don't know,' answered Denniston. 'Some people think he's alive, others not. At any rate he disappeared. And Mrs Fisher-King more or less handed over the problem to her brother, to our chief. That in fact was why she gave him the money. He was to collect a company round him to watch for this danger, and to strike when it came.'

'That's not quite right, Arthur,' said Camilla. 'He was told that a company would in fact collect round him and he was to be its Head.'

'I don't think we need go into that,' said Arthur. 'But I agree. And now, Mrs Studdock, this is where you come in.'

Jane waited.

'The Sura said that when the time came we should find what he called a seer: a person with second sight.'

'Not that we'd *get* a seer, Arthur,' said Camilla, 'that a seer would turn up. Either we or the other side would get her.'

'And it looks,' said Denniston to Jane, 'as if you were the seer.'

'But, please,' said Jane smiling, 'I don't want to be anything so exciting.'

'No,' said Denniston. 'It's rough luck on you.' There was just the right amount of sympathy in his tone.

Camilla turned to Jane and said, 'I gathered from Grace Ironwood that you weren't quite convinced you *were* a seer. I mean you thought it might be just ordinary dreams. Do you still think that?'

'It's all so strange and – *beastly*,' said Jane. She liked these people, but her habitual inner prompter was whispering, 'Take care. Don't get drawn in. Don't commit yourself to anything. You've got your own life to live.' Then an impulse of honesty forced her to add:

'As a matter of fact, I've had another dream since then. And it turns out to have been true. I saw the murder – Mr Hingest's murder.'

'There you are,' said Camilla. 'Oh, Mrs Studdock, you *must* come in. You must, you must. That means we're right on top of it now. Don't you see? We've been wondering all this time exactly where the trouble is going to begin, and now your dream gives us a clue. You've seen something within a few miles of Edgestow. In fact, we are apparently in the thick of it already – whatever it is. And we can't move an inch without your help. You are our secret service, our eyes. It's all been arranged long before we were born. Don't spoil everything. Do join us.'

'No, Cam, don't,' said Denniston. 'The Pendragon – the Head, I mean, wouldn't like us to do that. Mrs Studdock must come in freely.'

'But,' said Jane, 'I don't know anything about all this. Do I? I don't want to take sides in something I don't understand.'

'But don't you see,' broke in Camilla, 'that you can't be neutral? If you don't give yourself to us, the enemy will use you.'

The words 'give yourself to us' were ill-chosen. The very muscles of Jane's body stiffened a little: if the speaker had been anyone who attracted her less than Camilla she would have become like stone to any further appeal. Denniston laid a hand on his wife's arm.

'You must see it from Mrs Studdock's point of view, dear,' he said. 'You forget she knows practically nothing at all about us. And that is the real difficulty. We can't tell her much until she has joined. We are in fact asking her to take a leap in the dark.' He turned to Jane with a slightly quizzical smile on his face which was, nevertheless, grave. 'It *is* like that,' he said, 'like getting married, or going into the Navy as a boy, or becoming a monk, or trying a new thing to eat. You can't know what it's like until you take the plunge.' He did not perhaps know (or again perhaps he did) the complicated resentments and resistances which his choice of illustrations awoke in Jane, nor could she herself analyse them. She merely replied in a colder voice than she had yet used:

'In that case, it is rather difficult to see why one should take it at all.'

'I admit frankly,' said Denniston, 'that you can only take it on trust. It all depends really, I suppose, what impression the Dimbles and Grace and we two have made on you: and, of course, the Head himself, when you meet *him*.'

Jane softened again.

'What exactly are you asking me to do?' she said.

'To come and see our chief, first of all. And then – well, to join. It would involve making certain promises to him. He is really a Head, you see. We have all agreed to take his orders. Oh – there's one other thing. What view would Mark take about it? – he and I are old friends, you know.'

'I wonder,' said Camilla. 'Need we go into that for the moment?'

'It's bound to come up sooner or later,' said her husband.

There was a little pause.

'Mark?' said Jane. 'How does he come into it? I can't imagine what he'd say about all this. He'd probably think we were all off our heads.'

'Would he object, though?' said Denniston. 'I mean, would he object to your joining us?'

'If he were at home, I suppose he'd be rather surprised if I announced I was going to stay indefinitely at St Anne's. Does "joining you" mean that?'

'Isn't Mark at home?' asked Denniston with some surprise.

'No,' said Jane. 'He's at Belbury. I think he's going to have a job in the NICE.' She was rather pleased to be able to say this for she was well aware of the distinction it implied. If Denniston was impressed he did not show it.

'I don't think,' he said, 'that "joining us" would mean, at the moment, coming to live at St Anne's, specially in the case of a married woman. Unless old Mark got really interested and came himself – '

'That is quite out of the question,' said Jane.

('He doesn't know Mark,' she thought.)

'Anyway,' continued Denniston, 'that is hardly the real point at the moment. Would he object to your joining – putting yourself under the Head's orders and making the promises and all that?'

'Would he object?' asked Jane. 'What on earth would it have to do with him?'

'Well,' said Denniston, hesitating a little, 'the Head – or the authorities he obeys – have rather old-fashioned notions. He wouldn't like a married woman to come in, if it could be avoided, without her husband's – without consulting –'

'Do you mean I'm to ask Mark's *permission*?' said Jane with a strained little laugh. The resentment which had been rising and ebbing, but rising each time a little more than it ebbed, for several minutes, had now overflowed. All this talk of promises and obedience to an unknown Mr Fisher-King had already repelled her. But the idea of this same person sending her back to get Mark's permission – as if she were a child asking leave to go to a party – was the climax. For a moment she looked on Mr Denniston with real dislike. She saw him, and Mark, and the Fisher-King man and this preposterous Indian fakir simply as Men – complacent, patriarchal figures making arrangements for women as if women were children or bartering them like cattle. ('And so the king promised that if anyone killed the dragon he would *give* him his daughter in marriage.') She was very angry.

'Arthur,' said Camilla, 'I see a light over there. Do you think it's a bonfire?'

'Yes, I should say it was.'

'My feet are getting cold. Let's go for a little walk and look at the fire. I wish we had some chestnuts.'

'Oh, do let's,' said Jane.

They got out. It was warmer in the open than it had by now become in the car – warm and full of leavy smells, and dampness, and the small noise of dripping branches. The fire was big and in its middle life – a smoking hillside of leaves on one side and great caves and cliffs of glowing red on the other. They stood round it and chatted of indifferent matters for a time.

'I'll tell you what I'll do,' said Jane presently. 'I won't join your – your – whatever it is. But I'll promise to let you know if I have any more dreams of that sort.'

'That is splendid,' said Denniston. 'And I think it is as much as we had a right to expect. I quite see your point of view. May I ask for one more promise?'

'What is that?'

'Not to mention us to anyone.'

'Oh, certainly.'

Later, when they had returned to the car and were driving back, Mr Denniston said, 'I hope the dreams will not *worry* you much, now, Mrs Studdock. No: I don't mean I hope they'll stop: and I don't think they will either. But now that you know they are not something in yourself but only things going on in the outer world (nasty things, no doubt, but no worse than lots you read in the papers), I believe you'll find them quite bearable. The less you think of them as *your dreams* and the more you think of them – well, as News – the better you'll feel about them.'

Fog

A night (with little sleep) and half another day dragged past before Mark was able to see the Deputy Director again. He went to him in a chastened frame of mind, anxious to get the job on almost any terms.

'I have brought back the Form, Sir,' he said.

'What Form?' asked the Deputy Director. Mark found he was talking to a new and different Wither. The absent-mindedness was still there, but the courtliness was gone. The man looked at him as if out of a dream, as if divided from him by an immense distance, but with a sort of dreamy distaste which might turn into active hatred if ever that distance were diminished. He still smiled, but there was something cat-like in the smile; an occasional alteration of the lines about the mouth which even hinted at a snarl. Mark in his hands was as a mouse. At Bracton the Progressive Element, having to face only scholars, had passed for very knowing fellows, but here at Belbury, one felt quite different. Wither said he had understood that Mark had already refused the job. He could not, in any event, renew the offer. He spoke vaguely and alarmingly of strains and frictions, of injudicious behaviour, of the danger of making enemies, of the impossibility that the NICE could harbour a person who appeared to have quarrelled with all its members in the first week. He spoke even more vaguely and alarmingly of conversations he had had with 'your colleagues at Bracton' which entirely confirmed this view. He doubted if Mark were really suited to a learned career, but disclaimed any intention of giving advice. Only after he had hinted and murmured Mark into a sufficient state of dejection did he throw him, like a bone to a dog, the suggestion of an appointment for a probationary period at (roughly – he could not commit the Institute) six hundred a year. And Mark took it. He attempted to get answers even then to some of his questions. From whom was he to take orders? Was he to reside at Belbury?

Wither replied, 'I think, Mr Studdock, we have already mentioned elasticity as the keynote of the Institute. Unless you are prepared to treat membership as – er – a vocation rather than a mere appointment, I could not conscientiously advise you to come to us. There are no water-tight compartments. I fear I could not persuade the Committee to invent for your benefit some cut and dried position in which you would discharge artificially limited duties and, apart from those, regard your time as your own. Pray allow me to finish, Mr Studdock. We are, as I have said before, more like a family, or even, perhaps, like a single personality. There must be no question of "taking your orders", as you (rather unfortunately) suggest, from some specified official and considering yourself free to adopt an intransigent attitude to your other colleagues. (I must ask you not to interrupt me, please.) That is not the spirit in which I would wish you to approach your duties. You must make yourself useful, Mr Studdock – generally useful. I do not think the Institute could allow anyone to remain in it who showed a disposition to stand on his rights – who grudged this or that piece of service because it fell outside some function which he had chosen to circumscribe by a rigid definition. On the other hand, it would be quite equally disastrous – I mean for yourself, Mr Studdock: I am thinking throughout of your own interests – quite equally disastrous if you allowed yourself ever to be distracted from your real work by unauthorised collaboration – or, worse still, interference – with the work of other members. Do not let casual suggestions distract you or dissipate your energies. Concentration, Mr Studdock, concentration. And the free spirit of give and take. If you avoid both the errors I have mentioned then – ah, I do not think I need despair of correcting on your behalf certain unfortunate impressions which (we must admit) your behaviour has already produced. No, Mr Studdock, I can allow no further discussion. My time is already fully occupied. I cannot be continually harassed by conversations of this sort. You must find your own level, Mr Studdock. Good morning, Mr Studdock, good morning. Remember what I have said. I am trying to do all I can for you. Good morning.'

Mark reimbursed himself for the humiliation of this interview by reflecting that if he were not a married man he would not have borne it for a moment. This seemed to him (though he did not put it into words) to throw the burden upon Jane. It also set him free to think of all the things he would have said to Wither if he hadn't had Jane to bother about – and would still say if ever he got a chance. This kept him in a sort of twilight happiness for several minutes; and when he went to tea he found that the reward for his submission had already begun. The Fairy signed to him to come and sit beside her.

'You haven't done anything about Alcasan yet?' she asked.

'No,' said Mark, 'because I hadn't really decided to stay, not until this morning. I could come up and look at your materials this afternoon – at least as far as I know, for I haven't yet really found out what I'm supposed to be doing.'

'Elasticity, Sonny, elasticity,' said Miss Hardcastle. 'You never will. Your line is to do whatever you're told and above all not to bother the old man.'

◆ ○ ◆

During the next few days several processes, which afterwards came to seem important, were steadily going on.

The fog, which covered Edgestow as well as Belbury, continued and grew denser. At Edgestow one regarded it as 'coming up from the river', but in reality it lay all over the heart of England. It blanketed the whole town so that walls dripped and you could write your name in the dampness on tables and men worked by artificial light at midday. The workings, where Bragdon Wood had been, ceased to offend conservative eyes and become mere clangings, thuddings, hootings, shouts, curses and metallic screams in an invisible world.

Some felt glad that the obscenity should thus be covered for all beyond the Wynd was now an abomination. The grip of the NICE on Edgestow was tightening. The river itself which had once been brownish green and amber and smooth-skinned silver, tugging at the reeds and playing with the red roots, now flowed opaque, thick with mud, sailed on by endless fleets of empty tins, sheets of paper, cigarette ends and fragments of wood, sometimes varied by rainbow patches of oil. Then, the invasion actually crossed it. The Institute had bought the land up to the left or eastern bank. But now Busby was summoned to meet Feverstone and a Professor Frost as the representatives of the NICE, and learned for the first time that the Wynd itself was to be diverted: there was to be no river in Edgestow. This was still strictly confidential, but the Institute had already powers to force it. This being so, a new adjustment of boundaries between it and the College was clearly needed. Busby's jaw fell when he realised that the Institute wanted to come right up to the College walls. He refused of course. And it was then that he first heard a hint of requisitioning. The College could sell today and the Institute offered a good price: if they did not, compulsion and a merely nominal compensation awaited them. Relations between Feverstone and the Bursar deteriorated during this interview. An extraordinary College Meeting had to be summoned, and Busby had to put the best face he could on things to his colleagues. He was almost physically shocked by the storm of hatred which met him. In vain did he point out that those who were now abusing him had themselves voted for the sale of the wood; but equally in vain did they abuse him. The College was caught in the net of necessity. They sold the little strip on their side of the Wynd which meant so much. It was no more than a terrace between the eastern walls and the water. Twenty-four hours later the NICE boarded over the doomed Wynd and converted the terrace into a dump. All day long workmen were trampling across the planks with heavy loads which they flung down against the very walls of Bracton till the pile had covered the boarded blindness which had once been the Henrietta Maria window and reached almost to the east window of chapel.

In these days many members of the Progressive Element dropped off and joined the opposition. Those who were left were hammered closer together by the unpopularity they had to face. And though the College was thus sharply divided within, yet for the very same reason it also took on a new unity perforce in its relations to the outer world. Bracton as a whole bore the blame for bringing the NICE to Edgestow at all. This was unfair, for many high authorities in the University had thoroughly approved Bracton's action in doing so, but now that the result was becoming apparent people refused to remember this. Busby, though he had heard the hint of requisitioning in confidence, lost no time in spreading it through Edgestow common rooms – 'It would have done no good if we *had* refused to sell,' he said. But nobody believed that this was why Bracton had sold, and the unpopularity of that College steadily increased. The undergraduates got wind of it, and stopped attending the lectures of Bracton dons. Busby, and even the wholly innocent Warden, were mobbed in the streets.

The Town, which did not usually share the opinions of the University, was also in an unsettled condition. The disturbance in which the Bracton windows had been broken was taken little notice of in the London papers or even in the *Edgestow Telegraph*. But it was followed by other episodes. There was an indecent assault in one of the mean streets down by the station. There were two 'beatings up' in a public house. There were increasing complaints of threatening and disorderly behaviour on the part of the NICE workmen. But these complaints never appeared in the papers. Those who had actually seen ugly incidents were surprised to read in the *Telegraph*, that the new Institute was settling down very comfortably in Edgestow and the most cordial relations developing between it and the natives. Those who had not seen them but only heard of them, finding nothing in the *Telegraph*, dismissed the stories as rumours or exaggerations. Those who had seen them wrote letters to it, but it did not print their letters.

But if episodes could be doubted, no one could doubt that nearly all the hotels of the town had passed into the hands of the Institute, so that a man could no longer drink with a friend in his accustomed bar; that familiar shops were crowded with strangers who seemed to have plenty of money, and that prices were higher; that there was a queue for every omnibus and a difficulty in getting into every cinema. Quiet houses that had looked out on quiet streets were shaken all day long by heavy and unaccustomed traffic: wherever one went one was jostled by crowds of strangers. To a little midland market town like Edgestow even visitors from the other side of the county had hitherto ranked as aliens: the day-long clamour of Northern, Welsh, and even Irish voices, the shouts, the cat-calls, the songs, the wild faces passing in the fog, were utterly detestable. 'There's going to be trouble here,' was the comment of many a citizen; and in a few days, 'You'd think they *wanted* trouble.' It is not recorded who first said, 'We need more police.' And then at last the *Edgestow Telegraph* took notice. A shy little article – a cloud no bigger than a man's hand – appeared suggesting that the local police were quite incapable of dealing with the new population.

Of all these things Jane took little notice. She was, during these days, merely 'hanging on'. Perhaps Mark would summon her to Belbury. Perhaps he would give up the whole Belbury scheme and come home – his letters were vague and unsatisfactory. Perhaps she would go out to St Anne's and see the Dennistons. The dreams continued. But Mr Denniston had been right: it was better when one had given in to regarding them as 'news'. If it had not been, she could hardly have endured her nights. There was one recurrent dream in which nothing exactly happened. She seemed indeed to be lying in her own bed. But there was someone beside the bed – someone who had apparently drawn a chair up to the bedside and then sat down to watch. He had a notebook in which he occasionally made an entry. Otherwise he sat perfectly still and patiently attentive – like a doctor. She knew his face already, and came to know it infinitely well: the pince-nez, the well-chiselled, rather white, features, and the little pointed beard. And presumably – if he could see her – he must by now know hers equally well: it was certainly herself whom he appeared to be studying. Jane did not write about this to the Dennistons the first time it occurred. Even after the second she delayed until it was too late to post the letter that day. She had a sort of hope that the longer she kept silent the more likely they would be to come in and see her again. She wanted comfort but she wanted it, if possible, without going out to St Anne's, without meeting this Fisher-King man and getting drawn into his orbit.

Mark meanwhile was working at the rehabilitation of Alcasan. He had never seen a police dossier before and found it difficult to understand. In spite of his efforts to conceal his ignorance, the Fairy soon discovered it. 'I'll put you onto the Captain,' she said. 'He'll show you the ropes.' That was how Mark came to spend most of his working hours with her second in command, Captain O'Hara, a big white-haired man with a handsome face, talking in what English people called a Southern brogue and Irish people 'a Dublin accent you could cut with a knife'. He claimed to be of ancient family and had a seat at Castlemortle. Mark did not really understand his explanations of the dossier, the Q Register, the Sliding File system, and what the Captain called 'weeding'. But he was ashamed to confess this and so it came about that the whole selection of facts really remained in O'Hara's hands and Mark found himself working merely as a writer. He did his best to conceal this from O'Hara and to make it appear that they were really working together; this naturally made it impossible for him to repeat his original protests against being treated as a mere journalist. He had, indeed, a taking style (which had helped his academic career much more than he would have liked to acknowledge) and his journalism was a success. His articles and letters about Alcasan appeared in papers where he would never have had the *entrée* over his own signature: papers read by millions. He could not help feeling a little thrill of pleasurable excitement.

He also confided to Captain O'Hara his minor financial anxieties. When was one paid? And in the meantime, he was short of petty cash. He had lost his wallet on his very first night at Belbury and it had never been recovered. O'Hara roared with laughter. 'Sure you can have any money you like by asking the Steward.'

'You mean it's then deducted from one's next cheque?' asked Mark.

'Man,' said the Captain, 'once you're in the Institute, God bless it, you needn't bother your head about that. Aren't we going to take over the whole currency question? It's we that *make* money.'

'Do you mean?' gasped Mark and then paused and added, 'But they'd come down on you for the lot if you left.'

'What do you want to be talking about leaving for at all?' said O'Hara. 'No one leaves the Institute. At least, the only one that ever I heard of was old Hingest.'

About this time Hingest's inquest came to an end with a verdict of murder by a person or persons unknown. The funeral service was held in the college chapel at Bracton.

It was the third and thickest day of the fog, which was now so dense and white that men's eyes smarted from looking at it and all distant sounds were annihilated; only the drip from eaves and trees and the shouts of the workmen outside chapel were audible within the College. Inside the chapel the candles burned with straight flames, each flame the centre of a globe of greasy luminosity, and cast almost no light on the building as a whole; but for the coughing and shuffling of feet, one would not have known that the stalls were quite full. Curry, black-suited and black-gowned and looming unnaturally large, went to and fro at the western end of the chapel, whispering and peering, anxious lest the fog might delay the arrival of what he called the Remains, and not unpleasingly conscious of the weight wherewith his responsibility for the whole ceremony pressed upon his shoulders. Curry was very great at College funerals. There was no taint of the undertaker about him; he was the restrained, manly friend, stricken by a heavy blow but still mindful that he was (in some undefined sense) the father of the

College and that amid all the spoils of mutability he, at any rate, must not give way. Strangers who had been present on such occasions often said to one another as they drove off, 'You could see that Sub-Warden chap felt it, though he wasn't going to show it.' There was no hypocrisy in this. Curry was so used to superintending the lives of his colleagues that it came naturally to him to superintend their deaths; and possibly, if he had possessed an analytic mind, he might have discovered in himself a vague feeling that his influence, his power of smoothing paths and pulling suitable wires, could not really quite cease once the breath was out of the body.

The organ began to play and drowned both the coughing within and the harsher noises without – the monotonously ill-tempered voices, the rattle of iron, and the vibrating shocks with which loads were flung from time to time against the chapel wall. But the fog had, as Curry feared, delayed the coffin, and the organist had been playing for half an hour before there came a stir about the door and the family mourners, the black-clad Hingests of both sexes with their ram-rod backs and country faces, began to be ushered into the stalls reserved for them. Then came maces and beadles and censors and the Grand Rector of Edgestow; then, singing, the choir, and finally the coffin – an island of flowers drifting indistinctly through the fog, which seemed to have poured in, thicker, colder and wetter, with the opening of the door. The service began.

Canon Storey took it. His voice was still beautiful, and there was beauty too in his isolation from all that company. He was isolated both by his faith and by his deafness. He felt no qualm about the appropriateness of the words which he read over the corpse of the proud old unbeliever, for he had never suspected his unbelief; and he was wholly unconscious of the strange antiphony between his own voice reading and the other voices from without. Glossop might wince when one of those voices, impossible to ignore in the silence of the chapel, was heard shouting, 'Take your bucking great foot out of the light or I'll let you have the whole lot on top of it'; but Storey, unmoved and unaware, replied, 'Thou fool, that which thou sowest is not quickened unless it die.'

'I'll give you one across your ugly face in a moment, see if I don't,' said the voice again.

'It is sown a natural body; it is raised a spiritual body,' said Storey.

'Disgraceful, disgraceful,' muttered Curry to the Bursar who sat next to him. But some of the junior Fellows saw, as they said, the funny side of it and thought how Feverstone (who had been unable to be present) would enjoy the story.

◆　○　◆

The pleasantest of the rewards which fell to Mark for his obedience was admission to the library. Shortly after his brief intrusion into it on that miserable morning he had discovered that this room, though nominally public, was in practice reserved for what one had learned, at school, to call 'bloods' and, at Bracton, 'the Progressive Element'. It was on the library hearthrug and during the hours between ten and midnight that the important and confidential talks took place; and that was why, when Feverstone one evening sidled up to Mark in the lounge and said, 'What about a drink in the library?' Mark smiled and agreed and harboured no resentment for the last conversation he had had with Feverstone. If he felt a little contempt of himself for doing so, he repressed and forgot it: that sort of thing was childish and unrealistic.

The circle in the library usually consisted of Feverstone, the Fairy, Filostrato and – more surprising – Straik. It was balm to Mark's wounds to find that Steele never appeared there. He had apparently got in beyond, or behind, Steele, as they had promised him he would; all was working according to programme. The one person whose frequent appearance in the library he did not understand was the silent man with the pince-nez and the pointed beard, Professor Frost. The Deputy Director – or, as Mark now called him, the DD, or the Old Man – was often there, but in a peculiar mode. He had a habit of drifting in and sauntering about the room, creaking and humming as usual. Sometimes he came up to the circle by the fire and listened and looked on with a vaguely parental expression on his face; but he seldom said anything and he never joined the party. He drifted away again, and then, perhaps, would return an hour later and once more potter about the empty parts of the room and once more go away. He had never spoken to Mark since the humiliating interview in his study, and Mark learned from the Fairy that he was still out of favour. 'The Old Man will thaw in time,' she said. 'But I told you he didn't like people to talk about leaving.'

The least satisfactory member of the circle in Mark's eyes was Straik. Straik made no effort to adapt himself to the ribald and realistic tone in which his colleagues spoke. He never drank nor smoked. He would sit silent, nursing a threadbare knee with a lean hand and turning his large unhappy eyes from one speaker to another, without attempting to combat them or to join in the joke when they laughed. Then – perhaps once in the whole evening – something said would start him off: usually something about the opposition of reactionaries in the outer world and the measures which the NICE would take to deal with it. At such moments he would burst into loud and prolonged speech, threatening, denouncing, prophesying. The strange thing was that the others neither interrupted him nor laughed. There was some deeper unity between this uncouth man and them which apparently held in check the obvious lack of sympathy, but what it was Mark did not discover. Sometimes Straik addressed him in particular, talking, to Mark's great discomfort and bewilderment, about resurrection. 'Neither a historical fact nor a fable, young man,' he said, 'but a prophecy. All the miracles – shadows of things to come. Get rid of false spirituality. It is all going to happen, here in this world, in the only world there is. What did the Master tell us? Heal the sick, cast out devils, raise the dead. We shall. The Son of Man – that is, Man himself, full grown – has power to judge the world – to distribute life without end, and punishment without end. You shall see. Here and now.' It was all very unpleasant.

It was on the day after Hingest's funeral that Mark first ventured to walk into the library on his own; hitherto he had always been supported by Feverstone or Filostrato. He was a little uncertain of his reception, and yet also afraid that if he did not soon assert his right to the *entrée*, this modesty might damage him. He knew that in such matters the error in either direction is equally fatal; one has to guess and take the risk.

It was a brilliant success. The circle were all there, and before he had closed the door behind him, all had turned with welcoming faces, and Filostrato had said, '*Ecco*' and the Fairy, 'Here's the very man.' A glow of sheer pleasure passed over Mark's whole body. Never had the fire seemed to burn more brightly nor the smell of the drinks to be more attractive. He was actually being waited for. He was wanted.

'How quick can you write two leading articles, Mark?' said Feverstone.

'Can you work all night?' asked Miss Hardcastle.

'I *have* done,' said Mark. 'What's it all about?'

'You are satisfied,' asked Filostrato, 'that it – the disturbance – must go forward at once, yes?'

'That's the joke of it,' said Feverstone. 'She's done her work too well. She hasn't read her Ovid. *Ad metam properate simul.*'

'We cannot delay it if we wished,' said Straik.

'What are we talking about?' said Mark.

'The disturbances at Edgestow,' answered Feverstone.

'Oh … I haven't been following them very much. Are they becoming serious?'

'They're going to become serious, Sonny,' said the Fairy. 'And that's the point. The real riot was timed for next week. All this little stuff was only meant to prepare the ground, But it's been going on too well, damn it. The balloon will have to go up tomorrow, or the day after, at latest.'

Mark glanced in bewilderment from her face to Feverstone's. The latter doubled himself up with laughter and Mark, almost automatically, gave a jocular turn to his own bewilderment.

'I think the penny hasn't dropped, Fairy,' he said.

'You surely didn't imagine,' grinned Feverstone, 'that the Fairy left the initiative with the natives?'

'You mean she herself is the Disturbance?' said Mark.

'Yes, yes,' said Filostrato, his little eyes glistening above his fat cheeks.

'It's all fair and square,' said Miss Hardcastle. 'You can't put a few hundred thousand imported workmen – '

'Not the sort you enrolled!' interjected Feverstone.

'Into a sleepy little hole like Edgestow,' Miss Hardcastle continued, 'without having trouble. I mean there'd have been trouble anyway. As it turns out, I don't believe my boys needed to do anything. But, since the trouble was bound to come, there was no harm in seeing it came at the right moment.'

'You mean you've *engineered* the disturbances?' said Mark. To do him justice, his mind was reeling from this new revelation. Nor was he aware of any decision to conceal his state of mind: in the snugness and intimacy of that circle he found his facial muscles and his voice, without any conscious volition, taking on the tone of his colleagues.

'That's a crude way of putting it,' said Feverstone.

'It makes no difference,' said Filostrato. 'This is how things have to be managed.'

'Quite,' said Miss Hardcastle. 'It's always done. Anyone who knows police work will tell you. And as I say, the real thing – the big riot – must take place within the next forty-eight hours.'

'It's nice to get the tip straight from the horse's mouth!' said Mark. 'I wish I'd got my wife out of the town, though.'

'Where does she live?' said the Fairy.

'Up at Sandown.'

'Ah. It'll hardly affect her. In the meantime, you and I have got to get busy about the account of the riot.'

'But – what's it all for?'

'Emergency regulations,' said Feverstone. 'You'll never get the powers we want at Edgestow until the Government declares that a state of emergency exists there.'

'Exactly,' said Filostrato. 'It is folly to talk of peaceful revolutions. Not that the *canaglia* would always resist – often they have to be prodded into it – but until there is the disturbance, the firing, the barricades – no one gets powers to act effectively. There is not enough what you call weigh on the boat to steer him.'

'And the stuff must be all ready to appear in the papers the very day after the riot,' said Miss Hardcastle. 'That means it must be handed in to the DD by six tomorrow morning, at latest.'

'But how are we to write it tonight if the thing doesn't even happen till tomorrow at the earliest?'

Everyone burst out laughing.

'You'll never manage publicity that way, Mark,' said Feverstone. 'You surely don't need to wait for a thing to happen before you tell the story of it!'

'Well, I admit,' said Mark, and his face was full of laughter, 'I had a faint prejudice for doing so, not living in Mr Dunne's sort of time nor in looking-glass land.'

'No good, Sonny,' said Miss Hardcastle. 'We've got to get on with it at once. Time for one more drink and you and I'd better go upstairs and begin. We'll get them to give us devilled bones and coffee at three.'

This was the first thing Mark had been asked to do which he himself, before he did it, clearly knew to be criminal. But the moment of his consent almost escaped his notice; certainly, there was no struggle, no sense of turning a corner. There may have been a time in the world's history when such moments fully revealed their gravity, with witches prophesying on a blasted heath or visible Rubicons to be crossed. But, for him, it all slipped past in a chatter of laughter, of that intimate laughter between fellow professionals, which of all earthly powers is strongest to make men do very bad things before they are yet, individually, very bad men. A few moments later he was trotting upstairs with the Fairy. They passed Cosser on the way and Mark, talking busily to his companion, saw out of the corner of his eye that Cosser was watching them. To think that he had once been afraid of Cosser!

'Who has the job of waking the DD up at six?' asked Mark.

'Probably not necessary,' said the Fairy. 'I suppose the old man must sleep sometime. But I've never discovered when he does it.'

◆ ○ ◆

At four o'clock Mark sat in the Fairy's office re-reading the last two articles he had written – one for the most respectable of our papers, the other for a more popular organ. This was the only part of the night's work which had anything in it to flatter literary vanity. The earlier hours had been spent in the sterner labour of concocting the news itself. These two Leaders had been kept for the end, and the ink was still wet. The first was as follows:

While it would be premature to make any final comment on last night's riot at Edgestow, two conclusions seem to emerge from the first accounts (which we publish elsewhere) with a clarity which is not likely to be shaken by subsequent developments. In the first place, the whole episode will administer a rude shock to any complacency which may still lurk among us as to the enlightenment of our own civilisation. It must, of course, be admitted that the transformation of a small university town into a centre of national research cannot be carried out without some friction and some cases of hardship to the local inhabitants. But the Englishman has always had his own quiet and humorous way of dealing with frictions and has never showed himself unwilling, when the issue is properly put before him, to make sacrifices much greater than those small alterations of habit and sentiment which progress demands of the people of Edgestow. It is gratifying to note that there is no suggestion in any authoritative quarter that the NICE has in any way exceeded its powers or failed in that consideration and courtesy which was expected of it; and there is little doubt that the actual starting point of the disturbances was some quarrel, probably in a public house, between one of the NICE workmen and some local Sir Oracle. But as the Stagyrite said long ago, disorders which have trivial occasions have deeper causes, and there seems little doubt that this petty *fracas* must have been inflamed, if not exploited, by sectional interests or widespread prejudice.

It is disquieting to be forced to suspect that the old distrust of planned efficiency and the old jealousy of what is ambiguously called 'Bureaucracy' can be so easily (though, we hope, temporarily) revived; though at the same time, this very suspicion, by revealing the gaps and weaknesses in our national level of education, emphasises one of the very diseases which the National Institute exists to cure. That it will cure it we need have no doubt. The will of the nation is behind this magnificent 'peace-effort', as Mr Jules so happily described the Institute, and any ill-informed opposition which ventures to try conclusions with it will be, we hope, gently, but certainly firmly, resisted.

The second moral to be drawn from last night's events is a more cheering one. The original proposal to provide the NICE with what is misleadingly called its own 'police force' was viewed with distrust in many quarters. Our readers will remember that while not sharing that distrust, we extended to it a certain sympathy. Even the false fears of those who love liberty should be respected as we respect even the ill-grounded anxieties of a mother. At the same time we insisted that the complexity of modern society rendered it an anachronism to confine the actual execution of the will of society to a body of men whose real function was the prevention and detection of crime: that the police, in fact, must be relieved sooner or later of that growing body of coercive functions which do not properly fall within their sphere. That this problem has been solved by other countries in a manner which proved fatal to liberty and justice, by creating a real *imperium in imperio*, is a fact which no one is likely to forget. The so-called 'Police' of the NICE – who should rather be called its 'Sanitary Executive' – is the characteristically English solution. Its relation to the National Police cannot, perhaps, be defined with perfect logical accuracy; but, as a nation, we have never been much enamoured of logic. The executive of the NICE has no connection with politics; and if it ever comes into relation with criminal justice, it does so in the gracious role of a rescuer – a rescuer who can remove the criminal from the harsh sphere of punishment into that of remedial treatment. If any doubt as to the value of such a force existed, it has been amply set at rest by the episodes at Edgestow. The happiest relations seem to have been maintained throughout between the officers of the Institute and the National Police, who, but for the assistance of the Institute, would have found themselves faced with an impossible situation. As an eminent police officer observed to one of our representatives this morning, 'But for the NICE Police, things would have taken quite a different turn.' If in the light of these events it is found convenient to place the whole Edgestow area under the exclusive control of the Institutional 'police' for some limited period, we do not believe that the British people – always realists at heart – will have the slightest objection. A special tribute is due to the female members of the force, who appear to have acted throughout with that mixture of courage and common sense which the last few years have taught us to expect of English women almost as a matter of course. The wild rumours, current in London this morning, of machine-gun fire in the streets and casualties by the hundred, remain to be sifted. Probably, when accurate details are available, it will be found (in the words of a recent Prime Minister) that 'when blood flowed, it was generally from the nose'.

The second ran thus:

What is happening at Edgestow?

That is the question which John Citizen wants to have answered. The Institute which has settled at Edgestow is a

National Institute. That means it is yours and mine. We are not scientists and we do not pretend to know what the master-brains of the Institute are thinking. We do know what each man or woman expects of it. We expect a solution of the unemployment problem, the cancer problem, the housing problem, the problems of currency, of war, of education. We expect from it a brighter, cleaner and fuller life for our children, in which we and they can march ever onward and onward and develop to the full urge of life which God has given each one of us. The NICE is the people's instrument for bringing about all the things we fought for.

Meanwhile – what is happening at Edgestow?

Do you believe this riot arose simply because Mrs Snooks or Mr Buggins found that the landlord had sold their shop or their allotment to the NICE? Mrs Snooks and Mr Buggins know better. They know that the Institute means more trade in Edgestow, more public amenities, a larger population, a burst of undreamed-of prosperity. I say these disturbances have been ENGINEERED.

This charge may sound strange, but it is true.

Therefore I ask yet again: What is happening at Edgestow?

There are traitors in the camp. I am not afraid to say so, whoever they may be. They may be so-called religious people. They may be financial interests. They may be the old cobweb-spinning professors and philosophers of Edgestow University itself. They may be Jews. They may be lawyers. I don't care who they are, but I have one thing to tell them. Take care. The people of England are not going to stand this. We are not going to have the Institute sabotaged.

What is to be done at Edgestow?

I say, put the whole place under the Institutional Police. Some of you may have been to Edgestow for a holiday. If so, you'll know as well as I do what it is like – a little, sleepy, country town with half a dozen policemen who have had nothing to do for ten years but stop cyclists because their lamps have gone out. It doesn't make sense to expect these poor old Bobbies to deal with an ENGINEERED RIOT. Last night the NICE police showed that they could. What I say is – Hats off to Miss Hardcastle and her brave boys, yes, and her brave girls too. Give them a free hand and let them get on with the job. Cut out the Red Tape.

I've one bit of advice. If you hear anyone backbiting the NICE police, tell him where he gets off. If you hear anyone comparing them to the Gestapo or the Ogpu, tell him you've heard that one before. If you hear anyone talking about the liberties of England (by which he means the liberties of the obscurantists, the Mrs Grundies, the Bishops, and the capitalists), watch that man. He's the enemy. Tell him from me that the NICE is the boxing glove on the democracy's fist, and if he doesn't like it, he'd best get out of the way.

Meanwhile – WATCH EDGESTOW.

It might be supposed that after enjoying these articles in the heat of composition, Mark would awake to reason, and with it to disgust, when reading through the finished product. Unfortunately the process had been almost the reverse. He had become more and more reconciled to the job the longer he worked at it.

The complete reconciliation came when he fair-copied both articles. When a man has crossed the T's and dotted the I's, and likes the look of his work, he does not wish it to be committed to the wastepaper basket. The more often he re-read the articles the better he liked them. And, anyway, the thing was a kind of joke. He had in his mind a picture of himself, old and rich (probably with a peerage, certainly very distinguished) when all this – all the unpleasant side of the NICE – was over, regaling his juniors with wild, unbelievable tales of this present time. ('Ah … it was a rum show in those early days. I remember once …') And then, too, for a man whose writings had hitherto appeared only in learned periodicals or at best in books which only other dons would read, there was an all but irresistible lure in the thought of the daily press – editors waiting for copy – readers all over Europe – something really depending on his words. The idea of the immense dynamo which had been placed for the moment at his disposal, thrilled through his whole being. It was, after all, not so long ago that he had been excited by admission to the Progressive Element at Bracton. But what was the Progressive Element to this? It wasn't as if he were taken in by the articles himself. He was writing with his tongue in his cheek – a phrase that somehow comforted him by making the whole thing appear like a practical joke. And anyway, if he didn't do it, someone else would. And all the while the child inside him whispered how splendid and how triumphantly grown up it was to be sitting like this, so full of alcohol and yet not drunk, writing (with his tongue in his cheek) articles for great newspapers, against time, 'with the printer's devil at the door' and all the inner ring of the NICE depending on him, and nobody ever again having the least right to consider him a nonentity or cipher.

◆ ○ ◆

Jane stretched out her hand in the darkness but did not feel the table which ought to have been there at her bed's head. Then with a shock of surprise she discovered that she was not in bed at all, but standing. There was utter darkness all about her and it was intensely cold. Groping, she touched what appeared to be uneven surfaces of stone. The air, also, had some odd quality about it – dead air, imprisoned air, it seemed. Somewhere far away, possibly overhead, there were noises which came to her muffled and shuddering as if through earth. So the worst had happened – a bomb had fallen on the house and she was buried alive. But before she had time to feel the full impact of this idea she remembered that the war was over … oh, and all sorts of things had happened since then … she had married Mark … she had seen Alcasan in his cell … she had met Camilla. Then, with great and swift relief she thought, 'It is one of my dreams. It is a piece of news. It'll stop presently. There's nothing to be frightened of.'

The place, whatever it was, did not seem to be very large. She groped all along one of the rough walls and then, turning at the corner, struck her foot against something hard. She stooped down and felt. There was a sort of raised platform or table of stone, about three feet high. And on it? Did she dare to explore? But it would be worse not to. She began trying the surface of the table with her hand, and next moment bit her lip to save herself from screaming, for she had touched a human foot. It was a naked foot, and dead to judge by its coldness. To go on groping seemed the hardest thing she had ever done but somehow she was impelled to do it. The corpse was clothed in some very coarse stuff which was also uneven, as though it were heavily embroidered, and very volumi-nous. It must be a very large man, she thought, still groping upwards towards his head. On his chest the texture suddenly changed – as if the skin of some hairy animal had been laid over the coarse robe. So she thought at first; then she realised that the hair really belonged to a beard. She hesitated about feeling the face; she had a fear lest the man should stir or wake or speak if she did so. She therefore became still for a moment. It was only a dream; she could bear it; but it was so dreary and it all seemed to be happen-ing so long ago, as if she had slipped through a cleft in the present, down into some cold, sunless pit of the remote past. She hoped they wouldn't leave her here long. If only someone would come quickly and let her out. And immediately she had a picture of someone, someone bearded but also (it was odd) divinely young, someone all golden and strong and warm coming with a mighty earth-shaking tread down into that black place. The dream became chaotic at this point. Jane had an impression that she ought to courtesy to this person (who never actually arrived though the impression of him lay bright and heavy on her mind), and felt great consternation on realising that some dim memories of dancing lessons at school were not sufficient to show her how to do so. At this point she woke.

She went into Edgestow immediately after breakfast to hunt, as she now hunted every day, for someone who would replace Mrs

Maggs. At the top of Market Street something happened which finally determined her to go to St Anne's that very day and by the ten-twenty-three train. She came to a place where a big car was standing beside the pavement, an NICE car. Just as she reached it a man came out of a shop, cut across her path to speak to the chauffeur of the car, and then got in. He was so close to her that, despite the fog, she saw him very clearly, in isolation from all other objects: the background was all grey fog and passing feet and the harsh sounds of that unaccustomed traffic which now never ceased in Edgestow. She would have known him, anywhere: not Mark's face, not her own face in a mirror, was by now more familiar. She saw the pointed beard, the pince-nez, the face which somehow reminded her of a waxworks face. She had no need to think what she would do. Her body, walking quickly past, seemed of itself to have decided that it was heading for the station and thence for St Anne's. It was something different from fear (though she was frightened too, almost to the point of nausea) that drove her so unerringly forward. It was a total rejection of, or revulsion from, this man on all levels of her being at once. Dreams sank into insignificance compared with the blinding reality of the man's presence. She shuddered to think that their hands might have touched as she passed him.

The train was blessedly warm, her compartment empty, the fact of sitting down delightful. The slow journey through the fog almost sent her to sleep. She hardly thought about St Anne's until she found herself there: even as she walked up the steep hill she made no plans, rehearsed nothing that she meant to say, but only thought of Camilla and Mrs Dimble. The childish levels, the undersoil of the mind, had been turned up. She wanted to be with Nice people, away from Nasty people – that nursery distinction seeming at the moment more important than any later categories of Good and Bad or Friend and Enemy.

She was roused from this state by noticing that it was lighter. She looked ahead: surely that bend in the road was more visible than it ought to be in such a fog? Or was it only that a country fog was different from a town one? Certainly what had been grey was becoming white, almost dazzlingly white. A few yards further and luminous blue was showing overhead, and trees cast shadows (she had not seen a shadow for days), and then all of a sudden the enormous spaces of the sky had become visible and the pale golden sun, and looking back, as she took the turn to the Manor, Jane saw that she was standing on the shore of a little green sunlit island looking down on a sea of white fog, furrowed and ridged yet level on the whole, which spread as far as she could see. There were other islands too. That dark one to the west was the wooded hills above Sandown where she had picnicked with the Dennistons; and the far bigger and brighter one to the north was the many caverned hills – mountains one could nearly call them – in which the Wynd had its source. She took a deep breath. It was the *size* of this world above the fog which impressed her. Down in Edgestow all these days one had lived, even when out-of-doors, as if in a room, for only objects close at hand were visible. She felt she had come near to forgetting how big the sky is, how remote the horizon.

7

The Pendragon

Before she reached the door in the wall Jane met Mr Denniston and he guided her into the Manor, not by that door but by the main gate which opened on the same road a few hundred yards further on. She told him her story as they walked. In his company she had that curious sensation which most married people know of being with someone whom (for the final but wholly mysterious reason) one could never have married but who is nevertheless more of one's own world than the person one has married in fact. As they entered the house they met Mrs Maggs.

'What? Mrs Studdock! Fancy!' said Mrs Maggs.

'Yes, Ivy,' said Denniston, 'and bringing great news. Things are beginning to move. We must see Grace at once. And is MacPhee about?'

'He's out gardening hours ago,' said Mrs Maggs. 'And Dr Dimble's gone in to College. And Camilla's in the kitchen. Shall I send her along?'

'Yes, do. And if you can prevent Mr Bultitude from butting in —'

'That's right. I'll keep him out of mischief all right. You'd like a cup of tea, Mrs Studdock, wouldn't you? Coming by train and all that.'

A few minutes later Jane found herself once more in Grace Ironwood's room. Miss Ironwood and the Dennistons all sat facing her so that she felt as if she were the candidate in a *viva voce* examination. And when Ivy Maggs brought in the tea she did not go away again but sat down as if she also were one of the examiners.

'Now!' said Camilla, her eyes and nostrils widened with a sort of fresh mental hunger – it was too concentrated to be called excitement.

Jane glanced round the room.

'You need not mind Ivy, young lady,' said Miss Ironwood. 'She is one of our company.'

There was a pause. 'We have your letter of the 10th,' continued Miss Ironwood, 'describing your dream of the man with the pointed beard sitting making notes in your bedroom. Perhaps I ought to tell you that he wasn't really there: at least, the Director does not think it possible. But he was really studying *you*. He was getting information about you from some other source which, unfortunately, was not visible to you in the dream.'

'Will you tell us, if you don't mind,' said Mr Denniston, 'what you were telling me as we came along?'

Jane told them about the dream of the corpse (if it was a corpse) in the dark place and how she had met the bearded man that morning in Market Street; and at once she was aware of having created intense interest.

'Fancy!' said Ivy Maggs. 'So we were right about Bragdon Wood!' said Camilla. 'It is really Belbury,' said her husband. 'But in that case, where does Alcasan come in?'

'Excuse me,' said Miss Ironwood in her level voice, and the others became instantly silent. 'We must not discuss the matter here. Mrs Studdock has not yet joined us.'

'Am I to be told nothing?' asked Jane.

'Young lady,' said Miss Ironwood. 'You must excuse me. It would not be wise at the moment: indeed, we are not at liberty to do so. Will you allow me to ask you two more questions?'

'If you like,' said Jane, a little sulkily, but only a very little. The presence of Camilla and Camilla's husband somehow put her on her best behaviour.

Miss Ironwood had opened a drawer and for a few moments there was silence while she hunted in it. Then she handed a photograph across to Jane and asked,

'Do you recognise that person?'

'Yes,' said Jane in a low voice. 'That is the man I've dreamed of and the man I saw this morning in Edgestow.'

It was a good photograph and beneath it was the name Augustus Frost, with a few other details which Jane did not at the moment take in.

'In the second place,' continued Miss Ironwood, holding out her hand for Jane to return the photograph, 'are you prepared to see the Director – *now*?'

'Well – yes, if you like.'

'In that case, Arthur,' said Miss Ironwood to Denniston, 'you had better go and find out if he is well enough to meet Mrs Studdock.'

Denniston at once rose.

'In the meantime,' said Miss Ironwood, 'I would like a word with Mrs Studdock alone.' At this the others rose also and preceded Denniston out of the room. A very large cat which Jane had not noticed before jumped up and occupied the chair which Ivy Maggs had just vacated.

'I have very little doubt,' said Miss Ironwood, 'that the Director will see you.'

Jane said nothing.

'And at that interview,' continued the other, 'you will, I presume, be called upon to make a final decision.'

Jane gave a little cough which had no other purpose than to dispel a certain air of unwelcome solemnity which seemed to have settled on the room as soon as she and Miss Ironwood were left alone.

'There are also certain things,' said Miss Ironwood, 'which you ought to know about the Director before you see him. He will appear to you, Mrs Studdock, to be a very young man: younger than yourself. You will please understand that this is not the case. He is nearer fifty than forty. He is a man of very great experience, who has travelled where no other human being ever travelled before and mixed in societies of which you and I have no conception.'

'That is very interesting,' said Jane, though displaying no interest.

'And thirdly,' said Miss Ironwood, 'I must ask you to remember that he is often in great pain. Whatever decision you come to, I trust you will not say or do anything that may put an unnecessary strain upon him.'

'If Mr Fisher-King is not well enough to see visitors … ' said Jane vaguely.

'You must excuse me,' said Miss Ironwood, 'for impressing these points upon you. I am a doctor, and I am the only doctor in our company. I am therefore responsible for protecting him as far as I can. If you will now come with me I will show you to the Blue Room.'

She rose and held the door open for Jane. They passed out into the plain, narrow passage and thence up shallow steps into a large entrance hall whence a fine Georgian staircase led to the upper floors. The house, larger than Jane had at first supposed, was warm and very silent, and after so many days spent in fog, the autumn sunlight, falling on soft carpets and on walls, seemed to her bright and golden. On the first floor, but raised above it by six steps, they found a little square place with white pillars where Camilla, quiet and alert, sat waiting for them. There was a door behind her.

'He will see her,' she said to Miss Ironwood, getting up.

'Is he in much pain this morning?'

'It is not continuous. It is one of his good days.'

As Miss Ironwood raised her hand to knock on the door, Jane thought to herself, 'Be careful. Don't get let in for anything. All these long passages and low voices will make a fool of you, if you don't look out. You'll become another of this man's female adorers.' Next moment she found herself going in. It was light – it seemed all windows. And it was warm – a fire blazed on the hearth. And blue was the prevailing colour. Before her eyes had taken it in she was annoyed, and in a way ashamed, to see that Miss Ironwood was courtesying. 'I won't,' contended in Jane's mind with 'I can't': for it had been true in her dream, she couldn't.

'This is the young lady, sir,' said Miss Ironwood.

Jane looked; and instantly her world was unmade.

On a sofa before her, with one foot bandaged as if he had a wound, lay what appeared to be a boy, twenty years old.

On one of the long window sills a tame jackdaw was walking up and down. The light of the fire with its weak reflection, and the light of the sun with its weak reflection, and the light of the sun with its stronger reflection, contended on the ceiling. But all the light in the room seemed to run towards the gold hair and the gold beard of the wounded man.

Of course he was not a boy – how could she have thought so? The fresh skin on his forehead and cheeks and, above all, on his hands, had suggested the idea. But no boy could have so full a beard. And no boy could be so strong. She had expected to see an invalid. Now it was manifest that the grip of those hands would be inescapable, and imagination suggested that those arms and shoulders could support the whole house. Miss Ironwood at her side struck her as a little old woman, shrivelled and pale – a thing you could have blown away.

The sofa was placed on a kind of dais divided from the rest of the room by a step. She had an impression of massed hangings of blue – later, she saw that it was only a screen – behind the man, so that the effect was that of a throne room. She would have called it silly if, instead of seeing it, she had been told of it by another. Through the window she saw no trees nor hills nor shapes of other houses: only the level floor of mist, as if this man and she were perched in a blue tower overlooking the world.

Pain came and went in his face: sudden jabs of sickening and burning pain. But as lightning goes through the darkness and the darkness closes up again and shows no trace, so the tranquillity of his countenance swallowed up each shock of torture. How could she have thought him young? Or old either? It came over her, with a sensation of quick fear, that this face was of no age at all. She had (or so she had believed) disliked bearded faces except for old men with white hair. But that was because she had long since forgotten the imagined Arthur of her childhood – and the imagined Solomon too. Solomon – for the first time in many years the bright solar blend of king and lover and magician which hangs about that name stole back upon her mind. For the first time in all those years she tasted the word *king* itself with all linked associations of battle, marriage, priesthood, mercy and power. At that moment, as her eyes first rested on his face, Jane forgot who she was, and where, and her faint grudge against Grace Ironwood, and her more obscure grudge against Mark, and her childhood and her father's house. It was, of course, only for a flash. Next moment she was once more the ordinary social Jane, flushed and confused to find that she had been staring rudely (at least she hoped that rudeness would be the main impression produced) at a total stranger. But her world was unmade; she knew that. Anything might happen now.

'Thank you, Grace,' the man was saying. 'Is this Mrs Studdock?'

And the voice also seemed to be like sunlight and gold. Like gold not only as gold is beautiful but as it is heavy: like sunlight not only as it falls gently on English walls in autumn but as it beats down on the jungle or the desert to engender life or destroy it. And now it was addressing her.

'You must forgive me for not getting up, Mrs Studdock,' it said. 'My foot is hurt.'

And Jane heard her own voice saying, 'Yes Sir,' soft and chastened like Miss Ironwood's voice. She had meant to say, 'Good morning, Mr Fisher-King,' in an easy tone that would have counteracted the absurdity of her behaviour on first entering the room. But the other was what actually came out of her mouth. Shortly after this she found herself seated before the Director. She was shaken: she was even shaking. She hoped intensely that she was not going to cry, or be unable to speak, or do anything silly. For her world was unmade: anything might happen now. If only the conversation were over! – so that she could get out of that room without disgrace, and go away, not for good, but for a long time.

'Do you wish me to remain, Sir?' said Miss Ironwood.

'No, Grace,' said the Director, 'I don't think you need stay. Thank you.'

'And now,' thought Jane, 'it's coming – it's coming – it's coming now.' All the most intolerable questions he might ask, all the most extravagant things he might make her do, flashed through her mind in a fatuous medley. For all power of resistance seemed to have been drained away from her and she was left without protection.

◆ ○ ◆

For the first few minutes after Grace Ironwood had left them alone, Jane hardly took in what the Director was saying. It was not that her attention wandered; on the contrary, her attention was so fixed on him that it defeated itself. Every tone, every look (how could they have supposed she would think him young?), every gesture, was printing itself upon her memory; and it was not until she found that he had ceased speaking and was apparently awaiting an answer, that she realised she had taken in so little of what he had been saying.

'I – I beg your pardon,' she said, wishing that she did not keep on turning red like a schoolgirl.

'I was saying,' he answered, 'that you have already done us the greatest possible service. We knew that one of the most dangerous attacks ever made upon the human race was coming very soon and in this island. We had an idea that Belbury might be connected with it. But we were not certain. We certainly did not know that Belbury was so important. That is why your information is so valuable. But in another way, it presents us with a difficulty. I mean a difficulty as far as you are concerned. We had hoped you would be able to join us – to become one of our army.'

'Can I not, Sir?' said Jane.

'It is difficult,' said the Director after a pause. 'You see, your husband is in Belbury.'

Jane glanced up. It had been on the tip of her tongue to say, 'Do you mean that Mark is in any danger?' But she had realised that anxiety about Mark did not, in fact, make any part of the complex emotions she was feeling, and that to reply thus would be hypocrisy. It was a sort of scruple she had not often felt before. Finally, she said, 'What do you mean?'

'Why,' said the Director, 'it would be hard for the same person to be the wife of an official in the NICE and also a member of my company.'

'You mean you couldn't trust me?'

'I mean nothing we need be afraid to speak of. I mean that, in the circumstances, you and I and your husband could not all be trusting one another.'

Jane bit her lip in anger, not at the Director but at Mark. Why should he and his affairs with the Feverstone man intrude themselves at such a moment as this?

'I must do what I think right, musn't I?' she said softly. 'I mean – if Mark – if my husband – is on the wrong side, I can't let that make any difference to what *I* do. Can I?'

'You are thinking about what is *right*?' said the Director. Jane started, and flushed. She had not, she realised, been thinking about that.

'Of course,' said the Director, 'things might come to such a point that you would be justified in coming here, even wholly against his will, even secretly. It depends on how close the danger is – the danger to us all, and to you personally.'

'I thought the danger was right on top of us now – from the way Mrs Denniston talked.'

'That is just the question,' said the Director, with a smile. 'I am not allowed to be *too* prudent. I am not allowed to use desperate remedies until desperate diseases are really apparent. Otherwise we become just like our enemies – breaking all the rules whenever we imagine that it might possibly do some vague good to humanity in the remote future.'

'But will it do anyone any harm if I come here?' asked Jane.

He did not directly answer this. Presently he spoke again.

'It looks as if you will have to go back; at least for the present.

You will, no doubt, be seeing your husband again fairly soon. I think you must make at least one effort to detach him from the NICE.'

'But how can I, Sir?' said Jane. 'What have I to say to him. He'd think it all nonsense. He wouldn't believe all that about an attack on the human race.' As soon as she had said it she wondered, 'Did that sound cunning?' then, more disconcertingly, '*Was* it cunning?'

'No,' said the Director. 'And you must not tell him. You must not mention me nor the company at all. We have put our lives in your hands. You must simply ask him to leave Belbury. You must put it on your own wishes. You are his wife.'

'Mark never takes any notice of what I say,' answered Jane. She and Mark each thought that of the other.

'Perhaps,' said the Director, 'You have never asked anything as you will be able to ask this. Do you not *want* to save him as well as yourself?'

Jane ignored this question. Now that the threat of expulsion from the house was imminent, she felt a kind of desperation. Heedless of that inner commentator, who had more than once during this conversation shown her her own words and wishes in such a novel light, she began speaking rapidly.

'Don't send me back,' she said, 'I am all alone at home, with terrible dreams. It isn't as if Mark and I saw much of one another at the best of times. I am so unhappy. He won't care whether I come here or not. He'd only laugh at it all if he knew. Is it fair that my whole life should be spoiled just because he's got mixed up with some horrible people? You don't think a woman is to have no life of her own just because she's married?'

'Are you unhappy *now*?' said the Director. A dozen affirmatives died on Jane's lips as she looked up in answer to his question. Then suddenly, in a kind of deep calm, like the stillness at the centre of a whirlpool, she saw the truth, and ceased at last to think how her words might make him think of her, and answered, 'No.'

'But,' she added after a short pause, 'It will be worse now, if I go back.'

'Will it?'

'I don't know. No. I suppose not.' And for a little time Jane was hardly conscious of anything but peace and well-being, the comfort of her own body in the chair where she sat, and a sort of clear beauty in the colours and proportions of the room. But soon she began thinking to herself, 'This is the end. In a moment he will send for the Ironwood woman to take you away.' It seemed to her that her fate depended on what she said in the next minute.

'But is it really necessary?' she began. 'I don't think I look on marriage quite as you do. It seems to me extraordinary that everything should hang on what Mark says … about something he doesn't understand.'

'Child,' said the Director, 'it is not a question of how you or I look on marriage but how my Masters look on it.'

'Someone said they were very old fashioned. But –'

'That was a joke. They are not old fashioned; but they are very, very old.'

'They would never think of finding out first whether Mark and I believed in their ideas of marriage?'

'Well – no,' said the Director with a curious smile. 'No. Quite definitely they wouldn't think of doing that.'

'And would it make no difference to them what a marriage was actually like – whether it was a success? Whether the woman loved her husband?'

Jane had not exactly intended to say this: much less to say it in the cheaply pathetic tone which, it now seemed to her, she had used. Hating herself, and fearing the Director's silence, she added, 'But I suppose you will say I oughtn't to have told you that.'

'My dear child,' said the Director, 'you have been telling me that ever since your husband was mentioned.'

'Does it make no difference?'

'I suppose,' said the Director, 'it would depend on how he lost your love.'

Jane was silent. Though she could not tell the Director the truth, and indeed did not know it herself, yet when she tried to explore her inarticulate grievance against Mark, a novel sense of her own injustice and even of pity for her husband, arose in her mind. And her heart sank, for now it seemed to her that this conversation, to which she had vaguely looked for some sort of deliverance from all problem was in fact involving her in new ones.

'It was not his fault,' she said at last. 'I suppose our marriage was just a mistake.'

The Director said nothing.

'What would you – what would the people you are talking of – say about a case like that?'

'I will tell you if you really want to know,' said the Director.

'Please,' said Jane reluctantly.

'They would say,' he answered, 'that you do not fail in obedience through lack of love, but have lost love because you never attempted obedience.'

Something in Jane that would normally have reacted to such a remark with anger or laughter was banished to a remote distance (where she could still, but only just, hear its voice) by the fact that the word Obedience – but certainly not obedience to Mark – came over her, in that room and in that presence, like a strange oriental perfume, perilous, seductive and ambiguous ...

'Stop it!' said the Director, sharply.

Jane stared at him, open mouthed. There were a few moments of silence during which the exotic fragrance faded away.

'You were saying, my dear?' resumed the Director.

'I thought love meant equality,' she said, 'and free companionship.'

'Ah, equality!' said the Director. 'We must talk of that some other time. Yes, we must all be guarded by equal rights from one another's greed, because we are fallen. Just as we must all wear clothes for the same reason. But the naked body should be there underneath the clothes, ripening for the day when we shall need them no longer. Equality is not the deepest thing, you know.'

'I always thought that was just what it was. I thought it was in their souls that people were equal.'

'You were mistaken,' said he gravely. 'That is the last place where they are equal. Equality before the law, equality of incomes – that is very well. Equality guards life; it doesn't make it. It is medicine, not food. You might as well try to warm yourself with a blue-book.'

'But surely in marriage …?'

'Worse and worse,' said the Director. 'Courtship knows nothing of it; nor does fruition. What has free companionship to do with that? Those who are enjoying something, or suffering something together, are companions. Those who enjoy or suffer one another, are not. Do you not know how bashful friendship is? Friends – comrades – do not look *at* each other. Friendship would be ashamed… '

'I thought,' said Jane and stopped.

'I see,' said the Director. 'It is not your fault. They never warned you. No one has ever told you that obedience – humility – is an erotic necessity. You are putting equality just where it ought not to be. As to your coming here, that may admit of some doubt. For the present, I must send you back. You can come out and see us. In the meantime, talk to your husband and I will talk to my authorities.'

'When will you be seeing them?'

'They come to me when they please. But we've been talking too solemnly about obedience all this time. I'd like to show you some of its drolleries. You are not afraid of mice, are you?'

'Afraid of what?' said Jane in astonishment.

'Mice,' said the Director.

'No,' said Jane in a puzzled voice.

The Director struck a little bell beside his sofa which was almost immediately answered by Mrs Maggs.

'I think,' said the Director, 'I should like my lunch now, if you please. They will give you lunch downstairs, Mrs Studdock – something more substantial than mine. But if you will sit with me while I eat and drink, I will show you some of the amenities of our house.'

Mrs Maggs presently returned with a tray, bearing a glass, a small flacon of red wine, and a roll of bread. She set it down on a table at the Director's side and left the room.

'You see,' said the Director, 'I live like the King in *Curdie*. It is a surprisingly pleasant diet.' With these words he broke the bread and poured himself out a glass of wine.

'I never read the book you are speaking of,' said Jane.

They talked of the book a little while the Director ate and drank; but presently he took up the plate and tipped the crumbs off onto the floor. 'Now, Mrs Studdock,' he said, 'you shall see a diversion. But you must be perfectly still.' With these words he took from his pocket a little silver whistle and blew a note on it. And Jane sat still till the room became filled with silence like a solid thing and there was first a scratching and then a rustling and presently she saw three plump mice working their passage across what was to them the thick undergrowth of the carpet, nosing this way and that so that if their course had been drawn it would have resembled that of a winding river, until they were so close that she could see the twinkling of their eyes and even the palpitation of their noses. In spite of what she had said she did not really care for mice in the neighbourhood of her feet and it was with an effort that she sat still. Thanks to this effort she saw mice for the first time as they really are – not as creeping things but as dainty quadrupeds, almost, when they sat up, like tiny kangaroos, with sensitive kid-gloved forepaws and transparent ears. With quick, inaudible movements they ranged to and fro till not a crumb was left on the floor. Then he blew a second time on his whistle and with a sudden whisk of tails all three of them were racing for home and in a few seconds had disappeared behind the coal box. The Director looked at her with laughter in his eyes. ('It is impossible,' thought Jane, 'to regard him as old.') 'There,' he said, 'a very simple adjustment. Humans want crumbs removed; mice are anxious to remove them. It ought never to have been a cause of war. But you see that obedience and rule are more like a dance than a drill – specially between man and woman where the roles are always changing.'

'How huge we must seem to them,' said Jane.

This inconsequent remark had a very curious cause. Hugeness was what she was thinking of and for one moment it had seemed she was thinking of her own hugeness in comparison with the mice. But almost at once this identification collapsed. She was really thinking simply of hugeness. Or rather, she was not thinking of it. She was, in some strange fashion, experiencing it. Something intolerably big, something from Brobdingnag was pressing on her, was approaching, was almost in the room. She felt herself shrinking, suffocated, emptied of all power and virtue. She darted a glance at the Director which was really a cry for help, and that glance, in some inexplicable way, revealed him as being, like herself, a very small object. The whole room was a tiny place, a mouse's hole, and it seemed to her to be tilted aslant – as though the insupportable mass and splendour of this formless hugeness, in approaching, had knocked it askew. She heard the Director's voice.

'Quick,' he said gently, 'you must leave me now. This is no place for us small ones, but I am inured. Go!'

◆ ◯ ◆

When Jane left the hill-top village of St Anne's and came down to the station she found that, even down there, the fog had begun to lift. Great windows had opened in it, and as the train carried her on it passed repeatedly through pools of afternoon sunlight.

During this journey she was so divided against herself that one might say there were three, if not four, Janes in the compartment.

The first was a Jane simply receptive of the Director, recalling every word and every look, and delighting in them – a Jane taken utterly off her guard, shaken out of the modest little outfit of contemporary ideas which had hitherto made her portion of wisdom, and swept away on the flood tide of an experience which she did not understand and could not control. For she was trying to control it; that was the function of the second Jane. This second Jane regarded the first with disgust, as the kind of woman, in fact, whom she had always particularly despised. Once, coming out of a cinema, she had heard a little shop girl say to her friend, 'Oh, wasn't he lovely! If he'd looked at me the way he looked at her, I'd have followed him to the end of the world.' A little, tawdry, made-up girl, sucking a peppermint. Whether the second Jane was right in equating the first Jane with that girl, may be questioned, but she did. And she found her intolerable. To have surrendered without terms at the mere voice and look of this stranger, to have abandoned (without noticing it) that prim little grasp on her own destiny, that perpetural reservation, which she thought essential to her status as a grown-up, integrated, intelligent person ... the thing was utterly degrading, vulgar, uncivilised.

The third Jane was a new and unexpected visitant. Of the first there had been traces in girlhood, and the second was what Jane took to be her 'real' or normal self. But the third one, this moral Jane, was one whose existence she had never suspected. Risen from some unknown region of grace or heredity, it uttered all sorts of things which Jane had often heard before but which had never, till that moment, seemed to be connected with real life. If it had simply told her that her feelings about the Director were wrong, she would not have been very surprised, and would have discounted it as the voice of tradition. But it did not. It kept on blaming her for not having similar feelings about Mark. It kept on pressing into her mind those new feelings about Mark, feelings of guilt and pity, which she had first experienced in the Director's room. It was Mark who had made the fatal mistake; she must, must, must be 'nice' to Mark. The Director obviously insisted on it. At the very moment when her mind was most filled with another man there arose, clouded with some undefined emotion, a resolution to give Mark much more than she had ever given him before, and a feeling that in so doing she would be really giving it to the Director. And this produced in her such a confusion of sensations that the whole inner debate became indistinct and flowed over into the larger experience of the fourth Jane, who was Jane herself and dominated all the rest at every moment without effort and even without choice.

This fourth and supreme Jane was simply in the state of joy. The other three had no power upon her, for she was in the sphere of Jove, amid light and music and festal pomp, brimmed with life and radiant in health, jocund and clothed in shining garments. She thought scarcely at all of the curious sensations which had immediately preceded the Director's dismissal of her and made that dismissal almost a relief. When she tried to, it immediately led her thoughts back to the Director himself. Whatever she tried to think of led back to the Director himself and, in him, to joy. She saw from the windows of the train the outlined beams of sunlight pouring over stubble or burnished woods and felt that they were like the notes of a trumpet. Her eyes rested on the rabbits and cows as they flitted by and she embraced them in heart with merry, holiday love. She delighted in the occasional speech of the one wizened old man who shared her compartment and saw, as never before, the beauty of his shrewd and sunny old mind, sweet as a nut and English as a chalk down. She reflected with surprise how long it was since music had played any part in her life, and resolved to listen to many chorales by Bach on the gramophone that evening. Or else – perhaps – she would read a great many Shakespeare sonnets. She rejoiced also in her hunger and thirst and decided that she would make herself buttered toast for tea – a great deal of buttered toast. And she rejoiced also in the consciousness of her own beauty; for she had the sensation – it may have been false in fact, but it had nothing to do with vanity – that it was growing and expanding like a magic flower with every minute that passed. In such a mood it was only natural, after the old countryman had got out at Cure Hardy, to stand up and look at herself in the mirror which confronted her on the wall of the compartment. Certainly she was looking well: she was looking unusually well. And, once more, there was little vanity in this. For beauty was made for others. Her beauty belonged to the Director. It belonged to him so completely that he could even decide not to keep it for himself but to order that it be given to another, by an act of obedience lower, and therefore higher, more unconditional and therefore more delighting, than if he had demanded it for himself.

As the train came into Edgestow Station Jane was just deciding that she would not try to get a bus. She would enjoy the walk up to Sandown. And then – what on earth was all this? The platform, usually almost deserted at this hour, was like a London platform on a bank holiday. 'Here you are, mate!' cried a voice as she opened the door, and half a dozen men crowded into her carriage so roughly that for a moment she could not get out. She found difficulty in crossing the platform. People seemed to be going in all directions at once – angry, rough and excited people, 'Get back into the train, quick!' shouted someone. 'Get out of the station, if you're not travelling,' bawled another voice. 'What the devil?' asked a third just beside her, and then a woman's voice said, 'Oh dear, oh dear! Why don't they *stop* it!' And from outside, beyond the station came a great roaring noise like the noise of a football crowd. There seemed to be a lot of unfamiliar lights about.

◆   ○   ◆

Hours later, bruised, frightened, and tired to death, Jane found herself in a street she did not even know, surrounded by NICE policemen and a few of their females, the Waips. Her course had been like that of a man trying to get home along the beach when the tide is coming in. She had been driven out of her natural route along Warwick Street – they were looting shops and making bonfires there – and forced to take a much wider circle, up by the Asylum, which would have brought her home in the end. Then even that wider circle had proved impracticable, for the same reason. She had been forced to try a still longer way round; and each time the tide had got there before her. Finally she had seen Bone Lane, straight and empty and still, and apparently her last chance of getting home that night at all. A couple of NICE police – one seemed to meet them everywhere except where the rioting was most violent – had shouted out, 'You can't go down there, Miss.' But as they then turned their backs on her, and it was poorly lit, and because she was now desperate, Jane had made a bolt for it. They caught her. And that was how she found herself being taken into a lighted room and questioned by a uniformed woman with short grey hair, a square face, and an unlighted cheroot. The room was in disorder

– as if a private house had been suddenly and roughly converted into a temporary police station. The woman with the cheroot took no particular interest until Jane had given her name. Then Miss Hardcastle looked her in the face for the first time. And Jane felt quite a new sensation. She was already tired and frightened, but this was different. The face of the other woman affected her as the face of some men – fat men with small greedy eyes and strange disquieting smiles – had affected her when she was in her teens. It was dreadfully quiet and yet dreadfully interested in her. And Jane saw that some quite new idea was dawning on the woman as she stared at her: some idea that the woman found attractive, and then tried to put aside, and then returned to dally with, and then finally, with a little sigh of contentment, accepted. Miss Hardcastle lit her cheroot and blew a cloud of smoke towards her. If Jane had known how seldom Miss Hardcastle actually smoked she would have been even more alarmed. The policemen and policewomen who surrounded her probably did. The whole atmosphere of the room became a little different.

'Jane Studdock,' said the Fairy. 'I know all about you, honey. You'll be the wife of my friend Mark.' While she spoke she was writing something on a green form.

'*That's* all right,' said Miss Hardcastle. 'You'll be able to see Hubby again now. We'll take you out to Belbury tonight. Now just one question, dear. What were you doing down here at this time of night?'

'I had just come off a train.'

'And where had you been, Honey?'

Jane said nothing.

'You hadn't been getting up to mischief while Hubby was away, had you?'

'Will you please let me go?' said Jane. 'I want to get home. I am very tired and it's very late.'

'But you're not going home,' said Miss Hardcastle. 'You're coming out to Belbury.'

'My husband has said nothing about my joining him there.'

Miss Hardcastle nodded. 'That was one of his mistakes. But you're coming with *us*.'

'What do you mean?'

'It's an arrest, Honey,' said Miss Hardcastle, holding out the piece of green paper on which she had been writing. It appeared to Jane as all official forms always appeared – a mass of compartments, some empty, some full of small print, some scrawled with signatures in pencil, and one bearing her own name; all meaningless.

'Oh!' screamed Jane suddenly, overcome with a sensation of nightmare, and made a dash for the door. Of course she never reached it. A moment later she came to her senses and found herself held by the two policewomen.

'What a naughty temper!' said Miss Hardcastle playfully. 'But we'll put the nasty men outside, shall we?' She said something and the policemen removed themselves and shut the door behind them. As soon as they were gone Jane felt that a protection had been withdrawn from her.

'Well,' said Miss Hardcastle, addressing the two uniformed girls. 'Let's see. Quarter to one … and all going nicely. I think, Daisy, we can afford ourselves a little stand-easy. Be careful, Kitty, make your top grip under her shoulder just a little tighter. That's right.' While she was speaking Miss Hardcastle was undoing her belt, and when she had finished she removed her tunic and flung it on the sofa, revealing a huge torso, uncorseted (as Bill the Blizzard had complained), rank, floppy and thinly clad: such things as Rubens might have painted in delirium. Then she resumed her seat, removed the cheroot from her mouth, blew another cloud of smoke in Jane's direction, and addressed her.

'Where had you been by that train?' she said.

And Jane said nothing, partly because she could not speak, and partly because she now knew beyond all doubt that these were the enemies of the human race whom the Director was fighting against and one must tell them nothing. She did not feel heroic in making this decision. The whole scene was becoming unreal to her; and it was as if between sleeping and waking that she heard Miss Hardcastle say, 'I think, Kitty dear, you and Daisy had better bring her round here.' And it was still only half real when the two women forced her round to the other side of the table, and she saw Miss Hardcastle sitting with her legs wide apart and settling herself in the chair as if in the saddle; long leather-clad legs projecting from beneath her short skirt. The women forced her on, with a skilled, quiet increase of pressure whenever she resisted, until she stood between Miss Hardcastle's feet, whereupon Miss Hardcastle brought her feet together so that she had Jane's ankles piniqued between her own. This proximity to the ogress affected Jane with such horror that she had no fears left for what they might be going to do with her. And for what seemed an endless time Miss Hardcastle stared at her, smiling a little and blowing smoke in her face.

'Do you know,' said Miss Hardcastle at last, 'you're rather a pretty little thing in your way.'

There was another silence.

'Where had you been by that train?' said Miss Hardcastle.

And Jane stared as if her eyes would start out of her head and said nothing. Then suddenly Miss Hardcastle leant forward and, after very carefully turning down the edge of Jane's dress, thrust the lighted end of the cheroot against her shoulder. After that there was another pause and another silence.

'Where had you been by that train?' said Miss Hardcastle.

How many times this happened Jane could never remember. But somehow or other there came a time when Miss Hardcastle was talking not to her but to one of the women. 'What *are* you fussing about, Daisy?' she was saying.

'I was only saying, Ma'am, it was five past one.'

'How time flies, doesn't it, Daisy? But what if it is? Aren't you comfortable, Daisy? You're not getting tired, holding a little bit of a thing like her?'

'No Ma'am, thank you. But you did say, Ma'am, you'd meet Captain O'Hara at one sharp.'

'Captain O'Hara?' said Miss Hardcastle dreamily at first, and then louder, like one waking from a dream. Next moment she had jumped up and was putting on her tunic. 'Bless the girl!' she said. 'What a pair of blockheads you are! Why didn't you remind me before?'

'Well, Ma'am, I didn't exactly like to.'

'Like to! What do you think you're there for?'

'You don't like us to interrupt, Ma'am, sometimes, when you're examining,' said the girl sulkily.

'Don't argue!' shouted Miss Hardcastle, wheeling round and hitting her cheek a resounding blow with the palm of her hand. 'Look sharp. Get the prisoner into the car. Don't wait to button up her dress, idiots. I'll be after you the moment I've dipped my face in cold water.'

A few seconds later, pinioned between Daisy and Kitty, but still close to Miss Hardcastle (there seemed to be room for five in the back of the car), Jane found herself gliding through the darkness. 'Better go through the town as little as possible, Joe,' said Miss Hardcastle's voice. 'It'll be pretty lively by now. Go on to the Asylum and work down those little streets at the back of the close.' There seemed to be all sorts of strange noises and lights about. At places, too, there seemed to be a great many people. Then there came a moment when Jane found that the car had drawn up. 'What the hell are you stopping for?' said Miss Hardcastle. For a second or two there was no answer from the driver except grunts and the noise of unsuccessful attempts to start up the engine. 'What's the matter?' repeated Miss Hardcastle sharply. 'Don't know, Ma'am,' said the driver, still working away. 'God!' said Miss Hardcastle. 'Can't you even look after a car? Some of you people want a little humane remedial treatment yourselves.' The street in which they were was empty but, to judge by the noise, it was near some other street which was very full and very angry. The man got out, swearing under his breath, and opened the bonnet of the car. 'Here,' said Miss Hardcastle. 'You two hop out. Look round for another car – anywhere within five minutes' walk – commandeer it. If you don't find one, be back here in ten minutes whatever happens. Sharp.' The two other policemen alighted, and disappeared at the double. Miss Hardcastle continued pouring abuse on the driver and the driver continued working at the engine. The noise grew louder. Suddenly the driver straightened himself and turned his face (Jane saw the sweat shining on it in the lamplight) towards Miss Hardcastle. 'Look here, Miss,' he said, 'that's about enough, see? You keep a civil tongue in your head, or else come and mend the bloody car yourself if you're so bloody clever.' 'Don't you try taking that line with me, Joe,' said Miss Hardcastle, 'or you'll find me saying a little word about you to the ordinary police.' 'Well, suppose you do?' said Joe, 'I'm beginning to think I might as well be in clink as in your bucking tea-party. 'Struth! I've been in the military police and I've been in the Black and Tans and I've been in the BUF, but they were all ruddy picnics to this lot. A man got some decent treatment there. And he had men over him, not a bloody lot of old women.' 'Yes, Joe,' said Miss Hardcastle, 'but it wouldn't be clink for you this time if I passed the word to the ordinary cops.'

'Oh, it wouldn't, wouldn't it? I might have a story or two to tell about yourself if it came to that.'

'For the lord's sake, speak to him nicely, Ma'am,' wailed Kitty. 'They're coming. We'll catch it proper.' And in fact men running, by twos and threes, had begun to trickle into the street.

'Foot it, girls,' said Miss Hardcastle. 'Sharp's the word. This way.'

Jane found herself hustled out of the car and hurried along between Daisy and Kitty. Miss Hardcastle moved in front. The little party darted across the street and up an alley on the far side.

'Any of you know the way here?' asked Miss Hardcastle when they had walked a few steps.

'Don't know, I'm sure, Ma'am,' said Daisy.

'I'm a stranger here myself, Ma'am,' said Kitty.

'Nice useful lot I've got,' said Miss Hardcastle. 'Is there anything you do know?'

'It doesn't seem to go no further, Ma'am,' said Kitty.

The alley had indeed turned out to be a dead end. Miss Hardcastle stood still for a moment. Unlike her subordinates, she did not seem to be frightened, but only pleasantly excited, and rather amused at the white faces and shaky voices of the girls.

'Well,' she said, 'this is what I call a night out. You're seeing life, Daisy, aren't you? I wonder are any of these houses empty? All locked anyway. Perhaps we'd best stay where we are.'

The shouting in the street they had left had grown louder and they could see a confused mass of humanity surging vaguely in a westward direction. Suddenly it became much louder still and angrier.

'They've caught Joe,' said Miss Hardcastle. 'If he can make himself heard he'll send them up here. Blast! This means losing the prisoner. Stop blubbering Daisy, you little fool. Quick. We must go down into the crowd separately. We've a very good chance of getting through. Keep your heads. Don't shoot, whatever you do. Try to get to Billingham at the crossroads. Ta-ta, Babs! The quieter you keep the less likely we are to meet again.'

Miss Hardcastle set off at once. Jane saw her stand for a few seconds on the fringes of the crowd and then disappear into it. The two girls hesitated and then followed. Jane sat down on a doorstep. The burns were painful where her dress had rubbed against them, but what chiefly troubled her was extreme weariness. She was also deadly cold and a little sick. But above all tired; so tired she could drop asleep almost …

She shook herself. There was complete silence all about her: she was colder than she had ever been before and her limbs ached. 'I believe I *have* been asleep,' she thought. She rose, stretched herself, and walked down the desolate lamplit alley into the larger street. It was quite empty except for one man in a railway uniform who said, 'Good morning, Miss,' as he walked smartly past. She stood for a moment, undecided and then began to walk slowly to her right. She put her hand in the pocket of the coat which Daisy and Kitty had flung round her before leaving the flat and found three quarters of a large slab of chocolate. She was ravenous and began munching it. Just as she finished she was overtaken by a car which drew up shortly after it had passed her. 'Are you all right?' said a man, poking his head out.

'Were you hurt in the riot?' said a woman's voice from within.

'No … not much … I don't know,' said Jane stupidly.

The man stared at her and then got out. 'I say,' he said, 'you don't look too good. Are you sure you're quite well?' Then he turned and spoke to the woman inside. It seemed so long to Jane since she had heard kind, or even sane, voices that she felt like crying. The unknown couple made her sit in the car and gave her brandy and after that sandwiches. Finally they asked if they could give her a lift home. Where was home? And Jane, somewhat to her surprise, heard her own voice very sleepily answering, 'The Manor, at St Anne's.' 'That's fine,' said the man, 'we're making for Birmingham and we have to pass it.' Then Jane fell asleep at once again, and awoke only to find herself entering a lighted doorway and being received by a woman in pyjamas and an overcoat who turned out to be Mrs Maggs. But she was too tired to remember how or where she got to bed.

8

Moonlight at Belbury

'I am the last person, Miss Hardcastle,' said the Deputy Director, 'to wish to interfere with your – er – private pleasures. But really … !' It was some hours before breakfast time and the old gentleman was fully dressed and unshaved. But if he had been up all night, it was odd that he had let his fire out. He and the Fairy were standing by a cold and blackened grate in his study.

'She can't be far away,' said Fairy Hardcastle. 'We'll pick her up some other time. It was well worth trying. If I'd got out of her where she'd been – and I should have got it if I'd had a few minutes longer – why, it might have turned out to be enemy headquarters. We might have rounded up the whole gang.'

'It was hardly a suitable occasion …' began Wither, but she interrupted him.

'We haven't so much time to waste, you know. You tell me Frost is already complaining that the woman's mind is less accessible. And according to your own metapsychology, or whatever you call the damned jargon, that means she's falling under the influence of the other side. You told me that yourself! Where'll we be if you lose touch with her mind before I've got her body locked up here?'

'I am always, of course,' said Wither, 'most ready and – er – interested to hear expressions of your own opinions and would not for a moment deny that they are (in certain respects, of course, if not in all) of a very real value. On the other hand, there are matters on which your – ah – necessarily specialised experience does not entirely qualify you … An arrest was not contemplated at this stage. The Head will, I fear, take the view that you have exceeded your authority. Trespassed beyond your proper sphere, Miss Hardcastle. I do not say that I necessarily agree with him. But we must *all* agree that unauthorised action –'

'Oh, cut it out, Wither!' said the Fairy, seating herself on the side of the table. 'Try that game on the Steeles and Stones. I know too much about it. It's no bloody good trying the elasticity stunt on me. It was a golden opportunity, running into that girl. If I hadn't taken it, you'd have talked about lack of initiative; as I did, you talk about exceeding my authority. You can't frighten me. I know bloody well we're all for it if the NICE fails; and in the meantime, I'd like to see you do without me. We've got to get the girl, haven't we?'

'But not by an arrest. We have always deprecated anything like violence. If a mere arrest could have secured the – er – good will and collaboration of Mrs Studdock, we should hardly have embarrassed ourselves with the presence of her husband. And even supposing (merely, of course, for the purpose of argument) that your action in arresting her could be justified, I am afraid your conduct of the affair after that is open to serious criticism.'

'I couldn't tell that the bucking car was going to break down, could I?'

'I do not think,' said Wither, 'the Head could be induced to regard that as the only miscarriage. Once the slightest resistance on this woman's part developed, it was not, in my opinion, reasonable to expect success by the method you employed. As you are aware, I always deplore anything that is not perfectly humane; but that is quite consistent with the position that if more drastic expedients have to be used then they must be used thoroughly. *Moderate* pain, such as any ordinary degree of endurance can resist, is always a mistake. It is no true kindness to the prisoner. The more scientific and, may I add, more civilised facilities for coercive examination which we have placed at your disposal here, might have been successful. I am not speaking officially, Miss Hardcastle, and I would not in any sense attempt to anticipate the reactions of our Head.

But I should not be doing my duty if I failed to remind you that complaints from that quarter have already been made (though not, of course, minuted) as to your tendency to allow a certain – er – emotional excitement in the disciplinary or remedial side of your work to distract you from the demands of policy.'

'You won't find anyone can do a job like mine well unless they get some kick out of it,' said the Fairy sulkily.

The Deputy Director looked at his watch.

'Anyway,' said the Fairy, 'what does the Head want to see me *now* for? I've been on my feet the whole bloody night. I might be allowed a bath and some breakfast.'

'The path of duty, Miss Hardcastle,' said Wither, 'can never be an easy one. You will not forget that punctuality is one of the points on which emphasis has sometimes been laid.'

Miss Hardcastle got up and rubbed her face with her hands. 'Well, I must have something to drink before I go in,' she said. Wither held out his hands in deprecation.

'Come on, Wither. I *must*,' said Miss Hardcastle.

'You don't think he'll smell it?' said Wither.

'I'm not going in without it, anyway,' said she.

The old man unlocked his cupboard and gave her whiskey. Then the two left the study and went a long way, right over to the other side of the house where it joined onto the actual Blood Transfusion offices. It was all dark at this hour in the morning and they went by the light of Miss Hardcastle's torch – on through carpeted and pictured passages into blank passages with rubberoid floors and distempered walls and then through a door they had to unlock, and then through another. All the way Miss Hardcastle's booted feet made a noise but the slippered feet of the Deputy Director made no noise at all. At last they came to a place where the lights were on and there was a mixture of animal and chemical smells, and then to a door which was opened to them after they had parleyed through a speaking tube. Filostrato, wearing a white coat, confronted them in the doorway.

'Enter,' said Filostrato. 'He expect you for some time.'

'Is it in a bad temper?' said Miss Hardcastle.

'Sh!' said Wither. 'And in any case, my dear lady, I don't think that is quite the way in which one should speak of our Head. His sufferings – in his peculiar condition, you know –'

'You are to go in at once,' said Filostrato, 'as soon as you have made yourselves ready.'

'Stop. Half a moment,' said Miss Hardcastle suddenly.

'What is it? Be quick, please,' said Filostrato.

'I'm going to be sick.'

'You cannot be sick here. Go back. I will give you some X54 at once.'

'It's all right now,' said Miss Hardcastle. 'It was only momentary. It'd take more than this to upset me.'

'Silence, please,' said the Italian. 'Do not attempt to open the second door until my assistant has shut the first one behind you. Do not speak more than you can help. Do not even say yes when you are given an order. The Head will assume your obedience. Do not make sudden movements, do not get too close, do not shout, and above all do not argue. Now.'

◆ ○ ◆

Long after sunrise there came into Jane's sleeping mind a sensation which, had she put it into words, would have sung, 'Be glad thou sleeper and thy sorrow offcast. I am the gate to all good adventure.' And after she had wakened and found herself lying in pleasant languour with winter morning sunlight falling across her bed, the mood continued. 'He *must* let me stay here now,' she thought. Sometime after this Mrs Maggs came in and lit the fire and brought the breakfast. Jane winced as she sat up in bed for some of the burns had stuck to the strange nightdress (rather too large for her) in which she found herself clad. There was an indefinable difference in Mrs Maggs' behaviour. 'It's ever so nice us both being here, isn't it, Mrs Studdock?' she said, and somehow the tone seemed to imply a closer relation than Jane had envisaged between them. But she was too lazy to wonder much about it. Shortly after breakfast came Miss Ironwood. She examined and dressed the burns, which were not serious. 'You can get up in the afternoon if you like, Mrs Studdock,' she said. 'I should just take a quiet day till then. What would you like to read? There's a pretty large library.' 'I'd like the *Curdie* books, please,' said Jane, 'and *Mansfield Park* and Shakespeare's *Sonnets*.' Having thus been provided with reading matter for several hours, she very comfortably went to sleep again.

When Mrs Maggs looked in at about four o'clock to see if Jane was awake, Jane said she would like to get up. 'All right, Mrs Studdock,' said Mrs Maggs, 'just as you like. I'll bring you along a nice cup of tea in a minute and then I'll get the bathroom ready for you. There's a bathroom next door almost, only I'll have to get that Mr Bultitude out of it. He's that lazy and he *will* go in and sit there all day when it's cold weather.'

As soon as Mrs Maggs had gone, however, Jane decided to get up. She felt that her social abilities were quite equal to dealing with the eccentric Mr Bultitude and she did not want to waste any more time in bed. She had an idea that if once she were 'up and about' all sorts of pleasant and interesting things might happen. Accordingly she put on her coat, took her towel, and proceeded to explore; and that was why Mrs Maggs, coming upstairs with tea a moment later, heard a suppressed shriek and saw Jane emerge from the bathroom with a white face and slam the door behind her.

'Oh dear!' said Mrs Maggs bursting into laughter. 'I ought to have told you. Never mind. I'll soon have him out of that.' She set the tea tray down on the passage floor and turned to the bathroom.

'Is it safe?' asked Jane.

'Oh yes, he's *safe* all right,' said Mrs Maggs. 'But he's not that easy to shift. Not for you or me, Mrs Studdock. Of course if it was Miss Ironwood or the Director it would be another matter.' With that she opened the bathroom door. Inside, sitting up on its hunkers beside the bath and occupying most of the room was a great, snuffly, wheezy, beady-eyed, loose-skinned, gor-bellied brown bear, which, after a great many reproaches, appeals, exhortations, pushes and blows from Mrs Maggs, heaved up its enormous bulk and came very slowly out into the passage.

'Why don't you go out and take some exercise that lovely afternoon, you great lazy thing?' said Mrs Maggs. 'You ought to be ashamed of yourself, sitting there getting in everyone's way. Don't be frightened, Mrs Studdock. He's as tame as tame. He'll let you stroke him. Go on, Mr Bultitude. Go and say how do you do to the lady!'

Jane extended a hesitant and unconvincing hand to touch the animal's back, but Mr Bultitude was sulking and without a glance at Jane continued his slow walk along the passage to a point about ten yards away where he quite suddenly sat down. The tea things rattled at Jane's feet, and everyone on the floor below must have known that Mr Bultitude had sat down.

'Is it really safe to have a creature like that loose about the house?' said Jane.

'Mrs Studdock,' said Ivy Maggs with some solemnity, 'if the Director wanted to have a tiger about the house it would be safe. That's the way he has with animals. There isn't a creature in the place that would go for another or for us once he's had his little talk with them. Just the same as he does with us. You'll see.'

'If you would put the tea in my room ...' said Jane rather coldly and went into the bathroom. 'Yes,' said Mrs Maggs, standing in the open doorway, 'you might have had your bath with Mr Bultitude sitting there beside you – though he's that big and that human I don't somehow feel it would be Nice myself.'

Jane made to shut the door.

'Well, I'll leave you *to* it, then,' said Mrs Maggs without moving.

'Thank you,' said Jane.

'Sure you got everything you want?' said Mrs Maggs.

'Quite sure,' said Jane.

'Well, I'll be getting along, then,' said Mrs Maggs, turning as if to go, but almost instantly turning back again to say, 'you'll find us in the kitchen, I expect, Mother Dimble and me and the rest.'

'Is Mrs Dimble staying in the house?' asked Jane with a slight emphasis on the *Mrs*.

'*Mother* Dimble, we all call her here,' said Mrs Maggs. 'And I'm sure she won't mind you doing the same. You'll get used to our ways in a day or two, *I'm* sure. It's a funny house really, when you come to think of it. Well. I'll be getting along then. Don't take too long or your tea won't be worth drinking. But I daresay you'd better not have a bath, not with those nasty places on your chest. Got all you want?'

When Jane had washed and had tea and dressed herself with as much care as strange hairbrushes and a strange mirror allowed, she set out to look for the inhabited rooms. She passed down one long passage, through that silence which is not quite like any other in the world – the silence upstairs, in a big house, on a winter afternoon. Presently, she came to a place where two passages met, and here the silence was broken by a faint irregular noise – *pob-pob-pob-pob*. Looking to her right she saw the explanation, for where the passage ended in a bay window stood Mr Bultitude, this time on his hind legs, meditatively boxing a punch-ball. Jane chose the way to her left and came to a gallery whence she looked down the staircase into a large hall where daylight mixed with firelight. On the same level with herself, but only to be reached by descending to a landing and ascending again, were shadowy regions which she recognised as leading to the Director's room. A sort of solemnity seemed to her to emanate from them and she went down into the hall almost on tiptoes, and now, for the first time, her memory of that last and curious experience in the blue room came back to her with a weight which even the thought of the Director himself could not counteract. When she reached the hall she saw at once where the back premises of the house must lie – down two steps and along a paved passage, past a stuffed pike in a glass case and then past a grandfather clock, and then, guided by voices and other sounds, to the kitchen itself.

A wide, open hearth glowing with burning wood lit up the comfortable form of Mrs Dimble who was seated in a kitchen chair at one side of it, apparently, from the basin in her lap and other indications on a table beside her, engaged in preparing vegetables. Mrs Maggs and Camilla were doing something at a stove – the hearth was apparently not used for cooking – and in a doorway which doubtless led to the scullery a tall grizzle-headed man who wore gum-boots and seemed to have just come from the garden, was drying his hands.

'Come in, Jane,' said Mother Dimble, cordially. 'We're not expecting you to do any work today. Come and sit on the other side of the fire and talk to me. This is Mr MacPhee – who has no right to be here, but he'd better be introduced to you.'

Mr MacPhee, having finished the drying process and carefully hung the towel behind the door, advanced rather ceremoniously and shook hands with Jane. His own hand was very large and coarse in texture and he had a shrewd hard-featured face.

'I am very glad to see you, Mrs Studdock,' he said in what Jane took to be a Scotch accent, though it was really that of an Ulsterman.

'Don't believe a word he says, Jane,' said Mother Dimble. 'He's your prime enemy in this House. He doesn't believe in your dreams.'

'Mrs Dimble!' said MacPhee, 'I have repeatedly explained to you the distinction between a personal feeling of confidence and a logical satisfaction of the claims of evidence. The one is a psychological event –'

'And the other a perpetual nuisance,' said Mrs Dimble.

'Never mind her, Mrs Studdock,' said MacPhee. 'I am, as I was saying, very glad to welcome you among us. The fact that I have found it my duty on several occasions to point out that no *experimentum crucis* has yet confirmed the hypothesis that your dreams are veridical, has no connection in the world with my personal attitude.'

'Of course,' said Jane vaguely, and a little confused. 'I'm sure you have a right to your own opinions.'

All the women laughed as MacPhee in a somewhat louder tone replied, 'Mrs Studdock, I have *no* opinions – on any subject in the world. I state the facts and exhibit the implications. If everyone indulged in fewer opinions' (he pronounced the word with emphatic disgust), 'there'd be less silly talking and printing in the world.'

'I know who talks most in this house,' said Mrs Maggs, somewhat to Jane's surprise. The Ulsterman eyed the last speaker with an unaltered face while producing a small pewter box from his pocket and helping himself to a pinch of snuff.

'What are you waiting for anyway?' said Mrs Maggs. 'Women's day in the kitchen today.'

'I was wondering,' said MacPhee, 'whether you had a cup of tea saved for me.'

'And why didn't you come in at the right time, then?' said Mrs Maggs. Jane noticed that she talked to him much as she talked to the bear.

'I was busy,' said the other seating himself at one end of the table; and added after a pause, 'trenching celery. The wee woman does the best she can but she has a poor notion of what needs doing in a garden.'

'What is "women's day" in the kitchen?' asked Jane of Mother Dimble.

'There are no servants here,' said Mother Dimble, 'and we all do the work. The women do it one day and the men the next. What? No, it's a very sensible arrangement. The Director's idea is that men and women can't do housework together without quarrelling. There's something in it. Of course, it doesn't do to look at the cups too closely on the men's day, but on the whole we get along pretty well.'

'But why should they quarrel?' asked Jane.

'Different methods, my dear. Men can't *help* in a job, you know. They can be induced to do it: not to help while you're doing it. At least, it makes them grumpy.'

'The cardinal difficulty,' said MacPhee, 'in collaboration between the sexes is that women speak a language without nouns. If two men are doing a bit of work, one will say to the other, "Put this bowl inside the bigger bowl which you'll find on the top shelf of the green cupboard." The female for this is, "Put that in the other one in there." And then if you ask them, "in where?" they say, "in *there*, of course." There is consequently a phatic hiatus.' He pronounced this so as to rhyme with 'get *at* us.'

'There's your tea now,' said Ivy Maggs, 'and I'll go and get you a piece of cake, which is more than you deserve. And when you've had it you can go upstairs and talk about nouns for the rest of the evening.'

'Not *about* nouns: *by means of* nouns,' said MacPhee, but Mrs Maggs had already left the room. Jane took advantage of this to say to Mother Dimble in a lower voice, 'Mrs Maggs seems to make herself very much at home here.'

'My dear, she *is* at home here.'

'As a maid, you mean?'

'Well, no more than anyone else. She's here chiefly because her house has been taken from her. She had nowhere else to go.'

'You mean she is – one of the Director's charities.'

'Certainly that. Why do you ask?'

'Well – I don't know. It *did* seem a little odd that she should call you Mother Dimble. I hope I'm not being snobbish …'

'You're forgetting that Cecil and I are another of the Director's charities.'

'Isn't that rather playing on words?'

'Not a bit. Ivy and Cecil and I are all here because we were turned out of our homes. At least Ivy and I are. It may be rather different for Cecil.'

'And does the Director know that Mrs Maggs talks to everyone like that?'

'My dear child, don't ask me what the Director knows.'

'I think what's puzzling me is that when I saw him he said something about equality not being the important thing. But his own house seems to be run on – well, on very democratic lines indeed.'

'I never attempt to understand what he says on that subject,' said Mother Dimble. 'He's usually talking either about spiritual ranks – and you were never goose enough to think yourself *spiritually* superior to Ivy – or else he's talking about marriage.'

'Did you understand his views on marriàge?'

'My dear, the Director is a very wise man. But he *is* a man, after all, and an unmarried man at that. Some of what he says, or what the Masters say, about marriage does seem to me to be a lot of fuss about something so simple and natural that it oughtn't to need saying at all. But I suppose there are young women now-a-days who need to be told it.'

'You haven't got much use for young women who do, I see.'

'Well, perhaps I'm unfair. Things were easier for us. We were brought up on stories with happy endings and on the Prayer Book. We always intended to love, honour and obey, and we had figures and we wore petticoats and we liked waltzes ...'

'Waltzes are ever so nice,' said Mrs Maggs who had just returned and given MacPhee his slab of cake, 'so old fashioned.'

At that moment the door opened and a voice from behind it said, 'Well, go in then, if you're going.' Thus admonished, a very fine jackdaw hopped into the room, followed firstly by Mr Bultitude and secondly by Arthur Denniston.

'I've told you before, Arthur,' said Ivy Maggs, 'not to bring that bear in here when we're cooking the dinner.' While she was speaking Mr Bultitude, who was apparently himself uncertain of his welcome, walked across the room in what he believed (erroneously) to be an unobtrusive manner and sat down behind Mrs Dimble's chair.

'Dr Dimble's just come back, Mother Dimble,' said Denniston. 'But he's had to go straight to the Blue Room. And the Director wants you to go to him too, MacPhee.'

◆ ○ ◆

Mark sat down to lunch that day in good spirits. Everyone reported that the riot had gone off most satisfactorily and he had enjoyed reading his own accounts of it in the morning papers. He enjoyed it even more when he heard Steele and Cosser talking about it in a way which showed that they did not even know how it had been engineered, much less who had written it up in the newspapers. And he had enjoyed his morning too. It had involved a conversation with Frost, the Fairy, and Wither himself, about the future of Edgestow. All were agreed that the government would follow the almost unanimous opinion of the nation (as expressed in the newspapers) and put it temporarily under the control of the Institutional Police. An emergency governor of Edgestow must be appointed. Feverstone was the obvious man. As a member of Parliament he represented the Nation, as a Fellow of Bracton he represented the University, as a member of the Institute he represented the Institute. All the competing claims that might otherwise have come into collision were reconciled in the person of Lord Feverstone; the articles on this subject which Mark was to write that afternoon would almost write themselves! But that had not been all. As the conversation proceeded it had become clear that there was really a double object in getting this invidious post for Feverstone. When the time came, and the local unpopularity of the NICE rose to its height, he could be sacrificed. This of course was not said in so many words, but Mark realised perfectly clearly that even Feverstone was no longer quite in the Inner Ring. The Fairy said that old Dick was a mere politician at heart and always would be. Wither, deeply sighing, confessed that his talents had been perhaps more useful at an earlier stage of the movement than they were likely to be in the period on which they were now entering. There was in Mark's mind no plan for undermining Feverstone nor even a fully formed wish that he should be undermined; but the whole atmosphere of the discussion became somehow more agreeable to him as he began to understand the real situation. He was also pleased that he had (as he would have put it) 'got to know' Frost. He knew by experience that there is in almost every organisation some quiet, inconspicuous person whom the small fry suppose to be of no importance but who is really one of the mainsprings of the whole machine. Even to recognise such people for what they are shows that one had made considerable progress.

There was, to be sure, a cold fish-like quality about Frost which Mark did not like and something even repulsive about the regularity of his features. But every word he spoke (he did not speak many) went to the root of what was being discussed, and Mark found it delightful to speak to him. The pleasures of conversation were coming, for Mark, to have less and less connection with his spontaneous liking or disliking of the people he talked to. He was aware of this change – which had begun when he joined the Progressive Element in College – and welcomed it as a sign of maturity.

Wither had thawed in a most encouraging manner. At the end of the conversation he had taken Mark aside, spoken vaguely but paternally of the great work he was doing, and finally asked after his wife. The DD hoped there was no truth in the rumour which had reached him that she was suffering from – er – some nervous disorder. 'Who the devil has been telling him that?' thought Mark. 'Because,' said Wither, 'it had occurred to me, in view of the great pressure of work which rests on you at present and the difficulty, therefore, of your being at home as much as we should all (for your sake) wish, that in *your* case the Institute might be induced ... I am speaking in a quite informal way ... that we should all be delighted to welcome Mrs Studdock here.'

Until the DD had said this Mark had not realised that there was nothing he would dislike so much as having Jane at Belbury. There were so many things that Jane would not understand: not only the pretty heavy drinking which was becoming his habit but – oh, everything from morning to night. For it is only justice both to Mark and to Jane to record that he would have found it impossible to conduct in her hearing any one of the hundred conversations which his life at Belbury involved. Her mere presence would have made all the laughter of the Inner Ring sound metallic, unreal; and what he now regarded as common prudence would seem to her, and through her to himself, mere flattery, back-biting and toad-eating. Jane in the middle of Belbury would turn the whole of Belbury into a vast vulgarity, flashy and yet furtive. His mind sickened at the thought of trying to teach Jane that she must help to keep Wither in a good temper and must play up to Fairy Hardcastle. He excused himself vaguely to the DD, with profuse thanks, and got away as quickly as he could.

That afternoon, while he was having tea, Fairy Hardcastle came and leaned over the back of his chair and said in his ear,

'*You've* torn it, Studdock.'

'What's the matter now, Fairy?' said he.

'I can't make out what's the matter with *you*, young Studdock, and that's a fact. Have you made up your mind to annoy the Old Man? Because it's a dangerous game, you know.'

'What on earth are you talking about?'

'Well, here we've all been working on your behalf and soothing him down and this morning we thought we'd finally succeeded. He was talking about giving you the appointment originally intended for you and waiving the probationary period. Not a cloud in the sky: and then you have five minutes' chat with him – barely five minutes, in fact – and in that time you've managed to undo it all. I begin to think you are mental.'

'What the devil's wrong with him this time?'

'Well *you* ought to know! Didn't he say something about bringing your wife here?'

'Yes, he did. What about it?'

'And what did you say?'

'I said not to bother about it – and, of course, thanked him very much and all that.' The Fairy whistled.

'Don't you see, Honey,' she said, gently rapping Mark's scalp with her knuckles, 'that you could hardly have made a worse bloomer? It was a most terrific concession for him to make. He's never done it to anyone else. You might have known he'd be offended if you cold-shouldered him. He's burbling away now about lack of confidence. Says he's "hurt": which means that somebody else soon will be! He takes your refusal as a sign that you are not really "settled" here.'

'But that is sheer madness. I mean ...'

'Why the blazes couldn't you tell him you'd have your wife here?'

'Isn't that my own business?'

'Don't you want to have her? You're not very polite to little wifie, Studdock. And they tell me she's a damned pretty girl.'

At that moment the form of Wither, slowly sauntering in their direction, became apparent to both and the conversation ended.

At dinner he sat next to Filostrato. There were no other members of the inner circle within earshot. The Italian was in good spirits and talkative. He had just given orders for the cutting down of some fine beech trees in the grounds.

'Why have you done that, Professor?' said a Mr Winter who sat opposite. 'I shouldn't have thought they did much harm at that distance from the house. I'm rather fond of trees myself.'

'Oh, yes, yes,' replied Filostrato. 'The pretty trees, the garden trees. But not the savages. I put the rose in my garden, but not the brier. The forest tree is a weed. But I tell you I have seen the civilised tree in Persia. It was a French *attaché* who had it because he was in a place where trees do not grow. It was made of metal. A poor, crude thing. But how if it were perfected? Light, made of aluminium. So natural, it would even deceive.'

'It would hardly be the same as a real tree,' said Winter.

'But consider the advantages! You get tired of him in one place: two workmen carry him somewhere else: wherever you please. It never dies. No leaves to fall, no twigs, no birds building nests, no muck and mess.'

'I suppose one or two, as curiosities, might be rather amusing.'

'Why one or two? At present, I allow, we must have forests, for the atmosphere. Presently we find a chemical substitute. And then, why *any* natural trees? I foresee nothing but the *art* tree all over the earth. In fact, we *clean* the planet.'

'Do you mean,' put in a man called Gould, 'that we are to have no vegetation at all?'

'Exactly. You shave your face: even, in the English fashion, you shave him every day. One day we shave the planet.'

'I wonder what the birds will make of it?'

'I would not have any birds either. On the art tree I would have the art birds all singing when you press a switch inside the house. When you are tired of the singing you switch them off. Consider again the improvement. No feathers dropped about, no nests, no eggs, no dirt.'

'It sounds,' said Mark, 'like abolishing pretty well all organic life.'

'And why not? It is simple hygiene. Listen, my friends. If you pick up some rotten thing and find this organic life crawling over it, do you not say, "Oh, the horrid thing. It is alive," and then drop it?'

'Go on,' said Winter.

'And you, especially you English, are you not hostile to any organic life except your own on your own body? Rather than permit it you have invented the daily bath.'

'That's true.'

'And what do you call dirty dirt? Is it not precisely the organic? Minerals are clean dirt. But the real filth is what comes from organisms – sweat, spittles, excretions. Is not your whole idea of purity one huge example? The impure and the organic are interchangeable conceptions.'

'What are you driving at, Professor?' said Gould. 'After all we are organisms ourselves.'

'I grant it. That is the point. In us organic life has produced Mind. It has done its work. After that we want no more of it. We do not want the world any longer furred over with organic life, like what you call the blue mould – all sprouting and budding and breeding and decaying. We must get rid of it. By little and little, of course. Slowly we learn how. Learn to make our brains live with less and less body: learn to build our bodies directly with chemicals, no longer have to stuff them full of dead brutes and weeds. Learn how to reproduce ourselves without copulation.'

'I don't think that would be much fun,' said Winter.

'My friend, you have already separated the Fun, as you call it, from fertility. The Fun itself begins to pass away. Bah! I know that is not what you think. But look at your English women. Six out of ten are frigid, are they not? You see? Nature herself begins to throw away the anachronism. When she has thrown it away, then real civilisation becomes possible. You would understand if you were peasants. Who would try to work with stallions and bulls? No, no; we want geldings and oxen. There will never be peace and order and discipline so long as there is sex. When man has thrown it away, then he will become finally governable.'

This brought them to the end of dinner and as they rose from the table Filostrato whispered in Mark's ear, 'I would not advise the Library for you tonight. You understand? You are not in favour. Come and have a little conversation with me in my room.'

Mark rose and followed him, glad and surprised that in this new crisis with the DD Filostrato was apparently still his friend. They went up to the Italian's sitting-room on the first floor. There Mark sat down before the fire, but his host continued to walk up and down the room.

'I am very sorry, my young friend,' said Filostrato, 'to hear of this new trouble between you and the Deputy Director. It must be stopped, you understand? If he invites you to bring your wife here, why do you not bring her?'

'Well, really,' said Mark, 'I never knew he attached so much importance to it. I thought he was merely being polite.'

His objection to having Jane at Belbury had been, if not removed, at least temporarily deadened by the wine he had drunk at dinner and by the sharp pang he had felt at the threat of expulsion from the library circle.

'It is of no importance in itself,' said Filostrato. 'But I have reason to believe it came not from Wither but from the Head himself.'

'The Head? You mean Jules?' said Mark in surprise. 'I thought he was a mere figurehead. And why should *he* care whether I bring my wife here or not?'

'You were mistaken,' said Filostrato. 'Our Head is no figurehead.' There was something odd about his manner, Mark thought. For some time neither man spoke.

'It is all true,' said Filostrato at last, 'what I said at dinner.'

'But about Jules,' said Mark. 'What business is it of his?'

'Jules?' said Filostrato. 'Why do you speak of him? I say it was all true. The world I look forward to is the world of perfect purity. The clean mind and the clean minerals. What are the things that most offend the dignity of man? Birth and breeding and death. How if we are about to discover that man can live without any of the three?'

Mark stared. Filostrato's conversation appeared so disjointed and his manner so unusual that he began to wonder if he were quite sane or quite sober.

'As for your wife,' resumed Filostrato, 'I attach no importance to it. What have I to do with men's wives? The whole subject disgusts me. But if they make a point of it … Look, my friend, the real question is whether you mean to be truly at one with us or not.'

'I don't quite follow,' said Mark.

'Do you want to be a mere hireling? But you have already come too far in for that. You are at the turning point of your career, Mr Studdock. If you try to go back you will be as unfortunate as the fool Hingest. If you come really in – the world … bah, what do I say? … the universe is at your feet.'

'But of course I want to come in,' said Mark. A certain excitement was stealing over him.

'The Head thinks that you cannot be really one of us if you will not bring your wife here. He will have all of you, and all that is yours – or nothing. You must bring the woman in too. She also must be one of us.'

This remark was like a shock of cold water in Mark's face. And yet … and yet … in that room and at that moment, fixed with the little, bright eyes of the Professor, he could hardly make the thought of Jane quite real to himself.

'You shall hear it from the lips of the Head himself,' said Filostrato suddenly.

'Is Jules *here*?' said Mark.

Instead of answering, Filostrato turned sharply from him and with a great scarping movement flung back the window curtains.

Then he switched off the light. The fog had all gone, the wind had risen. Small clouds were scudding across the stars and the full Moon – Mark had never seen her so bright – stared down upon them. As the clouds passed her she looked like a ball that was rolling through them. Her bloodless light filled the room.

'There is a world for you, no?' said Filostrato. 'There is cleanness, purity. Thousands of square miles of polished rock with not one blade of grass, not one fibre of lichen, not one grain of dust. Not even air. Have you thought what it would be like, my friend, if you could walk on that land? No crumbling, no erosion. The peaks of those mountains are real peaks: sharp as needles, they would go through your hand. Cliffs as high as Everest and as straight as the wall of a house. And cast by those cliffs, acres of shadow black as ebony, and in the shadow hundreds of degrees of frost. And then, one step beyond the shadow, light that would pierce your eyeballs like steel and rock that would burn your feet. The temperature is at boiling point. You would die, no? But even then you would not become filth. In a few moments you are a little heap of ash; clean, white powder. And mark, no wind to blow that powder about. Every grain in the little heap would remain in its place, just where you died, till the end of the world ... but that is nonsense. The universe will have no end.'

'Yes. A dead world,' said Mark gazing at the Moon.

'No!' said Filostrato. He had come close to Mark and spoke almost in a whisper, the bat-like whisper of a voice that is naturally high-pitched. 'No. There is life there.'

'Do we *know* that?' asked Mark.

'Oh, *si*. Intelligent life. Under the surface. A great race, further advanced than we. An inspiration. A *pure* race. They have cleaned their world, broken free (almost) from the organic.'

'But how – ?'

'They do not need to be born and breed and die; only their common people, their *canaglia* do that. The Masters live on. They retain their intelligence: they can keep it artificially alive after the organic body has been dispensed with – a miracle of applied biochemistry. They do not need organic food. You understand? They are almost free of Nature, attached to her only by the thinnest, finest cord.'

'Do you mean that all *that*,' Mark pointed to the mottled globe of the Moon, 'is their own doing?'

'Why not? If you remove all the vegetation, presently you have not atmosphere, no water.'

'But what was the purpose?'

'Hygiene. Why should they have their world all crawling with organisms? And specially, they would banish one organism. Her surface is not all as you see. There are still surface-dwellers – savages. One great dirty patch on the far side of her where there is still water and air and forests – yes, and germs and death. They are slowly spreading their hygiene over their whole globe. Disinfecting her. The savages fight against them. There are frontiers, and fierce wars, in the caves and galleries down below. But the great race presses on. If you could see the other side you would see year by year the clean rock – like this side of the Moon – encroaching: the organic stain, all the green and blue and mist, growing smaller. Like cleaning tarnished silver.'

'But how do we know all this?'

'I will tell you all that another time. The Head has many sources of information. For the moment, I speak only to inspire you. I speak that you may know what can be done: what shall be done here. This Institute – *Dio meo*; it is for something better than housing and vaccinations and faster trains and curing the people of cancer. It is for the conquest of death: or for the conquest of organic life, if you prefer. They are the same thing. It is to bring out of that cocoon of organic life which sheltered the babyhood of mind the New Man, the man who will not die, the artificial man, free from Nature. Nature is the ladder we have climbed up by, now we kick her away.'

'And you think that some day we shall really find a means of keeping the brain alive indefinitely?'

'We have begun already. The Head himself ...'

'Go on,' said Mark. His heart was beating wildly and he had forgotten both Jane and Wither. This at last was the real thing.

'The Head himself has already survived death, and you shall speak to him this night.'

'Do you mean that Jules has died?'

'Bah! Jules is nothing. He is not the Head.'

'Then who is?'

At this moment there was a knock on the door. Someone, without waiting for an answer came in.

'Is the young man ready?' asked the voice of Straik.

'Oh yes. You are ready, are you not, Mr Studdock?'

'You have explained it to him, then?' said Straik. He turned to Mark and the moonlight in the room was so bright that Mark could now partially recognise his face – its harsh furrows emphasised by that cold light and shade.

'Do you mean really to join us, young man?' said Straik. 'There is no turning back once you have set your hand to the plough. And there are no reservations. The Head has sent for you. Do you understand – *the Head*? You will look upon one who was killed and is still alive. The resurrection of Jesus in the Bible was a symbol: tonight you shall see what it symbolised. This is real Man at last, and it claims all our allegiance.'

'What the devil are you talking about?' said Mark. The tension of his nerves distorted his voice into a hoarse blustering cry.

'My friend is quite right,' said Filostrato. 'Our Head is the first of the New Men – the first that lives beyond animal life. As far as Nature is concerned he is already dead: if Nature had her way his brain would now be mouldering in the grave. But he will speak to you within this hour, and – a word in your ear, my friend – you will obey his orders.'

'But who *is* it?' said Mark.

'It is François Alcasan,' said Filostrato.

'You mean the man who was guillotined?' gasped Mark. Both the heads nodded. Both faces were close to him: in that disastrous light they looked like masks hanging in the air.

'You are frightened?' said Filostrato. 'You will get over that. We are offering to make you one of us. *Ahi* – if you were outside, if you were mere *canaglia* you would have reason to be frightened. It is the beginning of all power. He lives forever. The giant time is conquered. And the giant space – he was already conquered too. One of our company has already travelled in space. True, he was betrayed and murdered and his manuscripts are imperfect: we have not yet been able to reconstruct his space-ship. But that will come.'

'It is the beginning of Man Immortal and Man Ubiquitous,' said Straik. 'Man on the throne of the universe. It is what all the prophecies really meant.'

'At first, of course,' said Filostrato, 'the power will be confined to a number – a small number – of individual men. Those who are selected for eternal life.'

'And you mean,' said Mark, 'it will then be extended to all men?'

'No,' said Filostrato. 'I mean it will then be reduced to one man. You are not a fool, are you, my young friend? All that talk about the power of Man over Nature – Man in the abstract – is only for the *canaglia*. You know as well as I do that Man's power over Nature means the power of some men over other men with Nature as the instrument. There is no such thing as Man – it is a word. There are only men. No! It is not Man who will be omnipotent, it is some one man, some immortal man. Alcasan, our Head, is the first sketch of it. The completed product may be someone else. It may be you. It may be me.'

'A king cometh,' said Straik, 'who shall rule the universe with righteousness and the heavens with judgment. You thought all that was mythology, no doubt. You thought because fables had clustered about the phrase "Son of Man" that Man would never really have a son who will wield all power. But he will.'

'I don't understand, I don't understand,' said Mark.

'But it is very easy,' said Filostrato. 'We have found how to make a dead man live. He was a wise man even in his natural life. He lives now forever; he gets wiser. Later, we make them live

191

better – for at present, one must concede, this second life is probably not very agreeable to him who has it. You see? Later we make it pleasant for some – perhaps not so pleasant for others. For we can make the dead live whether they wish it or not. He who shall be finally king of the universe can give this life to whom he pleases. They cannot refuse the little present.'

'And so,' said Straik, 'the lessons you learned at your mother's knee return. God will have power to give eternal reward and eternal punishment.'

'God?' said Mark. 'How does He come into it? I don't believe in God.'

'But, my friend,' said Filostrato, 'does it follow that because there was no God in the past that there will be no God also in the future?'

'Don't you see,' said Straik, 'that we are offering you the unspeakable glory of being present at the creation of God Almighty? Here, in this house, you shall meet the first sketch of the real God. It is a man – or a being made by man – who will finally ascend the throne of the universe. And rule forever.'

'You will come with us?' said Filostrato. 'He has sent for you!'

'Of course, he will come,' said Straik. 'Does he think he could hold back and live?'

'And that little affair of the wife,' added Filostrato. 'You will not mention a triviality like that. You will do as you are told. One does not argue with the Head.'

Mark had nothing now to help him but the rapidly ebbing exhilaration of the alcohol taken at dinner time and some faint gleams of memory from hours with Jane and with friends made before he went to Bracton, during which the world had had a different taste from this exciting horror which now pressed upon him. These, and a merely instinctive dislike for both the moonlit faces which so held his attention. On the other side was fear. What would they do to him if he refused? And aiding fear was his young man's belief that if one gave in for the present things would somehow right themselves 'in the morning'. And, aiding the fear and the hope, there was still, even then, a not wholly disagreeable thrill at the thought of sharing so stupendous a secret.

'Yes,' he said, halting in his speech as if he were out of breath, 'Yes – of course – I'll come.'

They led him out. The passages were already still and the sound of talk and laughter from the public rooms on the ground floor had ceased. He stumbled, and they linked arms with him. The journey seemed long: passage after passage, passages he had never seen before, doors to unlock, and then into a place where all the lights were on, and there were strange smells. Then Filostrato spoke through a speaking tube and a door was opened to them.

Mark found himself in a surgical-looking room with glaring lights, and sinks, and bottles, and glittering instruments. A young man whom he hardly knew, dressed in a white coat, received them.

'Strip to your underclothes,' said Filostrato. While Mark was obeying he noticed that the opposite wall of the room was covered with dials. Numbers of flexible tubes came out of the floor and went into the wall just beneath the dials. The staring dial faces and the bunches of tubes beneath them, which seemed to be faintly pulsating, gave one the impression of looking at some creature with many eyes and many tentacles. The young man kept his eyes fixed on the vibrating needles of the dials. When the three new-comers had removed their outer clothes, they washed their hands and faces, and after that Filostrato plucked white clothes for them out of a glass container with a pair of forceps. When they had put these on he gave them also gloves and masks such as surgeons wear. There followed a moment's silence while Filostrato studied the dials. 'Yes, yes,' he said. 'A little more air. Not much: point nought three. Turn on the chamber air – slowly – to full. Now the lights. Now air in the lock. A little less of the solution. And now' (here he turned to Straik and Studdock) 'are you ready to go in?'

He led them to a door in the same wall as the dials.

9

The Saracen's Head

'It was the worst dream I've had yet,' said Jane next morning. She was seated in the Blue Room with the Director and Grace Ironwood.

'Yes,' said the Director. 'Yours is perhaps the hardest post: until the real struggle begins.'

'I dreamed I was in a dark room,' said Jane, 'with queer smells in it and a sort of low humming noise. Then the light came on – but not very much light, and for a long time I didn't realise what I was looking at. And when I made it out ... I should have waked up if I hadn't made a great effort not to. I thought I saw a face floating in front of me. A face, not a head, if you understand what I mean. That is, there was a beard and nose and eyes – at least, you couldn't see the eyes because it had coloured glasses on, but there didn't seem to be anything above the eyes. Not at first. But as I got used to the light, I got a horrible shock. I thought the face was a mask tied on to a kind of balloon thing. But it wasn't, exactly. Perhaps it looked a bit like a man wearing a sort of turban ... I'm telling this dreadfully badly. What it really was, was a head (the rest of a head) which had had the top part of the skull taken off and then ... then ... as if something inside had boiled over. A great big mass which bulged out from inside what was left of the skull. Wrapped in some kind of composition stuff, but very thin stuff. You could see it twitch. Even in my fright I remember thinking, "Oh kill it, kill it. Put it out of its pain." But only for a second because I thought the thing was real, really. It was green looking and the mouth was wide open and quite dry. You realise I was a

194

long time, looking at it, before anything else happened. And soon I saw that it wasn't exactly floating. It was fixed up on some kind of bracket, or shelf, or pedestal – I don't know quite what, and there were things hanging from it. From the neck, I mean. Yes, it had a neck and a sort of collar thing round it, but nothing below the collar; no shoulders or body. Only these hanging things. In the dream I thought it was some kind of new man that had only head and entrails: I thought all those tubes were its insides. But presently – I don't quite know how, I saw that they were artificial. Little rubber tubes and bulbs and little metal things too. I couldn't understand them. All the tubes went into the wall. Then at last something happened.'

'You're all right, Jane, are you?' said Miss Ironwood.

'Oh yes,' said Jane, 'as far as that goes. Only one somehow doesn't *want* to tell it. Well, quite suddenly, like when an engine is started, there came a puff of air out of its mouth, with a hard dry rasping sound. And then there came another, and it settled down into a sort of rhythm – *huff, huff, huff* – like an imitation of breathing. Then came a most horrible thing: the mouth began to dribble. I know it sounds silly but in a way I felt sorry for it because it had no hands and couldn't wipe its mouth. It seems a small thing compared with all the rest but that is how I felt. Then it began working its mouth about and even licking its lips. It was like someone getting a machine into working order. To see it doing that just as if it was alive, and at the same time dribbling over the beard which was all stiff and dead looking ... Then three people came into the room, all dressed up in white, with masks on, walking as carefully as cats on the top of a wall. One was a great fat man, and another was lanky and bony. The third ... ' here Jane paused involuntarily. 'The third ... I think it was Mark ... I mean my husband.'

'You are uncertain?' said the Director.

'No,' said Jane. 'It was Mark. I knew his walk. And I knew the shoes he was wearing. And his voice. It *was* Mark.'

'I am sorry,' said the Director.

'And then,' said Jane, 'all three of them came round and stood in front of the Head. They bowed to it. You couldn't tell if it was looking at them because of its dark glasses. It kept on with that rhythmical huffing noise. Then it spoke.'

'In English?' said Grace Ironwood.

'No, in French.'

'What did it say?'

'Well, my French wasn't quite good enough to follow it. It spoke in a queer way. In starts – like a man who's out of breath. With no proper expression. And of course it couldn't turn itself this way or that way as a – a real person – does.'

The Director spoke again.

'Did you understand any of what was said?'

'Not very much. The fat man seemed to be introducing Mark to it. It said something to him. Then Mark tried to answer. I could follow him all right: his French isn't much better than mine.'

'What did he say?'

'He said something about "doing it in a few days if it was possible".'

'Was that all?'

'Very nearly. You see Mark couldn't stand it. I knew he wouldn't be able to: I remember, idiotically, in the dream I wanted to tell him. I saw he was going to fall. I think I tried to shout out to the other two, "He's going to fall." But of course I couldn't. He was sick too. Then they got him out of the room.'

All three were silent for a few seconds.

'Was that all?' said Miss Ironwood.

'Yes,' said Jane.' That's all I remember. I think I woke up then.'

The Director took a deep breath. 'Well,' he said, glancing at Miss Ironwood, 'it becomes plainer and plainer. We must hold a council at once. Is everyone here?'

'No. Dr Dimble has had to go into Edgestow, into College, to take pupils. He won't be back till evening.'

'Then we must hold the council this evening. Make all arrangements.' He paused for a moment and then turned to Jane.

'I am afraid this is very bad for you, my dear,' he said – 'and worse for him.'

'You mean for Mark, Sir?'

The Director nodded.

'Yes. Don't think hardly of him. He is suffering. If we are defeated we shall all go down with him. If we win we will rescue him; he cannot be far gone yet.' He paused, smiled, and added, 'We are quite used to trouble about husbands here, you know. Poor Ivy's is in jail.'

'In jail?'

'Oh, yes – for ordinary theft. But quite a good fellow. He'll be all right again.'

Though Jane felt horror, even to the point of nausea, at the sight (in her dream) of Mark's real surroundings and associates, it had been horror that carried a certain grandeur and mystery with it. The sudden equation between his predicament and that of a common convict whipped the blood to her cheeks. She said nothing.

'One other thing,' continued the Director. 'You will not misunderstand it if I exclude you from our council tonight.'

'Of course not, Sir,' said Jane, in fact misunderstanding it very much.

'You see,' he said, 'MacPhee takes the line that if you hear things talked of, you will carry ideas of them into your sleep and that will destroy the evidential value of your dreams. And it's not very easy to refute him. He is our sceptic; a very important office.'

'I quite understand,' said Jane.

'That applies, of course,' said the Director, 'only to things we don't know yet. You mustn't hear our guesses, you mustn't be there when we're puzzling over the evidence. But we have no secrets from you about the earlier history of our family. In fact MacPhee himself will insist on being the one who tells you all that. He'd be afraid Grace's account, or mine, wouldn't be objective enough.'

'I see.'

'I want you to like him if you can. He's one of my oldest friends. And he'll be about our best man if we're going to be defeated. You couldn't have a better man at your side in a losing battle. What he'll do if we win, I can't imagine.'

◆ ○ ◆

Mark woke next morning to the consciousness that his head ached all over but specially at the back. He remembered that he had fallen – that was how he had hurt his head – fallen in that other room, with Filostrato and Straik … and then, as one of the poets says, he 'discovered in his mind an inflammation swollen and deformed, his memory'. Oh, but impossible, not to be accepted for a moment: it had been a nightmare, it must be shoved away, it would vanish away now that he was fully awake. It was an absurdity. Once in delirium he had seen the front part of a horse, by itself, with no body or hind legs, running across a lawn, had felt it ridiculous at the very moment of seeing it, but not the less horrible for that. This was an absurdity of the same sort. A Head without any body underneath. A Head that could speak when they turned on the air and the artificial saliva with taps in the next room. His own head began to throb so hard that he had to stop thinking.

But he knew it was true. And he could not, as they say, 'take it'. He was very ashamed of this, for he wished to be considered one of the tough ones. But the truth is that his toughness was only of the will, not of the nerves, and the virtues he had almost succeeded in banishing from his mind still lived, if only negatively and as weaknesses, in his body. He approved of vivisection, but had never worked in a dissecting room. He recommended that certain classes of people should be gradually eliminated: but he had never been there when a small shopkeeper went to the workhouse or a starved old woman of the governess type came to the very last day and hour and minute in the cold attic. He knew nothing about the last half cup of cocoa drunk slowly ten days before.

Meantime he must get up. He must do something about Jane. Apparently he would *have* to bring her to Belbury. His mind had made this decision for him at some moment he did not remember. He must get her, to save his life. All his anxieties about being in the

198

inner ring or getting a job had shrunk into insignificance. It was a question of life or death. They would kill him if he annoyed them; perhaps behead him … oh God, if only they would really kill that monstrous little lump of torture, that lump with a face, which they kept there talking on its steel bracket. All the minor fears at Belbury – for he knew now that all except the leaders were always afraid – were only emanations from that central fear. He must get Jane; he wasn't fighting against that now.

It must be remembered that in Mark's mind hardly one rag of noble thought, either Christian or Pagan, had a secure lodging. His education had been neither scientific nor classical – merely 'Modern'. The severities both of abstraction and of high human tradition had passed him by: and he had neither peasant shrewd-ness nor aristocratic honour to help him. He was a man of straw, a glib examinee in subjects that require no exact knowledge (he had always done well on Essays and General Papers) and the first hint of a real threat to his bodily life knocked him sprawling. And his head ached so terribly and he felt so sick. Luckily he now kept a bottle of whisky in his room. A stiff one enabled him to shave and dress.

He was late for breakfast, but that made little difference for he could not eat. He drank several cups of black coffee and then went into the writing room. Here he sat for a long time drawing things on the blotting paper. This letter to Jane proved almost impossible now that it came to the point. And why did they want Jane? Formless fears stirred in his mind. And Jane of all people! Would they take her to the Head? For almost the first time in his life a gleam of something like dis-interested love came into his mind; he wished he had never married her, never dragged her into this whole outfit of horrors which was, apparently, to be his life.

'Hello, Studdock!' said a voice. 'Writing to little wifie, eh?'

'Damn!' said Mark, 'You've made me drop my pen.'

'Then pick it up, Sonny,' said Miss Hardcastle, seating herself on the table. Mark did so, and then sat still without looking up at her. Not since he had been bullied at school had he known what it was to hate and dread anyone with every nerve of his body as he now hated and dreaded this woman.

'I've got bad news for you, Sonny,' she said presently. His heart gave a jump.

'Take it like a man, Studdock,' said the Fairy.

'What is it?'

She did not answer quite at once and he knew she was studying him, watching how the instrument responded to her playing.

'I'm worried about little wifie, and that's a fact,' she said at last.

'What do you mean?' said Mark sharply, this time looking up. The cheroot between her teeth was still unlit but she had got as far as taking out her matches.

'I looked her up,' said Miss Hardcastle, 'all on your account, too. I thought Edgestow wasn't too healthy a place for her to be at present.'

'What's wrong with her?' shouted Mark.

'Ssh!' said Miss Hardcastle. 'You don't want everyone to hear.'

'Can't you tell me what's wrong?'

She waited for a few seconds before replying. 'How much do you know about her family, Studdock?'

'Lots. What's that got to do with it?'

'Nothing … queer … on either side?'

'What the devil do you mean?'

'Don't be rude, Honey. I'm doing all I can for you. It's only – well, I thought she was behaving pretty oddly when I saw her.'

Mark well remembered his conversation with his wife on the morning he left for Belbury. A new stab of fear pierced him. Might not this detestable woman be speaking the truth?

'What did she say?' he asked.

'If there is anything wrong with her in that way,' said the Fairy, 'take my advice, Studdock, and have her over here at once. She'll be properly looked after here.'

'You haven't yet told me what she said or did.'

'I wouldn't like to have anyone belonging to me popped into Edgestow Asylum. Specially now that we're getting our emergency powers. They'll be using the ordinary patients experimentally, you know. Whereas if you'll just sign this form I'll run over after lunch and have her here this evening.'

Mark threw his pen on the desk.

'I shall do nothing of the sort. Specially as you haven't given me the slightest notion what's wrong with her.'

'I've been trying to tell you but you don't let me. She kept on talking about someone who'd broken into your flat – or else met her at the station (one couldn't make out which) and burned her with cigars. Then, most unfortunately, she noticed my cheroot, and, if you please, she identified *me* with this imaginary persecutor. Of course after that I could do not good.'

'I must go home at once,' said Mark getting up.

'Here – whoa! You can't do that,' said the Fairy also rising.

'Can't go home? I've bloody well got to, if all this is true.'

'Don't be a fool, Lovey,' said Miss Hardcastle. 'Honest! I know what I'm talking about. You're in a damn dangerous position already. You'll about do yourself in if you're absent without leave now. Send me. Sign the form. That's the sensible way to do it.'

'But a moment ago you said she couldn't stand you at any price.'

'Oh, that wouldn't make any odds. Of course, it would be easier if she hadn't taken a dislike to me. I say, Studdock, you don't think little wifie could be jealous, do you?'

'Jealous? Of you?' said Mark with uncontrollable disgust.

'Where are you off to?' said the Fairy sharply.

'To see the DD and then home.'

'Stop. You won't do that unless you mean to make me your enemy for life – and let me tell you, you can't afford many more enemies.'

'Oh, go to the devil,' said Mark.

'Come back, Studdock,' shouted the Fairy. 'Wait! Don't be a bloody fool.' But Mark was already in the hall. For the moment everything seemed to have become clear. He would look in on Wither, not to ask for leave but simply to announce that he had to go home at once because his wife was dangerously ill; he would be out of the room before Wither could reply – and then off. The further future was vague, but that did not seem to matter. He put on his hat and coat, ran upstairs and knocked at the door of the Deputy Director's office.

There was no answer. Then Mark noticed that the door was not quite shut. He ventured to push it open a little further and saw the Deputy Director sitting inside with his back to the door. 'Excuse me, Sir,' said Mark. 'Might I speak to you for a few minutes?' There was no answer. 'Excuse me, Sir,' said Mark in a louder voice, but the figure neither spoke nor moved. With some hesitation, Mark went into the room and walked around to the other side of the desk; but when he turned to look at Wither he caught his breath, for he thought he was looking into the face of a corpse. A moment later he recognised his mistake. In the stillness of the room he could hear the man breathing. He was not even asleep, for his eyes were open. He was not unconscious, for his eyes rested momentarily on Mark and then looked away. 'I beg your pardon, Sir,' began Mark and then stopped. The Deputy Director was not listening. He was so far from listening that Mark felt an insane doubt whether he was there at all, whether the soul of the Deputy Director were not floating far away, spreading and dissipating itself like a gas through formless and lightless worlds, waste lands and lumber rooms of the universe. What looked out of those pale watery eyes was, in a sense, infinity – the shapeless and the interminable. The room was still and cold: there was no clock and the fire had gone out. It was impossible to speak to a face like that. Yet it seemed impossible also to get out of the room, for the man had seen him. Mark was afraid; it was so unlike any experience he had ever had before.

When at last Mr Wither spoke, his eyes were not fixed on Mark but on some remote point beyond him, beyond the window, perhaps in the sky.

'I know who it is,' said Wither. 'Your name is Studdock. What do you mean by coming here? You had better have stayed outside. Go away.'

It was then that Mark's nerve suddenly broke. All the slowly mounting fears of the last few days ran together into one fixed determination and a few seconds later he was going downstairs three steps at a time. Then he was crossing the hall. Then he was out, and walking down the drive. Once again, his immediate course seemed quite plain to him. Opposite the entrance was a thick belt of trees pierced by a field path. That path would bring him in half an hour to Courthampton and there he could get a country bus to Edgestow. About the future he did not think at all. Only two things mattered: firstly, to get out of that house, and, secondly, to get back to Jane. He was devoured with a longing for Jane which was physical without being at all sensual: as if comfort and fortitude would flow from her body, as if her very skin would clean away all the filth that seemed to hang about him. The idea that she might be really mad had somehow dropped out of his mind. And he was still young enough to be incredulous of misery. He could not quite rid himself of the belief that if only he made a dash for it the net must somehow break, the sky must clear, and it would all end up with Jane and Mark having tea together as if none of all this had happened.

He was out of the grounds now; he was crossing the road: he had entered a belt of trees. He stopped suddenly. Something impossible was happening. There was a figure before him on the path: a tall, very tall, slightly stooping figure, sauntering and humming a little dreary tune: the Deputy Director himself. And in one moment all that brittle hardihood was gone from Mark's mood. He turned back. He stood in the road; this seemed to him the worst pain that he ever felt. Then, tired, so tired that he felt the weak tears filling his eyes, he walked very slowly back into Belbury.

◆ ○ ◆

Mr MacPhee had a little room on the ground floor at the Manor which he called his office and to which no woman was ever admitted except under his own conduct; and in this tidy but dusty apartment he sat with Jane Studdock shortly before dinner that evening, having invited her there to give her what he called 'a brief, objective outline of the situation'.

'I should premise at the outset, Mrs Studdock,' he said, 'that I have known the Director for a great many years and that for most of his life he was a philologist. I'm not just satisfied myself that philology can be regarded as an exact science, but I mention the fact as a testimony to his general intellectual capacity. And, not to forejudge any issue, I will not say, as I would in ordinary conversation, that he has always been a man of what you might call an imaginative turn. His original name was Ransom.'

'Not Ransom's *Dialect and Semantics*?' said Jane.

'Aye. That's the man,' said MacPhee. 'Well, about six years ago – I have all the dates in a wee book there, but it doesn't concern us at the moment – came his first disappearance. He was clean gone – not a trace of him – for about nine months. I thought he'd most likely been drowned bathing or something of the kind. And then one day what does he do but turn up again in his rooms at Cambridge and go down sick and into hospital for three months more. And he wouldn't say where he'd been except privately to a few friends.'

'Well?' said Jane eagerly.

'He said,' answered MacPhee, producing his snuff-box and laying great emphasis on the word *said*, 'he said he'd been to the planet Mars.'

'You mean he said this … while he was ill?'

'No, no. He says so still. Make what you can of it; that's his story.'

'I believe it,' said Jane.

MacPhee selected a pinch of snuff with as much care as if those particular grains had differed from all the others in his box and spoke before applying them to his nostrils.

'I'm giving you the facts,' he said. 'He told us he'd been to Mars, kidnapped, by Professor Weston and Mr Devine – Lord Feverstone as he now is. And by his own account he'd escaped from them – on Mars, you'll understand – and been wandering about there alone for a bit. Alone.'

'It's uninhabited, I suppose?'

'We have no evidence on that point except his own story. You are doubtless aware, Mrs Studdock, that a man in complete solitude even on this earth – an explorer, for example – gets into very remarkable states of consciousness. I'm told a man might forget his own identity.'

'You mean he might have imagined things on Mars that weren't there?'

'I'm making no comments,' said MacPhee. 'I'm merely recording. By his own accounts there are all kinds of creatures walking about there; that's may be why he has turned his house into a sort of menagerie, but no matter for that. But he also says he met one kind of creature there which specially concerns us at this moment. He called them *eldila*.'

'A kind of animal, do you mean?'

'Did ever you try to define the word Animal, Mrs Studdock?'

'Not that I remember. I meant, were these things … well, intelligent? Could they talk?'

'Aye. They could talk. They were intelligent, for-bye, which is not always the same thing.'

'In fact, these were the Martians?'

'That's just what they weren't, according to his account. They were on Mars but they didn't rightly belong there. He says they are creatures that live in empty space.'

'But there's no air.'

'I'm telling you his story. He says they don't breathe. He said also that they don't reproduce their species and don't die. But you'll observe that even if we assume the rest of his story to be correct this last statement could not rest on observation.'

'What on earth are they like?'

'I'm telling you how he described them.'

'I mean, what do they look like?'

'I'm not just exactly prepared to answer that question,' said MacPhee.

'Are they perfectly *huge*?' said Jane almost involuntarily. MacPhee blew his nose and continued.

'The point, Mrs Studdock,' he said, 'is this: Dr Ransom claims that he has received continual visits from these creatures since he returned to Earth. So much for his first disappearance. Then came the second. He was away for more than a year and that time he said he'd been in the planet Venus – taken there by these *eldila*.'

'Venus is inhabited by them too?'

'You'll forgive me observing that this remark shows you have not grasped what I'm telling you. These creatures are not planetary creatures at all. Supposing them to exist, you are to conceive them floating about the depth of space, though they may alight on a planet here and there, like a bird alighting on a tree, you understand. There's some of them, he says, are more or less permanently attached to particular planets, but they're not native there. They're just a clean different kind of thing.'

There were a few seconds of silence, and then Jane asked, 'They are, I gather, more or less friendly?'

'That is certainly the Director's idea about them, with one important exception.'

'What's that?'

'The *eldila* that have for many centuries concentrated on our own planet. We seem to have had no luck at all in choosing our particular complement of parasites. And that, Mrs Studdock brings me to the point.'

Jane waited. It was extraordinary how MacPhee's manner almost neutralised the strangeness of what he was telling her.

'The long and short of it is,' said he, 'that this house is dominated either by the creatures I'm talking about, or by a sheer delusion. It is by advices he thinks he has received from *eldila* that the Director has discovered the conspiracy against the human race; and what's more, it's on instructions from *eldila* that he's conducting the campaign – if you can call it conducting! It may have occurred to you to wonder, Mrs Studdock, how any man in his senses thinks we're going to defeat a powerful conspiracy by sitting here growing winter vegetables and training performing bears. It is a question I have propounded on more than one occasion. The answer is always the same; we're waiting for orders.'

'From the *eldila*? It was they he meant when he spoke of his Masters?'

'I doubt it would be, though he doesn't use that word in speaking to me.'

'But, Mr MacPhee, I don't understand. I thought you said the ones on our planet were hostile.'

'That's a very good question,' said MacPhee, 'but it's not our own ones that the Director claims to be in communication with. It's his friends from outer space. Our own crew, the terrestrial *eldila*, are at the back of the whole conspiracy. You are to imagine us, Mrs Studdock, living on a world where the criminal classes of the *eldila* have established their headquarters. And what's happening now, if the Director's views are correct, is that their own respectable kith and kin are visiting this planet to red the place up.'

'You mean that the other *eldila* out of space actually come here – to this house?'

'That is what the Director thinks.'

'But you must know whether it's true or not.'

'How?'

'Have you seen them?'

'That's not a question to be answered Aye or No. I've seen a good many things in my time that weren't there or weren't what they were letting on to be: rainbows and reflections and sunsets, not to mention dreams. And there's hetero-suggestion too. I will not deny that I have observed a class of phenomena in this house that I have not yet fully accounted for. But they never occurred at a moment when I had a notebook handy or any facilities for verification.'

'Isn't seeing believing?'

'It may be – for children or beasts,' said MacPhee.

'But not for sensible people, you mean?'

'My uncle, Dr Duncanson,' said MacPhee, 'whose name may be familiar to you – he was Moderator of the General Assembly over the water, in Scotland – used to say, "Show it to me in the word of God." And then he'd slap the big Bible on the table. It was a way he had of shutting up people that came to him blathering about religious experiences. And granting his premises, he was quite right. I don't hold his views, Mrs Studdock, you understand, but I work on the same principles. If anything wants Andrew MacPhee to believe in its existence, I'll be obliged if it will present itself in full daylight, with a sufficient number of witnesses present, and not get shy if you hold up a camera or a thermometer.'

MacPhee regarded his snuff-box meditatively.

'You have seen something, then.'

'Aye. But we must keep an open mind. It might be a hallucination. It might be a conjuring trick …'

'By the Director?' asked Jane angrily. Mr MacPhee once more had recourse to his snuff-box. 'Do you really expect me,' said Jane, 'to believe that the Director is that sort of man? A charlatan?'

'I wish, Ma'am,' said MacPhee, 'you could see your way to consider the matter without constantly using such terms as *believe*. Obviously, conjuring is one of the hypotheses that any impartial investigator must take into account. The fact that it is a hypothesis specially uncongenial to the emotions of this investigator or that, is neither here nor there. Unless, maybe, it is an extra ground for emphasising the hypothesis in question, just because there is a strong psychological danger of neglecting it.'

'There's such a thing as loyalty,' said Jane. MacPhee, who had been carefully shutting up the snuff-box, suddenly looked up with a hundred covenanters in his eyes.

'There is, Ma'am,' he said. 'As you get older you will learn that it is a virtue too important to be lavished on individual personalities.'

At that moment there was a knock at the door. 'Come in,' said MacPhee, and Camilla entered.

'Have you finished with Jane, Mr MacPhee?' she said. 'She promised to come out for a breath of air with me before dinner.'

'Och, breath of air your grandmother!' said MacPhee with a gesture of despair. 'Very well, ladies, very well. Away out to the garden. I doubt they're doing something more to the purpose on the enemy's side. They'll have all this country under their hands before we move, at this rate.'

'I wish you'd read the poem I'm reading,' said Camilla. 'For it says in one line just what I feel about this waiting: *Fool, All lies in a passion of patience, my lord's rule*.'

'What's that from?' asked Jane.

'*Taliessin through Logres*.'

'Mr MacPhee probably approves of no poets except Burns.'

'Burns!' said MacPhee with profound contempt, opening the drawer of his table with great energy and producing a formidable sheaf of papers. 'If you're going to the garden, don't let me delay you, ladies.'

'He's been telling you?' said Camilla, as the two girls went together down the passage. Moved by a kind of impulse which was rare to her experience, Jane seized her friend's hand as she answered, 'Yes!' Both were filled with some passion, but what passion they did not know. They came to the front door and as they opened it a sight met their eyes which, though natural, seemed at the moment apocalyptic.

All day the wind had been rising and they found themselves looking out on a sky swept almost clean. The air was intensely cold, the stars severe and bright. High above the last rags of scurrying clouds hung the Moon in all her wildness – not the voluptuous Moon of a thousand southern love-songs, but the huntress, the untameable virgin, the spear-head of madness. If that cold satellite had just then joined our planet for the first time, it could hardly have looked more like an omen. The wildness crept into Jane's blood.

'That Mr MacPhee … ' said Jane as they walked steeply uphill to the very summit of the garden.

'I know,' said Camilla. And then, '*You* believed it?'

'Of course.'

'How does Mr MacPhee explain the Director's age?'

'You mean his looking – or being – so young – if you call it young?'

'Yes. That is what people are like who come back from the stars. Or at least from Perelandra. Paradise is still going on there; make him tell you about it some time. He will never grow a year or a month older again.'

'Will he die?'

'He will be taken away, I believe. Back into Deep Heaven. It has happened to one or two people, perhaps about six, since the world began.'

'Camilla!'

'Yes.'

'What – what *is* he?'

'He's a man, my dear. And he is the Pendragon of Logres. This house, all of us here, and Mr Bultitude and Pinch, are all that's left of the Logres: all the rest has become merely Britain. Go on. Let's go right to the top. How it's blowing! They might come to him tonight.'

◆   ○   ◆

That evening Jane washed up under the attentive eye of Baron Corvo, the jackdaw, while the others held council in the Blue Room.

'Well,' said Ransom as Grace Ironwood concluded reading from her notes. 'That is the dream, and everything in it seems to be objective.'

'Objective?' said Dimble. 'I don't understand, Sir. You don't mean they could really have a thing like that?'

'What do you think, MacPhee?' asked Ransom.

'Oh aye, it's possible,' said MacPhee. 'You see it's an old experiment with animals' heads. They do it often in laboratories. You cut off a cat's head, maybe, and throw the body away. You can keep the head going a bit if you supply it with blood at the right pressure.'

'Fancy!' said Ivy Maggs.

'Do you mean, keep it *alive*,' said Dimble.

'*Alive* is an ambiguous word. You can keep all the functions. It's what would be popularly called alive. But a human head – and consciousness – I don't know what would happen if you tried that.'

'It has been tried,' said Miss Ironwood. 'A German tried it before the first war. With the head of a criminal.'

'Is that a fact?' said MacPhee with great interest. 'And do you know what result he got?'

'It failed. The head simply decayed in the ordinary way.'

'I've had enough of this, I have,' said Ivy Maggs rising and abruptly leaving the room.

'Then this filthy abomination,' said Dr Dimble, 'is real – not only a dream.' His face was white and his expression strained. His wife's face, on the other hand, showed nothing more than that controlled distaste with which a lady of the old school listens to any disgusting detail when its mention becomes unavoidable.

'We have no evidence of that,' said MacPhee. 'I'm only stating facts. What the girl has dreamed is possible.'

'And what about this turban business,' said Denniston, 'this sort of swelling on top of the head?'

'You see what it *might* be,' said the Director.

'I'm not sure that I do, Sir,' said Dimble.

'Supposing the dream to be veridical,' said MacPhee. 'You can guess what it would be. Once they'd got it kept alive, the first thing that would occur to boys like them would be to increase its brain. They'd try all sorts of stimulants. And then, maybe, they'd ease open the skull-cap and just – well, just let it boil over as you might say. That's the idea, I don't doubt. A cerebral hypertrophy artificially induced to support a superhuman power of ideation.'

'Is it at all probable,' said the Director, 'that a hypertrophy like that would increase thinking power?'

'That seems to me the weak point,' said Miss Ironwood. 'I should have thought it was just as likely to produce lunacy – or nothing at all. But it *might* have the opposite effect.'

There was a thoughtful silence.

'Then what we are up against,' said Dimble, 'is a criminal's brain swollen to super-human proportions and experiencing a mode of consciousness which we can't imagine, but which is presumably a consciousness of agony and hatred.'

'It's not certain,' said Miss Ironwood, 'that there would be very much actual pain. Some from the neck, perhaps, at first.'

'What concerns us much more immediately,' said MacPhee, 'is to determine what conclusions we can draw from these carryings on with Alcasan's head and what practical steps should be taken on our part – always and simply as a working hypothesis, assuming the dream to be veridical.'

'It tells us one thing straight away,' said Denniston.

'What's that?' asked MacPhee.

'That the enemy movement is international. To get that head they must have been hand in glove with at least one foreign police force.'

MacPhee rubbed his hands. 'Man,' he said, 'you have the makings of a logical thinker. But the deduction's not all that certain. Bribery might account for it without actual consolidation.'

'It tells us something in the long run even more important,' said the Director. 'It means that if this technique is really successful, the Belbury people have for all practical purposes discovered a way of making themselves immortal.' There was a moment's silence, and then he continued: 'It is the beginning of what is really a new species – the Chosen Heads who never die. They will call it the next step in evolution. And henceforward, all the creatures that you and I call human are mere candidates for admission to the new species or else its slaves – perhaps its food.'

'The emergence of the Bodiless Men!' said Dimble.

'Very likely, very likely,' said MacPhee, extending his snuff-box to the last speaker. It was refused and he took a very deliberate pinch before proceeding. 'But there's no good at all applying the forces of rhetoric to make ourselves skeery or daffing our own heads off our shoulders because some other fellows have had the shoulders taken from under their heads. I'll back the Director's Head, and yours, Dr Dimble, and my own, against this lad's whether the brains is boiling out of it or no. Provided we use them.

I should be glad to hear what practical measures on our side are suggested.'

With these words he tapped his knuckles gently on his knee and stared hard at the Director.

'It is,' said MacPhee, 'a question I have ventured to propound before.'

A sudden transformation, like the leaping up of a flame in embers, passed over Grace Ironwood's face. 'Can the Director not be trusted to produce his own plan in his own time, Mr MacPhee?' she said fiercely.

'By the same token, Doctor,' said he, 'can the Director's council not be trusted to hear his plan?'

'What do you mean, MacPhee?' asked Dimble.

'Mr Director,' said MacPhee. 'You'll excuse me for speaking frankly. Your enemies have provided themselves with this Head. They have taken possession of Edgestow and they're in a fair way to suspend the laws of England. And still you tell us it is not time to move. If you had taken my advice six months ago we would have had an organisation all over this island by now and maybe a party in the House of Commons. I know well what you'll say – that those are not the right methods. And maybe no. But if you can neither take our advice nor give us anything to do, what are we all sitting here for? Have you seriously considered sending us away and getting some other colleagues that you *can* work with?'

'Dissolve the Company, do you mean?' said Dimble.

'Aye, I do,' said MacPhee.

The Director looked up with a smile. 'But,' he said, 'I have no power to dissolve it.'

'In that case,' said MacPhee, 'I must ask what authority you had to bring it together?'

'I never brought it together,' said the Director. Then, after glancing round the company he added: 'There is some strange misunderstanding here! Were you all under the impression I had *selected* you?'

'Were you?' he repeated, when no one answered.

'Well,' said Dimble, 'as regards myself I fully realise that the thing has come about more or less unconsciously ... even accidentally. There was no moment at which you asked me to join a definite movement, or anything of that kind. That is why I have always regarded myself as a sort of camp follower. I had assumed that the others were in a more regular position.'

'You know why Camilla and I are here, Sir,' said Denniston. 'We certainly didn't intend or foresee how we were going to be employed.'

Grace Ironwood looked up with a set expression on her face which had grown rather pale. 'Do you wish ...?' she began.

The Director laid his hand on her arm. 'No,' he said, 'No. There is no need for all these stories to be told.'

MacPhee's stern features relaxed into a broad grin. 'I see what you're driving at,' he said. 'We've all been playing blind man's buff, I doubt. But I'll take leave to observe, Dr Ransom, that you carry things a wee bit high. I don't just remember how you came to be called Director: but from that title and from one or two other indications a man would have thought you behaved more like the leader of an organisation than the host at a house-party.'

'I am the Director,' said Ransom, smiling. 'Do you think I would claim the authority I do if the relation between us depended either on your choice or mine? You never chose me. I never chose you. Even the great Oyéresu whom I serve never chose me. I came into their worlds by what seemed, at first, a chance; as you came to me – as the very animals in this house first came to it. You and I have not started or devised this: it has descended on us – sucked us into itself, if you like. It is, no doubt, an organisation: but we are not the organisers. And that is why I have no authority to give any one of you permission to leave my household.'

For a time there was complete silence in the Blue Room, except for the crackling of the fire.

'If there is nothing more to discuss,' said Grace Ironwood presently, 'perhaps we had better leave the Director to rest.'

MacPhee rose and dusted some snuff off the baggy knees of his trousers – thus preparing a wholly novel adventure for the mice when they next came out in obedience to the Director's whistle.

'I have no notion,' he said, 'of leaving this house if anyone wishes me to stay. But as regards the general hypothesis on which the Director appears to be acting and the very peculiar authority he claims, I absolutely reserve my judgment. You know well, Mr Director, in what sense I have, and in what sense I have not, complete confidence in yourself.'

The Director laughed. 'Heaven forbid,' he said, 'that I should claim to know what goes on in the two halves of your head, MacPhee, much less how you connect them. But I know (what matters much more) the kind of confidence I have in you. But won't you sit down? There is much more to be said.'

MacPhee resumed his chair; Grace Ironwood, who had been sitting bolt upright in hers, relaxed; and the Director spoke.

'We have learned tonight,' he said, 'if not what the real power behind our enemies is doing, at least the form in which it is embodied at Belbury. We therefore know something about one of the two attacks which are about to be made on our race. But I'm thinking of the other.'

'Yes,' said Camilla earnestly. 'The other.'

'Meaning by that?' asked MacPhee.

'Meaning,' said Ransom, 'whatever is under Bragdon Wood.'

'You're still thinking about *that*?' said the Ulsterman.

A moment of silence ensued.

'I am thinking of almost nothing else,' said the Director. 'We knew already that the enemy wanted the wood. Some of us guessed why. Now Jane has seen – or rather felt – in a vision what it is they are looking for in Bragdon. It may be the greater danger of the two. But what is certain is that the greatest danger of all is the junction of the enemies' forces. He is staking everything on that. When the new power from Belbury joins up with the old power under Bragdon Wood, Logres – indeed Man – will be almost surrounded. For us everything turns on preventing that junction. That is the point at which we must be ready both to kill and die. But we cannot strike yet. We cannot get into Bragdon and start excavating for ourselves. There must be a moment when they find him – it. I have no doubt we shall be told in one way or another. Till then we must wait.'

'I don't believe a word of all that other story,' said MacPhee.

'I thought,' said Miss Ironwood, 'we weren't to use words like *believe*. I thought we were only to state facts and exhibit implications.'

'If you two quarrel much more,' said the Director, 'I think I'll make you marry one another.'

◆ ○ ◆

At the beginning the grand mystery for the Company had been why the enemy wanted Bragdon Wood. The land was unsuitable and could be made fit to bear a building on the scale they proposed only by the costliest preliminary work; and Edgestow itself was not an obviously convenient place. By intense study in collaboration with Dr Dimble, and despite the continued scepticism of MacPhee, the Director had at last come to a certain conclusion. Dimble and he and the Dennistons shared between them a knowledge of Arthurian Britain which orthodox scholarship will probably not reach for some centuries. They knew that Edgestow lay in what had been the very heart of ancient Logres, that the village of Cure Hardy preserved the name of Ozana le Coeur Hardi, and that a historical Merlin had once worked in what was now Bragdon Wood.

What exactly he had done there they did not know; but they had all, by various routes, come too far either to consider his art mere legend and imposture, or to equate it exactly with what the Renaissance called Magic. Dimble even maintained that a good critic, by his sensibility alone, could detect the difference between the traces which the two things had left on literature. 'What common measure is there,' he would ask, 'between ceremonial occultists like Faustus and Prospero and Archimago with their midnight studies, their forbidden books, their attendant fiends or elementals, and a figure like Merlin who seems to produce his results simply by being Merlin?' And Ransom agreed. He thought that Merlin's art was the last survival of something older and different – something brought to Western Europe after the fall of Numinor and going back to an era in which the general relations of mind and matter on this planet had been other than those we know. It had probably differed from Renaissance Magic profoundly. It had possibly (though this was doubtful) been less guilty: it had certainly been more effective. For Paracelsus and Agrippa and the rest had achieved little or nothing: Bacon himself – no enemy to magic except on this account – reported that the magicians 'attained not to greatness and certainty of works'. The whole Renaissance outburst of forbidden arts had, it seemed, been a method of losing one's soul on singularly unfavourable terms. But the older Art had been a different proposition.

But if the only possible attraction of Bragdon lay in its association with the last vestiges of Atlantean magic, this told the Company something else. It told them that the NICE, at its core, was not concerned solely with modern or materialistic forms of power. It told the Director, in fact, that there was eldilic energy and eldilic knowledge behind it. It was, of course, another question whether its human members knew of the dark powers who were their real organisers. And in the long run this question was not perhaps important. As Ransom himself had said more than once, 'Whether they know it or whether they don't, much the same sort of things are going to happen. It's not a question of how the Belbury people are going to act (the dark-*eldila* will see to that) but of how they will think about their actions. They'll go to Bragdon: it remains to be seen whether any of them will know the real reason why they're going there, or whether they'll all fudge up some theory of soils, or air, or etheric tensions, to explain it.'

Up to a certain point the Director had supposed that the powers for which the enemy hankered were resident in the mere site at Bragdon – for there is an old and wide-spread belief that locality itself is of importance in such matters. But from Jane's dream of the cold sleeper he had learned better. It was something much more definite, something located under the soil of Bragdon Wood, something to be discovered by digging. It was, in fact the body of Merlin. What the *eldila* had told him about the possibility of such discovery he had received, while they were with him, almost without wonder. It was no wonder to them. In their eyes the normal Tellurian modes of being – engendering and birth and death and decay – which are to use the framework of thought, were no less wonderful than the countless other patterns of being which were continually present to their unsleeping minds. To those high creatures whose activity builds what we call Nature, nothing is 'natural'. From their station the essential arbitrariness (so to call it) of every actual creation is ceaselessly visible; for them there are no basic assumptions: all springs with the willful beauty of a jest or a tune from that miraculous moment of self-limitation wherein the Infinite, rejecting a myriad possibilities, throws out of Himself the positive and elected invention. That a body should lie uncorrupted for fifteen hundred years, did not seem strange to them; they knew worlds where there was no corruption at all. That its individual life should remain latent in it all that time, was to them no more strange: they had seen innumerable different modes in which soul and matter could be combined and separated, separated without loss of reciprocal influence, combined without true incarnation, fused so utterly as to be a third thing, or periodically brought together in a union as short, and as momentous, as the nuptial embrace. It was not as a marvel in natural philosophy, but as an information in time of war, that they brought the Director their tidings. Merlin had not died. His life had been hidden, sidetracked, moved out of our one-dimensioned time, for fifteen centuries. But under certain conditions it would return to his body.

They had not told him this till recently because they had not known it. One of Ransom's greatest difficulties in disputing with MacPhee (who consistently professed to disbelieve the very existence of the *eldila*) was that MacPhee made the common, but curious assumption that if there are creatures wiser and stronger than man they must be forthwith omniscient and omnipotent. In vain did Ransom endeavor to explain the truth. Doubtless, the great beings who now so often came to him had power sufficient to sweep Belbury from the face of England and England from the face of the globe; perhaps, to blot the globe itself out of existence. But no power of that kind would be used. Nor had they any direct vision into the minds of men. It was in a different place, and approaching their knowledge from the other side, that they had discovered the state of Merlin: not from inspection of the thing that slept under Bragdon Wood, but from observing a certain unique configuration in that place where those things remain that are taken off time's mainroad, behind the invisible hedges, into the unimaginable fields. Not all the times that are outside the present are therefore past or future.

It was this that kept the Director wakeful, with knitted brow, in the small cold hours of that morning when the others had left him. There was no doubt in his mind now that the enemy had bought Bragdon to find Merlin: and if they found him they would re-awake him. The old druid would inevitably cast his lot with the new planners – what could prevent his doing so? A junction would be effected between two kinds of power which between them would determine the fate of our planet. Doubtless that had been the will of the dark-*eldila* for centuries. The physical sciences, good and innocent in themselves, had already, even in Ransom's own time, begun to be warped, had been subtly manœuvred in a certain direction. Despair of objective truth had been increasingly insinuated into the scientists; indifference to it, and a concentration upon mere power, had been the result. Babble about the *élan vital* and flirtations with panpsychism were bidding fair to restore the *Anima Mundi* of the magicians. Dreams of the far future destiny of man were dragging up from its shallow and unquiet grave the old dream of Man as God. The very experiences of the dissecting room and the pathological laboratory were breeding a conviction that the stifling of all deep-set repugnances was the first essential for progess. And now, all this had reached the stage at which its dark contrivers thought they could safely begin to bend it back so that it would meet that other and earlier kind of power. Indeed they were choosing the first moment at which this could have been done. You could not have done it with nineteenth-century scientists. Their firm objective materialism would have excluded it from their minds; and even if they could have been made to believe, their inherited morality would have kept them from touching dirt. MacPhee was a survivor from that tradition. It was different now. Perhaps few or none of the people at Belbury knew what was happening; but once it happened, they would be like straw in fire. What should they find incredible, since they believed no longer in a rational universe? What should they regard as too obscene, since they held that all morality was a mere subjective by-product of the physical and economic situations of men? The time was ripe. From the point of view which is accepted in Hell, the whole history of our Earth had led up to this moment. There was now at last a real chance for fallen Man to shake off that limitation of his powers which mercy had imposed upon him as a protection from the full results of his fall. If this succeeded, Hell would be at last incarnate. Bad men, while still in the body, still crawling on this little globe, would enter that state which, heretofore, they had entered only after death, would have the diuturnity and power of evil spirits. Nature, all over the globe of Tellus, would become their slave; and of that dominion no end, before the end of time itself, could be certainly foreseen.

· 10 ·

The Conquered City

Up till now, whatever his days had been like, Mark had usually slept well; this night sleep failed him. He had not written to Jane; he had spent the day keeping out of sight and doing nothing in particular. The wakeful night moved all his fears onto a new level. He was, of course, a materialist in theory; and (also in theory) he was past the age at which one can have night fears. But now, as the wind rattled his window hour after hour, he felt those old terrors again: the old exquisite thrill, as of cold fingers delicately travelling down his back. Materialism is in fact no protection. Those who seek it in that hope (they are not a negligible class) will be disappointed. The thing you fear is impossible. Well and good. Can you therefore cease to fear it? Not here and now. And what then? If you must see ghosts, it is better not to disbelieve in them.

He was called earlier than usual, and with his tea came a note. The Deputy Director sent his compliments and must ask Mr Studdock to call on him *instantly* about a most urgent and distressing matter. Mark dressed and obeyed.

In Wither's room he found Wither and Miss Hardcastle. To Mark's surprise and (momentarily) to his relief, Wither showed no recollection of their last meeting. Indeed, his manner was genial, even deferential, though extremely grave.

'Good morning, good morning, Mr Studdock,' he said. 'It is with the greatest regret that I – er – in short, I would not have kept you from your breakfast unless I had felt that in your own interests you should be placed in full possession of the facts at the earliest possible moment. You will, of course, regard all that I am about to say as strictly confidential. The matter is a distressing or at least an embarrassing one. I feel sure that as the conversation proceeds (pray be seated, Mr Studdock) you will realise in your present situation how very wise we have been in securing from the outset a police force – to give it that rather unfortunate name – of our own.'

Mark licked his lips and sat down.

'My reluctance to raise the question,' continued Wither, 'would however be very much more serious if I did not feel able to assure you – in *advance*, you understand – of the complete confidence which we all feel in you and which I very much hoped' (here for the first time he looked Mark in the eyes) 'you were beginning to reciprocate. We regard ourselves here as being so many brothers and – er sisters: so that whatever passes between us in this room can be regarded as confidential in the fullest possible sense of the word, and I take it we shall all feel entitled to discuss the subject I am about to mention in the most human and informal manner possible.'

Miss Hardcastle's voice, suddenly breaking in, had an effect not wholly unlike that of a pistol shot.

'You have lost your wallet, Studdock,' she said.

'My – my wallet?' said Mark.

'Yes. Wallet. Pocketbook. Thing you keep notes and letters in.'

'Yes. I have. Have you found it?'

'Does it contain three pounds ten, counterfoil of postal order for five shillings, letters from a woman signing herself Myrtle, from the Bursar of Bracton, from G. Hernshaw, F. A. Browne, M. Belcher, and a bill for a dress suit from Simonds and Son, 32a Market Street, Edgestow?'

'Well, more or less so.'

'There it is,' said Miss Hardcastle pointing to the table. 'No, you don't!' she added as Mark made a step towards it.

'What on earth is all this about?' said Mark. His tone was that which I think almost any man would have used in the circumstances but which policemen are apt to describe as 'blustering'.

'None of that,' said Miss Hardcastle. 'This wallet was found in the grass beside the road about five yards away from Hingest's body.'

'My God!' said Studdock. 'You don't mean … the thing's absurd.'

'There's no use appealing to *me*,' said Miss Hardcastle. 'I'm not a solicitor, nor a jury, nor a judge. I'm only a policewoman. I'm telling you the facts.'

'Do I understand that I'm suspected of murdering Hingest?'

'I don't really think,' said the Deputy Director, 'that you need have the slightest apprehension that there is, at this stage, any radical difference between your colleagues and yourself as to the light in which this very painful matter should be regarded. The question is really a constitutional one –'

'Constitutional?' said Mark angrily. 'If I understand her, Miss Hardcastle is accusing me of murder.'

Wither's eyes looked at him as if from an infinite distance.

'Oh,' said he, 'I don't really think that does justice to Miss Hardcastle's position. That element in the Institute which she represents would be strictly *ultra vires* in doing anything of the kind within the NICE – supposing, but purely of course for purposes of argument, that they wished, or should wish at a later stage, to do so – while in relation to the outside authorities their function, however we define it, would be quite inconsistent with any action of the sort; at least, in the sense in which I understand you to be using the words.'

'But it's the outside authorities with whom I'm concerned, I suppose,' said Mark. His mouth had become dry and he had difficulty in making himself audible. 'As far as I can understand, Miss Hardcastle means I'm going to be arrested.'

'On the contrary,' said Wither. 'This is precisely one of those cases in which you see the enormous value of possessing our own executive. Here is a matter which might, I fear, cause you very considerable inconvenience if the ordinary police had discovered the wallet or if we were in the position of an ordinary citizen who felt it his duty – as we should ourselves feel it our duty if we ever came to be in that very different situation – to hand over the wallet to them. I do not know if Miss Hardcastle has made it perfectly clear to you that it was her officers, and they only, who have made this – er – embarrassing discovery.'

'What on earth do you mean?' said Mark. 'If Miss Hardcastle does not think there's a *prima facie* case against me, why am I being arraigned in this way at all? And if she does, how can she avoid informing the authorities?'

'My dear friend,' said Wither in an antediluvian tone, 'there is not the slightest desire on the part of the Committee to insist on defining, in cases of this sort, the powers of action of our own police, much less (what is here in question) their powers of inaction. I do not think anyone had suggested that Miss Hardcastle should be *obliged* – in any sense that limited her own initiative – to communicate to outside authorities, who by their very organisation must be supposed to be less adapted for dealing with such imponderable and quasi-technical inquiries as will often arise, any facts acquired by her and her staff in the course of their internal functioning within the NICE.'

'Do I understand,' said Mark, 'that Miss Hardcastle thinks she has facts justifying my arrest for the murder of Mr Hingest, but is kindly offering to suppress them?'

'You got it now, Studdock,' said the Fairy. A moment later for the first time in Mark's experience, she actually lit her cheroot, blew a cloud of smoke, and smiled, or at least drew back her lips so that the teeth became visible.

'But that's not what I want,' said Mark. This was not quite true. The idea of having the thing hushed up in any way and on almost any terms when it first presented itself a few seconds ago had come like air to one suffocating. But something like citizenship was still alive in him and he proceeded, almost without noticing this emotion, to follow a different line. 'I don't want that,' he said, speaking rather too loud. 'I'm an innocent man. I think I'd better go to the police – the *real* police, I mean – at once.'

'If you *want* to be tried for your life,' said the Fairy, 'that's another matter.'

'I want to be vindicated,' said Mark. 'The charge would fall to pieces at once. There was no conceivable motive. And I have an *alibi*. Everyone knows I slept here that night.'

'Really?' said the Fairy.

'What do you mean?' said Mark.

'There's always a *motive*, you know,' said she. 'For anyone murdering anyone. The police are only human. When the machinery's started they naturally want a conviction.'

Mark assured himself he was not frightened. If only Wither didn't keep all his windows shut and then have a roaring fire!

'There's a letter you wrote,' said the Fairy.

'What letter?'

'A letter to a Mr Pelham, of your own College, dated six weeks ago, in which you say, "I wish Bill the Blizzard could be moved to a better world."'

Like a sharp physical pain the memory of that scribbled note came back to Mark. It was the sort of silly jocularity one used in the Progressive Element – the kind of thing that might be said a dozen times a day in Bracton about an opponent or even about a bore.

'How does that letter come to be in your hands?' said Mark.

'I think, Mr Studdock,' said the Deputy Director, 'it would be very improper to suggest that Miss Hardcastle should give any kind of exposition – in detail, I mean – of the actual working of the Institutional Police. In saying this, I do not mean for one moment to deny that the fullest possible confidence between all the members of the NICE is one of the most valuable characteristics it can have, and, indeed, a *sine qua non* of that really concrete and organic life which we expect it to develop. But there are necessarily certain spheres – not sharply defined, of course, but inevitably revealing themselves in response to the environment and obedience to the indwelling *ethos* or dialectic of the whole – in which a confidence that involved the verbal interchange of facts would – er – would defeat its own end.'

'You don't suppose,' said Mark, 'that anyone could take that letter to be meant seriously?'

'Ever tried to make a policeman understand anything?' said the Fairy. 'I mean what you call a *real* policeman.'

Mark said nothing.

'And I don't think the *alibi* is specially good,' said the Fairy. 'You were seen talking to Bill at dinner. You were seen going out of the front door with him when he left. You were not seen coming back. Nothing is known of your movements till breakfast time next morning. If you had gone with him by car to the scene of the murder you would have had ample time to walk back and go to bed by about two fifteen. Frosty night, you know. No reason why your shoes should have been specially muddy or anything of that sort.'

'If I might pick up a point made by Miss Hardcastle,' said Wither, 'this is a very good illustration of the immense importance of the Institutional Police. There are so many fine shades involved which it would be unreasonable to expect the ordinary authorities to understand but which, so long as they remain, so to speak, in our own family circle (I look upon the NICE, Mr Studdock, as one great family) need develop no tendency to lead to any miscarriage of justice.'

Owing to some mental confusion, which had before now assailed him in dentists' operating rooms and in the studies of Headmasters, Mark began almost to identify the situation which seemed to be imprisoning him with his literal imprisonment by the four walls of that hot room. If only he could once get out of it, on any terms, out into the free air and sunlight, away over the countryside, away from the recurrent creak of the Deputy Director's collar and the red stains on the end of Miss Hardcastle's cheroot and the picture of the King which hung above the fireplace!

'You really advise me, Sir,' he said, 'not to go to the police?'

'To the police?' said Wither as if this idea were completely new. 'I don't think, Mr Studdock, that any one had quite contemplated your taking any irrevocable action of that sort. It might even be argued that by such an action you would be guilty – unintentionally guilty, I hasten to add – of some degree of disloyalty to your colleagues and specially to Miss Hardcastle. You would, of course be placing yourself outside our protection …'

'That's the point, Studdock,' said the Fairy. 'Once you are in the hands of the police you are in the hands of the police.'

The moment of Mark's decision had passed by him without his noticing it.

'Well,' he said, 'what do you propose to do?'

'Me?' said the Fairy. 'Sit tight. It's lucky for you that it was we and not some outsider who found the wallet.'

'Not only fortunate for – er – Mr Studdock,' added Wither gently, 'but for the whole NICE. We could not have been indifferent …'

'There's only one snag,' said the Fairy, 'and that is that we haven't got your letter to Pelham. Only a copy. But with any luck, nothing will come of that.'

'Then there's nothing to be done at present?' said Mark.

'No,' said Wither. 'No. No immediate action of any official character. It is, of course, very advisable that you should act, as I am sure you will, with the greatest prudence and – er – er – caution for the next few months. As long as you are with us, Scotland Yard would, I feel, see the inconvenience of trying to act unless they had a very clear case indeed. It is no doubt probable that some – er – some trial of strength between the ordinary executive and our own organisation will take place within the next six months; but I think it very unlikely they would choose to make this a test case.'

Wither's attitude was paternal.

'But do you mean they suspect me already?' said Mark.

'We'll hope not,' said the Fairy. 'Of course, they want a prisoner – that's only natural. But they'd a damn sight rather have one who doesn't involve them in searching the premises of the NICE.'

'But look here, damn it!' said Mark. 'Aren't you hoping to catch the thief in a day or two? Aren't you going to do *anything*?'

'The thief?' said Wither. 'There has been no suggestion so far that the body was rifled.'

'I mean the thief who stole my wallet.'

'Oh – ah – your wallet,' said the other very gently stroking his refined, handsome face. 'I see. I understand, do I, that you are advancing a charge of theft against some person or persons unknown –'

'But good God!' shouted Mark. 'Were you not assuming that someone stole it? Do you think I was there myself? Do *you* both think I am a murderer?'

'Please!' said the Deputy Director. 'Please, Mr Studdock, you really must not shout. Quite apart from the indiscretion of it, I must remind you that you are in the presence of a lady. As far as I can remember, nothing has been said on our side about murder, and no charge of any sort has been made. My only anxiety is to make perfectly clear what we are all doing. There are, of course, certain lines of conduct and a certain mode of procedure which it would be theoretically possible for you to adopt and which would make it very difficult for us to continue the discussion. I am sure Miss Hardcastle agrees with me.'

'It's all one to me,' said the Fairy. 'Why Studdock should start bellowing at us because we are trying to keep him out of the dock, I don't know. But that's for him to decide. I've got a busy day and don't want to hang about here all morning.'

'Really,' said Mark, 'I should have thought it was excusable to …'

'Pray compose yourself, Mr Studdock,' said Wither. 'As I said before, we look upon ourselves as one family and nothing like a formal apology is required. We all understand one another and all dislike – er – scenes. I might perhaps be allowed to mention, in the friendliest possible manner, that any instability of temperament would be viewed by the Committee as – well, as not very favourable to the confirmation of your appointment. We are all speaking, of course, in the strictest confidence.'

Mark was far past bothering about the job for its own sake;

but he realised that the threat of dismissal was now a threat of hanging.

'I'm sorry if I was rude,' he said at last. 'What do you advise me to do?'

'Don't put your nose outside Belbury, Studdock,' said the Fairy.

'I do not think Miss Hardcastle could have given you better advice,' said Wither. 'And now that Mrs Studdock is going to join you here, this temporary captivity – I am using that word, you will understand, in a metaphorical sense – will not be a serious hardship. You must look upon this as your *home*, Mr Studdock.'

'Oh … that reminds me, Sir,' said Mark. 'I'm not really quite sure about having my wife here. As a matter of fact, she's not in very good health –'

'But surely, in that case, you must be all the more anxious to have her here?'

'I don't believe it would suit her, Sir.'

The DD's eyes wandered and his voice became lower.

'I had almost forgotten, Mr Studdock,' he said, 'to congratulate you on your introduction to our Head. It marks an important transition in your career. We all now feel that you are really one of us in a deeper sense. I am sure nothing is further from your intention than to repel the friendly – the almost fatherly – concern he feels about you. He is very anxious to welcome Mrs Studdock among us at the earliest opportunity.'

'Why?' said Mark suddenly.

Wither looked at Mark with an indescribable smile.

'My dear boy,' he said. 'Unity, you know. The family circle. She'd – she'd be company for Miss Hardcastle!' Before Mark had recovered from this staggeringly new conception, Wither rose and shuffled towards the door. He paused with one hand on the handle and laid the other on Mark's shoulder.

'You must be hungry for your breakfast,' he said. 'Don't let me delay you. Behave with the greatest caution. And – and –' here his face suddenly changed. The widely opened mouth looked all at once like the mouth of some enraged animal: what had been the senile vagueness of the eyes became an absence of all specifically human expression. 'And bring the girl. Do you understand? Get your wife,' he added. 'The Head ... he's not patient.'

◆ ○ ◆

As Mark closed the door behind him he immediately thought 'Now! They're both in there together. Safe for a minute at least.' Without even waiting to get his hat, he walked briskly to the front door and down the drive. Nothing but physical impossibility would stop him from going to Edgestow and warning Jane. After that he had no plans. Even the vague idea of escaping to America which, in a simpler age, comforted so many a fugitive, was denied him. He had already read in the papers the warm approval of the NICE and all its works which came from the United States and from Russia. Some poor tool just like himself had written them. Its claws were embedded in every country: on the liner, if he should ever succeed in sailing; on the tender, if he should ever make some foreign port; its ministers would be waiting for him.

Now he was past the road; he was in the belt of trees. Scarcely a minute had passed since he had left the DD's office and no one had overtaken him. But yesterday's adventure was happening over again. A tall, stooped, shuffling, creaking figure, humming a tune, barred his way. Mark had never fought. Ancestral impulses lodged in his body – that body which was in so many ways wiser than his mind – directed the blow which he aimed at the head of his senile obstructor. But there was no impact. The shape had suddenly vanished.

Those who know best were never fully agreed as to the explanation of this episode. It may have been that Mark, both then and on the previous day, being overwrought, saw a hallucination of Wither where Wither was not. It may be that the continual appearance of Wither which at almost all hours haunted so many rooms and corridors of Belbury was (in one well-verified sense of the word) a ghost – one of those sensory impressions which a strong personality in its last decay can imprint, most commonly after death but sometimes before it, on the very structure of a building, and which are removed not by exorcism but by architectural alterations. Or it may, after all, be that souls who have lost the intellectual good do indeed receive in return, and for a short period, the vain privilege of thus reproducing themselves in many places as wraiths. At any rate the thing, whatever it was, vanished.

The path ran diagonally across a field in grass, now powdered with frost, and the sky was hazy blue. Then came a stile; after that the path ran for three fields along the edge of a spinney. Then a little to the left, past the back parts of a farm, then along a ride through a wood. After that the spire of Courthampton was in sight; Mark's feet had now got warm and he was beginning to feel hungry. Then he went across a road, through a herd of cattle that put down their heads and snorted at him, across a stream by a foot bridge, and so into the frozen ruts of the lane that led him into Courthampton.

The first thing he saw as he came into the village street was a farm cart. A woman and three children sat beside the man who was driving it and in the cart were piled chests of drawers, bedsteads, mattresses, boxes, and a canary in a cage. Immediately after it came a man and woman and child on foot wheeling a perambulator; it also was piled with small household property. After that came a family pushing a handcart, and then a heavily loaded trap, and then an old car, blowing its horn incessantly but unable to get out of its place in the procession. A steady stream of such traffic was passing through the village. Mark had never seen war: if he had he would have recognised at once the signs of flight. In all those plodding horses and men and in all those loaded vehicles he would have read clearly the message, 'Enemy behind.'

The traffic was so continuous that it took him a long time to get to the crossroads by the pub where he could find a glazed and framed table of busses. There would not be one to Edgestow till twelve fifteen. He hung about, understanding nothing of what he saw, but wondering; Courthampton was normally a very quiet village. By a happy, and not uncommon illusion he felt less endangered now that Belbury was out of sight, and thought surprisingly little about his future. He thought sometimes about Jane, and sometimes about bacon and eggs, and fried fish, and dark, fragrant streams of coffee pouring into large cups. At eleven thirty the pub opened. He went in and ordered a pint and some bread and cheese.

The bar was at first empty. During the next half hour men dropped in one by one till about four were present. They did not at first talk about the unhappy procession which continued all this time to pass the windows. For some time indeed they did not talk at all. Then a very little man with a face like an old potato observed to no one in particular, 'I seen old Rumbold the other night.' No one replied for five minutes and then a very young man in leggings said, 'I reckon he's sorry he ever tried it.' In this way conversation about Rumbold trickled on for some time. It was only when the subject of Rumbold was thoroughly exhausted that the talk, very indirectly and by gradual stages, began to throw some light on the stream of refugees.

'Still coming out,' said one man.

'Ah,' said another.

'Can't be many left there by now.'

'Don't know where they'll all get in, I'm sure.'

Little by little the whole thing came out. These were the refugees from Edgestow. Some had been turned out of their houses, some scared by the riots and still more by the restoration of order. Something like a terror appeared to have been established in the town. 'They tell me there were two hundred arrests yesterday,' said the landlord. 'Ah,' said the young man. 'They're hard cases, those NICE police, every one of them. They put the wind up my old Dad proper, I tell 'ee.' He ended with a laugh. ''Taint the police so much as the workmen by what I hear,' said another. 'They never ought to have brought those Welsh and Irish.' But that was about as far as the criticism went. What struck Mark deeply was the almost complete absence of indignation among the speakers, or even of any distinct sympathy with the refugees. Everyone present knew of at least one outrage in Edgestow; but all agreed that these refugees must be greatly exaggerating. 'It says in this morning's paper that things are pretty well settling down,' said the landlord. 'That's right,' agreed the others. 'There'll always be some who get awkward,' said the potato-faced man. 'What's the good of getting awkward?' asked another, 'it's got to go on. You can't stop it.' 'That's what I say,' said the Landlord. Fragments of articles which Mark himself had written drifted to and fro. Apparently he and his kind had done their work well; Miss Hardcastle had rated too high the resistance of the working classes to propaganda.

When the time came he had no difficulty in getting onto the bus: it was indeed empty for all the traffic was going in the opposite direction. It put him down at the top of Market Street and he set out at once to walk up to the flat. The whole town wore a new expression. One house out of three was empty. About half the shops had their windows boarded up. As he gained height and came into the region of large villas with gardens, he noticed that many of these had been requisitioned and bore white placards with the NICE symbol – a muscular male nude grasping a thunderbolt. At every corner, and often in between, lounged or sauntered the NICE police, helmeted, swinging their clubs, with revolvers in holsters on their black shiny belts. Their round, white faces with open mouths slowly revolving as they chewed gum remained long in his memory. There were also notices everywhere which he did not stop to read: they were headed *Emergency Regulations* and bore the signature, Feverstone.

Would Jane be in? He felt he could not bear it if Jane should not be in. He was fingering his latchkey in his pocket long before he reached the house. The front door was locked. This meant that the Hutchinsons who occupied the ground floor were away. He opened it and went in. It seemed cold and damp on the staircase: cold and damp and dark on the landing. 'Ja-ane,' he shouted as he unlocked the door of the flat; but he had already lost hope. As soon as he was inside the door he knew the place was uninhabited. A pile of unopened letters lay on the inside door mat. There was no sound, not a tick of a clock. Everything was in order: Jane must have left some morning immediately after 'doing' all the rooms. The tea cloths hanging in the kitchen were bone dry: they clearly had not been used for at least twenty-four hours. The bread in the cupboard was stale. There was a jug half full of milk, but the milk had thickened and would not pour. He continued stumping from room to room long after he was quite certain of the truth, staring at the staleness and pathos which pervades deserted homes. But obviously it was no good hanging about here. A splutter of unreasonable anger arose. Why the hell hadn't Jane told him she was going away? Or had someone taken her away? Perhaps there was a note for him. He took a pile of letters off the mantlepiece, but they were only letters he had put there himself to be answered. Then on the table he noticed an envelope addressed to Mrs Dimble at her own house over beyond the Wynd. So that damned woman had been here! Those Dimbles had always, he felt, disliked him. They'd probably asked Jane to stay with them. Been interfering somehow, no doubt. He must go down to Northumberland and see Dimble.

The idea of being annoyed with the Dimbles occurred to Mark almost as an inspiration. To bluster a little as an injured husband in search of his wife would be a pleasant change for the attitudes he had recently been compelled to adopt. On the way down town he stopped to have a drink. As he came to the Bristol and saw the NICE placard on it, he had almost said, 'Oh, damn,' and turned away, before he suddenly remembered that he was himself a high official in the NICE and by no means a member of that general Public whom the Bristol now excluded. They asked him who he was at the door and became obsequious when he told them. There was a pleasant fire burning. After the gruelling day he had had, he felt justified in ordering a large whisky, and after it he had a second. It completed the change in his mental weather which had begun at the moment when he first conceived the idea of having a grievance against the Dimbles. The whole state of Edgestow had something to do with it. There was an element in him to which all these exhibitions of power suggested chiefly how much nicer and how much more appropriate it was, all said and done, to be part of the NICE than to be an outsider. Even now … had he been taking all this *démarche* about a murder trial too seriously? Of course, that was the way Wither managed things: he liked to have something hanging over everyone. It was only a way to keep him at Belbury and to make him send for Jane. And when one came to think of it, why not? She couldn't go on indefinitely living alone. And the wife of a man who meant to have a career and live at the centre of things would have to learn to be a woman of the world. Anyway, the first thing was to see that fellow Dimble.

He left the Bristol feeling, as he would have said, a different man. Indeed he was a different man. From now onwards till the moment of final decision should meet him, the different men in him appeared with startling rapidity and each seemed very complete while it lasted. Thus, skidding violently from one side to the other, his youth approached the moment at which he would begin to be a person.

◆ ○ ◆

'Come in,' said Dimble in his rooms at Northumberland. He had just finished with his last pupil for the day and was intending to start for St Anne's in a few minutes. 'Oh, it's you, Studdock,' he added as the door opened. 'Come in.' He tried to speak naturally but he was surprised at the visit and shocked by what he saw. Studdock's face appeared to him to have changed since they last met; it had grown fatter and paler and there was a new vulgarity in the expression.

'I've come to ask about Jane,' said Mark. 'Do you know where she is?'

'I can't give you her address, I'm afraid,' said Dimble.

'Do you mean you don't know it?'

'I can't give it,' said Dimble.

According to Mark's programme this was the point at which he should have begun to take a strong line. But he did not feel the same now that he was in the room. Dimble had always treated him with scrupulous politeness and Mark had always felt that Dimble disliked him. This had not made him dislike Dimble. It had only made him uneasily talkative in Dimble's presence and anxious to please. Vindictiveness was by no means one of Mark's vices. For Mark liked to be liked. A snub sent him away dreaming of not revenge but of brilliant jokes or achievements which would one day conquer the good will of the man who had snubbed him. If he were ever cruel it would be downwards, to inferiors and outsiders who solicited his regard, not upwards to those who rejected it. There was a good deal of the spaniel in him.

'What do you mean?' he asked. 'I don't understand.'

'If you have any regard for your wife's safety you will not ask me to tell you where she has gone,' said Dimble.

'Safety?'

'Safety,' repeated Dimble with great sternness.

'Safety from what?'

'Don't you know what has happened?'

'What's happend?'

'On the night of the big riot the Institutional Police attempted to arrest her. She escaped, but not before they had tortured her.'

'Tortured her? What do you mean?'

'Burned her with cigars.'

'That's what I've come about,' said Mark. 'Jane – I'm afraid she is on the verge of a nervous breakdown. That didn't really happen, you know.'

'The doctor who dressed the burns thinks otherwise.'

'Great Scot!' said Mark. 'So they really did? But, look here …'

Under the quiet stare of Dimble he found it difficult to speak.

'Why have I not been told of this outrage?' he shouted.

'By your colleagues?' asked Dimble drily. 'It is an odd question to ask me. You ought to understand the workings of the NICE better than I do.'

'Why didn't *you* tell me? Why has nothing been done about it? Have you been to the police?'

'The Institutional Police?'

'No, the ordinary police.'

'Do you really not know that there are no ordinary police left in Edgestow?'

'I suppose there are some magistrates.'

'There is the Emergency Commissioner, Lord Feverstone. You seem to misunderstand. This is a conquered and occupied city.'

'Then why, in Heaven's name, didn't you get on to me?'

'*You?*' said Dimble.

For one moment, the first for many years, Mark saw himself exactly as a man like Dimble saw him. It almost took his breath away.

'Look here,' he said. 'You don't … it's too fantastic! You don't imagine I knew about it. You don't really believe I send policemen about to man-handle my own wife!' He had begun on the note of indignation, but ended by trying to insinuate a little jocularity. If only Dimble would give even the ghost of a smile: anything to move the conversation onto a different level.

But Dimble said nothing and his face did not relax. He had not, in fact, been perfectly sure that Mark might not have sunk even to this, but out of charity he did not wish to say so.

'I know you've always disliked me,' said Mark. 'But I didn't know it was quite as bad as that.' And again Dimble was silent, but for a reason Mark could not guess. The truth was that his shaft had gone home. Dimble's conscience had for years accused him of a lack of charity towards Studdock and he had struggled to amend it: he was struggling now.

'Well,' said Studdock in a dry voice, after the silence had lasted for several second, 'there doesn't seem to be much more to say. I insist on being told where Jane is.'

'Do you *want* her to be taken to Belbury?'

Mark winced. It was as if the other had read the very thought he had had in the Bristol half an hour ago.

'I don't see, Dimble,' he said, 'why I should be cross-questioned in this way. Where is my wife?'

'I have no permission to tell you. She is not in my house nor under my protection. She is well and happy and safe. If you still have the slightest regard for her happiness you will make no attempt to get into touch with her.'

'Am I sort of leper or criminal that I can't even be trusted to know her address?'

'Excuse me. You are a member of the NICE who have already insulted, tortured and arrested her. Since her escape she has been left alone only because your colleagues do not know where she is.'

'And if it really was the NICE police, do you suppose I'm not going to have a very full explanation out of them? Damn it, what do you take me for?'

'I can only hope that you have no power in the NICE at all. If you have no power, then you cannot protect her. If you have, then you are identified with its policy. In neither case will I help you to discover where Jane is.'

'This is fantastic,' said Mark. 'Even if I do happen to hold a job in the NICE for the moment, you know *me*.'

'I do *not* know you,' said Dimble. 'I have no conception of your aims or motives.'

He seemed to Mark to be looking at him, not with anger or contempt, but with that degree of loathing which produces in those who feel it a kind of embarrassment – as if he were an obscenity which decent people are forced, for very shame, to pretend that they have not noticed. In this Mark was quite mistaken. In reality his presence was acting on Dimble as a summons to rigid self-control. Dimble was simply trying very hard not to hate, not to despise, above all not to enjoy hating and despising, and he had no idea of the fixed severity which this effort gave to his face. The whole of the rest of the conversation went on under this misunderstanding.

'There has been some ridiculous mistake,' said Mark. 'I tell you I'll look into it thoroughly. I'll make a row. I suppose some newly enrolled policeman got drunk or something. Well, he'll be broken. I –'

'It was the chief of your police, Miss Hardcastle herself, who did it.'

'Very well. I'll break *her* then. Did you suppose I was going to take it lying down? But there must be some mistake. It can't ...'

'Do you know Miss Hardcastle well?' asked Dimble. Mark was silenced. And he thought (quite wrongly) that Dimble was reading his mind to the bottom and seeing there his certainty that Miss Hardcastle had done this very thing and that he had no more power of calling her to account than of stopping the revolution of the Earth.

Suddenly the immobility of Dimble's face changed, and he spoke in a new voice. 'Have *you* the means to bring her to book?' he said. 'Are you already as near the centre of Belbury as that? If so, then you have consented to the murder of Hingest, the murder of Compton. If so, it was by your orders that Mary Prescott was raped and battered to death in the sheds behind the station. It is with your approval that criminals – honest criminals whose hands you are unfit to touch – are being taken from the jails to which British judges sent them on the conviction of British juries and packed off to Belbury to undergo for an indefinite period, out of reach of the law, whatever tortures and assaults on personal identity you call Remedial Treatment. It is you who have driven two thousand families from their homes to die of exposure in every ditch from here to Birmingham or Worcester. It is you who can tell us why Place and Rowley and Cunningham (at eighty years of age) have been arrested, and where they are. And if you are as deeply in it as that, not only will I not deliver Jane into your hands, but I would not deliver my dog.'

'Really – really,' said Mark. 'This is absurd. I know one or two high-handed things have been done. You always get some of the wrong sort in a police force – specially at first. But – I mean to say – what have I ever done that you should make me responsible for every action that any NICE official has taken – or is said to have taken in the gutter press?'

'Gutter press!' thundered Dimble, who seemed to Mark to be even physically larger than he was a few minutes before. 'What nonsense is this? Do you suppose I don't know that you have control of every paper in the country except one? And that one has not appeared this morning. Its printers have gone on strike. The poor dupes say they will not print articles attacking the people's Institute. Where the lies in all other papers come from you know better than I.'

It may seem strange to say that Mark, having long lived in a world without charity, had nevertheless very seldom met real anger. Malice in plenty he had encountered, but it all operated by snubs and sneers and stabbing in the back. The forehead and eyes and voice of this elderly man had an effect on him which was stifling and unnerving. At Belbury one used the words 'whining' and 'yapping' to describe any opposition which the actions of Belbury aroused in the outer world. And Mark had never had enough imagination to realise what the 'whining' would really be like if you met it face to face.

'I tell you I knew nothing about it,' he shouted. 'Damn it, I'm the injured party. The way you talk, anyone would think it was *your* wife who'd been ill-treated.'

'So it might have been. So it may be. It may be any man or woman in England. It was a woman and a citizen. What does it matter whose wife it was?'

'But I tell you I'll raise hell about it. I'll break the infernal bitch who did it, if it means breaking the whole NICE.'

Dimble said nothing. Mark knew that Dimble knew that he was talking nonsense. Yet Mark could not stop. If he did not bluster, he would not know what to say.

'Sooner than put up with this,' he shouted, 'I'll leave the NICE.'

'Do you mean that?' asked Dimble with a sharp glance. And to Mark, whose ideas were now all one fluid confusion of wounded vanity and jostling fears and shames, this glance once more appeared accusing and intolerable. In reality, it had been a glance of awakened hope: for charity hopes all things. But there was caution in it; and between hope and caution Dimble found himself once more reduced to silence.

'I see you don't trust me,' said Mark, instinctively summoning to his face the manly and injured expression which had often served him well in headmasters' studies.

Dimble was a truthful man. 'No,' he said after a longish pause. 'I don't quite.'

Mark shrugged his shoulders and turned away.

'Studdock,' said Dimble. 'This is not a time for foolery, or compliments. It may be that both of us are within a few minutes of death. You have probably been shadowed into the college. And I, at any rate, don't propose to die with polite insincerities in my mouth. I don't trust you. Why should I? You are (at least in some degree) the accomplice of the worst men in the world. Your very coming to me this afternoon may be only a trap.'

'Don't you know me better than *that*?' said Mark.

'Stop talking nonsense!' said Dimble. 'Stop posturing and acting, if only for a minute. Who are you to talk like that? They have corrupted better men than you or me before now. Straik was a good man once. Filostrato was at least a great genius. Even Alcasan – yes, yes, I know who your Head is – was at least a plain murderer: something better than they have now made of him. Who are you to be exempt?'

Mark gasped. The discovery of how much Dimble knew had suddenly inverted his whole picture of the situation. No logic was left in him.

'Nevertheless,' continued Dimble, 'knowing all this – knowing that you may be only the bait in the trap, I will take a risk. I will risk things compared with which both our lives are a triviality. If you seriously wish to leave the NICE, I will help you.'

One moment it was like the gates of Paradise opening – then, at once, caution and the incurable wish to temporise rushed back. The chink had closed again.

'I – I'd need to think that over,' he mumbled.

'There is no time,' said Dimble. 'And there is really nothing to think about. I am offering you a way back into the human family. But you must come at once.'

'It's a question affecting my whole future career.'

'Your career!' said Dimble. 'It's a question of damnation or – a last chance. But you must come at once.'

'I don't think I understand,' said Mark. 'You keep on suggesting some kind of danger. What is it? And what powers have you to protect me – or Jane – if I do bolt?'

'You must risk that,' said Dimble. 'I can offer you no security. Don't you understand? There is no security for anyone now. The battle has started. I'm offering you a place on the right side. I don't know which will win.'

'As a matter of fact,' said Mark, 'I *had* been thinking of leaving. But I must think it over. You put things in rather an odd way.'

'There is no time,' said Dimble.

'Supposing I look you up again tomorrow?'

'Do you know that you'll be able?'

'Or in an hour? Come, that's only sensible. Will you be here in an hour's time?'

'What can an hour do for you? You are only waiting in the hope that your mind will be less clear.'

'But will you be here?'

'If you insist. But no good can come of it.'

'I want to think. I want to think,' said Mark, and left the room without waiting for a reply.

Mark had said he wanted to think: in reality he wanted alcohol and tobacco. He had thoughts in plenty – more than he desired. One thought prompted him to cling to Dimble as a lost child clings to a grown-up. Another whispered to him, 'Madness. Don't *break* with the NICE. They'll be after you. How can Dimble save you! You'll be killed.' A third implored him not, even now, to write off as a total loss his hard won position in the Inner Ring at Belbury: there must, must be some middle course. A fourth recoiled from the idea of ever seeing Dimble again: the memory of every tone Dimble had used caused horrible discomfort. And he wanted Jane, and he wanted to punish Jane for being a friend of Dimble's, and he wanted never to see Wither again, and he wanted to creep back and patch things up with Wither somehow. He wanted to be perfectly safe and yet also very nonchalant and daring – to be admired for manly honesty among the Dimbles and yet also for realism and knowingness at Belbury – to have two more large whiskies and also to think everything out very clearly and collectedly. And it was beginning to rain and his head had begun to ache again. Damn the whole thing. Damn, damn! Why had he such a rotten heredity? Why had his education been so ineffective? Why was the system of society so irrational? Why was his luck so bad?

He began walking rapidly.

It was raining quite hard as he reached the College lodge. Some sort of van seemed to be standing in the street outside, and there were three or four uniformed men in capes. He remembered afterwards how the wet oilskin shone in the lamplight. A torch was flashed in his face.

'Excuse me, Sir,' said one of the men. 'I must ask for your name.'

'Studdock,' said Mark.

'Mark Gainsby Studdock,' said the man, 'it is my duty to arrest you for the murder of William Hingest.'

◆ ○ ◆

Dr Dimble drove out to St Anne's dissatisfied with himself, haunted with the suspicion that if he had been wiser, or more perfectly in charity with this very miserable young man, he might have done something for him. 'Did I give way to my temper? Was I self-righteous? Did I tell him as much as I dared?' he thought. Then came the deeper self-distrust that was habitual with him. 'Did you fail to make things clear because you really wanted not to? Just wanted to hurt and humiliate? To enjoy your own self-righteousness? Is there a whole Belbury inside you too?' The sadness that came over him had novelty in it. 'And thus,' he quoted from Brother Lawrence, 'thus I shall always do, whenever You leave me to myself.'

Once clear of the town, he drove slowly – almost sauntering on wheels. The sky was red to westward and the first stars were out.

Far down below him in a valley he saw the lights already lit in Cure Hardy. 'Thank Heaven it at any rate is far enough from Edgestow to be safe,' he thought. The sudden whiteness of a white owl flying low fluttered across the woody twilight on his left. It gave him a delicious feeling of approaching night. He was very pleasantly tired; he looked forward to an agreeable evening and an early bed.

'Here he is! Here's Dr Dimble,' shouted Ivy Maggs as he drove up to the front door of the Manor.

'Don't put the car away, Dimble,' said Denniston.

'Oh, Cecil!' said his wife; and he saw fear in her face. The whole household seemed to have been waiting for him.

A few moments later, blinking in the lighted kitchen, he saw that this was not to be a normal evening. The Director himself was there, seated by the fire, with the jackdaw on his shoulder and Mr Bultitude at his feet. There were signs that everyone else had had an early supper and Dimble found himself almost at once seated at the end of the table and being rather excitedly urged to eat and drink by his wife and Mrs Maggs.

'Don't stop to ask questions, dear,' said Mrs Dimble. 'Go on eating while they tell you. Make a good meal.'

'You have to go out again,' said Ivy Maggs.

'Yes,' said the Director. 'We're going into action at last. I'm sorry to send you out the moment you come in; but the battle has started.'

'I have already repeatedly urged,' said MacPhee, 'the absurdity of sending out an older man like yourself, that's done a day's work forbye, when here am I, a great strapping fellow sitting doing nothing.'

'It's no good, MacPhee,' said the Director, 'you can't go. For one thing you don't know the language. And for another – it's time for frankness – you have never put yourself under the protection of Maleldil.'

'I am perfectly ready,' said MacPhee, 'in and for this emergency, to allow the existence of these *eldila* of yours and of a being called Maleldil whom they regard as their king. And I –'

'You can't go,' said the Director. 'I will not send you. It would be like sending a three-year-old child to fight a tank. Put the other map on the table where Dimble can see it while he goes on with his meal. And now, silence. This is the situation, Dimble. What was under Bragdon was a living Merlin. Yes, asleep, if you like to call it sleep. And nothing has yet happened to show that the enemy have found him. Got that? No, don't talk, go on eating. Last night Jane Studdock had the most important dream she's had yet. You remember that in an earlier dream she saw (or so I thought) the very place where he lay under Bragdon. But – and this is the important thing – it's not reached by a shaft and a stair. She dreamed of going through a long tunnel with a very gradual ascent. Ah, you begin to see the point. You're right. Jane thinks she can recognise the entrance to that tunnel: under a heap of stones at the end of a copse with – what was it, Jane?'

'A white gate, Sir. An ordinary five-barred gate with a cross-piece. But the cross-piece was broken off about a foot from the top. I'd know it again.'

'You see, Dimble? There's a very good chance that this tunnel comes up *outside* the area held by the NICE.'

'You mean,' said Dimble, 'that we can now get *under* Bragdon without going *into* Bragdon.'

'Exactly. But that's not all.'

Dimble, steadily munching, looked at him.

'Apparently,' said the Director, 'we are almost too late. He was waked already.'

Dimble stopped eating.

'Jane found the place empty,' said Ransom.

'You mean the enemy have already found him?'

'No. Not quite as bad as that. The place had not been broken into. He seems to have waked of his own accord.'

'My God!' said Dimble.

'Try to eat, darling,' said his wife.

'But what does it mean?' he asked, covering her hand with his.

'I think it means that the whole thing has been planned and timed long, long ago,' said the Director. 'That he went out of Time, into the parachronic state, for the very purpose of returning at this moment.'

'A sort of human time-bomb,' observed MacPhee, 'which is why –'

'You can't go, MacPhee,' said the Director.

'Is he out?' asked Dimble.

'He probably is by now,' said the Director. 'Tell him what it was like, Jane.'

'It was the same place,' said Jane. 'A dark place, all stone, like a cellar. I recognised it at once. And the slab of stone was there, but no one lying on it; and this time it wasn't quite cold. Then I dreamed about this tunnel … gradually sloping up from the souterrain. And there was a man in the tunnel. Of course, I couldn't see him: it was pitch dark. But a great big man. Breathing heavily. At first I thought it was an animal. It got colder as we went up the tunnel. There was air – a little air – from outside. It seemed to end in a pile of loose stones. He was pulling them about just before the dream changed. Then I was outside, in the rain. That was when I saw the white gate.'

'It looks, you see,' said Ransom, 'as if they had not yet – or not then – established contact with him. That is our only chance now. To meet this creature before they do.'

'You will all have observed that Bragdon is very nearly water-logged,' put in MacPhee. 'Where exactly you'll find a dry cavity in which a body could be preserved all these centuries is a question worth asking. That is, if any of you are still concerned with evidence.'

'That's the point,' said the Director. 'The chamber must be under the high ground – the gravelly ridge on the south of the wood where it slopes up to the Eaton Road. Near where Storey used to live. That's where you'll have to look first for Jane's white gate. I suspect it opens on the Eaton Road. Or else that other road – look at the map – the yellow one that runs up into the Y of Cure Hardy.'

'We can be there in half an hour,' said Dimble, his hand still on his wife's hand. To everyone in that room, the sickening excitement of the last minutes before battle had come nearer.

'I suppose it must be tonight?' said Mrs Dimble, rather shame-facedly.

'I am afraid it must, Margaret,' said the Director. 'Every minute counts. We have practically lost the war if the enemy once make contact with him. Their whole plan probably turns on it.'

'Of course. I see. I'm sorry,' said Mrs Dimble.

'And what is our procedure, Sir?' said Dimble, pushing his plate away from him and beginning to fill his pipe.

'The first question is whether he's *out*,' said the Director. 'It doesn't seem likely that the entrance to the tunnel has been hidden all these centuries by nothing but a heap of loose stones. And if it has, they wouldn't be very loose by now. He may take hours get-ting out.'

'You'll need at least two strong men with picks –' began MacPhee.

'It's no good, MacPhee,' said the Director. 'I'm not letting you go. If the mouth of the tunnel is still sealed, you must just wait there. But he may have powers we don't know. If he's out, you must look for tracks. Thank God it's a muddy night. You must just hunt him.'

'If Jane is going, Sir,' said Camilla, 'couldn't I go too? I've had more experience of this sort of thing than –'

'Jane has to go because she is the guide,' said Ransom. 'I am afraid you must stay at home. We in this house are all that is left of Logres. You carry its future in your body. As I was saying, Dimble, you must hunt. I do not think he can get far. The country will, of course, be quite unrecognisable to him, even by daylight.'

'And ... if we do find him, Sir?'

'That is why it must be you, Dimble. Only you know the Great Tongue. If there was eldilic power behind the tradition he repre-sented he may understand it. Even if he does not understand it he will, I think, recognise it. That will teach him he is dealing with

Masters. There is a chance that he will think *you* are the Belbury people – his friends. In that case you will bring him here at once.'

'And if not?'

The Director spoke sternly.

'Then you must show your hand. That is the moment when the danger comes. We do not know what the powers of the old Atlantean circle were: some kind of hypnotism probably covered most of it. Don't be afraid; but don't let him try any tricks. Keep your hand on your revolver. You too Denniston.'

'I'm a good hand with a revolver myself,' said MacPhee. 'And why, in the name of all commonsense –'

'You can't go, MacPhee,' said the Director. 'He'd put *you* to sleep in ten seconds. The others are heavily protected as you are not. You understand, Dimble? Your revolver in your hand, a prayer on your lips, your mind fixed on Maleldil. Then, if he stands, conjure him.'

'What shall I say in the Great Tongue?'

'Say that you come in the name of God and all angels and in the power of the planets from one who sits today in the seat of the Pendragon and command him to come with you. Say it now.'

And Dimble, who had been sitting with his face drawn, and rather white, between the white faces of the two women, and his eyes on the table, raised his head, and great syllables of words that sounded like castles came out of his mouth. Jane felt her heart leap and quiver at them. Everything else in the room seemed to have been intensely quiet; even the bird, and the bear, and the cat, were still, staring at the speaker. The voice did not sound like Dimble's own: it was as if the words spoke themselves through him from some strong place at a distance – or as if they were not words at all but present operations of God, the planets, and the Pendragon. For this was the language spoken before the Fall and beyond the Moon and the meanings were not given to the syllables by chance, or skill, or long tradition, but truly inherent in them as the shape of the great Sun is inherent in the little waterdrop. This was Language herself, as she first sprang at Maleldil's bidding out of the molten quicksilver of the star called Mercury on Earth, but Viritrilbia in Deep Heaven.

'Thank you,' said the Director in English; and once again the warm domesticity of the kitchen flowed back upon them. 'And if he comes with you, all is well. If he does not – why then, Dimble, you must rely on your Christianity. Do not try any tricks. Say your prayers and keep your will fixed in the will of Maleldil. I don't know what he will do. But stand firm. You can't lose your soul, whatever happens; at least, not by any action of his.'

'Yes,' said Dimble. 'I understand.'

There was a longish pause. Then the Director spoke again.

'Don't be cast down, Margaret,' he said. 'If they kill Cecil, we shall none of us be let live many hours after him. It will be a shorter separation than you could have hoped for in the course of Nature. And now, gentlemen,' he said, 'you would like a little time, to say your prayers, and to say goodbye to your wives. It is eight now, as near as makes no matter. Suppose you all re-assemble here at ten past eight, ready to start?'

'Very good,' answered several voices. Jane found herself left alone in the kitchen with Mrs Maggs and the animals and MacPhee and the Director.

'*You* are all right, child?' said Ransom.

'I think so, Sir,' said Jane. Her actual state of mind was one she could not analyse. Her expectation was strung up to the height; something that would have been terror but for the joy, and joy but for the terror, possessed her – an all-absorbing tension of excitement and obedience. Everything else in her life seemed small and commonplace compared with this moment.

'Do you place yourself in the obedience,' said the Director, 'in obedience to Maleldil?'

'Sir,' said Jane, 'I know nothing of Maleldil. But I place myself in obedience to you.'

'It is enough for the present,' said the Director. 'This is the courtesy of Deep Heaven: that when you mean well, He always takes you to have meant better than you knew. It will not be enough for

249

always. He is very jealous. He will have you for no one but Himself in the end. But for tonight, it is enough.'

'This is the craziest business ever I heard of,' said MacPhee.

Battle Begun

'I can't see a thing,' said Jane.

'This rain is spoiling the whole plan,' said Dimble from the back seat. 'Is this still Eaton Road, Arthur?'

'I think … yes, there's the toll-house,' said Denniston who was driving.

'But what's the use?' said Jane. 'I can't see, even with the window down. We might have passed it any number of times. The only thing is to get out and walk.'

'I think she's right, Sir,' said Denniston.

'I say!' said Jane suddenly. 'Look! Look! What's that? Stop.'

'I can't see a white gate,' said Denniston.

'Oh, it's not that,' said Jane. 'Look over there.'

'I can't see anything,' said Dimble.

'Do you mean that light?' said Denniston.

'Yes, of course; that's the fire.'

'What fire?'

'It's the light,' she said, 'the fire in the hollow of the little wood. I'd forgotten all about it. Yes, I know: I never told Grace, or the Director. I'd forgotten that part of the dream till this moment. That was how it ended. It was the most important part really. That was where I found *him* – Merlin, you know. Sitting by a fire in a little wood. After I came out of the place underground. Oh, come quickly!'

'What do you think, Arthur?' said Dimble.

'I think we must go wherever Jane leads,' answered Denniston.

'Oh, do hurry,' said Jane. 'There's a gate here. Quick! It's only one field away.'

All three of them crossed the road and opened the gate and went into the field. Dimble said nothing. He was inwardly reeling under the shock and shame of the immense and sickening fear which had surged up inside him. He had, perhaps, a clearer idea than the others of what sort of things might happen when they reached the place.

Jane, as guide, went first, and Denniston beside her, giving her his arm and showing an occasional gleam of his torch on the rough ground. Dimble brought up the rear. No one was inclined to speak.

The change from the road to the field was as if one had passed from a waking into a phantasmal world. Everything became darker, wetter, more incalculable. Each small descent felt as if you might be coming to the edge of a precipice. They were following a track beside a hedge; wet and prickly tentacles seemed to snatch at them as they went. Whenever Denniston used his torch, the things that appeared within the circle of its light – tufts of grass, ruts filled with water, draggled yellow leaves clinging to the wet blackness of many-angled twigs, and once the two greenish-yellow fires in the eyes of some small animal – had the air of being more commonplace than they ought to have been; as if, for that moment's exposure, they had assumed a disguise which they would shuffle off again the moment they were left alone. They looked curiously small, too; when the light vanished the cold, noisy darkness seemed a huge thing.

The fear which Dimble had felt from the first began to trickle into the minds of the others as they proceeded – like water coming into a ship from a slow leak. They realised that they had not really believed in Merlin till now. They had thought they were believing the Director in the kitchen; but they had been mistaken. The shock was still to take. Out here with only the changing red light ahead and the black all round, one really began to accept as fact this tryst with something dead and yet not dead, something dug up, exhumed, from that dark pit of history which lies between the ancient Romans and the beginning of the English. 'The Dark Ages,' thought Dimble; how lightly one had read and written those words. But now they were going to step right into that Darkness. It was an age, not a man, that awaited them in the horrible little dingle.

And suddenly all that Britain which had been so long familiar to him as a scholar rose up like a solid thing. He could see it all. Little dwindling cities where the light of Rome still rested – little Christian sites, Camalodunum, Kaerleon, Glastonbury – a church, a villa or two, a huddle of houses, an earthwork. And then, beginning scarcely a stone's throw beyond the gates, the wet, tangled endless woods, silted with the accumulated decay of autumns that had been dropping leaves since before Britain was an island; wolves slinking, beavers building, wide shallow marshes, dim horns and drummings, eyes in the thickets, eyes of men not only Pre-Roman but Pre-British, ancient creatures, unhappy and dispossessed, who became the elves and ogres and wood-wooses of the later tradition. But worse than the forests, the clearings. Little strongholds with unheard-of kings. Little colleges and covines of Druids. Houses whose mortar had been ritually mixed with babies' blood. They had tried to do that to Merlin. And now all that age, horribly dislocated, wrenched out of its place in the time series and forced to come back and go through all its motions yet again with doubled monstrosity, was flowing towards them and would, in a few minutes, receive them into itself.

Then came a check. They had walked right into a hedge. They wasted a minute, with the aid of the torch, disentangling Jane's hair. They had come to the end of a field. The light of the fire, which kept on growing stronger and weaker in fitful alternations, was hardly visible from here. There was nothing for it but to set to work and find a gap or a gate. They went a long way out of their course before they found one. It was a gate that would not open: and as they came down on the far side, after climbing it, they went ankle deep into water. For a few minutes, plodding slightly up-hill, they were out of sight of the fire, and when it re-appeared it was well away on their left and much further off than anyone supposed.

Hitherto Jane had scarcely attempted to think of what might lie before them. As they went on, the real meaning of that scene in the kitchen began to dawn on her. He had sent the men to bid good-bye to their wives. He had blessed them all. It was likely, then, that this – this stumbling walk on a wet night across a ploughed field – meant death. Death – the thing one had always heard of (like love), the thing the poets had written about. So this was how it was going to be. But that was not the main point. Jane was trying to see death in the new light of all she had heard since she left Edgestow. She had long ceased to feel any resentment at the Director's tendency, as it were, to dispose of her – to give her, at one time or in one sense, to Mark, and in another to Maleldil – never, in any sense, to keep her for himself. She accepted that. And of Mark she did not think much, because to think of him increasingly aroused feelings of pity and guilt. But Maleldil. Up till now she had not thought of Maleldil either. She did not doubt that the *eldila* existed; nor did she doubt the existence of this stronger and more obscure being whom they obeyed ... whom the Director obeyed, and through him the whole household, even MacPhee. If it had ever occurred to her to question whether all these things might be the reality behind what she had been taught at school as 'religion', she had put the thought aside. The distance between these alarming and operative realities and the memory, say, of fat Mrs Dimble saying her prayers, was too wide. The things belonged, for her, to different worlds. On the one hand, terror of dreams, rapture of obedience, the tingling light and sound from under the Director's door, and the great struggle against an imminent danger; on the other, the smell of pews, horrible lithographs of the Saviour (apparently seven feet high, with the face of a consumptive girl), the embarrassment of confirmation classes, the nervous affability of clergymen. But this time, if it was really to be death, the thought would not be put aside. Because, really, it now appeared that almost anything might be true. The world had already turned out to be so very unlike what she had expected. The old ring-fence had been smashed completely. One might be in for anything. Maleldil might be, quite simply and crudely, God. There might be a life after death: a Heaven: a Hell. The thought glowed in her mind for a second like a spark that has fallen on shavings, and then a second later, like those shavings, her whole mind was in a blaze – or with just enough left outside the blaze to utter some kind of protest. 'But … but this is unbearable. I ought to have been told.' It did not, at that moment, occur to her even to doubt that if such things existed they would be totally and unchangeably adverse to her.

'Look out, Jane,' said Denniston. 'That's a tree.'

'I – I think it's a cow,' said Jane.

'No. It's a tree. Look. There's another.'

'Hush,' said Dimble. 'This is Jane's little wood. We are very close now.'

The ground rose in front of them for about twenty yards and there made an edge against the firelight. They could see the wood quite clearly now, and also each other's faces, white and blinking.

'I will go first,' said Dimble.

'I envy you your nerve,' said Jane.

'Hush,' said Dimble again.

They walked slowly and quietly up to the edge and stopped. Below them in a big fire wood was burning at the bottom of a little dingle. There were bushes all about, whose changing shadows, as the flames rose and fell, made it difficult to see clearly. Beyond the fire there seemed to be some rude kind of tent made out of sacking, and Denniston thought he saw an upturned cart. In the foreground, between them and the fire, there was certainly a kettle.

'Is there anyone here?' whispered Dimble to Denniston.

'I don't know. Wait a few seconds.'

'Look!' said Jane suddenly. 'There! When the flame blew aside.'

'What?' said Dimble.

'Didn't you see him?'

'I saw nothing.'

'I thought I saw a man,' said Denniston.

'I saw an ordinary tramp,' said Dimble. 'I mean a man in modern clothes.'

'What did he look like?'

'I don't know.'

'We must go down,' said Dimble.

'*Can* one get down?' said Denniston.

'Not this side,' said Dimble. 'It looks as if a sort of path came into it over there to the right. We must go along the edge till we find the way down.'

They had all been talking in low voices and the crackling of the fire was now the loudest sound, for the rain seemed to be stopping. Cautiously, like troops who fear the eye of the enemy, they began to skirt the lip of the hollow, stealing from tree to tree.

'Stop!' whispered Jane suddenly.

'What is it?'

'There's something moving.'

'Where?'

'In there. Quite close.'

'I heard nothing.'

'There's nothing now.'

'Let's go on.'

'Do you still think there's something, Jane?'

'It's quiet now. There *was* something.'

They made a few paces more.

'St!' said Denniston. 'Jane's right. There is something.'

'Shall I speak?' said Dimble.

'Wait a moment,' said Denniston. 'It's just there. Look! – damn it, it's only an old donkey!'

'That's what I said,' said Dimble. 'The man's a gypsy: a tinker or something. This is his donkey. Still, we must go down.'

They proceeded. In a few moments they found themselves descending a rutted grassy path which wound about till the whole hollow opened before them; and now the fire was no longer between them and the tent. 'There he is,' said Jane.

'Can you see him?' said Dimble. 'I haven't got your eyes.'

'I can see him all right,' said Denniston. 'It *is* a tramp. Can't you see him, Dimble? An old man with a ragged beard in what looks like the remains of a British Warm and a pair of black trousers. Don't you see his left foot, stuck out, and the toe a bit up in the air?'

'That?' said Dimble. 'I thought was a log. But you've better eyes than I have. Did you really see a man, Arthur?'

'Well, I thought I did, Sir. But I'm not certain now. I think my eyes are getting tired. He's sitting very still. If it *is* a man, he's asleep.'

'Or dead,' said Jane with a sudden shudder.

'Well,' said Dimble, 'We must go down.'

And in less than a minute all three walked down into the dingle and past the fire. And there was the tent, and a few miserable attempts at bedding inside it, and a tin plate, and some matches on the ground, and the dottle of a pipe, but they could see no man.

◆ ○ ◆

'What I can't understand, Wither,' said Fairy Hardcastle, 'is why you don't let me try my hand on the young pup. All these ideas of yours are so half-hearted – keeping him on his toes about the murder, arresting him, leaving him all night in the cells to think it over. Why do you keep messing about with things that may work or may not? – when twenty minutes of my treatment would turn his mind inside out. I know the type.'

Miss Hardcastle was talking, at about ten o'clock that same wet night, to the Deputy Director in his study. There was a third person present: Professor Frost.

'I assure you, Miss Hardcastle,' said Wither, fixing his eyes not on her but on Frost's forehead, 'you need not doubt that your views on this, or any other matter, will always receive the fullest consideration. But if I may say so, this is one of those cases where – ah – any grave degree of coercive examination might defeat its own end.'

'Why?' said the Fairy sulkily.

'You must excuse me,' said Wither, 'for reminding you – not, of course, that I assume you are neglecting the point, but simply on methodological grounds – it is so important to make everything *clear* – that we need the woman – I mean, that it would be of the greatest value to welcome Mrs Studdock among us – chiefly on account of the remarkable psychical faculty she is said to possess. In using the word *Psychical*, I am not, you understand, committing myself to any particular theory.'

'You mean these dreams?'

'It is very doubtful,' said Wither, 'what effect it might have on her if she were brought here under compulsion and then found her husband – ah – in the markedly, though no doubt temporarily, abnormal condition which we should have to anticipate as a result of your scientific methods of examination. One would run the risk of a profound emotional disturbance on her part. The faculty itself might disappear, at least for a long time.'

'We have not yet had Major Hardcastle's report,' said Professor Frost quietly.

'No good,' said the Fairy. 'He was shadowed into Northumberland. Only three possible people left the College after him – Lancaster, Lyly and Dimble. I put them in that order of probability. Lancaster is a Christian, and a very influential man. He's in the Lower House of Convocation. He had a lot to do with the Repton Conference. He's mixed up with several big clerical families. And he's written a lot of books. He has a real stake in their side. Lyly is rather the same type, but less of an organiser. As you will remember, he did a great deal of harm on that reactionary commission about Education last year. Both these are dangerous men. They are the sort of people who get things done – natural leaders of the other party. Dimble is quite a different type. Except that he's a Christian, there isn't really much against him. He's purely academic. I shouldn't think his name is much known, except to other scholars in his own subject. Not the kind that would make a public man. Impractical … he'd be too full of scruples to be much use to them. The others know a thing or two, Lancaster particularly. In fact, he's a man we could find room for on our own side if he held the right views.'

'You should tell Major Hardcastle that we have access to most of these facts already,' said Professor Frost.

'Perhaps,' said Wither, 'in view of the late hour – we don't wish to overtax your energies, Miss Hardcastle – we might go on to the more strictly narrative parts of your report.'

'Well,' said the Fairy, 'I had to follow all three. With the resources I had at the moment. You'll realise young Studdock was seen setting off for Edgestow only by good luck. It was a bomb-shell. Half my people were already busy on the hospital affair. I just had to lay my hands on anyone I could get. I posted a sentry and had six others out of sight of the College; in plain clothes, of course. As soon as Lancaster came out I told off the three best to keep him in sight. I've had a wire from them half an hour ago from London where Lancaster went off by train. We may be onto something there. Lyly gave the devil of a lot of trouble. He appeared to be calling on about fifteen different people in Edgestow. We've got them all noted – I sent the next two of my lads to deal with him. Dimble came out last. I would have sent my last man off to follow him, but a call came through at that moment from Captain O'Hara, who wanted another car. So I decided to let Dimble go for tonight and sent my man up with the one he had. Dimble can be got any time. He comes into College pretty regularly every day; and he's really a nonentity.'

'I do not quite understand,' said Frost, 'why you had no one inside the college to see what staircase Studdock went to.'

'Because of your damned Emergency Commissioner,' said the Fairy. 'We're not allowed into colleges now, if you please. I said at the time that Feverstone was the wrong man. He's trying to play on both sides. He's for us against the town, but when it comes to us against the University he's unreliable. Mark my words, Wither, you'll have trouble with him yet.'

Frost looked at the Deputy Director.

'I am far from denying,' said Wither, 'though without at all closing my mind to other possible explanations, that some of Lord Feverstone's measures may have been injudicious. It would be inexpressibly painful to me to suppose that –'

'Need we keep Major Hardcastle?' said Frost.

'Bless my soul!' said Wither. 'How very right of you! I had almost forgotten, my dear lady, how tired you must be, and how very valuable your time is. We must try to save you for that particular kind of work in which you have shown yourself indispensable. You must not allow us to impose on your good nature. There is a lot of duller and more routine work which it is only reasonable that you should be spared.' He got up and held the door open for her.

'You don't think,' said she, 'that I ought to let the boys have just a *little* go at Studdock? I mean, it seems so absurd to have all this trouble about getting an address.'

And suddenly, as Wither stood with his hand on the door-handle, courtly, patient and smiling, the whole expression faded out of his face. The pale lips, open wide enough to show his gums, the white curly head, the pouchy eyes, ceased to make up any single expression. Miss Hardcastle had the feeling that a mere mask of skin and flesh was staring at her. A moment later and she was gone.

'I wonder,' said Wither as he came back to his chair, 'whether we are attaching too much importance to this Studdock woman.'

'We are acting on an order dated the 1st of October,' said Frost.

'Oh … I wasn't questioning it,' said Wither with a gesture of deprecation.

'Allow me to remind you of the facts,' said Frost. 'The authorities had access to the woman's mind for only a very short time. They inspected one dream only – a most important dream, which revealed, though with some irrelevancies, an essential element in our programme. That warned us that if the woman fell into the hands of any ill-affected persons who knew how to exploit her faculty, she would constitute a grave danger.'

'Oh, to be sure, to be sure. I never intended to deny –'

'That was the first point,' said Frost, interrupting him. 'The second is that her mind became opaque to our authorities almost immediately afterwards. In the present state of our science we know only one cause for such occulations. They occur when the mind in question has placed itself, by some voluntary choice of its own, however vague, under the control of some hostile organism. The occultation, therefore, while cutting off our access to the dreams, also tells us that she has, in some mode or other, come under enemy influence. This is in itself a grave danger. But it also means that to find her would probably mean discovering the enemy's headquarters. Miss Hardcastle is probably right in maintaining that torture would soon induce Studdock to give up his wife's address. But as you pointed out, a round up at their headquarters, an arrest, and the discovery of her husband here in the condition in which the torture would leave him, would produce psychological conditions in the woman which might destroy her faculty. We should thus frustrate one of the purposes for which we want to get her. That is the first objection. The second is that an attack on enemy headquarters is very risky. They almost certainly have protection of a kind we are not prepared to cope with. And finally the man may not *know* his wife's address. In that case …'

'Oh,' said Wither, 'there is nothing I should more deeply deplore. Scientific examination (I cannot allow the word *Torture* in this context) in cases where the patient doesn't know the answer is always a fatal mistake. As men of humanity we should neither of us … and then, if you go on, the patient naturally does not recover … and if you stop, even an experienced operator is haunted by the fear that perhaps he *did* know after all. It is in every way unsatisfactory.'

'There is, in fact, no way of implementing our instructions except by inducing Studdock to bring his wife here himself.'

'Or else,' said Wither, a little more dreamily than usual, 'if it were possible, by inducing in him a much more radical allegiance to our side than he has yet shown. I am speaking, my dear friend, of a real change of heart.'

Frost slightly opened and extended his mouth, which was a very long one, so as to show his white teeth.

'That,' he said, 'is a subdivision of the plan I was mentioning. I was saying that he must be induced to send for the woman himself.

That, of course, can be done in two ways. Either by supplying him with some motive on the instinctive level, such as fear of us or desire for her; or else by conditioning him to identify himself so completely with the Cause that he will understand the real motive for securing her person and act on it.'

'Exactly ... exactly,' said Wither. 'Your expressions, as always, are a little different from those I would choose myself, but ...'

'Where is Studdock at present?' said Frost.

'In one of the cells here – on the other side.'

'Under the impression he has been arrested by the ordinary police?'

'That I cannot answer for. I presume he would be. It does not, perhaps, make much difference.'

'And how are you proposing to act?'

'We had proposed to leave him to himself for several hours – to allow the psychological results of the arrest to mature. I have ventured ... of course, with every regard for humanity ... to reckon on the value of some slight physical discomforts – he will not have dined, you understand. They have instructions to empty his pockets. One would not wish the young man to relieve any nervous tension that may have arisen by smoking. One wishes the mind to be thrown entirely on its own resources.'

'Of course. And what next?'

'Well, I suppose some sort of examination. That is a point on which I should welcome your advice. I mean, as to whether, I, personally, should appear in the first instance. I am inclined to think that the appearance of examination by the ordinary police should be maintained a little longer. Then at a later stage will come the discovery that he is still in our hands. He will probably misunderstand this discovery at first – for several minutes. It would be well to let him realise only gradually that this by no means frees him from the – er – embarrassments arising out of Hingest's death. I take it that some fuller realisation of his inevitable solidarity with the Institute would then follow ...'

'And then you mean to ask him again for his wife?'

'I shouldn't do it at all like that,' said Wither. 'If I might venture to say so, it is one of the disadvantages of that extreme simplicity and accuracy with which you habitually speak (much as we all admire it) that it leaves no room for fine shades. One had rather hoped for a spontaneous outburst of confidence on the part of the young man himself. Anything like a direct demand –'

'The weakness of the plan,' said Frost, 'is that you are relying wholly on fear.'

'Fear,' repeated Wither as if he had not heard the word before. 'I do not quite follow the connection of thought. I can hardly suppose you are following the opposite suggestion, once made, if I remember rightly, by Miss Hardcastle.'

'What was that?'

'Why,' said Wither, 'If I understand her aright, she thought of taking scientific measures to render the society of his wife more desirable in the young man's eyes. Some of the chemical resources …'

'You mean an aphrodisiac?'

Wither sighed gently and said nothing.

'That is nonsense,' said Frost. 'It isn't to his wife that a man turns under the influence of aphrodisiacs. But as I was saying, I think it is a mistake to rely wholly on fear. I have observed, over a number of years, that its results are incalculable: especially when the fear is complicated. The patient may get too frightened to move, even in the desired direction. If we have to despair of getting the woman here with her husband's good will, we must use torture and take the consequences. But there are other alternatives. There is desire.'

'I am not sure that I am following you. You have rejected the idea of any medical or chemical approach.'

'I was thinking of stronger desires.'

Neither at this stage of the conversation nor at any other did the Deputy Director look much at the face of Frost; his eyes, as usual, wandered over the whole room or fixed themselves on distant objects. Sometimes they were shut. But either Frost or Wither – it was difficult to say which – had been gradually moving his chair, so that by this time the two men sat with their knees almost touching.

'I had my conversation with Filostrato,' said Frost in his low, clear voice. 'I used expressions which must have made my meaning clear if he had any notion of the truth. His senior assistant. Wilkins, was present too. The fact is that neither is really interested. What interests them is the fact that they have succeeded – as they think – in keeping the Head alive and getting it to talk. What it says does not really interest them. As to any question about *what* is really speaking, they have no curiosity. I went very far. I raised questions about its mode of consciousness – its sources of information. There was no response.'

'You are suggesting, if I understand you,' said Wither, 'a movement towards this Mr Studdock along *those* lines. If I remember rightly, you rejected fear on the ground that its effects could not really be predicted with the accuracy one might wish. But – ah – would the method now envisaged be any *more* reliable? I need hardly say that I fully realise a certain disappointment which serious-minded people must feel with such colleagues as Filostrato and his subordinate Mr Wilkins.'

'That is the point,' said Frost. 'One must guard against the error of supposing that the political and economic dominance of England by the NICE is more than a subordinate object: it is individuals that we are really concerned with. A hard unchangeable core of individuals really devoted to the same cause as ourselves – that is what we need and what, indeed, we are under orders to supply. We have not succeeded so far in bringing many people in – really *in*.'

'There is still no news from Bragdon Wood?'

'No.'

'And you believe that Studdock might really be a suitable person? … '

'You must not forget,' said Frost, 'that his value does not rest solely on his wife's clairvoyance. The couple are eugenically interesting. And secondly, I think he can offer no resistance. The hours of fear in the cell, and then an appeal to desires that undercut the fear, will have an almost certain effect on a character of that sort.'

'Of course,' said Wither, 'nothing is so much to be desired as the greatest possible unity. You will not suspect me of under-rating that aspect of our orders. Any fresh individual brought into that unity would be a source of the most intense satisfaction to – ah – all concerned. I desire the closest possible bond. I would welcome an interpenetration of personalities so close, so irrevocable, that it almost transcends individuality. You need not doubt that I would open my arms to receive – to absorb – to assimilate this young man.'

They were now sitting so close together that their faces almost touched, as if they had been lovers about to kiss. Frost's pince-nez caught the light so that they made his eyes invisible: only his mouth, smiling but not relaxed in the smile, revealed his expression. Wither's mouth was open, the lower lip hanging down, his eyes wet, his whole body hunched and collapsed in his chair as if the strength had gone out of it. A stranger would have thought he had been drinking. Then his shoulders twitched and gradually he began to laugh. And Frost did not laugh, but his smile grew moment by moment brighter and also colder, and he stretched out his hand and patted his colleague on the shoulder. Suddenly in that silent room there was a crash. *Who's Who* had fallen off the table, swept onto the floor as, with sudden swift convulsive movement, the two old men lurched forward towards each other and sat swaying to and fro, locked in an embrace from which each seemed to be struggling to escape. And as they swayed and scrabbled with hand and nail, there arose, shrill and faint at first, but then louder and louder, a cackling noise that seemed in the end rather an animal than a senile parody of laughter.

◆ ○ ◆

When Mark was bundled out of the police wagon into the dark and rain and hurried indoors between two constables and left at length alone in a little lighted room, he had no idea that he was at Belbury. Nor would he have cared greatly if he had known, for the moment he was arrested he had despaired of his life. He was going to be hanged.

He had never till now been at close quarters with death. Now, glancing down at his hand (because his hands were cold and he had been automatically rubbing them), it came to him as a totally new idea that this very hand, with its five nails and the yellow tobacco stain on the inside of the second finger, would one day be the hand of a corpse, and later the hand of a skeleton. He did not exactly feel horror, though on the physical level he was aware of a choking sensation; what made his brain reel was the preposterousness of the idea. This was something incredible, yet at the same time quite certain.

There came a sudden uprush of grisly details about execution, supplied long since by Miss Hardcastle. But that was a dose too strong for the consciousness to accept. It hovered before his imagination for a fraction of a second, agonising him to a kind of mental scream, and then sank away in a blur. Mere death returned as the object of attention. The question of immortality came before him. He was not in the least interested. What had an after life to do with it? Happiness in some other and disembodied world (he never thought of unhappiness) was totally irrelevant to a man who was going to be killed. The killing was the important thing. On any view, this body – this limp, shaking, desperately vivid thing, so intimately his own – was going to be returned into a *dead* body. If there were such things as souls, this cared nothing about them. The choking, smothering sensation gave the body's view of the matter with an intensity which excluded all else.

Because he felt that he was choking, he looked round the cell for any sign of ventilation. There was, in fact, some sort of grating above the door. That ventilator and the door itself were the only objects to detain the eye. All else was white floor, white ceiling, white wall, without a chair or table or book or peg, and with one hard white light in the centre of the ceiling.

Something in the look of the place now suggested to him for the first time the idea that he might be at Belbury and not in an ordinary police station. But the flash of hope aroused by this idea was so brief as to be instantaneous. What difference did it make whether Wither and Miss Hardcastle and the rest had decided to get rid of him by handing him over to the ordinary police or by making away with him in private – as they had doubtless done with Hingest? The meaning of all the ups and downs he had experienced at Belbury now appeared to him perfectly plain. They were all his enemies, playing upon his hopes and fears to reduce him to complete servility, certain to kill him if he broke away, and certain to kill him in the long run when he had served the purpose for which they wanted him. It appeared to him astonishing that he could ever have thought otherwise. How could he have supposed that any real conciliation of these people could be achieved by anything he did?

What a fool – a blasted, babyish, gullible fool – he had been! He sat down on the floor, for his legs felt weak, as if he had walked twenty-five miles. Why had he come to Belbury in the first instance? Ought not his very first interview with the Deputy Director to have warned him, as clearly as if the truth were shouted through a megaphone or printed on a poster in letters six feet high, that here was the world of plot within plot, crossing and double-crossing, of lies and graft and stabbing in the back, of murder and a contemptuous guffaw for the fool who lost the game? Feverstone's guffaw, that day he had called him an 'incurable romantic', came back to his mind. Feverstone … that was how he had come to believe in Wither: on Feverstone's recommendation. Apparently his folly went further back. How on earth had he come to trust Feverstone – a man with a mouth like a shark, with his flash manners, a man who never looked you in the face? Jane, or Dimble, would have seen through him at once. He had 'crook' written all over him. He was fit only to deceive puppets like Curry and Busby. But then, at the time when he first met Feverstone, he had not thought Curry and Busby puppets. With extraordinary clarity, but with renewed astonishment, he remembered how he had felt about the Progressive Element at Bracton when he was first admitted to its confidence; he remembered, even more incredulously, how he had felt as a very junior Fellow while he was outside it – how he had looked almost with awe at the heads of Curry and Busby bent close together in Common Room, hearing occasional fragments of their whispered conversation, pretending himself the while to be absorbed in a periodical but longing – oh, so intensely longing – for one of them to cross the room and speak to him. And then, after months and months, it had happened. He had a picture of himself, the odious little outsider who wanted to be an insider, the infantile gull, drinking in the husky and unimportant confidences, as if he were being admitted to the government of the planet. Was there *no* beginning to his folly? Had he been utter fool all through from the very day of his birth? Even as a schoolboy, when he had ruined his work and half broken his heart trying to get into the society called Grip, and lost his only real friend in doing so? Even as a child, fighting Myrtle because she *would* go and talk secrets with Pamela next door?

He himself did not understand why all this, which was now so clear, had never previously crossed his mind. He was unaware that such thoughts had often knocked for entrance, but had always been excluded for the very good reason that if they were once entertained it involved ripping up the whole web of his life, cancelling almost every decision his will had ever made, and really beginning over again as though he were an infant. The indistinct mass of problems which would have to be faced if he admitted such thoughts, the innumerable 'something' about which 'something' would have to be done, had deterred him from ever raising these questions. What had now taken the blinkers off was the fact that nothing *could* be done. They were going to hang him. His story was at an end. There was no harm in ripping up the web now for he was not going to use it any more; there was no bill to be paid (in the shape of arduous decision and reconstruction) for truth. It was a result of the approach of death which the Deputy Director and Professor Frost had possibly not foreseen.

There were no moral considerations at this moment in Mark's mind. He looked back on his life not with shame, but with a kind of disgust at its dreariness. He saw himself as a little boy in short trousers, hidden in the shrubbery beside the paling, to overhear Myrtle's conversation with Pamela, and trying to ignore the fact that it was not at all interesting when overheard. He saw himself making believe that he enjoyed those Sunday afternoons with the athletic heroes of Grip while all the time (as he now saw) he was almost homesick for one of the old walks with Pearson – Pearson whom he had taken such pains to leave behind. He saw himself in his teens laboriously reading rubbishy grown-up novels and drinking beer when he really enjoyed John Buchan and stone ginger. The hours that he had spent learning the very slang of each new circle that attracted him, the perpetual assumption of interest in things he found dull and of knowledge he did not possess, the almost heroic sacrifice of nearly every person and thing he actually enjoyed, the miserable attempt to pretend that one *could* enjoy Grip, or the Progressive Element, or the NICE – all this came over him with a kind of heart-break. When had he ever done what he wanted? Mixed with the people whom he liked? Or even eaten and drunk what took his fancy? The concentrated insipidity of it all filled him with self-pity.

In his normal condition, explanations that laid on impersonal forces outside himself the responsibility for all this life of dust and broken bottles would have occurred at once to his mind and been at once accepted. It would have been 'the system' or 'an inferiority complex' due to his parents, or the peculiarities of the age. None of these things occurred to him now. His 'scientific' outlook had never been a real philosophy believed with blood and heart. It had lived only in his brain, and was a part of that public self which was now falling off him. He was aware, without even having to think of it, that it was he himself – nothing else in the whole universe –

that had chosen the dust and broken bottles, the heap of old tin cans, the dry and choking places.

An unexpected idea came into his head. This – this death of his – would be lucky for Jane. Myrtle long ago, Pearson at school, Denniston while they were undergraduates, and lastly Jane had been the four biggest invasions of his life by something from beyond the dry and choking places. Myrtle he had conquered by becoming the clever brother who won scholarships and mixed with important people. They were really twins, but after a short period in childhood during which she had appeared as an elder sister, she had become more like a younger sister and had remained so ever since. He had wholly drawn her into his orbit: it was her large wondering eyes and naif answers to his accounts of the circle he was now moving in which had provided at each stage most of the real pleasure of his career. But for the same reason she had ceased to mediate life from beyond the dry places. The flower, once safely planted among the tin cans, had turned into a tin can itself. Pearson and Denniston he had thrown away. And he now knew, for the first time, what he had secretly meant to do with Jane. If all had succeeded, if he had become the sort of man he hoped to be, she was to have been the great hostess – the secret hostess in the sense that only the very esoteric few would know who that striking-looking woman was and why it mattered so enormously to secure her good will. Well … it was lucky for Jane. She seemed to him, as he now thought of her, to have in herself deep wells and knee-deep meadows of happiness, rivers of freshness, enchanted gardens of leisure, which he could not enter but could have spoiled. She was one of those other people – like Pearson, like Denniston, like the Dimbles – who could enjoy things for their own sake. She was not like him. It was well that she should be rid of him.

At that moment came the sound of a key turning in the lock of the cell-door. Instantly all these thoughts vanished; mere physical terror of death, drying the throat, rushed back upon him. He scrambled to his feet and stood with his back against the furthest wall, staring as hard as if he could escape hanging by keeping whoever entered steadily in sight.

It was not a policeman who came in. It was a man in a grey suit whose *pince-nez* as he glanced toward Mark and towards the light become opaque windows concealing his eyes. Mark knew him at once and knew that he was at Belbury. It was not this that made him open his own eyes even wider and almost forget his terror in his astonishment. It was the change in the man's appearance – or rather the change in the eyes with which Mark saw him. In one sense everything about Professor Frost was as it had always been – the pointed beard, the extreme whiteness of forehead, the regularity of features, and the bright Arctic smile. But what Mark could not understand was how he had ever managed to overlook something about the man so obvious that any child would have shrunk away from him and any dog would have backed into the corner with raised hackles and bared teeth. Death itself did not seem more frightening than the fact that only six hours ago he would in some measure have trusted this man, welcomed his confidence, and even made believe that his society was not disagreeable.

Wet and Windy Night

'Well,' said Dimble. 'There's no one here.'

'He was here a moment ago,' said Denniston.

'You're sure you *did* see someone?' said Dimble.

'I thought I saw someone,' said Denniston. 'I'm not positive.'

'If there was anyone he must still be quite close,' said Dimble.

'What about giving him a call?' suggested Denniston.

'Hush! Listen!' said Jane. They were all silent for a few moments.

'That's only the old donkey,' said Dimble presently, 'moving about at the top.'

There was another silence.

'He seems to have been pretty extravagant with his matches,' said Denniston, presently, glancing at the trodden earth in the firelight. 'One would expect a tramp –'

'On the other hand,' said Dimble, 'one would not expect Merlin to have brought a box of matches with him from the fifth century.'

'But what are we to *do*?' said Jane.

'One hardly likes to think what MacPhee will say if we return with no more success than this. He will at once point out a plan we ought to have followed,' said Denniston with a smile.

'Now that the rain's over,' said Dimble, 'we'd better get back to the car and start looking for your white gate. What are you looking at, Denniston?'

'I'm looking at this mud,' said Denniston who had moved a few paces away from the fire and in the direction of the path by which they had descended into the dingle. He had been stooping and using his torch. Now he suddenly straightened himself. 'Look!' he said, 'there have been several people here. No, don't walk on it and mess up all the tracks. Look. Can't you see, Sir?'

'Aren't they our own footprints?' said Dimble.

'Some of them are pointing the wrong way. Look at that – and that.'

'Might they be the tramp himself?' said Dimble. 'If it was a tramp.'

'He couldn't have walked up that path without our seeing him,' said Jane.

'Unless he did it before we arrived,' said Denniston.

'But we all saw him,' said Jane.

'Come,' said Dimble. 'Let's follow them up to the top. I don't suppose we shall be able to follow them far. If not, we must get back to the road and go on looking for the gate.'

As they reached the lip of the hollow, mud changed into grass under foot and the footprints disappeared. They walked twice round the dingle and found nothing; then they set out to return to the road. It had turned into a fine night: Orion dominated the whole sky.

◆ ○ ◆

The Deputy Director hardly ever slept. When it became absolutely necessary for him to do so, he took a drug, but the necessity was rare, for the mode of consciousness he experienced at most hours of day or night had long ceased to be exactly like what other men call waking. He had learned to withdraw most of his consciousness from the task of living, to conduct business, even, with only a quarter of his mind. Colours, tastes, smells and tactual sensations no doubt bombarded his physical senses in the normal manner: they did not now reach his ego. The manner and outward attitude to men which he had adopted half a century ago were now an organisation which functioned almost independently like a gramophone and to which he could hand over his whole routine of interviews and committees. While the brain and lips carried on this work, and built up day by day for those around him the vague and formidable personality which they knew so well, his inmost self was free to pursue its own life. That detachment of the spirit, not only from the senses, but even from the reason, which has been the goal of some mystics, was now his.

Hence he was still, in a sense, awake – that is, he was certainly not sleeping – an hour after Frost had left him to visit Mark in his cell. Anyone who had looked into the study during that hour would have seen him sitting motionless at his table, with bowed head and folded hands. But his eyes were not shut. The face had no expression; the real man was far away suffering, enjoying, or inflicting whatever such souls do suffer, enjoy or inflict when the cord that binds them to the natural order is stretched out to its utmost but not yet snapped. When the telephone rang at his elbow he took up the receiver without a start.

'Speaking,' he said.

'This is Stone, Sir,' came a voice. 'We have found the chamber.'

'Yes.'

'It was empty, Sir.'

'Empty?'

'Yes, Sir.'

'Are you sure, my dear Mr Stone, that you have found the right place? It is possible ...'

'Oh yes, Sir. It is a little kind of crypt. Stonework and some Roman brick. And a kind of slab in the middle, like an altar or a bed.'

'And am I to understand there was no one there? No sign of occupation?'

'Well, Sir, it seemed to us to have been recently disturbed.'

'Pray be as explicit as possible, Mr Stone.'

'Well, Sir, there was an exit – I mean a tunnel, leading out of it to the South. We went up this tunnel at once. It comes out about eight hundred yards away, outside the area of the wood.'

'Comes out? Do you mean there is an arch – a gate – a tunnel-mouth?'

'Well, that's just the point. We got out to the open air all right. But obviously something had been smashed-up there quite recently. It looked as if it had been done by explosives. As if the end of the tunnel had been walled up and had some depth of earth on top of it, and as if someone had recently blasted his way out. There was no end of a mess.'

'Continue, Mr Stone. What did you do next?'

'I used the order you had given me, Sir, to collect all the police available and have sent off search parties for the man you described.'

'I see. And how did *you* describe him to them?'

'Just as you did, Sir: an old man with either a very long beard or a beard very roughly trimmed, probably in a mantle, but certainly in some kind of unusual clothes. It occurred to me at the last moment to add that he might have no clothes at all.'

'Why did you add that, Mr Stone?'

'Well, Sir, I didn't know how long he'd been there, and it isn't my business. I'd heard things about clothes preserved in a place like that and all falling to pieces as soon as the air was admitted. I hope you won't imagine for a moment that I'm trying to find out anything you don't choose to tell me. But I just thought it would be as well to …'

'You were quite right, Mr Stone,' said Wither, 'in thinking that anything remotely resembling inquisitiveness on your part might have the most disastrous consequences. I mean, for yourself, for, of course, it is your interests I have chiefly had in view in my choice of methods. I assure you that you can rely on my support in the very – er – delicate position you have – no doubt unintentionally – chosen to occupy.'

'Thank you very much, Sir. I am so glad you think I was right in saying he might be naked.'

'Oh, as to *that*,' said the Director, 'there are a great many considerations which cannot be raised at the moment. And what did you instruct your search parties to do on finding any such – er – person?'

'Well, that was another difficulty, Sir. I sent my own assistant, Father Doyle, with one party, because he knows Latin. And I gave Inspector Wrench the ring you gave me and put him in charge of the second. The best I could do for the third party was to see that it contained someone who knew Welsh.'

'You did not think of accompanying a party yourself?'

'No, Sir. You'd told me to ring up without fail the moment we found anything. And I didn't want to delay the search parties until I'd got you.'

'I see. Well, no doubt your action (speaking quite without prejudice) could be interpreted along those lines. You made it quite clear that this – ah – Personage – when found, was to be treated with the greatest deference and – if you won't misunderstand me – caution?'

'Oh yes, Sir.'

'Well, Mr Stone, I am, on the whole, and with certain inevitable reservations, moderately satisfied with your conduct of this affair. I believe that I may be able to present it in a favourable light to those of my colleagues whose good will you have, unfortunately, not been able to retain. If you can bring it to a successful conclusion you would very much strengthen your position. If not … it is inexpressibly painful to me that there should be these tensions and mutual recriminations among us. But you quite understand me, my dear boy. If only I could persuade – say Miss Hardcastle and Mr Studdock – to share my appreciation of your very real qualities, you would need to have no apprehensions about your career or – ah – your security.'

'But what do you want me to *do*, Sir?'

'My dear young friend, the golden rule is very simple. There are only two errors which would be fatal to one placed in the peculiar situation which certain parts of your previous conduct have unfortunately created for you. On the one hand, anything like a lack of initiative or enterprise would be disastrous. On the other, the slightest approach to unauthorised action – anything which suggested that you were assuming a liberty of decision which, in all the circumstances, is not really yours – might have consequences from which even I could not protect you. But as long as you keep quite clear of these two extremes, there is no reason (speaking unofficially) why you should not be perfectly safe.'

Then, without waiting for Mr Stone to reply, he hung up the receiver and rang his bell.

◆ ○ ◆

'Oughtn't we to be nearly at the gate we climbed over?' said Dimble.

It was a good deal lighter now that the rain had stopped, but the wind had risen and was roaring about them so that only shouted remarks could be heard. The branches of the hedge beside which they were tramping swayed and dipped and rose again so that they looked as if they were lashing the bright stars.

'It's a good deal longer than I remembered,' said Denniston.

'But not so muddy,' said Jane.

'You're right,' said Denniston, suddenly stopping. 'It's all stony. It wasn't like this at all one the way up. We're in the wrong field.'

'I *think*,' said Dimble mildly, 'we must be right. We turned half left along this hedge as soon as we came out of the trees, and I'm sure I remember –'

'But did we come out of the copse on the right side?' said Denniston.

'If we once start changing course,' said Dimble, 'we shall go round and round in circles all night. Let's keep straight on. We're bound to come to the road in the end.'

'Hullo!' said Jane sharply. 'What's this?'

All listened. Because of the wind, the unidentified rhythmic noise which they were straining to hear seemed quite distant at one moment, and then, next moment, with shouts of 'Look out!' – 'Go away, you great brute!' – 'Get back!' – and the like, all were shrinking back into the hedge as the *plosh-plosh* of a horse cantering on soft ground passed close beside them. A cold gobbet of mud flung up from its hoofs struck Denniston in the face.

'Oh look! Look!' cried Jane. 'Stop him. Quick!'

'Stop him?' said Denniston who was trying to clean his face. 'What on earth for? The less I see of that great clodhopping quadruped, the better –'

'Oh, shout out to him, Dr Dimble,' said Jane in an agony of impatience. 'Come on. Run! Didn't you see?'

'See what?' panted Dimble as the whole party, under the influence of Jane's urgency, began running in the direction of the retreating horse.

'There's a man on his back,' gasped Jane. She was tired and out of breath and had lost a shoe.

'A man?' said Denniston; and then: 'by God, Sir, Jane's right. Look, look there! Against the sky … to your left.'

'We can't overtake him,' said Dimble.

'Hi! Stop! Come back! Friends – *amis* – *amici*,' bawled Denniston.

Dimble was not able to shout for the moment. He was an old man, who had been tired before they set out, and now his heart and lungs were doing things to him of which his doctor had told him the meaning some years ago. He was not frightened, but he could not shout with a great voice (least of all in the Old Solar language) until he had breathed. And while he stood trying to fill his lungs all the others suddenly cried, 'Look!' yet again; for high among the stars, looking unnaturally large and many legged, the shape of the horse appeared as it leaped a hedge some twenty yards away, and on its back, with some streaming garment blown far out behind him in the wind, the great figure of a man. It seemed to Jane that he was looking back over his shoulder as though he mocked. Then came a splash and thud as the horse alighted on the far side; and then nothing but wind and starlight again.

◆ ○ ◆

'You are in danger,' said Frost when he had finished locking the door of Mark's cell, 'but you are also within reach of a great opportunity.'

'I gather,' said Mark, 'I am at the Institute after all and not in a police station.'

'Yes. That makes no difference to the danger. The Institute will soon have official powers of liquidation. It has anticipated them. Hingest and Carstairs have both been liquidated. Such actions are demanded of us.'

'If you are going to kill me,' said Mark, 'why all this farce of a murder charge?'

'Before going on,' said Frost, 'I must ask you to be strictly objective. Resentment and fear are both chemical phenomena. Our reactions to one another are chemical phenomena. Social relations are chemical relations. You must observe these feelings in yourself in an objective manner. Do not let them distract your attention from the facts.'

'I see,' said Mark. He was acting while he said it – trying to sound at once faintly hopeful and slightly sullen, ready to be worked upon. But within, his new insight into Belbury kept him resolved not to believe one word the other said, not to accept (though he might feign acceptance) any offer he made. He felt that he must at all costs hold onto the knowledge that these men were unalterable enemies; for already he felt the old tug towards yielding, towards semi-credulity, inside him.

'The murder charge against you and the alterations in your treatment have been part of a planned programme with a well-defined end in view,' said Frost. 'It is a discipline through which everyone is passed before admission to the Circle.'

Again Mark felt a spasm of retrospective terror. Only a few days ago he would have swallowed any hook with that bait on it; and nothing but the imminence of death could have made the hook so obvious and the bait so insipid as it now was. At least, so comparatively insipid. For even now …

'I don't quite see the purpose of it,' he said aloud.

'It is, again, to promote objectivity. A circle bound together by subjective feelings of mutual confidence and liking would be useless. Those, as I have said, are chemical phenomena. They could all in principle be produced by injections. You have been made to pass through a number of conflicting feelings about the Deputy Director and others in order that your future association with us may not be based on feelings at all. In so far as there must be social relations between members of the circle it is, perhaps, better that they should be feelings of dislike. There is less risk of their being confused with the real *nexus*.'

'My future association?' said Studdock, acting a tremulous eagerness. But it was perilously easy for him to act it. The reality might re-awake at any moment.

'Yes,' said Frost. 'You have been selected as a possible candidate for admission. If you do not gain admission, or if you reject it, it will be necessary to destroy you. I am not, of course, attempting to work on your fears. They only confuse the issue. The process would be quite painless, and your present reactions to it are inevitable physical events.'

Mark considered this thoughtfully.

'It – it seems rather a formidable decision,' said Mark.

'That is merely a proposition about the state of your own body at the moment. If you please, I will go on to give you the necessary information. I must begin by telling you that neither the Deputy Director, nor I, are responsible for shaping the policy of the Institute.'

'The Head?' said Mark.

'No. Filostrato and Wilkins are quite deceived about the Head. They have, indeed, carried out a remarkable experiment by preserving it from decay. But Alcasan's mind is not the mind we are in contact with when the Head speaks.'

'Do you mean Alcasan is really … *dead*?' asked Mark. His surprise at Frost's last statement needed no acting.

'In the present state of our knowledge,' said Frost, 'there is no answer to that question. Probably it has no meaning. But the cortex and vocal organs in Alcasan's head are used by a different mind. And now, please, attend very carefully. You have probably not heard of macrobes.'

'Microbes?' said Mark in bewilderment. 'But of course –'

'I did not say *microbes;* I said *macrobes.* The formation of the word explains itself. Below the level of animal life, we have long known that there are microscopic organisms. Their actual results on human life, in respect of health and disease, have of course made up a large part of history: the secret cause was not known till we invented the microscope.'

'Go on,' said Mark. Ravenous curiosity was moving like a sort of groundswell beneath his conscious determination to stand on guard.

'I have now to inform you that there are similar organisms *above* the level of animal life. When I say, "above", I am not speaking biologically. The structure of the macrobe, so far as we know it, is of extreme simplicity. When I say that it is above the animal level, I mean that it is more permanent, disposes of more energy, and has greater intelligence.'

'More intelligent than the highest anthropoids?' said Mark. 'It must be pretty nearly human, then.'

'You have misunderstood me. When I say it transcended the animals, I was, of course, including the most efficient animal, Man. The macrobe is more intelligent than Man.'

Frowningly, Mark studied this theory.

'But how is it in that case that we have had no communication with them?'

'It is not certain that we have not. But in primitive times it was spasmodic, and was opposed by numerous prejudices. Moreover, the intellectual development of man had not reached the level at which intercourse with our species could offer any attractions to a macrobe. But though there has been little intercourse, there has been profound influence. Their effect on human history has been far greater than that of the microbes, though, of course, equally unrecognised. In the light of what we now know, all history will have to be re-written. The real causes of all the principal events are quite unknown to historians; that, indeed, is why history has not yet succeeded in becoming a science.'

'I think I'll sit down, if you don't mind,' said Mark resuming his seat on the floor. Frost remained, throughout the whole conversation, standing perfectly still with his arms hanging down straight at his sides. But for the periodic upward tilt of his head and flash of his teeth at the end of a sentence, he used no gestures.

'The vocal organs and brain taken from Alcasan,' he continued, 'have become the conductors of a regular intercourse between the Macrobes and our own species. I do not say that we have discovered this technique; the discovery was theirs, not ours. The circle to which you may be admitted is the organ of that co-operation between the two species which has already created a new situation for humanity. The change, you will see, is far greater than that which turned the sub-man into the man. It is more comparable to the first appearance of organic life.'

'These organisms, then,' said Mark, 'are friendly to humanity?'

'If you reflect for a moment,' said Frost, 'you will see that your question has no meaning except on the level of the crudest popular thought. Friendship is a chemical phenomenon; so is hatred. Both of them presuppose organisms of our own type. The first step towards intercourse with the macrobes is the realisation that one must go outside the whole world of our subjective emotions. It is only as you begin to do so, that you discover how much of what you mistook for your thought was merely a by-product of your blood and nervous tissues.'

'Oh, of course. I didn't quite mean, "friendly", in that sense. I really meant, were their aims compatible with our own?'

'What do you mean by our own aims?'

'Well – I suppose – the scientific reconstruction of the human race in the direction of increased efficiency – the elimination of war and poverty and other forms of waste – a fuller exploitation of Nature – the preservation and extension of our species, in fact.'

'I do not think this pseudo-scientific language really modifies the essentially subjective and instinctive basis of the ethics you are describing. I will return to the matter at a later stage. For the moment, I would merely remark that your view of war and your reference to the preservation of the species suggest a profound misconception. They are mere generalisations from affectional feelings.'

'Surely,' said Mark, 'one requires a pretty large population for the full exploitation of Nature, if for nothing else? And surely war is disgenic and reduces efficiency? Even if population needs thinning, is not war the worst possible method of thinning it?'

'That idea is a survival from conditions which are rapidly being altered. A few centuries ago, war did not operate in the way you describe. A large agricultural population was essential; and war destroyed types which were then still useful. But every advance in industry and agriculture reduces the number of work-people who are required. A large, unintelligent population is now becoming a deadweight. The real importance of scientific war is that scientists have to be reserved. It was not the great technocrats of Koenigsberg or Moscow who supplied the casualties in the siege of Stalingrad: it was superstitious Bavarian peasants and low-grade Russian agricultural workers. The effect of modern war is to eliminate retrogressive types, while sparing the technocracy and increasing its hold upon public affairs. In the new age, what has hitherto been merely the intellectual nucleus of the race is to become, by gradual stages, the race itself. You are to conceive the species as an animal which has discovered how to simplify nutrition and locomotion to such a point that the old complex organs and the large body which contained them are no longer necessary. That large body is therefore to disappear. Only a tenth part of it will now be needed to support the brain. The individual is to become all head. The human race is to become all Technocracy.'

'I see,' said Mark. 'I had thought rather vaguely – that the intelligent nucleus would be extended by education.'

'That is pure chimera. The great majority of the human race can be educated only in the sense of being given knowledge: they cannot be trained into the total objectivity of mind which is now necessary. They will always remain animals, looking at the world through the haze of their subjective reactions. Even if they could, the day for a large population has passed. It has served its function by acting as a kind of cocoon for Technocratic and Objective Man. Now, the macrobes, and the selected humans who can co-operate with them, have no further use for it.'

'The two last wars, then, were not disasters in your view?'

'On the contrary, they were simply the beginning of the programme – the first two of the sixteen major wars which are scheduled to take place in this century. I am aware of the emotional (that is, the chemical) reactions which a statement like this produces in you, and you are wasting your time in trying to conceal them from me. I do not expect you to control them. That is not the path to objectivity. I deliberately raise them in order that you may become accustomed to regard them in a purely scientific light and distinguish them as sharply as possible from the *facts*.'

Mark sat with his eyes fixed on the floor. He had felt, in fact, very little emotion at Frost's programme for the human race; indeed, he almost discovered at that moment how little he had ever really cared for those remote futures and universal benefits whereon his co-operation with the Institute had at first been theoretically based. Certainly, at the present moment there was no room in his mind for such considerations. He was fully occupied with the conflict between his resolution not to trust these men, never again to be lured by any bait into a real co-operation, and the terrible strength – like a tide sucking at the shingle as it goes out – of an opposite emotion. For here, here surely at last (so his desire whispered to him) was the true inner circle of all, the circle whose centre was outside the human race – the ultimate secret, the supreme power, the last initiation. The fact that it was almost completely horrible did not in the least diminish its attraction. Nothing that lacked the tang of horror would have been quite strong enough to satisfy the delirious excitement which now set his temples hammering. It came into his mind that Frost knew all about this excitement, and also about the opposite determination, and reckoned securely on the excitement as something which was certain to carry the day in his victim's mind.

A rattling and knocking which had been obscurely audible for some time now became so loud that Frost turned to the door. 'Go away,' he said, raising his voice. 'What is the meaning of this impertinence?' The indistinct noise of someone shouting on the other side of the door was heard, and the knocking went on. Frost's smile widened as he turned and opened it. Instantly a piece of paper was put into his hand. As he read it, he started violently. Without glancing at Mark, he left the cell. Mark heard the door locked again behind him.

◆ ○ ◆

'What friends those two are!' said Ivy Maggs. She was referring to Pinch the cat and Mr Bultitude the bear. The latter was sitting up with his back against the warm wall by the kitchen fire. His cheeks were so fat and his eyes so small that he looked as if he were smiling. The cat after walking to and fro with erected tail and rubbing herself against his belly had finally curled up and gone to sleep between his legs. The jackdaw, still on the Director's shoulder, had long since put its head beneath its wing.

Mrs Dimble, who sat further back in the kitchen, darning as if for dear life, pursed her lips a little as Ivy Maggs spoke. She could not go to bed. She wished they would all keep quiet. Her anxiety had reached that pitch at which almost every event, however small, threatens to become an irritation. But then, if anyone had been watching her expression, they would have seen the little grimace rapidly smoothed out again. Her will had many years of practice behind it.

'When we use the word Friends of those two creatures,' said MacPhee, 'I doubt we are being merely anthropomorphic. It is difficult to avoid the illusion that they have personalities in the human sense. But there's no evidence for it.'

'What's she go making up to him for, then?' asked Ivy.

'Well,' said MacPhee, 'maybe there'd be a desire for warmth – she's away in out of the draught there. And there'd be a sense of security from being near something familiar. And likely enough some obscure transferred sexual impulses.'

'Really, Mr MacPhee,' said Ivy with great indignation, 'it's a shame for you to say those things about two dumb animals. I'm sure I never did see Pinch – or Mr Bultitude either, the poor thing –'

'I said *transferred*,' interrupted MacPhee drily. 'And anyway, they like the mutual friction of their fur as a means of rectifying irritations set up by parasites. Now, you'll observe –'

'If you mean they have fleas,' said Ivy, 'you know as well as anyone that they have no such thing.' She had reason on her side, for it was MacPhee himself who put on overalls once a month and solemnly lathered Mr Bultitude from rump to snout in the wash-house and poured buckets of tepid water over him, and finally dried him – a day's work in which he allowed no one to assist him.

'What do you think, Sir?' said Ivy, looking at the Director.

'Me?' said Ransom. 'I think MacPhee is introducing into animal life a distinction that doesn't exist there, and then trying to determine on which side of that distinction the feelings of Pinch and Bultitude fall. You've got to become human before the physical cravings are distinguishable from affections – just as you have to become spiritual before affections are distinguishable from charity. What is going on in the cat and the bear isn't one or other of these two things: it is a single undifferentiated thing in which you can find the germ of what we call friendship and of what we call physical need. But it isn't either at that level. It is one of Barfield's "ancient unities."'

'I never denied they liked being together,' said MacPhee.

'Well, that's what I said,' retorted Mrs Maggs.

'The question is worth raising, Mr Director,' said MacPhee, 'because I submit that it points to an essential falsity in the whole system of this place.'

Grace Ironwood who had been sitting with her eyes half-closed suddenly opened them wide and fixed them on the Ulsterman, and Mrs Dimble leaned her head towards Camilla and said in a whisper, 'I do wish Mr MacPhee could be persuaded to go to bed. It's perfectly unbearable at a time like this.'

'How do you mean, MacPhee?' asked the Director.

'I mean that there is a half-hearted attempt to adopt an attitude towards irrational creatures which cannot be consistently maintained. And I'll do the justice to say that you've never tried. The bear is kept in the house and given apples and golden syrup till it's near bursting –'

'Well, I like that!' said Mrs Maggs. 'Who is it that's always giving him apples? That's what I'd like to know.'

'The bear, as I was observing,' said MacPhee, 'is kept in the house and pampered. The pigs are kept in a stye and killed for bacon. I would be interested to know the philosophical *rationale* of the distinction.'

Ivy Maggs looked in bewilderment from the smiling face of the Director to the unsmiling face of MacPhee.

'I think it's just silly,' she said. 'Who ever heard of trying to make bacon out of a bear?'

MacPhee made a little stamp of impatience and said something which was drowned first by Ransom's laughter, and then by a great clap of wind which shook the window as if it would blow it in.

'What a dreadful night for them!' said Mrs Dimble.

'I love it,' said Camilla. 'I'd love to be out in it. Out on a high hill. Oh, I do wish you'd let me go with them, Sir.'

'You *like* it?' said Ivy. 'Oh I don't! Listen to it round the corner of the house. It'd make me feel kind of creepy if I were alone. Or even if you was upstairs, Sir. I always think it's on nights like this that they – you know – come to you.'

'They don't take any notice of weather one way or the other, Ivy,' said Ransom.

'Do you know,' said Ivy in a low voice, 'that's a thing I don't quite understand. They're so eerie, these ones that come to visit you. I wouldn't go near that part of the house if I thought there was anything there, not if you paid me a hundred pounds. But I don't feel like that about God. But He ought to be worse, if you see what I mean.'

'He was, once,' said the Director. 'You are quite right about the Powers. Angels in general are not good company for men in

287

general, even when they are good angels and good men. It's all in St Paul. But as for Maleldil Himself, all that has changed: it was changed by what happened at Bethlehem.'

'It's getting ever so near Christmas now,' said Ivy addressing the company in general.

'We shall have Mr Maggs with us before then,' said Ransom.

'In a day or two, Sir,' said Ivy.

'Was that only the wind?' said Grace Ironwood.

'It sounded to me like a horse,' said Mrs Dimble.

'Here,' said MacPhee jumping up. 'Get out of the way, Mr Bultitude, till I get my gum boots. It'll be those two horses of Broad's again, tramping all over my celery trenches. If only you'd let me go to the police in the first instance. Why the man can't keep them shut up – ' He was bundling himself into his mackintosh as he spoke and the rest of the speech was inaudible.

'My crutch please, Camilla,' said Ransom. 'Come back, MacPhee. We will go to the door together, you and I. Ladies, stay where you are.'

There was a look on his face which some of those present had not seen before. The four women sat as if they had been turned to stone, with their eyes wide and staring. A moment later Ransom and MacPhee stood alone in the scullery. The back door was so shaking on its hinges with the wind that they did not know whether someone were knocking at it or not.

'Now,' said Ransom, 'open it. And stand back behind it yourself.'

For a second MacPhee worked with the bolts. Then, whether he meant to disobey or not (a point which must remain doubtful), the storm flung the door against the wall and he was momentarily pinned behind it. Ransom, standing motionless, leaning forward on his crutch, saw in the light from the scullery, outlined against the blackness, a huge horse, all in a lather of sweat and foam, its yellow teeth laid bare, its nostrils wide and red, its ears flattened against its skull, and its eyes flaming. It had been ridden so close up to the door that its front hoofs rested on the doorstep. It had neither saddle, stirrup nor bridle; but at that very moment a man leapt off its back. He seemed both very tall and very fat, almost a giant. His reddish-grey hair and beard were blown all about his face so that it was hardly visible; and it was only after he had taken a step forward that Ransom noticed his clothes – the ragged, ill-fitting khaki coat, baggy trousers, and boots that had lost the toes.

◆　○　◆

In a great room at Belbury, where the fire blazed and wine and silver sparkled on side-tables and a great bed occupied the centre of the floor, the Deputy Director watched in profound silence while four young men with reverential or medical heedfulness carried in a burden on a stretcher. As they removed the blankets and transferred the occupant of the stretcher to the bed, Wither's mouth opened wider. His interest became so intense that for the moment the chaos of his face appeared ordered and he looked like an ordinary man. What he saw was a naked human body, alive, but apparently unconscious. He ordered the attendants to place hot water bottles at its feet and raise the head with pillows: when they had done so and withdrawn, he drew a chair to the foot of the bed and sat down to study the face of the sleeper. The head was very large, though perhaps it looked larger than it was because of the unkempt grey beard and the long and tangled grey hair. The face was weatherbeaten in the extreme and the neck, where visible, already lean and scraggy with age. The eyes were shut and the lips wore a very slight smile. The total effect was ambiguous. Wither gazed at it for a long time and sometimes moved his head to see how it looked from a different angle – almost as if he searched for some trait he could not find and were disappointed. For nearly a quarter of an hour he sat thus; then the door opened and Professor Frost came softly into the room.

He walked to the bedside, bent down and looked closely into the stranger's face. Then he walked round to the far side of the bed and did the same.

'Is he asleep?' whispered Wither.

'I think not. It is more like some kind of a trance. What kind, I don't know.'

'You have no doubts, I trust?'

'Where did they find him?'

'In a dingle about quarter of a mile from the entrance to the souterrain. They had the track of bare feet almost all the way.'

'The souterrain itself was empty?'

'Yes. I had a report on that from Stone shortly after you left me.'

'You will make provisions about Stone?'

'Yes. But what do you think?' – he pointed with his eyes to the bed.

'I think it is he,' said Frost. 'The place is right. The nudity is hard to account for on any other hypothesis. The skull is the kind I expected.'

'But the face.'

'Yes. There are certain traits which are a little disquieting.'

'I could have sworn,' said Wither, 'that I knew the look of a Master – even the look of one who could be made into a Master. You understand me … one sees at once that Straik or Studdock might do; that Miss Hardcastle, with all her excellent qualities, would not.'

'Yes. Perhaps we must be prepared for great crudities in … *him*. Who knows what the technique of the Atlantean Circle was really like?'

'Certainly, one must not be – ah – narrow-minded. One can suppose that the Masters of that age were not quite so sharply divided from the common people as we are. All sorts of emotional and even instinctive, elements were perhaps still tolerated in the Great Atlantean which we have had to discard.'

'One not only *may* suppose it, one *must*. We should not forget that the whole plan consists in the reunion of different kinds of the art.'

'Exactly. Perhaps one's association with the Powers – their different time scale and all that – tends to make one forget how enormous the gap in time is by our human standards.'

'What we have here,' said Frost pointing to the sleeper, 'is not, you see, something from the fifth century. It is the last vestige, surviving into the fifth century, of something much more remote. Something that comes down from long before the Great Disaster, even from before primitive druidism; something that takes us back to Numinor, to pre-glacial periods.'

'The whole experiment is perhaps more hazardous than we realised.'

'I have had occasion before,' said Frost, 'to express the wish that you would not keep on introducing these emotional pseudo-statements into our scientific discussions.'

'My dear friend,' said Wither without looking at him, 'I am quite aware that the subject you mention has been discussed between you and the Powers themselves. Quite aware. And I don't doubt that you are equally well aware of certain discussions they have held with me about aspects of your own methods which are open to criticism. Nothing would be more futile – I might say more dangerous – than any attempt to introduce between ourselves those modes of oblique discipline which we properly apply to our inferiors. It is in your own interest that I venture to touch on this point.'

Instead of replying, Frost signalled to his companion. Both men became silent, their gaze fixed on the bed: for the Sleeper had opened his eyes.

The opening of the eyes flooded the whole face with meaning, but it was a meaning they could not interpret. The Sleeper seemed to be looking at them, but they were not quite sure that he saw them. As the seconds passed, Wither's main impression of the face was its caution. But there was nothing intense or uneasy about it. It was a habitual, unemphatic defensiveness which seemed to have behind it years of hard experience, quietly – perhaps even humorously – endured.

Wither rose to his feet, and cleared his throat. '*Magister Merline,*' he said, '*Sapientissime Britonum, secreti secretorum possessor, incredibili quodam gaudio afficimur quod te in domum nostram* *accipere nobis – ah – contingit. Scito nos etiam haud imperitos esse magnae artis – et – ut ita dicam ...*"*

But his voice died away. It was too obvious that the Sleeper was taking no notice of what he said. It was impossible that a learned man of the fifth century should not know Latin. Was there, then, some error in his own pronunciation? But he felt by no means sure that this man could not understand him. The total lack of curiosity, or even interest, in his face, suggested rather that he was not listening.

Frost took a decanter from the table and poured out a glass of red wine. He then returned to the bedside, bowed deeply, and handed it to the stranger. The latter looked at it with an expression that might (or might not) be interpreted as one of cunning; then he suddenly sat up in bed, revealing a huge hairy chest and lean, muscular arms. His eyes turned to the table and he pointed. Frost went back to it and touched a different decanter. The stranger shook his head and pointed again.

'I think,' said Wither, 'that our very distinguished guest is trying to indicate the jug. I don't quite know what was provided. Perhaps –'

'It contains beer,' said Frost.

'Well, it is hardly appropriate – still, perhaps – we know so little of the customs of that age ...'

While he was still speaking Frost had filled a pewter mug with beer and offered it to their guest. For the first time a gleam of interest came into that cryptic face. The man snatched the mug eagerly, pushed back his disorderly moustache from his lips, and began to drink. Back and back went the grey head; up and up went the bottom of the tankard; the moving muscles of the lean throat made the act of drinking visible. At last the man, having completely

* Master Merlin, wisest of the Britons, possessor of the secrets, it is with inexpressible pleasure that we embrace the opportunity of – ah – welcoming you in our house. You will understand that we also are not unskilled in the Great Art, and, if I may say so ...

inverted the tankard, set it down, wiped his wet lips with the back of his hand, and heaved a long sigh – the first sound he had uttered since his arrival. Then he turned his attention once more to the table.

For about twenty minutes the two old men fed him – Wither with tremulous and courtly deference, Frost with the deft, noiseless movements of a trained servant. All sorts of delicacies had been provided, but the stranger devoted his attention entirely to cold beef, chicken, pickles, bread, cheese and butter. The butter he ate neat, off the end of a knife. He was apparently unacquainted with forks, and took the chicken bones in both hands to gnaw them, placing them under the pillow when he had done. His eating was noisy and animal. When he had eaten, he signalled for a second pint of beer, drank it at two long draughts, wiped his mouth on the sheet and his nose on his hand, and seemed to be composing himself for further slumber.

'*Ah – er – domine*', said Wither with deprecating urgency, '*nihil magis mihi displiceret quam ut tibi ullo modo – ah – molestior essem. Attamen, venia tua …*'*

But the man was taking no notice at all. They could not tell whether his eyes were shut or whether he was still looking at them under half-closed lids; but clearly he was not intending to converse. Frost and Wither exchanged enquiring glances.

'There is no approach to this room, is there?' said Frost, 'except through the next one.'

'No,' said Wither.

'Let us go out there and discuss the situation. We can leave the door ajar. We shall be able to hear if he stirs.'

◆ ○ ◆

When Mark found himself left suddenly alone by Frost, his first sensation was an unexpected lightness of heart. It was not that he had any release from fears about the future. Rather, in the very

---

* Ah – er – Sir – nothing would be further from my wish than to be in any way troublesome to you. At the same time, with your pardon …

midst of those fears, a strange sense of liberation had sprung up. The relief of no longer trying to win these men's confidence, the shuffling off of miserable hopes, was almost exhilarating. The straight fight, after the long series of diplomatic failures, was tonic. He might lose the straight fight. But at least it was now his side against theirs. And he could talk of 'his side' now. Already he was with Jane and with all she symbolised. Indeed, it was he who was in the front line: Jane was almost a non-combatant ...

The approval of one's own conscience is a very heady draught; and specially for those who are not accustomed to it. Within two minutes Mark passed from that first involuntary sense of liberation to a conscious attitude of courage, and thence into unrestrained heroics. The picture of himself as hero and martyr, as Jack the Giant-Killer still coolly playing his hand even in the giant's kitchen, rose up before him, promising that it could blot out for-ever those other, and unendurable pictures of himself which had haunted him for the last few hours. It wasn't everyone, after all, who could have resisted an invitation like Frost's. An invitation that beckoned you right across the frontiers of human life ... into something that people had been trying to find since the beginning of the world ... a touch on that infinitely secret cord which was the real nerve of all history. How it would have attracted him once!

Would have attracted him once ... Suddenly, like a thing that leaped to him across infinite distances with the speed of light, desire (salt, black, ravenous, unanswerable desire) took him by the throat. The merest hint will convey to those who have felt it the quality of the emotion which now shook him, like a dog shaking a rat; for others, no description perhaps will avail. Many writers speak of it in terms of lust: a description admirably illuminating from within, totally misleading from without. It has nothing to do with the body. But it is in two respects like lust as lust shows itself to be in the deepest and darkest vault of its labyrinthine house. For like lust, it disenchants the whole universe. Everything else that Mark had ever felt – love, ambition, hunger, lust itself – appeared to have been mere milk and water, toys for children, not worth one throb of the nerves. The infinite attraction of this dark thing sucked all other passions into itself: the rest of the world appeared blenched, etiolated, insipid, a world of white marriages and white masses, dishes without salt, gambling for counters. He could not now think of Jane except in terms of appetite: and appetite here made no appeal. That serpent, faced with the true dragon, became a fangless worm. But it was like lust in another respect also. It is idle to point out to the perverted man the horror of his perversion: while the fierce fit is on, that horror is the very spice of his craving. It is ugliness itself that becomes, in the end, the goal of his lechery; beauty has long since grown too weak a stimulant. And so it was here. These creatures of which Frost had spoken – and he did not doubt now that they were locally present with him in the cell – breathed death on the human race and on all joy. Not despite this but because of this, the terrible gravitation sucked and tugged and fascinated him towards them. Never before had he known the fruitful strength of the movement opposite to Nature which now had him in its grip; the impulse to reverse all reluctances and to draw every circle anti-clockwise. The meaning of certain pictures, of Frost's talk about 'objectivity', of the things done by witches in old times, became clear to him. The image of Wither's face rose to his memory; and this time he did not merely loathe it. He noted, with shuddering satisfaction, the signs it bore of a shared experience between them. Wither also knew. Wither understood …

At the same moment, it came back to him that he would probably be killed. As soon as he thought of that, he became once more aware of the cell – the little hard white empty place with the glaring light, in which he found himself sitting on the floor. He blinked his eyes. He could not remember that it had been visible for the last few minutes. Where had he been? His mind was clear now at any rate. This idea of something in common between him and Wither was all nonsense. Of course they meant to kill him in the end unless he could rescue himself by his own wits. What had he been thinking and feeling while he forgot that?

Gradually he realised that he had sustained some sort of attack, and that he had put up no resistance at all; and with that realisation a quite new kind of dread entered his mind. Though he was theoretically a materialist, he had all his life believed quite inconsistently, and even carelessly, in the freedom of his own will. He had seldom made a moral resolution, and when he had resolved some hours ago to trust the Belbury crew no further, he had taken it for granted that he would be able to do what he resolved. He knew, to be sure, that he might 'change his mind'; but till he did so, of course he would carry out his plan. It had never occurred to him that his mind could thus be changed for him, all in an instant of time, changed beyond recognition. If that sort of thing could happen … It was unfair. Here was a man trying (for the first time in his life) to do what was obviously the right thing – the thing that Jane and the Dimbles and Aunt Gilly would have approved of. You might have expected that when a man behaved in that way the universe would back him up. For the relics of such semi-savage versions of Theism as Mark had picked up in the course of his life were stronger in him than he knew, and he felt, though he would not have put it into words, that it was 'up to' the universe to reward his good resolutions. Yet, the very first moment you tried to be good, the universe let you down. It revealed gaps you had never dreamed of. It invented new laws for the express purpose of letting you down. That was what you got for your pains.

The cynics, then, were right. But at this thought, he stopped sharply. Some flavour that came with it had given him pause. Was this the other mood beginning again? Oh not that, at any price. He clenched his hands. No, no, no. He could not stand this much longer. He wanted Jane; he wanted Mrs Dimble; he wanted Denniston. He wanted somebody or something. 'Oh don't, don't let me go back into it,' he said; and then louder, 'don't, don't.' All that could in any sense be called himself went into that cry; and the dreadful consciousness of having played his last card began to turn slowly into a sort of peace. There was nothing more to be done. Unconsciously he allowed his muscles to relax. His young body was very tired by this time and even the hard floor was grateful to it. The cell also seemed to be somehow emptied and purged, as if it too were tired after the conflicts it had witnessed – emptied like a sky after rain, tired like a child after weeping. A dim consciousness that the night must be nearly ended stole over him, and he fell asleep.

·13·

They Have Pulled Down
Deep Heaven on Their Heads

'Stand! Stand where you are and tell me your name and business,' said Ransom.

The ragged figure on the threshold tilted its head a little sideways like one who cannot quite hear. At the same moment the wind from the opened door had its way with the house. The inner door, between the scullery and the kitchen, clapped to with a loud bang, isolating the three men from the women, and a large tin basin fell clattering into the sink. The stranger took a pace further into the room.

'*Sta*,' said Ransom in a loud voice. '*In nomine Patris et Filii et Spiritus Sancti, dic mihi qui sis et quam ob causam veneris.*'*

The Stranger raised his hand and flung back the dripping hair from his forehead. The light fell full on his face, from which Ransom had the impression of an immense quietness. Every muscle of this man's body seemed as relaxed as if he were asleep, and he stood absolutely still. Each drop of rain from the khaki coat struck the tiled floor exactly where the drop before it had fallen.

His eyes rested on Ransom for a second or two with no particular interest. Then he turned his head to his left, to where the door was flung back almost against the wall. MacPhee was concealed behind it.

'Come out,' said the Stranger in Latin. The words were spoken almost in a whisper, but so deep that even in that windshaken

---

* Stand. In the name of the Father and the Son and the Holy Ghost, tell me who you are and why you come.

room they made a kind of vibration. But what surprised Ransom much more was the fact that MacPhee immediately obeyed. He did not look at Ransom but at the Stranger. Then, unexpectedly, he gave an enormous yawn. The Stranger looked him up and down and then turned to the Director.

'Fellow,' he said in Latin, 'tell the Lord of this House that I am come.' As he spoke, the wind from behind him was whipping the coat about his legs and blowing his hair over his forehead; but his great mass stood as if it had been planted like a tree and he seemed in no hurry. And the voice, too, was such as one might imagine to be the voice of a tree, large and slow and patient, drawn up through roots and clay and gravel from the depths of the Earth.

'I am the Master here,' said Ransom, in the same language.

'To be sure!' answered the Stranger. 'And yonder whipper-snapper [*mastigia*] is without doubt your Bishop.' He did not exactly smile, but a look of disquieting amusement came into his keen eyes. Suddenly he poked his head forward so as to bring his face much nearer to the Director's.

'Tell your master that I am come,' he repeated in the same voice as before.

Ransom looked at him without the flicker of an eyelid.

'Do you really wish,' he said at last, 'that I call upon my Masters?'

'A daw that lives in a hermit's cell has learned before now to chatter book-Latin,' said the other. 'Let us hear your calling, man-nikin' (*homuncio*).

'I must use another language for it,' said Ransom.

'A daw could have Greek also in its bill.'

'It is not Greek.'

'Let us hear your Hebrew, then.'

'It is not Hebrew.'

'Nay,' answered the other with something like a chuckle, a chuckle deep hidden in his enormous chest and betrayed only by a slight movement of his shoulders, 'if you come to the gabble of barbarians, it will go hard but I shall out-chatter you. Here is excellent sport.'

'It may happen to seem to you the speech of barbarians,' said Ransom, 'for it is long since it has been heard. Not even in Numinor was it heard in the streets.'

The Stranger gave no start and his face remained as quiet as before, if it did not become quieter. But he spoke with a new interest.

'Your Masters let you play with dangerous toys,' he said. 'Tell me, slave, what is Numinor?'

'The true West,' said Ransom.

'Well,' said the other. Then, after a pause, he added, 'You have little courtesy to guests in this house. It is a cold wind on my back, and I have been long in bed. You see, I have already crossed the threshold.'

'I value that at a straw,' said Ransom. 'Shut the door, MacPhee,' he added in English. But there was no response; and looking round for the first time, he saw that MacPhee had sat down in the one chair which the scullery contained and was fast asleep.

'What is the meaning of this foolery?' said Ransom looking sharply at the Stranger.

'If you are indeed the Master of this house, you have no need to be told. If not, why should I give account of myself to such as you? Do not fear; your horse-boy will be none the worse.'

'This shall be seen to shortly,' said Ransom. 'In the meantime, I do not fear your entering the house. I have more cause to fear your escaping. Shut the door if you will, for you see my foot is hurt.'

The Stranger without ever taking his eyes off Ransom swept back his left hand behind him, found the door handle, and slammed the door to. MacPhee never stirred. 'Now,' he said, 'what of these Masters of yours?'

'My Masters are the Oyéresu.'

'Where did you hear that name?' asked the Stranger. 'Or, if you are truly of the College, why do they dress you like a slave?'

'Your own garments,' said Ransom, 'are not those of a druid.'

'That stroke was well put by,' answered the other. 'Since you have knowledge, answer me three questions, if you dare.'

'I will answer them, if I can. But as for daring, we shall see.'

The Stranger mused for a few seconds; then, speaking in a slightly sing-song voice, as though he repeated an old lesson, he asked, in two Latin hexameters, the following question:

'Who is called Sulva? What road does she walk? Why is the womb barren on one side? Where are the cold marriages?'

Ransom replied, 'Sulva is she whom mortals call the Moon. She walks in the lowest sphere. The rim of the world that was wasted goes through her. Half of her orb is turned towards us and shares our curse. Her other half looks to Deep Heaven; happy would he be who could cross that frontier and see the fields on her further side. On this side, the womb is barren and the marriages cold. There dwell an accursed people, full of pride and lust. There when a young man takes a maiden in marriage, they do not lie together, but each lies with a cunningly fashioned image of the other, made to move and to be warm by devilish arts, for real flesh will not please them, they are so dainty [*delicati*] in their dreams of lust. Their real children they fabricate by vile arts in a secret place.'

'You have answered well,' said the Stranger. 'I thought there were but three men in the world that knew this question. But my second may be harder. Where is the ring of Arthur the King? What Lord has such a treasure in his house?'

'The ring of the King,' said Ransom, 'is on Arthur's finger where he sits in the House of Kings in the cup-shaped land of Abhalljin, beyond the seas of Lur in Perelandra. For Arthur did not die; but Our Lord took him, to be in the body till the end of time and the shattering of Sulva, with Enoch and Elias and Moses and Melchisedec the King. Melchisedec is he in whose hall the steep-stoned ring sparkles on the fore-finger of the Pendragon.'

'Well answered,' said the Stranger. 'In my college it was thought that only two men in the world knew this. But as for my third question, no man knew the answer but myself. Who shall be Pendragon in the time when Saturn descends from his sphere? In what world did he learn war?'

'In the sphere of Venus I learned war,' said Ransom. 'In this age Lurga shall descend. I am the Pendragon.'

When he had said this, he took a step backwards for the big man had begun to move and there was a new look in his eyes. Any who had seen them as they stood thus face to face would have thought that it might come to fighting at any moment. But the Stranger had not moved with hostile purpose. Slowly, ponderously, yet not awkwardly, as though a mountain sank like a wave, he sank on one knee; and still his face was almost on a level with the Director's.

* ○ *

'This throws a quite unexpected burden on our resources,' said Wither to Frost, where they both sat in the outer room with the door ajar. 'I must confess I had not anticipated any serious difficulty about language.'

'We must get a Celtic scholar at once,' said Frost. 'We are regrettably weak on the philological side. I do not at the moment know who has discovered most about ancient British. Ransom would be the man to advise us if he were available. I suppose nothing has been heard of him by your department?'

'I need hardly point out,' said Wither, 'that Dr Ransom's philological attainments are by no means the only ground on which we are anxious to find him. If the least trace had been discovered, you may rest assured that you would have long since had the – ah – gratification of seeing him here in person.'

'Of course. He may not be in the Earth at all.'

'I met him once,' said Wither, half-closing his eyes. 'He was a most brilliant man in his way. A man whose penetrations and intuitions might have been of infinite value, if he had not embraced the cause of reaction. It is a saddening reflection …'

'Of course,' said Frost, interrupting him. 'Straik knows modern Welsh. His mother was a Welsh woman.'

'It would certainly be much more satisfactory,' said Wither, 'if we could, so to speak, keep the whole matter in the family. There would be something very disagreeable to me – and I am sure you would feel the same way yourself – about introducing a Celtic expert from outside.'

'The expert would, of course, be provided for as soon as we could dispense with his services,' replied Frost. 'It is the waste of time that is the trouble. What progress have you made with Straik?'

'Oh, really excellent,' said the Deputy Director. 'Indeed I am almost a little disappointed. I mean, my pupil is advancing so rapidly that it may be necessary to abandon an idea which, I confess, rather attracts me. I had been thinking while you were out of the room that it would be specially fitting and – ah – proper and gratifying if your pupil and mine could be initiated together. We should both, I am sure, have felt … But, of course, if Straik is ready some time before Studdock, I should not feel myself entitled to stand in his way. You will understand, my dear fellow, that I am not trying to make this anything like a test case as to the comparative efficacy of our very different methods.'

'It would be impossible for you to do so,' said Frost, 'since I have interviewed Studdock only once, and that one interview has had all the success that could be expected. I mentioned Straik only to find out whether he were already so far committed that he might properly be introduced to our guest.'

'Oh … as to being *committed*,' said Wither, 'in some sense … ignoring certain fine shades for the moment, while fully recognising their ultimate importance … I should not hesitate … we should be perfectly justified.'

'I was thinking,' said Frost, 'that there must be someone on duty here. He may wake at any moment. Our pupils – Straik and Studdock – could take it in turns. There is no reason why they should not be useful even before their full initiation. They would, of course, be under orders to ring us up the moment anything happened.'

'You think Mr – ah – Studdock is far enough on?'

'It doesn't matter,' said Frost. 'What harm can he do? He can't get *out*. And, in the meantime, we only want someone to watch. It would be a useful test.'

◆ ○ ◆

MacPhee who had just been refuting both Ransom and Alcasan's head by a two-edged argument which seemed unanswerable in the dream but which he never afterwards remembered, found himself violently waked by someone shaking his shoulder. He suddenly perceived that he was cold and his left foot was numb. Then he saw Denniston's face looking into his own. The scullery seemed full of people – Denniston and Dimble and Jane. They appeared extremely bedraggled, torn and muddy and wet.

'Are you all right?' Denniston was saying. 'I've been trying to wake you for several minutes.'

'All right?' said MacPhee swallowing once or twice and licking his lips. 'Aye. I'm all right.' Then he sat upright. 'There's been a – a man here,' he said.

'What sort of a man?' asked Dimble.

'Well,' said MacPhee. 'As to that … it's not just so easy … I fell asleep talking to him, to tell you the truth. I can't just bring to mind what we were saying.'

The others exchanged glances. Though MacPhee was fond of a little hot toddy on winter nights, he was a sober man: they had never seen him like this before. Next moment he jumped to his feet.

'Lord save us!' he exclaimed. 'He had the Director here. Quick! We must search the house and the garden. It was some kind of impostor or spy. I know now what's wrong with me. I've been hypnotised. There was a horse too. I mind the horse.'

This last detail had an immediate effect on his hearers. Denniston flung open the kitchen door and the whole party surged in after him. For a second they saw indistinct forms in the deep, red light of a large fire which had not been attended to for some hours; then, as Denniston found the switch and turned on the light, all drew a deep breath. The four women sat fast asleep. The jack-daw slept, perched on the back of an empty chair. Mr Bultitude, stretched out on his side across the hearth, slept also; his tiny, child-like snore, so disproportionate to his bulk, was audible in the momentary silence. Mrs Dimble, bunched in what seemed an uncomfortable position, was sleeping with her head on the table, a half-darned sock still clasped on her knees. Dimble looked at her with that incurable pity which men feel for any sleeper, but specially for a wife. Camilla, who had been in the rocking chair, was curled up in an attitude which was full of grace, like that of an animal accustomed to sleep anywhere. Mrs Maggs slept with her kind, commonplace mouth wide open; and Grace Ironwood, bolt upright as if she were awake, but with her head sagging a little to one side, seemed to submit with austere patience to the humiliation of unconsciousness.

'They're all right,' said MacPhee from behind. 'It's just the same as he did to me. We've no time to wake them. Get on.'

They passed from the kitchen into the flagged passage. To all of them except MacPhee the silence of the house seemed intense after their buffeting in the wind and rain. The lights as they switched them on successively revealed empty rooms and empty passages which wore the abandoned look of indoor midnight – fires dead in the grates, an evening paper on a sofa, a clock that had stopped. But no one had really expected to find much else on the ground floor. 'Now for upstairs,' said Dimble.

'The lights are on upstairs,' said Jane as they all came to the foot of the staircase.

'We turned them on ourselves from the passage,' said Dimble.

'I don't think we did,' said Denniston.

'Excuse me,' said Dimble to MacPhee, 'I think perhaps I'd better go first.'

Up to the first landing they were in darkness; on the second and last the light from the first floor fell. At each landing the stair made a right-angled turn, so that till you reached the second you could not see the lobby on the floor above. Jane and Denniston, who were last, saw MacPhee and Dimble stopped dead on the second landing; their faces in profile lit up, the backs of their heads in darkness. The Ulsterman's mouth was shut like a trap, his expression hostile and afraid. Dimble was open-mouthed. Then, forcing her tired limbs to run, Jane got up beside them and saw what they saw.

Looking down on them from the balustrade were two men, one clothed in sweepy garments of red and the other in blue. It was the Director who wore blue, and for one instant a thought that was pure nightmare crossed Jane's mind. The two robed figures looked to be two of the same sort ... and what, after all, did she know of this Director who had conjured her into his house and made her dream dreams and taught her the fear of Hell that very night? And there they were, the pair of them, talking their secrets and doing whatever such people would do, when they had emptied the house or laid its inhabitants to sleep. The man who had been dug up out of the earth and the man who had been in outer space ... and the one had told them that the other was an enemy, and now, the moment they met, here were the two of them, run together like two drops of quicksilver. All this time she had hardly looked at the Stranger. The Director seemed to have laid aside his crutch, and Jane had hardly seen him standing so straight and still before. The light so fell on his beard that it became a kind of halo; and on top of his head also she caught the glint of gold. Suddenly, while she thought of these things, she found that her eyes were looking straight into the eyes of the Stranger. Next moment she had noticed his size. The man was monstrous. And the two men were allies. And the Stranger was speaking and pointing at her as he spoke.

She did not understand the words; but Dimble did, and heard Merlin saying in what seemed to him a rather strange kind of Latin:

'Sir, you have in your house the falsest lady of any at this time alive.'

And Dimble heard the Director answer him in the same language:

'Sir, you are mistaken. She is doubtless like all of us a sinner; but the woman is chaste.'

'Sir,' said Merlin, 'know well that she has done in Logres a thing of which no less sorrow shall come than came of the stroke that Balinus struck. For, Sir, it was the purpose of God that she and her lord should between them have begotten a child by whom the enemies should have been put out of Logres for a thousand years.'

'She is but lately married,' said Ransom. 'The child may yet be born.'

'Sir,' said Merlin, 'be assured that the child will never be born, for the hour of its begetting is passed. Of their own will they are barren: I did not know till now that the usages of Sulva were so common among you. For a hundred generations in two lines the begetting of this child was prepared; and unless God should rip up the work of time, such seed, and such an hour, in such a land, shall never be again.'

'Enough said,' answered Ransom. 'The woman perceives that we are speaking of her.'

'It would be great charity,' said Merlin, 'if you gave order that her head should be cut from her shoulders; for it is a weariness to look at her.'

Jane, though she had a smattering of Latin, had not understood their conversation. The accent was unfamiliar, and the old druid used a vocabulary that was far beyond her reading – the Latin of a man to whom Apuleius and Martianus Capella were the primary classics and whose elegances resembled those of the *Hisperica Famina*. But Dimble had followed it. He thrust Jane behind him and called out, 'Ransom! What in Heaven's name is the meaning of this?'

Merlin spoke again in Latin and Ransom was just turning to answer him, when Dimble interrupted,

'Answer *us*,' he said. 'What has happened? Why are you dressed up like that? What are you doing with that bloodthirsty old man?'

MacPhee, who had followed the Latin even less than Jane, but who had been staring at Merlin as an angry terrier stares at a Newfoundland dog which has invaded its own garden, broke into the conversation: 'Dr Ransom,' he said. 'I don't know who the big man is and I'm no Latinist. But I know well that you've kept me under your eyes all this night against my own expressed will, and allowed me to be drugged and hypnotised. It gives me little pleasure, I assure you, to see yourself dressed up like something out of a pantomime and standing there hand in glove with that yogi, or shaman, or priest, or whatever he is. And you can tell him he need not look at me the way he's doing. I'm not afraid of him. And as for my own life and limb – if you, Dr Ransom, have changed sides after all that's come and gone, I don't know that I've much more use for either. But though I may be killed, I'm not going to be made a fool of. We're waiting for an explanation.'

The Director looked down on them in silence for a few seconds.

'Has it really come to this?' he said. 'Does not one of you trust me?'

'I do, Sir,' said Jane suddenly.

'These appeals to the passions and emotions,' said MacPhee, 'are nothing to the purpose. I could cry as well as anyone this moment if I gave my mind to it.'

'Well,' said the Director after a pause, 'there is some excuse for you all for we have all been mistaken. So has the enemy. This man is Merlinus Ambrosius. They thought that if he came back he would be on their side. I find he is on ours. You, Dimble, ought to realise that this was always a possibility.'

'That is true,' said Dimble. 'I suppose it was – well, the look of the thing – you and he standing there together: like *that*. And his appalling bloodthirstiness.'

'I have been startled by it myself,' said Ransom. 'But after all we had no right to expect that his penal code would be that of the nineteenth century. I find it difficult, too, to make him understand that I am not an absolute monarch.'

'Is – is he a Christian?' asked Dimble.

'Yes,' said Ransom. 'As for my clothes, I have for once put on the dress of my office to do him honour, and because I was ashamed. He mistook MacPhee and me for scullions or stable-boys. In his days, you see, men did not, except for necessity, go about in shapeless sacks of cloth, and drab was not a favourite colour.'

At this point Merlin spoke again. Dimble and the Director who alone could follow his speech heard him say, 'Who are these people? If they are your slaves, why do they do you no reverence? If they are enemies, why do we not destroy them?'

'They are my friends,' began Ransom in Latin, but MacPhee interrupted,

'Do I understand, Dr Ransom,' he said, 'that you are asking us to accept this person as a member of our organisation?'

'I am afraid,' said the Director, 'I cannot put it that way. He *is* a member of the organisation. And I must command you all to accept him.'

'And secondly,' continued MacPhee, 'I must ask what enquiries have been made into his credentials.'

'I am fully satisfied,' answered the Director. 'I am as sure of his good faith as of yours.'

'But the grounds of your confidence?' persisted MacPhee. 'Are we not to hear them?'

'It would be hard,' said the Director, 'to explain to you my reasons for trusting Merlinus Ambrosius; but no harder than to explain to him why, despite many appearances which might be misunderstood, I trust you.' There was just the ghost of a smile about his mouth as he said this. Then Merlin spoke to him again in Latin and he replied. After that Merlin addressed Dimble.

'The Pendragon tells me,' he said in his unmoved voice, 'that you accuse me for a fierce and cruel man. It is a charge I never heard before. A third part of my substance I gave to widows and poor men. I never sought the death of any but felons and heathen Saxons. As for the woman, she may live for me. I am not Master in this house. But would it be such a great matter if her head were struck off? Do not queens and ladies who would disdain her as their tire-woman go to the fire for less? Even that gallows bird [*cruciarius*] beside you – I mean you, fellow, though you speak nothing but your own barbarous tongue; you with the face like sour milk and the voice like a saw in a hard log and the legs like a crane's – even that cutpurse [*sector zonarius*], though I would have him to the gatehouse, yet the rope should be used on his back not his throat.'

MacPhee who realised, though without understanding the words, that he was the subject of some unfavourable comment, stood listening with that expression of entirely suspended judgment which is commoner in Northern Ireland and the Scotch lowlands than in England.

'Mr Director,' he said when Merlin had finished, 'I would be very greatly obliged if – '

'Come,' said the Director suddenly, 'we have none of us slept tonight. Arthur, will you come and light a fire for our guest in the big room at the North end of this passage? And would someone wake the women? Ask them to bring him up refreshments. A bottle of Burgundy and whatever you have cold. And then, all to bed. We need not stir early in the morning. All is going to be very well.'

◆ ○ ◆

'We're going to have difficulties with that new colleague of ours,' said Dimble. He was alone with his wife in their room at St Anne's late on the following day.

'Yes,' he repeated after a pause. 'What you'd call a strong colleague.'

'You look very tired, Cecil,' said Mrs Dimble.

'Well, it's been rather a gruelling conference,' said he. 'He's – he's a tiring man. Oh, I know we've all been fools. I mean, we've all been imagining that because he came back in the twentieth century he'd be a twentieth century man. Time is more important than we thought, that's all.'

'I felt that at lunch, you know,' said his wife. 'It was so silly not to have realised that he wouldn't know about forks. But what surprised me even more (after the first shock) was how – well, how *elegant* he was without them. I mean you could see it wasn't a case of having no manners but of having different ones.'

'Oh, the old boy's a gentleman in his own way – anyone can see that. But ... well, I don't know. I suppose it's all right.'

'What happened at the meeting?'

'Well, you see, everything had to be explained on both sides. We'd the dickens of a job to make him understand that Ransom isn't the king of this country or trying to become king. And then we had to break it to him that we weren't the British at all, but the English – what he'd call Saxons. It took him some time to get over that.'

'I see.'

'And then MacPhee had to choose that moment for embarking on an interminable explanation of the relations between Scotland and Ireland and England. All of which, of course, had to be translated. It was all nonsense too. Like a good many people, MacPhee imagines he's a Celt when, apart from his name, there's nothing Celtic about him any more than about Mr Bultitude. By the way Merlinus Ambrosius made a prophecy about Mr Bultitude.'

'Oh? What was that?'

'He said that before Christmas this bear would do the best deed that any bear had done in Britain except some other bear that none of us had ever heard of. He keeps on saying things like that. They just pop out when we're talking about something else, and in a rather different voice. As if he couldn't help it. He doesn't seem to know any *more* than the bit he tells you at the moment, if you see what I mean. As if something like a camera shutter opened at the back of his mind and closed again immediately and just one little item came through. It has rather a disagreeable effect.'

'He and MacPhee didn't quarrel again, I hope.'

'Not exactly. I'm afraid Merlinus Ambrosius wasn't taking MacPhee very seriously. From the fact that MacPhee is always being obstructive and rather rude and yet never gets sat on, I think Merlinus has concluded that he is the Director's fool. He seems to have got over his dislike for him. But I don't think MacPhee is going to like Merlinus.'

'Did you get down to actual business?' asked Mrs Dimble.

'Well, in a way,' said Dimble, wrinkling his forehead. 'We were all at cross-purposes, you see. The business about Ivy's husband being in prison came up, and Merlinus wanted to know why we hadn't rescued him. He seemed to imagine us just riding off and taking the County Jail by storm. That's the sort of thing one was up against all the time.'

'Cecil,' said Mrs Dimble suddenly. 'Is he going to be any use?'

'He's going to be able to *do* things, if that's what you mean. In that sense there's more danger of his being too much use than too little.'

'What sort of things?' asked his wife.

'The universe is so very complicated,' said Dr Dimble.

'So you have said rather often before, dear,' replied Mrs Dimble.

'Have I?' he said with a smile. 'How often, I wonder? As often as you've told the story of the pony and trap at Dawlish?'

'Cecil! I haven't told it for years.'

'My dear, I heard you telling it to Camilla the night before last.'

'Oh, *Camilla*. That was quite different. She'd never heard it before.'

'I don't know that we can be certain even about that … the universe being so complicated and all.' For a few minutes there was silence between them.

'But about Merlin?' asked Mrs Dimble presently.

'Have you ever noticed,' said Dimble, 'that the universe, and every little bit of the universe, is always hardening and narrowing and coming to a point?'

His wife waited as those wait who know by long experience the mental processes of the person who is talking to them.

'I mean this,' said Dimble in answer to the question she had not asked. 'If you dip into any college, or school, or parish, or family – anything you like – at a given point in its history, you always find that there was a time before that point when there was more elbow room and contrasts weren't quite so sharp; and that there's going to be a time after that point when there is even less room for indecision and choices are even more momentous. Good is always getting better and bad is always getting worse: the possibilities of even apparent neutrality are always diminishing. The whole thing is sorting itself out all the time, coming to a point, getting sharper and harder. Like in the poem about Heaven and Hell eating into merry Middle Earth from opposite sides … how does it go? Something about "eat every day" … "till all is *somethinged away*". It can't be *eaten*; that wouldn't scan. My memory has failed dreadfully these last few years. Do you know the bit, Margery?'

'What you were saying reminded me more of the bit in the Bible about the winnowing fan. Separating the wheat and the chaff. Or like Browning's line: "Life's business being just the terrible choice." '

'Exactly! Perhaps the whole time-process means just that and nothing else. But it's not only in questions of moral choice. Everything is getting more itself and more different from everything else all the time. Evolution means species getting less and less like one another. Minds get more and more spiritual, matter more and more material. Even in literature, poetry and prose draw further and further apart.'

Mrs Dimble with the ease born of long practice averted the danger, ever present in her house, of a merely literary turn being given to the conversation.

'Yes,' she said. 'Spirit and matter, certainly. That explains why people like the Studdocks find it so difficult to be happily married.'

'The Studdocks?' said Dimble, looking at her rather vaguely. The domestic problems of that young couple had occupied his mind a good deal less than they had occupied his wife's. 'Oh, I see. Yes. I daresay that has something to do with it. But about Merlin. What it comes to, as far as I can make out, is this. There were still possibilities for a man of that age which there aren't for a man of ours. The Earth itself was more like an animal in those days. And mental processes were much more like physical actions. And there were – well, Neutrals, knocking about.'

'Neutrals?'

'I don't mean, of course, that anything can be a *real* neutral. A conscious being is either obeying God or disobeying Him. But there might be things neutral in relation to us.'

'You mean *eldila* – angels?'

'Well, the word *angel* rather begs the question. Even the Oyéresu aren't exactly angels in the same sense as our guardian angels are. Technically they are Intelligences. The point is that while it may be true at the end of the world to describe every eldil either as an angel or a devil, and may even be true now, it was much less true in Merlin's time. There used to be things on this Earth pursuing their own business, so to speak. They weren't ministering spirits sent to help fallen humanity; but neither were they enemies preying upon us. Even in St Paul one gets glimpses of a population that won't exactly fit into our two columns of angels and devils. And if you go back further ... all the gods, elves, dwarfs, water-people, *fate*, *longaevi*. You and I know too much to think they are just illusions.'

'You think there are things like that?'

'I think there were. I think there was room for them then, but the universe has come more to a point. Not all rational things perhaps. Some would be mere wills inherent in matter, hardly conscious. More like animals. Others – but I don't really know. At any rate, that is the sort of situation in which one got a man like Merlin.'

'It all sounds rather horrible to me.'

'It was *rather* horrible. I mean even in Merlin's time (he came at the extreme tail end of it) though you could still use that sort of life in the universe innocently, you couldn't do it safely. The things weren't bad in themselves, but they were already bad for us. They sort of withered the man who dealt with them. Not on purpose. They couldn't help doing it. Merlinus is withered. He's quite pious and humble and all that, but something has been taken out of him. That quietness of his is just a little deadly, like the quiet of a gutted building. It's the result of having laid his mind open to something that broadens the environment just a bit too much. Like polygamy. It wasn't wrong for Abraham, but one can't help feeling that even he lost something by it.'

'Cecil,' said Mrs Dimble. 'Do you feel quite comfortable about the Director's using a man like this? I mean, doesn't it look a little bit like fighting Belbury with its own weapons?'

'No. I *had* thought of that. Merlin is the reverse of Belbury. He's at the opposite extreme. He is the last vestige of an old order in which matter and spirit were, from our modern point of view, confused. For him every operation on Nature is a kind of personal contact, like coaxing a child or stroking one's horse. After him came the modern man to whom Nature is something dead – a machine to be worked, and taken to bits if it won't work the way he pleases. Finally, come the Belbury people, who take over that view from the modern man unaltered and simply want to increase their power by tacking onto it the aid of spirits – extra-natural, anti-natural spirits. Of course they hoped to have it both ways. They thought the old *magia* of Merlin, which worked in with the spiritual qualities of Nature, loving and reverencing them and knowing them from within, could be combined with the new *goeteia* – the brutal surgery from without. No. In a sense Merlin represents what we've got to get back to in some different way. Do you know that he is forbidden by the rules of his order to use any edged tool on any growing thing?'

'Good gracious!' said Mrs Dimble. 'There's six o'clock. I'd promised Ivy to be in the kitchen at quarter to. There's no need for *you* to move, Cecil.'

'Do you know,' said Dimble, 'I think you are a wonderful woman.'

'Why?'

'How many women who had had their own house for thirty years would be able to fit into this menagerie as you do?'

'That's nothing,' said Mrs Dimble. 'Ivy had her own house too, you know. And it's much worse for her. After all, I haven't got my husband in jail.'

'You jolly soon will have,' said Dimble, 'if half the plans of Merlinus Ambrosius are put into action.'

◆ ○ ◆

Merlin and the Director were meanwhile talking in the Blue Room. The Director had put aside his robe and circlet and lay on his sofa. The druid sat in a chair facing him, his legs uncrossed, his pale large hands motionless on his knees, looking to modern eyes like an old conventional carving of a king. He was still robed and beneath the robe, as Ransom knew, had surprisingly little clothing, for the warmth of the house was to him excessive and he found trousers uncomfortable. His loud demands for oil after his bath had involved some hurried shopping in the village which had finally produced, by Denniston's exertions, a tin of Brilliantine. Merlinus had used it freely so that his hair and beard glistened and the sweet sticky smell filled the room. That was why Mr Bultitude had pawed so insistently at the door that he was finally admitted and now sat as near the magician as he could possibly get, his nostrils twitching. He had never smelled such an interesting man before.

'Sir,' said Merlin in answer to the question which the Director had just asked him. 'I give you great thanks. I cannot indeed understand the way you live and your house is strange to me. You give me a bath such as the Emperor himself might envy, but no one attends me to it; a bed softer than sleep itself, but when I rise from it I find I must put on my own clothes with my own hands as if I were a peasant. I lie in a room with windows of pure crystal so that you can see the sky as clearly when they are shut as when they are open, and there is not wind enough within the room to blow out an unguarded taper; but I lie in it alone with no more honour than a prisoner in a dungeon. Your people eat dry and tasteless flesh but it is off plates as smooth as ivory and as round as the sun. In all the house there are warmth and softness and silence that might put a man in mind of paradise terrestrial; but no hangings, no beautified pavements, no musicians, no perfumes, no high seats, not a gleam of gold, not a hawk, not a hound. You seem to me to live neither like a rich man nor a poor one: neither like a lord nor a hermit. Sir, I tell you these things because you have asked me. They are of no importance. Now that none hears us save the last of the seven bears of Logres, it is time that we should open counsels to each other.'

He glanced at the Director's face as he spoke and then, as if startled by what he saw there, leaned sharply forward.

'Does your wound pain you?' he asked.

Ransom shook his head. 'No,' he said, 'it is not the wound. We have terrible things to talk of.'

The big man stirred uneasily.

'Sir,' said Merlinus in a deeper and softer voice, 'I could taken all the anguish from your heel as though I were wiping it out with a sponge. Give me but seven days to go in and out and up and down and to and fro, to renew old acquaintance. These fields and I, this wood and I, have much to say to one another.'

As he said this, he was leaning forward so that his face and the bear's were almost side by side, and it almost looked as if those two might have been engaged in some kind of furry and grunted conversation. The druid's face had a strangely animal appearance: not sensual nor fierce but full of the patient, unarguing sagacity of a beast. Ransom's, meanwhile, was full of torment.

'You might find the country much changed,' he said, forcing a smile.

'No,' said Merlin. 'I do not reckon to find it much changed.' The distance between the two men was increasing every moment. Merlin was like something that ought not to be indoors. Bathed and anointed though he was, a sense of mould, gravel, wet leaves, weedy water, hung about him.

'Not *changed*,' he repeated in an almost inaudible voice. And in that deepening inner silence of which his face bore witness, one might have believed that he listened continually to a murmur of evasive sounds: rustling of mice and stoats, thumping progression of frogs, the small shock of falling hazel nuts, creaking of branches, runnels trickling, the very growing of grass. The bear had closed its eyes. The whole room was growing heavy with a sort of floating anæsthesia.

'Through me,' said Merlin, 'you can suck up from the Earth oblivion of all pains.'

'Silence,' said the Director sharply. He had been sinking down into the cushions of his sofa with his head drooping a little towards his chest. Now he suddenly sat bolt upright. The magician started and straightened himself likewise. The air of the room was cleared. Even the bear opened its eyes again.

'No,' said the Director. 'God's glory, do you think you were dug out of the earth to give me a plaster for my heel? We have drugs that could cheat the pain as well as your earth-magic or better, if it were not my business to bear it to the end. I will hear no more of that. Do you understand?'

'I hear and obey,' said the magician. 'But I meant no harm. If not to heal your own wound, yet for the healing of Logres, you will need my commerce with field and water. It must be that I should go in and out, and to and fro, renewing old acquaintance. It will not be changed, you know. Not what you would call *changed*.'

Again that sweet heaviness, like the smell of hawthorn, seemed to be flowing back over the Blue Room.

'No,' said the Director in a still louder voice, 'that cannot be done any longer. The soul has gone out of the wood and water. Oh, I daresay you could awake them; a little. But it would not be enough. A storm, or even a river-flood would be of little avail against our present enemy. Your weapon would break in your hands. For the Hideous Strength confronts us and it is as in the days when Nimrod built a tower to reach heaven.'

'Hidden it may be,' said Merlinus. 'But not *changed*. Leave me to work, Lord. I will wake it. I will set a sword in every blade of grass to wound them and the very clods of earth shall be venom to their feet. I will –'

'No,' said the Director. 'I forbid you to speak of it. If it were possible, it would be unlawful. Whatever of spirit may still linger in the earth has withdrawn fifteen hundred years further away from us since your time. You shall not speak a word to it. You shall not lift your little finger to call it up. I command you. It is in this age utterly unlawful.' Hitherto, he had been speaking sternly and coldly. Now he leaned forward and said in a different voice, 'It never was *very* lawful, even in your day. Remember, when we first knew that you would be awaked, we thought you would be on the side of the enemy. And because Our Lord does all things for each, one of the purposes of your reawakening was that your own soul should be saved.'

Merlin sank back into his chair like a man unstrung. The bear licked his hand where it hung, pale and relaxed, over the arm of the chair.

'Sir,' said Merlin presently, 'if I am not to work for you in that fashion, then you have taken into your house a silly bulk of flesh. For I am no longer much of a man of war. If it comes to point and edge I avail little.'

'Not that way either,' said Ransom, hesitating like a man who is reluctant to come to the point. 'No power that is merely earthly,' he continued at last, 'will serve against the Hideous Strength.'

'Then let us all to prayers,' said Merlinus. 'But there also ... I was not reckoned of much account ... they called me a devil's son, some of them. It was a lie. But I do not know why I have been brought back.'

'Certainly, let us stick to our prayers,' said Ransom. 'Now and always. But that was not what I meant. There are celestial powers: created powers, not in this Earth, but in the Heavens.'

Merlinus looked at him in silence.

'You know well what I am speaking of,' said Ransom. 'Did not I tell you when we first met that the Oyéresu were my Masters?'

'Of course,' said Merlin. 'And that was how I knew you were of the College. Is it not our pass-word all over the Earth?'

'A pass-word?' exclaimed Ransom with a look of surprise. 'I did not know that.'

'But ... but,' said Merlinus, 'if you knew not the pass-word, how did you come to say it?'

'I said it because it was true.'

The magician licked his lips which had become very pale.

'True as the plainest things are true,' repeated Ransom. 'True as it is true that you sit here with my bear beside you.'

Merlin spread out his hands. 'You are my father and mother,' he said. His eyes, steadily fixed on Ransom, were large as those of an awe-struck child, but for the rest he looked a smaller man than Ransom had first taken him to be.

'Suffer me to speak,' he said at last, 'or slay me if you will, for I am in the hollow of your hand. I had heard of it in my own days – that some had spoken with the gods. Blaise my Master knew a few words of that speech. Yet these were, after all, powers of Earth. For – I need not teach you, you know more than I – it is not the very Oyéresu, the true powers of Heaven, whom the greatest of our craft meet, but only their earthly wraiths, their shadows. Only the earth-Venus, the earth-Mercurius; not Perelandra herself, not Viritrilbia himself. It is only …'

'I am not speaking of the wraiths,' said Ransom. 'I have stood before Mars himself in the sphere of Mars and before Venus herself in the sphere of Venus. It is their strength, and the strength of some greater than they, which will destroy our enemies.'

'But, Lord,' said Merlin, 'how can this be? Is it not against the Seventh Law?'

'What law is that?' asked Ransom.

'Has not our Fair Lord made it a law for Himself that He will not send down the Powers to mend or mar in this Earth until the end of all things? Or is this the end that is even now coming to pass?'

'It may be the beginning of the end,' said Ransom. 'But I know nothing of that. Maleldil may have made it a law not to send down the Powers. But if men by enginry and natural philosophy learn to fly into the Heavens, and come, in the flesh, among the heavenly powers and trouble them, He has not forbidden the Powers to react. For all this is within the natural order. A wicked man did learn so to do. He came flying, by a subtle engine, to where Mars dwells in Heaven and to where Venus dwells, and took me with him as a captive. And there I spoke with the true Oyéresu face to face. You understand me?'

Merlin inclined his head.

'And so the wicked man had brought about, even as Judas brought about, the thing he least intended. For now there was one man in the world – even myself – who was known to the Oyéresu and spoke their tongue, neither by God's miracle nor by magic from Numinor, but naturally, as when two men meet in a road. Our enemies had taken away from themselves the protection of the Seventh Law. They had broken by natural philosophy the barrier which God of His own power would not break. Even so they sought you as a friend and raised up for themselves a scourge. And that is why Powers of Heaven have come down to this house, and in this chamber where we are now discoursing Malacandra and Perelandra have spoken to me.'

Merlin's face became a little paler. The bear nosed at his hand, unnoticed.

'I have become a bridge,' said Ransom.

'Sir,' said Merlin, 'what will come of this? If they put forth their power, they will unmake all Middle Earth.'

'Their naked power, yes,' said Ransom. 'That is why they will work only through a man.'

The magician drew one large hand across his forehead.

'Through a man whose mind is opened to be so invaded,' said Ransom, 'one who by his own will once opened it. I take Our Fair Lord to witness that if it were my task, I would not refuse it. But he will not suffer a mind that still has its virginity to be so violated. And through a black magician's mind their purity neither can nor will operate. One who has dabbled … in the days when dabbling had not begun to be evil, or was only just beginning … and also a Christian man and a penitent. A tool (I must speak plainly) good enough to be so used and not too good. In all these Western parts of the world there was only one man who had lived in those days and could still be recalled. You –'

He stopped, shocked at what was happening. The huge man had risen from his chair, and stood towering over him. From his horribly opened mouth there came a yell that seemed to Ransom utterly bestial, though it was in fact only the yell of primitive Celtic lamentation. It was horrifying to see that withered and bearded face all blubbered with undisguised tears like a child's. All the

Roman surface in Merlinus had been scraped off. He had become a shameless, archaic monstrosity babbling out entreaties in a mixture of what sounded like Welsh and what sounded like Spanish.

'Silence,' shouted Ransom. 'Sit down. You put us both to shame.'

As suddenly as it had begun the frenzy ended. Merlin resumed his chair. To a modern it seemed strange that, having recovered his self-control, he did not show the slightest embarrassment at his temporary loss of it. The whole character of the two-sided society in which this man must have lived became clearer to Ransom than pages of history could have made it.

'Do not think,' said Ransom, 'that for me either it is child's play to meet those who will come down for your empowering.'

'Sir,' faltered Merlin, 'you have been in Heaven. I am but a man. I am not the son of one of the Airish Men. That was a lying story. How can I? ... You are not as I. You have looked upon their faces before.'

'Not on all of them,' said Ransom. 'Greater spirits than Malacandra and Perelandra will descend this time. We are in God's hands. It may unmake us both. There is no promise that either you or I will save our lives or our reason. I do not know how we can dare to look upon their faces; but I know we cannot dare to look upon God's if we refuse this enterprise.'

Suddenly the magician smote his hand upon his knee.

'*Mehercule*!' he cried. 'Are we not going too fast? If you are the Pendragon, I am the High Council of Logres and I will counsel you. If the Powers must tear me in pieces to break our enemies, God's will be done. But is it yet come to that? This Saxon king of yours who sits at Windsor, now. Is there no help in him?'

'He has no power in this matter.'

'Then is he not weak enough to be overthrown?'

'I have no wish to overthrow him. He is the king. He was crowned and anointed by the Archbishop. In the order of Logres I may be Pendragon, but in the order of Britain I am the King's man.'

'Is it then his great men – the counts and legates and bishops – who do the evil and he does not know of it?'

'It is – though they are not exactly the sort of great men you have in mind.'

'And are we not big enough to meet them in plain battle?'

'We are four men, some women, and a bear.'

'I saw the time when Logres was only myself and one man and two boys, and one of those was a churl. Yet we conquered.'

'It could not be done now. They have an engine called the Press whereby the people are deceived. We should die without even being heard of.'

'But what of the true clerks? Is there no help in them? It cannot be that *all* your priests and bishops are corrupted.'

'The Faith itself is torn in pieces since your day and speaks with a divided voice. Even if it were made whole, the Christians are but a tenth part of the people. There is no help there.'

'Then let us seek help from over sea. Is there no Christian prince in Neustria or Ireland or Benwick who would come in and cleanse Britain if he were called?'

'There is no Christian prince left. These other countries are even as Britain, or else sunk deeper still in the disease.'

'Then we must go higher. We must go to him whose office it is to put down tyrants and give life to dying kingdoms. We must call on the Emperor.'

'There is no Emperor.'

'No Emperor ...' began Merlin, and then his voice died away. He sat still for some minutes wrestling with a world which he had never envisaged. Presently he said, 'A thought comes into my mind and I do not know whether it is good or evil. But because I am the High Council of Logres I will not hide it from you. This is a cold age in which I have awaked. If all this West part of the world is apostate, might it not be lawful, in our great need, to look farther ... beyond Christendom? Should we not find some even among the heathen who are not wholly corrupt? There were tales in my day of some such: men who knew not the articles of our most holy

Faith, but who worshipped God as they could and acknowledged the Law of Nature. Sir, I believe it would be lawful to seek help even there. Beyond Byzantium. It was rumoured also that there was knowledge in those lands – an Eastern circle and wisdom that came West from Numinor. I know not where – Babylon, Arabia or Cathay. You said your ships had sailed all round the earth, above and beneath.'

Ransom shook his head. 'You do not understand' he said. 'The poison was brewed in these West lands but it has spat itself everywhere by now. However far you went you would find the machines, the crowded cities, the empty thrones, the false writings, the barren beds: men maddened with false promises and soured with true miseries, worshipping the iron works of their own hands, cut off from Earth their mother and from the Father in Heaven. You might go East so far that East became West and you returned to Britain across the great Ocean, but even so you would not have come out anywhere into the light. The shadow of one dark wing is over all Tellus.'

'Is it then the end?' asked Merlin.

'And this,' said Ransom, ignoring the question, 'is why we have no way left at all save the one I told you. The Hideous Strength holds all this Earth in its fist to squeeze as it wishes. But for their one mistake, there would be no hope left. If of their own evil will they had not broken the frontier and let in the celestial Powers, this would be their moment of victory. Their own strength has betrayed them. They have gone to the gods who would not have come to them, and pulled down Deep Heaven on their heads. Therefore, they will die. For though you search every cranny to escape, now that you see all crannies closed, you will not disobey me.'

And then, very slowly, there crept back into Merlin's white face, first closing his dismayed mouth and finally gleaming in his eyes, that almost animal expression, earthy and healthy and with a glint of half-humorous cunning.

'Well,' he said, 'if the Earths are stopped, the fox faces the hounds. But had I known who you were at our first meeting,

I think I would have put the sleep on you as I did on your Fool.'

'I am a very light sleeper since I have travelled in the Heavens,' said Ransom.

'Real Life Is Meeting'

Since the day and night of the outer world made no difference in Mark's cell, he did not know whether it was minutes or hours later that he found himself once more awake, once more confronting Frost, and still fasting. The Professor came to ask if he had thought over their recent conversation. Mark, who judged that some decent show of reluctances would make his final surrender more convincing, replied that only one thing was still troubling him. He did not quite understand what he in particular or humanity in general stood to gain by co-operation with the Macrobes. He saw clearly that the motives on which most men act, and which they dignify by the names of patriotism or duty to humanity, were mere products of the animal organism, varying according to the behaviour pattern of different communities. But he did not yet see what was to be substituted for these irrational motives. On what ground henceforward were actions to be justified or condemned?

'If one insists on putting the question in those terms,' said Frost, 'I think Waddington has given the best answer. Existence is its own justification. The tendency to developmental change which we call Evolution is justified by the fact that it is a general characteristic of biological entities. The present establishment of contact between the highest biological entities and the Macrobes is justified by the fact that it is occurring, and it ought to be increased because an increase is taking place.'

'You think, then,' said Mark, 'that there would be no sense in asking whether the general tendency of the universe might be in the direction we should call Bad?'

'There could be no sense at all,' said Frost. 'The judgment you are trying to make turns out on inspection to be simply an expression of emotion. Huxley himself, could only express it by using emotive terms such as "gladiatorial" or "ruthless". I am referring to the famous Romanes lecture. When the so-called struggle for existence is seen simply as an actuarial theorem, we have, in Waddington's words, "a concept as unemotional as a definite integral" and the emotion disappears. With it disappears that preposterous idea of an external standard of value which the emotion produced.'

'And the actual tendency of events,' said Mark, 'would still be self-justified and in that sense "good" when it was working for the extinction of all organic life, as it presently will?'

'Of course,' replied Frost, 'if you insist on formulating the problem in those terms. In reality the question is meaningless. It presupposes a means-and-end pattern of thought which descends from Aristotle, who in his turn was merely hypostatising elements in the experience of an iron-age agricultural community. Motives are not the causes of action but its by-products. You are merely wasting your time by considering them. When you have attained real objectivity you will recognise, not *some* motives, but *all* motives as merely animal, subjective epiphenomena. You will then have no motives and you will find that you do not need them. Their place will be supplied by something else which you will presently understand better than you do now. So far from being impoverished your action will become much more efficient.'

'I see,' said Mark. The philosophy which Frost was expounding was by no means unfamiliar to him. He recognised it at once as the logical conclusion of thoughts which he had always hitherto accepted and which at this moment he found himself irrevocably rejecting. The knowledge that his own assumptions led to Frost's position combined with what he saw in Frost's face and what he had experienced in this very cell, effected a complete conversion. All the philosophers and evangelists in the world might not have done the job so neatly.

'And that,' continued Frost, 'is why a systematic training in objectivity must be given to you. Its purpose is to eliminate from your mind one by one the things you have hitherto regarded as grounds for action. It is like killing a nerve. That whole system of instinctive preferences, whatever ethical, aesthetic, or logical disguise they wear, is to be simply destroyed.'

'I get the idea,' said Mark though with an inward reservation that his present instinctive desire to batter the Professor's face into a jelly would take a good deal of destroying.

After that, Frost took Mark from the cell and gave him a meal in some neighbouring room. It also was lit by artificial light and had no window. The Professor stood perfectly still and watched him while he ate. Mark did not know what the food was and did not much like it, but he was far too hungry by now to refuse it if refusal had been possible. When the meal was over Frost led him to the ante-room of the Head and once more he was stripped and re-clothed in surgeon's overalls and a mask. Then he was brought in, into the presence of the gaping and dribbling Head. To his surprise, Frost took not the slightest notice of it. He led him across the room to a narrower little door with a pointed arch, in the far wall. Here he paused and said, 'Go in. You will speak to no one of what you find here. I will return presently.' Then he opened the door and Mark went in.

The room, at first sight, was an anticlimax. It appeared to be an empty committee room with a long table, eight or nine chairs, some pictures, and (oddly enough) a large stepladder in one corner. Here also there were no windows; it was lit by an electric light which produced, better than Mark had ever seen it produced before, the illusion of daylight – of a cold, grey place out of doors. This, combined with the absence of a fireplace, made it seem chilly though the temperature was not in fact very low.

A man of trained sensibility would have seen at once that the room was ill-proportioned, not grotesquely so, but sufficiently to produce dislike. It was too high and too narrow. Mark felt the effect without analysing the cause and the effect grew on him as time passed. Sitting staring about him he next noticed the door – and thought at first that he was the victim of some optical illusion. It took him quite a long time to prove to himself that he was not. The point of the arch was not in the centre: the whole thing was lop-sided. Once again, the error was not gross. The thing was near enough to the true to deceive you for a moment and to go on teasing the mind even after the deception had been unmasked. Involuntarily one kept shifting the head to find positions from which it would look right after all. He turned round and sat with his back to it … one mustn't let it become an obsession.

Then he noticed the spots on the ceiling. They were not mere specks of dirt or discolouration. They were deliberately painted on: little round black spots placed at irregular intervals on the pale mustard-coloured surface. There were not a great many of them: perhaps thirty … or was it a hundred? He determined that he would not fall into the trap of trying to count them. They would be hard to count, they were so irregularly placed. Or weren't they? Now that his eyes were growing used to them (and one couldn't help noticing that there were five in that little group to the right), their arrangement seemed to hover on the verge of regularity. They suggested some kind of pattern. Their peculiar ugliness consisted in the very fact that they kept on suggesting it and then frustrating the expectation thus aroused. Suddenly he realised that this was another trap. He fixed his eyes on the table.

There were spots on the table too: white ones. Shiny white spots, not quite round. And arranged, apparently, to correspond to the spots on the ceiling. Or were they? No, of course not … ah, now he had it! The pattern (if you could call it a pattern) on the table was an exact reversal of that on the ceiling. But with certain exceptions. He found he was glancing rapidly from one to the other, trying to puzzle it out. For the third time he checked himself. He got up and began to walk about. He had a look at the pictures.

Some of them belonged to a school of art with which he was already familiar. There was a portrait of a young woman who held her mouth wide open to reveal the fact that the inside of it was thickly overgrown with hair. It was very skilfully painted in the photographic manner so that you could almost feel that hair; indeed you could not avoid feeling it however hard you tried. There was a giant mantis playing a fiddle while being eaten by another mantis, and a man with corkscrews instead of arms bathing in a flat, sadly coloured sea beneath a summer sunset. But most of the pictures were not of this kind. At first, most of them seemed rather ordinary, though Mark was a little surprised at the predominance of scriptural themes. It was only at the second or third glance that one discovered certain unaccountable details – something odd about the positions of the figures' feet or the arrangement of their fingers or the grouping. And who was the person standing between the Christ and the Lazarus? And why were there so many beetles under the table in the Last Supper? What was the curious trick of lighting that made each picture look like something seen in delirium? When once these questions had been raised the apparent ordinariness of the pictures became their supreme menace – like the ominous surface innocence at the beginning of certain dreams. Every fold of drapery, every piece of architecture, had a meaning one could not grasp but which withered the mind. Compared with these the other, surrealistic, pictures were mere foolery. Long ago Mark had read somewhere of 'things of that extreme evil which seem innocent to the uninitiate', and had wondered what sort of things they might be. Now he felt he knew.

He turned his back on the pictures and sat down. He understood the whole business now. Frost was not trying to make him insane; at least not in the sense Mark had hitherto given to the word 'insanity'. Frost had meant what he said. To sit in the room was the first step towards what Frost called objectivity – the process whereby all specifically human reactions were killed in a man so that he might become fit for the fastidious society of the Macrobes. Higher degrees in the asceticism of anti-Nature would doubtless follow: the eating of abominable food, the dabbling in dirt and blood, the ritual performances of calculated obscenities.

They were, in a sense, playing quite fair with him – offering him the very same initiation through which they themselves had passed and which had divided them from humanity, distending and dissipating Wither into a shapeless ruin while it condensed and sharpened Frost into the hard, bright, little needle that he now was.

But after an hour or so this long, high coffin of a room began to produce on Mark an effect which his instructor had probably not anticipated. There was no return of the attack which he had suffered last night in the cell. Whether because he had already survived that attack, or because the imminence of death had drawn the tooth of his lifelong desire for the esoteric, or because he had (in a fashion) called very urgently for help, the built and painted perversity of this room had the effect of making him aware, as he had never been aware before, of this room's opposite. As the desert first teaches men to love water, or as absence first reveals affection, there rose up against this background of the sour and the crooked some kind of vision of the sweet and the straight. Something else – something he vaguely called the 'Normal' – apparently existed. He had never thought about it before. But there it was – solid, massive, with a shape of its own, almost like something you could touch, or eat, or fall in love with. It was all mixed up with Jane and fried eggs and soap and sunlight and the rooks cawing at Cure Hardy and the thought that, somewhere outside, daylight was going on at that moment. He was not thinking in moral terms at all; or else (what is much the same thing) he was having his first deeply moral experience. He was choosing a side: the Normal. 'All that', as he called it, was what he chose. If the scientific point of view led away from 'all that', then be damned to the scientific point of view! The vehemence of his choice almost took his breath away; he had not had such a sensation before. For the moment he hardly cared if Frost and Wither killed him.

I do not know how long this mood would have lasted; but while it was still at its height Frost returned. He led Mark to a bedroom where a fire blazed and an old man lay in bed. The light gleaming on glasses and silver and the soft luxury of the room so raised

Mark's spirits that he found it difficult to listen while Frost told him that he must remain here on duty till relieved and must ring up the Deputy Director if the patient spoke or stirred. He himself was to say nothing; indeed, it would be useless if he did for the patient did not understand English.

Frost retired. Mark glanced round the room. He was reckless now. He saw no possibility of leaving Belbury alive unless he allowed himself to be made into a dehumanised servant of the Macrobes. Meanwhile, do or die for it, he was going to have a meal. There were all sorts of delights on that table. Perhaps a smoke first, with his feet on the fender.

'Damn!' he said as he put his hand into his pocket and found it empty. At the same moment he noticed that the man in the bed had opened his eyes and was looking at him. 'I'm sorry,' said Mark, 'I didn't mean –' and then stopped.

The man sat up in bed and jerked his head towards the door.

'Ah?' he said enquiringly.

'I beg your pardon', said Mark.

'Ah?' said the man again. And then, 'Foreigners, eh?'

'You *do* speak English, then?' said Mark.

'Ah,' said the man. After a pause of several seconds he said, 'Guv'ner.' Mark looked at him. 'Guv'ner,' repeated the patient with great energy, 'you ha'nt got such a thing as a bit of baccy about you? Ah?'

◆ ○ ◆

'I think that's all we can do for the present,' said Mother Dimble. 'We'll do the flowers this afternoon.' She was speaking to Jane and both were in what was called the Lodge – a little stone house beside the garden door at which Jane had been first admitted to the Manor. Mrs Dimble and Jane had been preparing it for the Maggs family. For Mr Maggs's sentence expired today and Ivy had gone off by train on the previous afternoon to spend the night with an aunt in the town where he was imprisoned and to meet him at the prison gate.

When Mrs Dimble had told her husband how she would be engaged that morning he had said, 'Well, it can't take you very long just lighting a fire and making a bed.' I share Dr Dimble's sex and his limitation. I have no idea what the two women found to do in the Lodge for all the hours they spent there. Even Jane had hardly anticipated it. In Mrs Dimble's hands the task of airing the little house and making the bed for Ivy Maggs and her jail-bird husband became something between a game and a ritual. It woke in Jane vague memories of helping at Christmas or Easter decorations in church when she had been a small child. But it also suggested to her literary memory all sorts of things out of sixteenth-century epithalamiums: age-old superstitions, jokes, and sentimentalities about bridal beds and marriage bowers, with omens at the threshold and fairies upon the hearth. It was an atmosphere extraordinarily alien to that in which she had grown up. A few weeks ago she would have disliked it. Was there not something absurd about that stiff, twinkling archaic world – the mixture of prudery and sensuality, the stylised ardours of the groom and the conventional bashfulness of the bride, the religious sanction, the permitted salacities of Fescennine song, and the suggestion that everyone except the principals might be expected to be rather tipsy? How had the human race ever come to imprison in such a ceremony the most unceremonious thing in the world? But she was no longer sure of her reaction. What she was sure of was the dividing line that included Mother Dimble in that world and left her outside. Mother Dimble, for all her nineteenth-century propriety, or perhaps because of it, struck her this afternoon as being herself an archaic person. At every moment she seemed to join hands with some solemn yet roguish company of busy old women who had been tucking young lovers into beds since the world began with an incongruous mixture of nods and winks and blessings and tears – quite impossible old women in ruffs or wimples who would be making Shakespearian jokes about codpieces and cuckoldry at one moment and kneeling devoutly at altars the next. It was very odd; for, of course, as far as their conversation was concerned the difference between them was reversed. Jane, in a literary argument, could have talked about codpieces with great *sang-froid*, while Mother Dimble was an Edwardian lady who would simply have ignored such a subject out of existence if any modernised booby had been so unfortunate as to raise it in her presence. Perhaps the weather had some bearing on Jane's curious sensations. The frost had ended and it was one of those days of almost piercingly sweet mildness which sometimes occur in the very beginning of winter.

Ivy had discussed her own story with Jane only the day before. Mr Maggs had stolen some money from the laundry that he worked for. He had done this before he met Ivy and at a time when he had got into bad company. Since he and Ivy had started going out together he had gone 'as straight, as straight'; but the little crime had been unearthed and come out of the past to catch him, and he had been arrested about six weeks after their marriage. Jane had said very little during the telling of the story. Ivy had not seemed conscious of the purely social stigma attaching to petty theft and a term of imprisonment, so that Jane would have had no opportunity to practise, even if she had wished, that almost technical 'kindness' which some people reserve for the sorrows of the poor. On the other hand, she was given no chance to be revolutionary or speculative – to suggest that theft was no more criminal than all wealth was criminal. Ivy seemed to take traditional morality for granted. She had been 'ever so upset' about it. It seemed to matter a great deal in one way, and not to matter at all in another. It had never occurred to her that it should alter her relations with her husband – as though theft, like ill health, were one of the normal risks one took in getting married.

'I always say, you can't expect to know everything about a boy till you're married, not really,' she had said.

'I suppose not,' said Jane.

'Of course, it's the same for them,' added Ivy. 'My old Dad used often to say he'd never have married Mum, not if he'd known how she snored. And she said herself, "No, Dad, that you wouldn't!"'

'That's rather different, I suppose,' said Jane.

'Well, what I say is, if it wasn't one thing it'd be something else. That's how I look at it. And it isn't as if they hadn't a lot to put up with too. Because they've sort of got to get married if they're the right sort, poor things, but, whatever we say, Jane, a woman takes a lot of living with. I don't mean what you'd call a bad woman. I remember one day – it was before you came – Mother Dimble was saying something to the Doctor; and there he was sitting reading something, you know the way he does, with his fingers under some of the pages and a pencil in his hand – not the way you or I'd read – and he just said, "Yes dear," and we both of us knew he hadn't been listening. And I said, "There you are, Mother Dimble," said I, "that's how they treat us once they're married. They don't even listen to what we say," I said. And do you know what she said? "Ivy Maggs," said she, "did it ever come into your mind to ask whether anyone *could* listen to all we say?" Those were her very words. Of course I wasn't going to give in to it, not before him, so I said, "Yes, they could." But it was a fair knock-out. You know often I've been talking to my husband for a long time and he's looked up and asked me what I've been saying and, do you know? I haven't been able to remember myself!'

'Oh, that's different,' said Jane. 'It's when people drift apart – take up quite different opinions – join different sides … '

'You must be ever so anxious about Mr Studdock,' replied Ivy. 'I'd never be able to sleep a wink if I were in your shoes. But the Director'll bring it all right in the end. You see if he don't.'

Mrs Dimble went back to the house presently to fetch some little nicety which would put the finishing-touch to the bedroom in the Lodge. Jane, feeling a little tired, knelt on the window seat and put her elbows on the sill and her chin in her hands. The sun was almost hot. The thought of going back to Mark if Mark were ever rescued from Belbury was one which her mind had long accepted; it was not horrifying to her, but flat and insipid. It was not the less so because at this moment she fully forgave him for his conjugal crime of sometimes apparently preferring her person to her conversation and sometimes his own thoughts to both. Why should anyone be particularly interested in what she said? This new humility would even have been pleasant to her if it had been directed to anyone more exciting than Mark. She must, of course, be very different with him when they met again. But it was that 'again' which so took the savour out of the good resolution – like going back to a sum one had already got wrong and working it out afresh on the same scrawled page of the exercise book. 'If they met again . . .' she felt guilty at her lack of anxiety. Almost the same moment she found that she was a little anxious. For hitherto she had always somehow assumed that Mark would come back. The possibility of his death now presented itself. She had no direct emotions about herself living afterwards; she just saw the image of Mark dead, that face dead, in the middle of a pillow, that whole body rigid, those hands and arms (for good and ill so different from all other hands and arms) stretched out straight and useless like a doll's. She felt very cold. Yet the sun was hotter than ever – almost impossibly hot for the time of year. It was very still too, so still that she could hear the movements of a small bird which was hopping along the path outside the window. This path led to the door in the garden wall by which she had first entered. The bird hopped on to the threshold of that door, and onto someone's foot. For now Jane saw that someone was sitting on a little seat just inside the door. This person was only a few yards away, and she must have been sitting very quiet for Jane not to have noticed her.

A flame-coloured robe, in which her hands were hidden, covered this person from the feet to where it rose behind her neck in a kind of high ruff-like collar, but in front it was so low or open that it exposed her large breasts. Her skin was darkish and Southern and glowing, almost the colour of honey. Some such dress Jane had seen worn by a Minoan priestess on a vase from old Cnossus. The head, poised motionless on the muscular pillar of her neck, stared straight at Jane. It was a red-cheeked, wet-lipped face, with black eyes – almost the eyes of a cow – and an enigmatic expression. It was not by ordinary standards at all like the face of Mother Dimble; but Jane recognised it at once. It was, to speak like the musicians, the full statement of that theme which had elusively haunted Mother Dimble's face for the last few hours. It was Mother Dimble's face with something left out, and the omission shocked Jane. 'It is brutal,' she thought, for its energy crushed her; but then she half changed her mind and thought, 'It is I who am weak, trumpery.' 'It is mocking me,' she thought, but then once more changed her mind and thought, 'It is ignoring me. It doesn't see me'; for though there was an almost ogre-ish glee in the face, Jane did not seem to be invited to share the joke. She tried to look aside from the face – succeeded – and saw for the first time that there were other creatures present – four or five of them – no, more – a whole crowd of ridiculous little men: fat dwarfs in red caps with tassels on them, chubby, gnome-like little men, quite insufferably familiar, frivolous and irrepressible. For there was no doubt that they, at any rate, were mocking her. They were pointing at her, nodding, mimicking, standing on their heads, turning somersaults. Jane was not yet frightened, partly because the extreme warmth of the air at this open window made her feel drowsy. It was really quite ridiculous for the time of year. Her main feeling was one of indignation. A suspicion which had crossed her mind once or twice before now returned to her with irresistible force – the suspicion that the real universe might be simply silly. It was closely mixed up with the memories of that grown-up laughter – loud, careless, masculine laughter on the lips of bachelor uncles – which had often infuriated her in childhood, and from which the intense seriousness of her school debating society had offered such a grateful escape.

But a moment later she was very frightened indeed. The giantess rose. They were all coming at her. With a great glow and a noise like fire the flame-robed woman and the malapert dwarfs had all come into the house. They were in the room with her. The strange woman had a torch in her hand. It burned with terrible, blinding brightness, crackling, and sent up a cloud of dense black smoke, and filled the bedroom with a sticky, resinous smell. 'If they're not careful,' thought Jane, 'they'll set the house on fire.' But she had hardly time to think of that for her whole attention was fixed by the outrageous behaviour of the little men. They began making hay of the room. In a few seconds the bed was a mere chaos, the sheets on the floor, the blankets snatched up and used by the dwarfs for tossing the fattest of their company, the pillows hurtling through the air, feathers flying everywhere. 'Look out! Look out, can't you?' shouted Jane, for the giantess was beginning to touch various parts of the room with her torch. She touched a vase on the mantlepiece. Instantly there rose from it a streak of colour which Jane took for fire. She was just moving to try to put it out when she saw that the same thing had happened to a picture on the wall. And then it happened faster and faster all round her. The very topknots of the dwarfs were now on fire. But just as the terror of this became unbearable, Jane noticed that what was curling up from everything the torch had touched was not flame after all, but vegetation. Ivy and honeysuckle was growing up the legs of the bed, red roses were sprouting from the caps of the little men, and from every direction huge lilies rose to her knees and waist, shooting out their yellow tongues at her. The smells, the heat, the crowding, and the strangeness made her feel faint. It never occurred to her to think she was dreaming. People mistake dreams for visions: no one ever mistook a vision for a dream …

'Jane! Jane!' said the voice of Mrs Dimble suddenly. 'What on earth is the matter?'

Jane sat up. The room was empty, but the bed had all been pulled to pieces. She had apparently been lying on the floor. She felt cold and very tired.

'What *has* happened?' repeated Mrs Dimble.

'I don't know,' said Jane.

'Are you ill, child?' asked Mother Dimble.

'I must see the Director at once,' said Jane. 'It's all right. Don't bother. I can get up by myself … really. But I'd like to see the Director at once.'

◆ ○ ◆

Mr Bultitude's mind was as furry and as unhuman in shape as his body. He did not remember, as a man in his situation would have remembered, the provincial zoo from which he had escaped during a fire, not his first snarling and terrified arrival at the Manor, not the slow stages whereby he had learned to love and trust its inhabitants. He did not know that he loved and trusted them now. He did not know that they were people, nor that he was a bear. Indeed, he did not know that he existed at all: everything that is represented by the words *I* and *Me* and *Thou* was absent from his mind. When Mrs Maggs gave him a tin of golden syrup, as she did every Sunday morning, he did not recognise either a giver or a recipient. Goodness occurred and he tasted it. And that was all. Hence his loves might, if you wished, be all described as cupboard loves: food and warmth, hands that caressed, voices that reassured, were their objects. But if by a cupboard love you meant something cold or calculating you would be quite misunderstanding the real quality of the beast's sensations. He was no more like a human egoist than he was like a human altruist. There was no prose in his life. The appetencies which a human mind might disdain as cupboard loves were for him quivering and ecstatic aspirations which absorbed his whole being, infinite yearnings, stabbed with the threat of tragedy and shot through with the colour of Paradise. One of our race, if plunged back for a moment in the warm, trembling, iridescent pool of that pre-Adamite consciousness, would have emerged believing that he had grasped the absolute: for the states below reason and the states above it have, by their common contrast to the life we know, a certain superficial resemblance. Sometimes there returns to us from infancy the memory of a nameless delight or terror, unattached to any delightful or dreadful thing, a potent adjective floating in a nounless void, a pure quality. At such moments we have experience of the shallows of that pool. But fathoms deeper than any memory can take us, right down in the central warmth and dimness, the bear lived all its life.

Today an unusual thing had happened to him – he had got out into the garden without being muzzled. He was always muzzled out of doors, not because there was any fear of his becoming dangerous but because of his partiality for fruit and for the sweeter kinds of vegetables. ' 'Tisn't that he's not tame,' as Ivy Maggs had explained to Jane Studdock, 'but that he isn't honest. He wouldn't leave us a thing if we let him have the run of his teeth.' But today the precaution had been forgotten and the bear had passed a very agreeable morning investigating the turnips. Now – in the early afternoon – he had approached the garden wall. There was a chestnut tree within the wall which the bear could easily climb, and from its branches he could drop down on the far side. He was standing looking up at this tree. Mrs Maggs would have described his state of mind by saying, 'He knows perfectly well he's not allowed out of the garden.' That was not how it appeared to Mr Bultitude. He had no morals; but the Director had given him certain inhibitions. A mysterious reluctance arose, a clouding of the emotional weather, when the wall was too close; but mixed with this there was an opposite impulse to get beyond that wall. He did not, of course, know why, and was incapable even of raising the question. If the pressure behind this impulse could be translated into human terms at all, it would appear as something more like a mythology than a thought. One met bees in the garden, but never found a bee-hive. The bees all went away, over the wall. And to follow bees was the obvious thing to do. I think there was a sense in the bear's mind – one could hardly call it a picture – of endless green lands beyond the wall, and hives innumerable, and bees the size of sparrows, and waiting there, or else walking, trickling, oozing to meet one, something or someone stickier, sweeter, more golden than honey itself.

Today, this unrest was upon him in an unusual degree. He was missing Ivy Maggs. He did not know that there was any such person and he did not remember her as we know remembering, but there was an unspecified lack in his experience. She and the Director were, in their different ways, the two main factors in his existence. He felt, in his own fashion, the supremacy of the Director. Meetings with him were to the bear what mystical experiences are to men, for the Director had brought back with him from Venus some shadow of man's lost prerogative to ennoble beasts. In his presence Mr Bultitude trembled on the very borders of personality, thought the unthinkable and did the impossible, was troubled and enraptured with gleams from beyond his own woolly world, and came away tired. But with Ivy he was perfectly at home – as a savage who believes in some remote High God is more at home with the little deities of wood and water. It was Ivy who fed him, chased him out of forbidden places, cuffed him, and talked to him all day long. It was her firm conviction that the creature 'understood every word she said'. If you took this literally it was untrue; but in another sense it was not so wide of the mark. For much of Ivy's conversation was the expression not of thought but of feeling and of feelings Mr Bultitude almost shared – feelings of alacrity, snugness, and physical affection. In their own way they understood one another pretty well.

Three times Mr Bultitude turned away from the tree and the wall, but each time he came back. Then, very cautiously and quietly, he began to climb the tree. When he got up into the fork he sat there for a long time. He saw beneath him a steep grassy bank descending to a road. The desire and the inhibition were now both very strong. He sat there for nearly half an hour. Sometimes his mind wandered from the point and once he nearly went to sleep. In the end he got down on the outside of the wall. When he found that the thing had really happened, he became so frightened that he sat still at the bottom of the grassy bank on the very edge of the road. Then he heard a noise.

A motor van came into sight. It was driven by a man in the livery of the NICE and another man in the same livery sat beside him.

'Hullo … I say!' said the second man. 'Pull up, Sid. What about *that*?'

'What?' said the driver.

'Haven't you got eyes in your head?' said the other.

'Gor,' said Sid, pulling up. 'A bloody great bear. I say – it couldn't be our own bear, could it?'

'Get on,' said his mate. 'She was in her cage all right this morning.'

'You don't think she could have done a bunk? There'd be hell to pay for you and me ...'

'She couldn't have got there if she *had* done a bunk. Bears don't go forty miles an hour. That ain't the point. But hadn't we better pinch this one?'

'We haven't got no orders,' said Sid.

'No. And we haven't failed to get that blasted wolf either, have we?'

'Wasn't our fault. The old woman what said she'd sell wouldn't sell, as you're there to witness, young Len. We did our best. Told her that experiments at Belbury weren't what she thought. Told her the brute would have the time of its life and be made no end of a pet. Never told so many lies in one morning in my life. She'd been got at by someone.'

'Course it wasn't our fault. But the boss won't take no notice of that. It's get on or get out at Belbury.'

'Get out?' said Sid. 'I wish to hell I knew how to.'

Len spat over the side and there was a moment's silence.

'Anyway,' said Sid presently, 'what's the good of taking a bear back?'

'Well, isn't it better than coming back with nothing?' said Len. 'And bears cost money. I know they want another one. And here it is free.'

'All right,' said Sid ironically, 'if you're so keen on it, just hop out and ask him to step in.'

'Dope,' said Len.

'Not on my bit of dinner, you don't,' said Sid.

'You're a bucking good mate to have,' said Len, groping in a greasy parcel. 'It's a good thing for you I'm not the sort of chap who'd split on you.'

'You done it already,' said the driver. 'I know all your little games.'

Len had by this time produced a thick sandwich and was dabbing it with some strong smelling liquid from a bottle. When it was thoroughly saturated, he opened the door and went a pace forward, still holding the door in one hand. He was now about six yards from the bear, which had remained perfectly still ever since it saw them. He threw the sandwich to it.

Quarter of an hour later Mr Bultitude lay on his side, unconscious and breathing heavily. They had no difficulty in tying up his mouth and all four paws, but they had great difficulty in lifting him into the van.

'That's done something to my ticker,' said Sid, pressing his hand to his left side.

'Curse your ticker,' said Len, rubbing the sweat out of his eyes. 'Come on.'

Sid climbed back into the driving seat, sat still for a few seconds, panting and muttering 'Christ' at intervals. Then he started his engine up and they drove away.

♦　○　♦

For some time now Mark's waking life was divided between periods by the Sleeper's bedside and periods in the room with the spotted ceiling. The training in objectivity which took place in the latter cannot be described fully. The reversal of natural inclination which Frost inculcated was not spectacular or dramatic, but the details would be unprintable and had, indeed, a kind of nursery fatuity about them which is best ignored. Often Mark felt that one good roar of coarse laughter would have blown away the whole atmosphere of the thing; but laughter was unhappily out of the question. There indeed lay the horror – to perform petty obscenities which a very silly child might have thought funny all under the unchangingly serious inspection of Frost, with a stop watch and a note book and all the ritual of scientific experiment. Some of the things he had to do were merely meaningless. In one exercise he had to mount the stepladder and touch some one spot on the ceiling, selected by Frost: just touch it with his forefinger and then come down again. But either by association with the other exercises or because it really concealed some significance, this proceeding

343

always appeared to Mark to be the most indecent and even inhuman of all his tasks. And day by day, as the process went on, that idea of the Straight or the Normal which had occurred to him during his first visit to this room, grew stronger and more solid in his mind till it had become a kind of mountain. He had never before known what an Idea meant: he had always thought till now that they were things inside one's own head. But now, when his head was continually attacked and often completely filled with the clinging corruption of the training, this Idea towered up above him – something which obviously existed quite independently of himself and had hard rock surfaces which would not give, surfaces he could cling to.

The other thing that helped to save him was the Man in the Bed. Mark's discovery that he really could speak English had led to a curious acquaintance with him. It can hardly be said that they conversed. Both spoke but the result was hardly conversation as Mark had hitherto understood the term. The man was so very allusive and used gesture so extensively that Mark's less sophisticated modes of communication were almost useless. Thus when Mark explained that he had no tobacco, the man had slapped an imaginary tobacco pouch on his knee at least six times and struck an imaginary match about as often, each time jerking his head sideways with a look of such relish as Mark had seldom seen on a human face. Then Mark went on to explain that though 'they' were not foreigners, they were extremely dangerous people and that probably the Stranger's best plan would be to preserve his silence.

'Ah,' said the Stranger jerking his head again. 'Ah. Eh?' And then, without exactly laying his finger on his lips, he went through an elaborate pantomime which clearly meant the same thing. And it was impossible for a long time to get him off this subject. He went back and back to the theme of secrecy. 'Ah,' he said, 'don't get nothing out of me. I tell 'ee. Don't get nothing out of me. Eh? I tell 'ee. You and me knows. Ah?' And his look embraced Mark in such an apparently gleeful conspiracy that it warmed the heart. Believing this matter to be now sufficiently clear, Mark began, 'But, as regards the future –' only to be met by another pantomime of secrecy, followed by the word 'eh?' in a tone which demanded an answer.

'Yes, of course,' said Mark. 'We are both in considerable danger. And –'

'Ah,' said the man. 'Foreigners. Eh?'

'No, no,' said Mark. 'I told you they weren't. They seem to think *you* are, though. And that's why –'

'That's right,' interrupted the man. 'I know. Foreigners, I call them. I know. They get nothing out of me. You and me's all right. Ah.'

'I've been trying to think out some sort of plan,' said Mark.

'Ah,' said the man approvingly.

'And I was wondering,' began Mark when the man suddenly leaned forwards and said with extraordinary energy, 'I tell 'ee.'

'What?' said Mark.

'I got a plan.'

'What is it?'

'Ah,' said the man, winking at Mark with infinite knowingness and rubbing his belly.

'Go on. What is it?' said Mark.

'How'd it be,' said the man, sitting up and applying his left thumb to his right fore-finger as if about to propound the first step in a philosophical argument, 'how'd it be now if you and I made ourselves a nice bit of toasted cheese?'

'I meant a plan for escape,' said Mark.

'Ah,' replied the man. 'My old Dad now. He never had a day's illness in his life. Eh? How's that for a bit of all right? Eh?'

'It's a remarkable record,' said Mark.

'Ah. You may say so,' replied the other. 'On the road all his life. Never had a stomach-ache. Eh?' And here, as if Mark might not know that malady, he went through a long extraordinarily vivid dumb show.

'Open-air life suited him, I suppose,' said Mark.

'And what did he attribute his health to?' asked the man. He pronounced the word *attribute* with great relish, laying the accent

345

on the first syllable. 'I ask everyone, what did he attribute his health to?'

Mark was about to reply when the man indicated by a gesture that the question was purely rhetorical and that he did not wish to be interrupted.

'He attributed his health,' continued the speaker with great solemnity, 'to eating toasted cheese. Keeps the water out of the stomach. That's what it does. Eh? Makes a lining. Stands to reason. Ah!'

In several later interviews, Mark endeavoured to discover something of the Stranger's own history, and particularly how he had been brought to Belbury. This was not easy to do, for though the tramp's conversation was very autobiographical, it was filled almost entirely with accounts of conversations in which he had made stunning repartees whose points remained wholly obscure. Even where it was less intellectual in character, the allusions were too difficult for Mark, who was quite ignorant of the life of the roads though he had once written a very authoritative article on Vagrancy. But by repeated and (as he got to know his man) more cautious, questioning, he couldn't help getting the idea that the tramp had been made to give up his clothes to a total stranger and then put to sleep. He never got the story in so many words. The tramp insisted on talking as if Mark knew it already, and any pressure for a more accurate account produced only a series of nods, winks and highly confidential gestures. As for the identity or appearance of the person who had taken his clothes, nothing whatever could be made out. The nearest Mark ever got to it, after hours of talk and deep potations, was some such statement as 'Ah. He was a one!' or 'He was a kind of – eh? *You* know?' or 'That was a customer, that was.' These statements were made with enormous gusto as though the theft of the tramp's clothes had excited his deepest admiration.

Indeed, throughout the man's conversation this gusto was the most striking characteristic. He never passed any kind of moral judgment on the various things that had been done to him in the

346

course of his career nor did he even try to explain them. Much that was unjust and still more that was simply unintelligible seemed to be accepted, not only without resentment, but with a certain satisfaction provided only that it was striking. Even about his present situation he showed very much less curiosity than Mark would have thought possible. It did not make sense, but then the man did not expect things to make sense. He deplored the absence of tobacco and regarded the 'Foreigners' as very dangerous people; but the main thing, obviously, was to eat and drink as much as possible while the present conditions lasted. And gradually Mark fell into line. The man's breath, and indeed his body, were malodorous, and his methods of eating were gross. But the sort of continual picnic which the two shared carried Mark back into the realm of childhood which we have all enjoyed before nicety began. Each understood perhaps an eighth part of what the other said, but a kind of intimacy grew between them. Mark never noticed until years later that here, where there was no room for vanity and no more power or security than that of 'children playing in a giant's kitchen', he had unawares become a member of a 'circle', as secret and as strongly fenced against outsiders as any that he had dreamed of.

Every now and then their *tête-à-tête* was interrupted. Frost or Wither or both would come in introducing some stranger who addressed the tramp in an unknown language, failed completely to get any response, and was ushered out again. The tramp's habit of submission to the unintelligible, mixed with a kind of animal cunning, stood him in good stead during these interviews. Even without Mark's advice, it would never have occurred to him to undeceive his captors by replying in English. Undeceiving was an activity wholly foreign to his mind. For the rest, his expression of tranquil indifference, varied occasionally by extremely sharp looks but never by the least sign of anxiety or bewilderment, left his interrogators mystified. Wither could never find in his face the evil he was looking for; but neither could he find any of that virtue which would, for him, have been the danger signal. The tramp was a type of man he had never met. The dupe, the terrified victim, the toady, the would-be accomplice, the rival, the honest man with loathing and hatred in his eyes, were all familiar to him. But not this.

And then, one day, there came an interview that was different.

◆ ○ ◆

'It sounds rather like a mythological picture by Titian come to life,' said the Director with a smile when Jane had described her experience in the lodge.

'Yes, but …' said Jane; and then stopped. 'I see,' she began again, 'it was very like that. Not only the woman and the … the dwarfs … but the glow. As if the air were on fire. But I always thought I liked Titian. I suppose I wasn't really taking the pictures seriously enough. Just chattering about "the Renaissance" the way one did.'

'You didn't like it when it came out into real life?'

Jane shook her head.

'Was it real, Sir?' she asked presently. 'Are there such things?'

'Yes,' said the Director, 'it was real enough. Oh, there are thousands of things within this square mile that I don't know about yet. And I daresay that the presence of Merlinus brings out certain things. We are not living *exactly* in the twentieth century as long as he's here. We overlap a bit; the focus is blurred. And you yourself … you are a seer. You were perhaps bound to meet her. She's what you'll get if you won't have the other.'

'How do you mean, Sir?' said Jane.

'You said she was a little like Mother Dimble. So she is. But Mother Dimble with something left out. Mother Dimble is friends with all that world as Merlinus is friends with the woods and rivers. But he isn't a wood or a river himself. She has not rejected it, but she has baptised it. She is a Christian wife. And you, you know, are not. Neither are you a virgin. You have put yourself where you must meet that Old Woman and you have rejected all that has happened to her since Maleldil came to Earth. So you get her raw – not stronger than Mother Dimble would find her, but untransformed, demoniac. And you don't like it. Hasn't that been the history of your life?'

'You mean,' said Jane slowly, 'I've been repressing something?'

The Director laughed; just that loud, assured, bachelor laughter which had often infuriated her on other lips.

'Yes,' he said. 'But don't think I'm talking of Freudian repressions. He knew only half the facts. It isn't a question of inhibitions – inculcated shame – against natural desire. I'm afraid there's no niche in the world for people that won't be either Pagan or Christian. Just imagine a man who was too dainty to eat with his fingers and yet wouldn't use forks!'

His laughter rather than his words had reddened Jane's cheeks, and she was staring at him open-mouthed. Assuredly, the Director was not in the least like Mother Dimble; but an odious realisation that he was, in this matter, on Mother Dimble's side – that he also, though he did not belong to that hot-coloured, archaic world, stood somehow in good diplomatic relations with it, from which she was excluded – had struck her like a blow. Some old female dream of finding a man who 'really understood' was being insulted. She took it for granted, half-unconsciously, that the Director was the most virginal of his sex; but she had not realised that this would leave his masculinity still on the other side of the stream from herself and even steeper, more emphatic, than that of common men. Some knowledge of a world beyond Nature she had already gained from living in his house, and more from fear of death that night in the dingle. But she had been conceiving this world as 'spiritual' in the negative sense – as some neutral, or democratic, vacuum where differences disappeared, where sex and sense were not transcended but simply taken away. Now the suspicion dawned upon her that there might be differences and contrasts all the way up, richer, sharper, even fiercer, at every rung of the ascent. How if this invasion of her own being in marriage from which she had recoiled, often in the very teeth of instinct, were not, as she had supposed, merely a relic of animal life or patriarchal barbarism, but rather the lowest, the first, and the easiest form of some shocking contact with reality which would have to be repeated – but in ever larger and more disturbing modes – on the highest levels of all?

'Yes,' said the Director. 'There is no escape. If it were a virginal rejection of the male, he would allow it. Such souls can bypass the male and go on to meet something far more masculine, higher up, to which they must make a yet deeper surrender. But your trouble has been what old poets called *Daungier*. We call it Pride. You are offended by the masculine itself: the loud, irruptive, possessive thing – the gold lion, the bearded bull – which breaks through hedges and scatters the little kingdom of your primness as the dwarfs scattered the carefully made bed. The male you could have escaped, for it exists only on the biological level. But the masculine none of us can escape. What is above and beyond all things is so masculine that we are all feminine in relation to it. You had better agree with your adversary quickly.'

'You mean I shall have to become a Christian?' said Jane.

'It looks like it,' said the Director.

'But – I still don't see what that has to do with … with Mark,' said Jane. This was perhaps not perfectly true. The vision of the universe which she had begun to see in the last few minutes had a curiously stormy quality about it. It was bright, darting and over-powering. Old Testament imagery of eyes and wheels for the first time in her life took on some possibility of meaning. And mixed with this was the sense that she had been manoeuvered into a false position. It ought to have been she who was saying these things to the Christians. Hers ought to have been the vivid, perilous world brought against their grey formalised one; hers the quick, vital movements and theirs the stained-glass attitudes. That was the antithesis she was used to. This time, in a sudden flash of purple and crimson, she remembered what stained glass was really like. And where Mark stood in all this new world she did not know. Certainly not quite in his old place. Something which she liked to think of as the opposite of Mark had been taken away. Something civilised, or modern, or scholarly, or (of late) 'spiritual' which did not want to possess her, which valued her for the odd collection of qualities she called 'herself', something without hands that gripped and without demands upon her. But if there were no such thing? Playing for time, she asked, 'Who was that Huge Woman?'

'I'm not sure,' said the Director. 'But I think I can make a guess. Did you know that all the planets are represented in each?'

'No, Sir. I didn't.'

'Apparently they are. There is no Oyarsa in Heaven who has not got his representative on Earth. And there is no world where you could not meet a little unfallen partner of our own black Archon, a kind of other self. That is why there was an Italian Saturn as well as a Heavenly one, and a Cretan Jove as well as an Olympian. It was these earthly wraiths of the high intelligences that men met in old times when they reported that they had seen the gods. It was with those that a man like Merlin was (at times) conversant. Nothing from beyond the Moon ever really descended. What concerns you more, there is a terrestrial as well as a celestial Venus – Perelandra's wraith as well as Perelandra.'

'And you think …?'

'I do: I have long known that this house is deeply under her influence. There is even copper in the soil. Also – the earth Venus will be specially active here at present. For it is tonight that her heavenly archetype will really descend.'

'I had forgotten,' said Jane.

'You will not forget it once it has happened. All of you had better stay together – in the kitchen, perhaps. Do not come upstairs. Tonight I will bring Merlin before my Masters, all five of them – Viritrilbia, Perelandra, Malacandra, Glund, and Lurga. He will be opened. Powers will pass into him.'

'What will he *do*, Sir?'

The Director laughed. 'The first step is easy. The enemies at Belbury are already looking for experts in archaic Western dialects, preferably Celtic. We shall send them an interpreter! Yes, by the splendour of Christ, we will send them one. "Upon them He a spirit of frenzy sent To call in haste for their destroyer." They have advertised in the papers for one! And after the first step … well, you know, it will be easy. In fighting those who serve devils one always has this on one's side; their Masters hate them as much as they hate us. The moment we disable the human pawns enough to make them useless to Hell, their own Masters finish the work for us. They break their tools.'

There was a sudden knock on the door and Grace Ironwood entered.

'Ivy is back, Sir,' she said. 'I think you'd better see her. No; she's alone. She never saw her husband. The sentence is over but they haven't released him. He's been sent on to Belbury for remedial treatment. Under some new regulation. Apparently, it does not require a sentence from a court … but she's not very coherent. She is in great distress.'

♦ ○ ♦

Jane had gone into the garden to think. She accepted what the Director had said, yet it seemed to her nonsensical. His comparison between Mark's love and God's (since apparently there was a God) struck her nascent spirituality as indecent and irreverent. 'Religion' ought to mean a realm in which her haunting female fear of being treated as a thing, an object of barter and desire and possession, would be set permanently at rest and what she called her 'true self' would soar upwards and expand in some freer and purer world. For still she thought that 'Religion' was a kind of exhalation or a cloud of incense, something steaming up from specially gifted souls towards a receptive Heaven. Then, quite sharply, it occurred to her that the Director never talked about Religion; nor did the Dimbles nor Camilla. They talked about God. They had no picture in their minds of some mist steaming upward: rather of strong, skilful hands thrust down to make, and mend, perhaps even to destroy. Supposing one were a *thing* after all – a thing designed and invented by Someone Else and valued for qualities quite different from what one had decided to regard as one's true self? Supposing all those people who, from the bachelor uncles down to Mark and Mother Dimble, had infuriatingly found her sweet and fresh when she wanted them to find her also interesting and important, had all along been simply right and perceived the sort of thing she was? Supposing Maleldil on this subject agreed with them and not with her? For one moment she had a ridiculous and scorching vision of a world in which God Himself would never understand, never take her with full seriousness. Then, at one particular corner of the gooseberry patch, the change came.

What awaited her there was serious to the degree of sorrow and beyond. There was no form nor sound. The mould under the bushes, the moss on the path, and the little brick border, were not visibly changed. But they were changed. A boundary had been crossed. She had come into a world, or into a Person, or into the presence of a Person. Something expectant, patient, inexorable, met her with no veil or protection between. In the closeness of that contact she perceived at once that the Director's words had been entirely misleading. This demand which now pressed upon her was not, even by analogy, like any other demand. It was the origin of all right demands and contained them. In its light you could understand them; but from them you could know nothing of it. There was nothing, and never had been anything, like this. And now there was nothing except this. Yet also, everything had been like this; only by being like this had anything existed. In this height and depth and breadth the little idea of herself which she had hitherto called *me* dropped down and vanished, unfluttering, into bottomless distance, like a bird in a space without air. The name *me* was the name of a being whose existence she had never suspected, a being that did not yet fully exist but which was demanded. It was a person (not the person she had thought), yet also a thing, a made thing, made to please Another and in Him to please all others, a thing being made at this very moment, without its choice, in a shape it had never dreamed of. And the making went on amidst a kind of splendour or sorrow or both, whereof she could not tell whether it was in the moulding hands or in the kneaded lump.

Words take too long. To be aware of all this and to know that it had already gone made one single experience. It was revealed only in its departure. The largest thing that had ever happened to her had, apparently, found room for itself in a moment of time too short to be called time at all. Her hand closed on nothing but a memory. And as it closed, without an instant's pause, the voices of those who have not joy rose howling and chattering from every corner of her being.

'Take care. Draw back. Keep your head. Don't commit yourself,' they said. And then more subtly, from another quarter, 'You have had a religious experience. This is very interesting. Not everyone does. How much better you will now understand the Seventeenth-Century poets!' Or from a third direction, more sweetly, 'Go on. Try to get it again. It will please the Director.'

But her defences had been captured and these counter-attacks were unsuccessful.

The Descent of the Gods

The whole house at St Anne's was empty, but for two rooms. In the kitchen, drawn a little closer than usual about the fire and with the shutters closed, sat Dimble and MacPhee and Denniston and the women. Removed from them by many a long vacancy of stair and passage, the Pendragon and Merlin were together in the Blue Room.

If anyone had gone up the stairs and on to the lobby outside the Blue Room, he would have found something other than fear that barred his way – an almost physical resistance. If he had succeeded in forcing his way forward against it, he would have come into a region of tingling sounds that were clearly not voices though they had articulation; and if the passage were quite dark he would probably have seen a faint light, not like fire or moon, under the Director's door. I do not think he could have reached the door itself unbidden. Already the whole house would have seemed to him to be tilting and plunging like a ship in a Bay of Biscay gale. He would have been horribly compelled to feel this Earth not as the bottom of the universe but as a ball spinning, and rolling onwards, both at delirious speed, and not through emptiness but through some densely inhabited and intricately structured medium. He would have known sensuously, until his outraged senses forsook him, that the visitants in that room were in it, not because they were at rest but because they glanced and wheeled through the packed reality of Heaven (which men call empty space), to keep their beams upon this spot of the moving Earth's hide.

The druid and Ransom had begun to wait for these visitors soon after sundown. Ransom was on his sofa. Merlin sat beside him, his hands clasped, his body a little bent forward. Sometimes a drop of sweat trickled coldly down his grey cheek. He had at first addressed himself to kneel but Ransom forbade him. 'See thou do it not!' he had said. 'Have you forgotten that they are our fellow servants?' The windows were uncurtained and all the light that there was in the room came thence: frosty red when they began their waiting, but later lit with stars.

Long before anything happened in the Blue Room the party in the kitchen had made their ten o'clock tea. It was while they sat drinking it that the change occurred. Up till now they had instinctively been talking in subdued voices, as children talk in a room where their elders are busied about some august incomprehensible matter, a funeral, or the reading of a will. Now of a sudden they all began talking loudly at once, each, not contentiously but delightedly, interrupting the others. A stranger coming into the kitchen would have thought they were drunk, not soddenly but gaily drunk: would have seen heads bent close together, eyes dancing, an excited wealth of gesture. What they said, none of the party could ever afterwards remember. Dimble maintained that they had been chiefly engaged in making puns. MacPhee denied that he had ever, even that night, made a pun, but all agreed that they had been extraordinarily witty. If not plays upon words, yet certainly plays upon thoughts, paradoxes, fancies, anecdotes, theories laughingly advanced yet (on consideration) well worth taking seriously, had flowed from them and over them with dazzling prodigality. Even Ivy forgot her great sorrow. Mother Dimble always remembered Denniston and her husband as they had stood, one on each side of the fireplace, in a gay intellectual duel, each capping the other, each rising above the other, up and up, like birds or aeroplanes in combat. If only one could have remembered what they said! For never in her life had she heard such talk – such eloquence, such melody (song could have added nothing to it), such toppling structures of double meaning, such skyrockets of metaphor and allusion.

A moment after that and they were all silent. Calm fell, as suddenly as when one goes out of the wind behind a wall. They sat staring upon one another, tired and a little self-conscious.

Upstairs this first change had a different operation. There came an instant at which both men braced themselves. Ransom gripped the side of his sofa; Merlin grasped his own knees and set his teeth. A rod of coloured light, whose colour no man can name or picture, darted between them: no more to see than that, but seeing was the least part of their experience. Quick agitation seized them: a kind of boiling and bubbling in mind and heart which shook their bodies also. It went to a rhythm of such fierce speed that they feared their sanity must be shaken into a thousand fragments. And then it seemed that this had actually happened. But it did not matter: for all the fragments – needle-pointed desires, brisk merriments, lynx-eyed thoughts – went rolling to and fro like glittering drops and reunited themselves. It was well that both men had some knowledge of poetry. The doubling, splitting and recombining of thoughts which now went on in them would have been unendurable for one whom that art had not already instructed in the counterpoint of the mind, the mastery of doubled and trebled vision. For Ransom, whose study had been for many years in the realm of words, it was heavenly pleasure. He found himself sitting within the very heart of language, in the white-hot furnace of essential speech. All fact was broken, splashed into cataracts, caught, turned inside out, kneaded, slain, and reborn as meaning. For the lord of Meaning himself, the herald, the messenger, the slayer of Argus, was with them: the angel that spins nearest the sun. Viritrilbia, whom men call Mercury and Thoth.

Down in the kitchen drowsiness stole over them after the orgy of speaking had come to an end. Jane, having nearly fallen asleep, was startled by her book falling from her hand, and looked about her. How warm it was … how comfortable and familiar. She had always liked wood fires but tonight the smell of the logs seemed more than ordinarily sweet. She began to think it was sweeter than it could possibly be, that a smell of burning cedar or of incense pervaded the room. It thickened. Fragrant names hovered in her mind – nard and cassia's balmy smells and all Arabia breathing from a box; even something more subtly sweet, perhaps maddening – why not forbidden? – but she knew it was commanded. She was too drowsy to think deeply how this could be. The Dimbles were talking together but in so low a voice that others could not hear. Their faces appeared to her transfigured. She could no longer see that they were old – only mature, like ripe fields in August, serene and golden with the tranquility of fulfilled desire. On her other side, Arthur said something in Camilla's ear. There too ... but as the warmth and sweetness of that rich air now fully mastered her brain, she could hardly bear to look on them: not through envy (that thought was far away), but because a sort of brightness flowed from them that dazzled her, as if the god and goddess in them burned through their bodies and through their clothes and shone before her in a young double-natured nakedness of rose-red spirit that overcame her. And all about them danced (as she half saw), not the gross and ridiculous dwarfs which she had seen that afternoon, but grave and ardent spirits, bright winged, their boyish shapes smooth and slender like ivory rods.

In the Blue Room also Ransom and Merlin felt about this time that the temperature had risen. The windows, they did not see how or when, had swung open; at their opening the temperature did not drop, for it was from without that the warmth came. Through the bare branches, across the ground which was once more stiffening with frost, a summer breeze was blowing into the room, but the breeze of such a summer as England never has. Laden like heavy barges that glide nearly gunwale under, laden so heavily you would have thought it could not move, laden with ponderous fragrance of night-scented flowers, sticky gums, groves that drop odours, and with cool savour of midnight fruit, it stirred the curtains, it lifted a letter that lay on the table, it lifted the hair which had a moment before been plastered on Merlin's forehead. The room was rocking. They were afloat. A soft tingling and shivering as of foam and breaking bubbles ran over their flesh. Tears ran down Ransom's cheeks. He alone knew from what seas and what islands that breeze blew. Merlin did not; but in him also the inconsolable wound with which man is born waked and ached at this touching.

Low syllables of pre-historic Celtic self-pity murmured from his lips. These yearnings and fondlings were however only the fore-runners of the goddess. As the whole of her virtue seized, focussed and held that spot of the rolling Earth in her long beam, something harder, shriller, more perilously ecstatic, came out of the centre of all the softness. Both the humans trembled – Merlin because he did not know what was coming, Ransom because he knew. And now it came. It was fiery, sharp, bright and ruthless, ready to kill, ready to die, outspeeding light: it was Charity, not as mortals imagine it, not even as it has been humanised for them since the Incarnation of the Word, but the translunary virtue, fallen upon them direct from the Third Heaven, unmitigated. They were blinded, scorched, deafened. They thought it would burn their bones. They could not bear that it should continue. They could not bear that it should cease. So Perelandra, triumphant among planets, whom men call Venus, came and was with them in the room.

Down in the kitchen MacPhee sharply drew back his chair so that it grated on the tiled floor like a pencil squeaking on a slate. 'Man!' he exclaimed. 'It's a shame for us to be sitting here looking at the fire. If the Director hadn't got a game leg himself, I'll bet you he'd have found some other way for us to go to work.' Camilla's eyes flashed towards him. 'Go on!' she said. 'Go on!' 'What do you mean MacPhee?' said Dimble. 'He means fighting,' said Camilla. 'They'd be too many for us, I'm afraid,' said Arthur Denniston. 'Maybe that!' said MacPhee. 'But maybe they'll be too many for us this way too. But it would be grand to have one go at them before the end. To tell you the truth I sometimes feel I don't greatly care what happens. But I wouldn't be easy in my grave if I knew they'd won and I'd never had my hands on them. I'd like to be able to say as an old sergeant said to me in the first war, about a bit of a raid we did near Monchy. Our fellows did it all with the butt end, you know. "Sir," says he, "did ever you hear anything like the way their heads cracked."' 'I think that's disgusting,' said Mother Dimble. 'That part is, I suppose,' said Camilla. 'But … oh if one could have a charge in the old style. I don't mind anything once I'm on a horse.' 'I don't understand it,' said Dimble. 'I'm not like you, MacPhee. I'm not brave. But I was just thinking as you spoke that I don't feel afraid of being killed and hurt as I used to do. Not tonight.' 'We may be, I suppose,' said Jane. 'As long as we're all together,' said Mother Dimble. 'It might be … no, I don't mean anything heroic … it might be a *nice* way to die.' And suddenly all their faces and voices were changed. They were laughing again, but it was a different kind of laughter. Their love for one another became intense. Each, looking on all the rest, thought, 'I'm lucky to be here. I could die with these.' But MacPhee was humming to himself:

King William said, Be not dismayed, for the loss of one commander.

Upstairs it was, at first, much the same. Merlin saw in memory the wintry grass of Badon Hill, the long banner of the Virgin fluttering above the heavy British-Roman cataphracts, the yellow-haired barbarians. He heard the snap of the bows, the *click-click* of steel points in wooden shields, the cheers, the howling, and the ring of struck mail. He remembered also the evening, fires twinkling along the hill, frost making the gashes smart, starlight on a pool fouled with blood, eagles crowding together in the pale sky. And Ransom, it may be, remembered his long struggle in the caves of Perelandra. But all this passed. Something tonic and lusty and cheerily cold, like a sea breeze, was coming over them. There was no fear anywhere: the blood inside them flowed as if to a marching-song. They felt themselves taking their places in the ordered rhythm of the universe, side by side with punctual seasons and patterned atoms and the obeying Seraphim. Under the immense weight of their obedience their wills stood up straight and untiring like caryatids. Eased of all fickleness and all protestings they stood: gay, light, nimble, and alert. They had outlived all anxieties; care was a word without meaning. To live meant to share in this processional pomp. Ransom knew, as a man knows when he touches iron, the clear, taut splendour of that celestial spirit which now flashed between them: vigilant Malacandra, captain of a cold orb, whom men call Mars and Mavors, and Tyr who put his hand in the wolf-mouth. Ransom greeted his guests in the tongue of Heaven. But he warned Merlin that now the time was coming when he must play the man. The three gods who had already met in the Blue Room were less unlike humanity than the two whom they still awaited. In Viritrilbia and Venus and Malacandra were represented those two of the Seven Genders which bear a certain analogy to the biological sexes and can therefore be in some measure understood by men. It would not be so with those who were now preparing to descend. These also doubtless had their genders, but we have no clue to them. These would be mightier energies: ancient *eldila*, steersman of giant worlds which have never from the beginning been subdued to the sweet humiliations of organic life.

'Stir the fire, Denniston, for any sake. That's a cold night,' said MacPhee. 'It must be cold outside,' said Dimble. All thought of that: of stiff grass, hen-roosts, dark places in the middle of woods, graves. Then of the sun's dying, the Earth gripped, suffocated, in airless cold, the black sky lit only with stars. And then, not even stars: the heat-death of the universe, utter and final blackness of nonentity from which Nature knows no return. Another life? 'Possibly,' thought MacPhee. 'I believe,' thought Denniston. But the old life gone, all its times, all its hours and days, gone. Can even Omnipotence *bring back*? Where do years go, and why? Man never would understand it. The misgiving deepened. Perhaps there was nothing to be understood.

Saturn, whose name in the heavens is Lurga, stood in the Blue Room. His spirit lay upon the house, or even on the whole Earth, with a cold pressure such as might flatten the very orb of Tellus to a wafer. Matched against the lead-like burden of his antiquity the other gods themselves perhaps felt young and ephemeral. It was a mountain of centuries sloping up from the highest antiquity we can conceive, up and up like a mountain whose summit never comes into sight, not to eternity where the thought can rest, but into more and still more time, into freezing wastes and silence of unnameable numbers. It was also strong like a mountain; its age was no mere morass of time where imagination can sink in reverie, but a living, self-remembering duration which repelled lighter intelligences from its structure as granite flings back waves, itself unwithered and undecayed but able to wither any who approach it unadvised. Ransom and Merlin suffered a sensation of unendurable cold; and all that was strength in Lurga became sorrow as it entered them. Yet Lurga in that room was overmatched. Suddenly a greater spirit came – one whose influence tempered and almost transformed to his own quality the skill of leaping Mercury, the clearness of Mars, the subtler vibration of Venus, and even the numbing weight of Saturn.

In the kitchen his coming was felt. No one afterwards knew how it happened but somehow the kettle was put on, the hot toddy was brewed. Arthur – the only musician among them – was bidden to get out his fiddle. The chairs were pushed back, the floor cleared. They danced. What they danced no one could remember. It was some round dance, no modern shuffling: it involved beating the floor, clapping of hands, leaping high. And no one while it lasted thought himself or his fellows ridiculous. It may, in fact, have been some village measure, not ill-suited to the tiled kitchen: the spirit in which they danced it was not so. It seemed to each that the room was filled with kings and queens, that the wildness of their dance expressed heroic energy and its quieter movements had seized the very spirit behind all noble ceremonies.

Upstairs his mighty beam turned the Blue Room into a blaze of lights. Before the other angels a man might sink: before this he might die, but if he lived at all, he would laugh. If you had caught one breath of the air that came from him, you would have felt yourself taller than before. Though you were a cripple, your walk would have became stately: though a beggar, you would have worn your rags magnanimously. Kingship and power and festal pomp and courtesy shot from him as sparks fly from an anvil. The pealing of bells, the blowing of trumpets, the spreading out of banners, are means used on earth to make a faint symbol of his quality. It was like a long sunlit wave, creamy-crested and arched with emerald, that comes on nine feet tall, with roaring and with terror and unquenchable laughter. It was like the first beginning of music in the halls of some King so high and at some festival so solemn that a tremor akin to fear runs through young hearts when they hear it. For this was great Glund-Oyarsa, King of Kings, through whom the joy of creation principally blows across these fields of Arbol, known to men in old times as Jove and under that name, by fatal but not inexplicable misprision, confused with his Maker – so little did they dream by how many degrees the stair even of created being rises above him.

At his coming there was holiday in the Blue Room. The two mortals, momentarily caught up into the *Gloria* which those five excellent Natures perpetually sing, forgot for a time the lower and more immediate purpose of their meeting. Then they proceeded to operation. Merlin received the power into him.

He looked different next day. Partly because his beard had been shaved; but also, because he was no longer his own man. No one doubted that his final severance from the body was near. Later in the day MacPhee drove him off and dropped him in the neighborhood of Belbury.

◆ ○ ◆

Mark had fallen into a doze in the tramp's bedroom that day, when he was startled, and driven suddenly to collect himself, by the arrival of visitors. Frost came in first and held the door open. Two others followed. One was the Deputy Director; the other was a man whom Mark had not seen before.

This person was dressed in a rusty cassock and carried in his hand a wide-brimmed black hat such as priests wear in many parts of the continent. He was a very big man and the cassock perhaps made him look bigger. He was clean shaven, revealing a large face with heavy and complicated folds in it, and he walked with his head a little bowed. Mark decided that he was a simple soul, probably an obscure member of some religious order who happened to be an authority on some even more obscure language. And it was to Mark rather odious to see him standing between those two birds of prey – Wither, effusive and flattering on his right and Frost, on his left, stiff as a ramrod, waiting with scientific attention but also, as Mark could now see, with a certain cold dislike, for the result of the new experiment.

Wither talked to the stranger for some moments in a language which Mark could not follow but which he recognised as Latin. 'A priest, obviously,' thought Mark. 'But I wonder where from? Wither knows most of the ordinary languages. Would the old chap be a Greek? Doesn't look like a Levantine. More probably a Russian.' But at this point Mark's attention was diverted. The tramp, who had closed his eyes when he heard the door handle turning had suddenly opened them, seen the stranger, and then shut them tighter than before. After this his behaviour was peculiar. He began emitting a series of very exaggerated snores and turned his back to the company. The stranger took a step nearer to the bed and spoke two syllables in a low voice. For a second or two the tramp lay as he was but seemed to be afflicted with a shivering fit; then, slowly but with continuous movement, as when the bows of a ship come round in obedience to the rudder, he rolled round and lay staring up into the other's face. His mouth and his eyes were both opened very wide. From certain jerkings of his head and hands and from certain ghastly attempts to smile, Mark concluded that he was trying to say something, probably of a deprecatory and insinuating kind. What next followed took his breath away. The stranger spoke again; and then, with much facial contortion, mixed with coughs and stammers and spluttering and expectoration, there came out of the tramp's mouth, in a high unnatural voice, syllables, words, a whole sentence, in some language that was neither Latin nor English. All this time the stranger kept his eyes fixed on those of the tramp.

The stranger spoke again. This time the tramp replied at much greater length and seemed to manage the unknown language a little more easily, though his voice remained quite unlike that in which Mark had heard him talking for the last few days. At the end of his speech he sat up in bed and pointed to where Wither and Frost were standing. Then the stranger appeared to ask him a question. The tramp spoke for the third time.

At this reply the stranger started back, crossed himself several times, and exhibited every sign of terror. He turned and spoke rapidly in Latin to the other two. Something happened to their faces when he spoke. They looked like dogs who have just picked up a scent. Then, with a loud exclamation the stranger caught up his skirts and made a bolt for the door. But the scientists were too quick for him. For a few minutes all three were wrangling there, Frost's teeth bared like an animal's, and the loose mask of Wither's face wearing, for once, a quite unambiguous expression. The old priest was being threatened. Mark found that he himself had taken a step forward. But before he could make up his mind how to act, the stranger, shaking his head and holding out his hands, had come timidly back to the bedside. It was an odd thing that the tramp who had relaxed during the struggle at the door should suddenly stiffen again and fix his eyes on this frightened old man as if he were awaiting orders.

More words in the unknown language followed. The tramp once more pointed at Wither and Frost. The stranger turned and spoke to them in Latin, apparently translating. Wither and Frost looked at one another as if each waited for his fellow to act. What followed was pure lunacy. With infinite caution, wheezing and creaking, down went the whole shaky senility of the Deputy Director, down onto its knees; and half a second later, with a jerky, metallic movement, Frost got down beside him. When he was down, he suddenly looked over his shoulder to where Mark was standing. The flash of pure hatred in his face, but hatred, as it were, crystallised so that it was no longer a passion and had no heat in it, was like touching metal in the Arctic where metal burns. 'Kneel,' he bleated, and instantly turned his head. Mark never could remember afterwards whether he simply forgot to obey this order or whether his real rebellion dated from that moment.

The tramp spoke again, always with his eyes fixed on those of the man in the cassock. And again the latter translated, and then stood aside. Wither and Frost began going forward on their knees till they reached the bedside. The tramp's hairy, dirty hand with its bitten nails was thrust out to them. They kissed it. Then it seemed that some further order was given them. They rose and Mark perceived that Wither was gently expostulating in Latin against this order. He kept on indicating Frost. The words *venia tua** (each time emended to *venia vestra*) recurred so often that Mark could pick them out. But apparently the expostulation was unsuccessful: a few moments later Frost and Wither had both left the room.

As the door shut, the tramp collapsed like a deflated balloon. He rolled himself to and fro on the bed muttering,

'Gor' blimey. Couldn't have believed it. It's a knock-out. A fair knock-out.' But Mark had little leisure to attend to this. He found that the stranger was addressing him and though he could not understand the words, he looked up. Instantly, he wished to look away again and found that he could not. He might have claimed with some reason that he was by now an expert in the endurance of alarming faces. But that did not alter the fact that when he looked on this he felt himself afraid. Almost before he had time to realise this he felt himself drowsy. A moment later he fell into his chair and slept.

'Well?' said Frost as soon as they found themselves outside the door.

'It is ... er ... profoundly perplexing,' said the Deputy Director.

They walked down the passage conversing in low tones as they went.

'It certainly looked – I say *looked*,' continued Frost, 'as if the man in the bed were hypnotised and the Basque priest were in charge of the situation.'

* 'With your kind permission,' or 'if you will pardon me.'

'Oh, surely, my dear friend, that would be a most disquieting hypothesis.'

'Excuse me. I have made no hypothesis. I am describing how it looked.'

'And how, on your hypothesis – forgive me, but that is what it is – would a Basque priest come to invent the story that our guest was Merlinus Ambrosius?'

'That is the point. If the man in the bed is *not* Merlinus then someone else, and someone quite outside our calculations, namely the priest, knows our whole plan of campaign.'

'And that, my dear friend, is why the retention of both these persons and a certain extreme delicacy in our attitude to both is required – at least, until we have some further light.'

'They must, of course, be detained.'

'I should hardly say *detained*. It has implications ... I do not venture to express any doubt at present as to the identity of our distinguished guest. There is no question of detention. On the contrary, the most cordial welcome, the most meticulous courtesy ...'

'Do I understand that you had always pictured Merlinus entering the Institute as a Dictator rather than a colleague?'

'As to that,' said Wither, 'my conception of the personal, or even official, relations between us had always been elastic and ready for all necessary adaptations. It would be a very real grief to me if I thought you were allowing any misplaced sense of your own dignity ... ah, in short, provided he *is* Merlinus ... you understand me?'

'Where are you taking us at the moment?'

'To my apartments. If you remember, the request was that we should provide our guest with some clothes.'

'There was no request. We were ordered.'

To this the Deputy Director made no reply. When both men were in his bedroom and the door was shut, Frost said:

'I am not satisfied. You do not seem to realise the dangers of the situation. We must take into account the possibility that the man is not Merlinus. And if he is not Merlinus, then the priest knows things he ought not to know. To allow an imposter and a spy to remain at large in the Institute is out of the question. We must find out at once where that priest gets his knowledge from. And where did you get the priest from?'

'I think that is the kind of shirt which would be most suitable,' said Wither laying it on the bed. 'The suits are in here. The … ah … clerical personage said he had come in answer to our advertisement. I wish to do full justice to the point of view you have expressed, my dear Frost. On the other hand, to reject the real Merlinus … to alienate a power which is an integral factor in our plan … would be at least equally dangerous. It is not even certain that the priest would in any event be an enemy. He may have made independent contact with the Macrobes. He may be a potential ally.'

'Did you think he looked like it? His priesthood is against him.'

'All that we now want,' said Wither, 'is a collar and tie. Forgive me for saying that I have never been able to share your root and branch attitude to religion. I am not speaking of dogmatic Christianity in its primitive form. But within religious circles – ecclesiastical circles – types of spirituality of very real value do from time to time arise. When they do, they sometimes reveal great energy. Father Doyle, though not very talented, is one of our soundest colleagues; and Mr Straik has in him the germs of that total allegiance (*objectivity* is, I believe, the term you prefer) which is so rare. It doesn't do to be in any way narrow.'

'What do you actually propose to do?'

'We will, of course, consult the Head at once. I use that term, you understand, purely for convenience.'

'But how can you? Have you forgotten that this is the night of the inaugural banquet, and that Jules is coming down? He may be here in an hour. You will be dancing attendance on him till midnight.'

For a moment Wither's face remained still, the mouth wide open. He had indeed forgotten that the puppet Director, the dupe of the Institute by whom it duped the public, was coming that night. But the realisation that he had forgotten troubled him more than it would have troubled another. It was like the first cold breath of winter – the first little hint of a crack in that great secondary self or mental machine which he had built up to carry on the business of living while he, the real Wither, floated far away on the indeterminate frontiers of ghosthood.

'God bless my soul!' he said.

'You have therefore to consider at once,' said Frost, 'what to do with these two men this very evening. It is out of the question that they should attend the banquet. It would be madness to leave them to their own devices.'

'Which reminds me that we have already left them alone – and with Studdock too – for over ten minutes. We must go back with the clothes at once.'

'And without a plan?' inquired Frost, though following Wither out of the room as he said it.

'We must be guided by circumstances,' said Wither.

They were greeted on their return by a babble of imploring Latin from the man in the cassock. 'Let me go,' he said, 'I intreat you do not, for your mothers' sakes, do not do violence to a poor harmless old man. I will tell nothing – God forgive me – but I cannot stay here. This man who says he is Merlinus come back from the dead – he is a diabolist, a worker of infernal miracles. Look! Look what he did to the poor young man the moment you had left the room.' He pointed to where Mark lay unconscious in his chair. 'He did it with his eye, only by looking at him. The evil eye, the evil eye.'

'Silence!' said Frost in the same language, 'and listen. If you do what you are told, no harm will come to you. If you do not, you will be destroyed. I think that if you are troublesome you may lose your soul as well as your life, for you do not sound likely to be a martyr.'

The man whimpered, covering his face with his hands. Suddenly, not as if he wished to but as if he were a machine that had been worked, Frost kicked him. 'Get on,' he said. 'Tell him we have brought such clothes as men wear now.' The man did not stagger when he was kicked.

The end of it was that the tramp was washed and dressed. When this had been done, the man in the cassock said, 'He is saying that he must now be taken for a journey through all your house and shown the secrets.' 'Tell him,' said Wither, 'that it will be a very great pleasure and privilege –' But here the tramp spoke again. 'He says,' translated the big man, 'first that he must see the Head and the beasts and the criminals who are being tormented. Secondly, that he will go with one of you alone. With you, Sir,' and here he turned to Wither.

'I will allow no such arrangement,' said Frost in English.

'My dear Frost,' said Wither, 'this is hardly the moment … and *one* of us must be free to meet Jules.'

The tramp had spoken again. 'Forgive me,' said the man in the cassock, 'I must follow what he says. The words are not mine. He forbids you to talk in his presence in a tongue which he cannot, even through me, understand. And he says it is an old habit of his to be obeyed. He is asking now whether you wish to have him for a friend or an enemy.'

Frost took a pace nearer to the pseudo-Merlin so that his shoulder touched the rusty cassock of the real one. Wither thought that Frost had intended to say something but had grown afraid. In reality, Frost found it impossible to remember any words. Perhaps it was due to the rapid shifts from Latin to English which had been going on. He could not speak. Nothing but nonsense syllables would occur to his mind. He had long known that his continued intercourse with the beings he called Macrobes might have effects on his psychology which he could not predict. In a dim sort of way, the possibility of complete destruction was never out of his thoughts. He had schooled himself not to attend to it. Now, it seemed to be descending on him. He reminded himself that fear was only a chemical phenomenon. For the moment, clearly, he must step out of the struggle, come to himself, and make a new start later in the evening. For, of course, this could not be final. At the very worst it could only be the first hint of the end. Probably he had years of work before him. He would outlast Wither. He would kill the priest. Even Merlin, if it was Merlin, might not stand better with the Macrobes than himself. He stood aside, and the tramp, accompanied by the real Merlin and the Deputy Director, left the room.

Frost had been right in thinking that the aphasia would be only temporary. As soon as they were alone he found no difficulty in saying, as he shook Mark by the shoulder, 'Get up. What do you mean by sleeping here? Come with me to the Objective Room.'

◆　○　◆

Before proceeding to their tour of inspection Merlin demanded robes for the tramp, and Wither finally dressed him as a Doctor of Philosophy of the University of Edgestow. Thus arrayed, walking with his eyes half shut, and as delicately as if he were treading on eggs, the bewildered tinker was led upstairs and downstairs and through the zoo and into the cells. Every now and then his face underwent a kind of spasm as if he were trying to say something; but he never succeeded in producing any words except when the real Merlin asked him a question and fixed him with his eye. Of course, all this was not to the tramp what it would have been to anyone who made an educated and wealthy man's demands upon the universe. It was, no doubt, a 'rum do' – the rummest do that had ever befallen him. The mere sensation of being clean all over would have made it that even apart from the crimson robe and the fact that his own mouth kept on uttering sounds he did not understand and without his own consent. But it was not by any means the first inexplicable thing that had been done to him.

Meanwhile, in the Objective Room, something like a crisis had developed between Mark and Professor Frost. As soon as they arrived there Mark saw that the table had been drawn back. On the floor lay a large crucifix, almost life size, a work of art in the Spanish tradition, ghastly and realistic. 'We have half an hour to pursue our exercises,' said Frost looking at his watch. Then he instructed Mark to trample on it and insult it in other ways.

Now whereas Jane had abandoned Christianity in early childhood, along with her belief in fairies and Santa Claus, Mark had never believed in it at all. At this moment, therefore, it crossed his mind for the very first time that there might conceivably be something in it. Frost who was watching him carefully knew perfectly well that this might be the result of the present experiment. He knew it for the very good reason that his own training by the Macrobes had, at one point, suggested the same odd idea to himself. But he had no choice. Whether he wished it or not this sort of thing was part of the initiation.

'But, look here,' said Mark.

'What is it?' said Frost. 'Pray be quick. We have only a limited time at our disposal.'

'This,' said Mark, pointing with an undefined reluctance to the horrible white figure on the cross. 'This is all surely a pure superstition.'

'Well?'

'Well, if so, what is there objective about stamping on the face? Isn't it just as subjective to spit on a thing like this as to worship it? I mean – damn it all – if it's only a bit of wood, why do anything about it?'

'That is superficial. If you had been brought up in a non-Christian society, you would not be asked to do this. Of course, it is a superstition; but it is that particular superstition which has pressed upon our society for a great many centuries. It can be experimentally shown that it still forms a dominant system in the subconscious of many individuals whose conscious thought appears to be wholly liberated. An explicit action in the reverse direction is therefore a necessary step towards complete objectivity. It is not a question for *a priori* discussion. We find it in practice that it cannot be dispensed with.'

Mark himself was surprised at the emotions he was undergoing. He did not regard the image with anything at all like a religious feeling. Most emphatically it did not belong to that idea of the Straight or Normal or Wholesome which had, for the last few days, been his support against what he now knew of the innermost circle at Belbury. The horrible vigour of its realism was, indeed, in its own way as remote from that Idea as anything else in the room. That was one source of his reluctance. To insult even a carved image of such agony seemed an abominable act. But it was not the only source. With the introduction of this Christian symbol the whole situation had somehow altered. The thing was becoming incalculable. His simple antithesis of the Normal and the Diseased had obviously failed to take something into account. Why was the crucifix there? Why were more than half the poison-pictures religious? He had the sense of new parties to the conflict – potential allies and enemies which he had not suspected before. 'If I take a step in any direction,' he thought, 'I may step over a precipice.' A donkey-like determination to plant hoofs and stay still at all costs arose in his mind.

'Pray make haste,' said Frost.

The quiet urgency of the voice, and the fact that he had so often obeyed it before, almost conquered him. He was on the verge of obeying, and getting the whole silly business over, when the defencelessness of the figure deterred him. The feeling was a very illogical one. Not because its hands were nailed and helpless, but because they were only made of wood and therefore even more helpless, because the thing, for all its realism, was inanimate and could not in any way hit back, he paused. The unretaliating face of a doll – one of Myrtle's dolls – which he had pulled to pieces in boyhood had affected him in the same way and the memory, even now, was tender to the touch.

'What are you waiting for, Mr Studdock?' said Frost.

Mark was well aware of the rising danger. Obviously, if he disobeyed, his last chance of getting out of Belbury alive might be gone. Even of getting out of this room. The smothering sensation once again attacked him. He was himself, he felt, as helpless as the wooden Christ. As he thought this, he found himself looking at the crucifix in a new way – neither as a piece of wood nor a monument of superstition but as a bit of history. Christianity was nonsense, but one did not doubt that the man had lived and had been executed thus by the Belbury of those days. And that, as he suddenly saw, explained why this image, though not itself an image of the Straight or Normal, was yet in opposition to crooked Belbury. It was a picture of what happened when the Straight met the Crooked, a picture of what the Crooked did to the Straight – what it would do to him if he remained straight. It was, in a more emphatic sense than he had yet understood, a *cross*.

'Do you intend to go on with the training or not?' said Frost. His eye was on the time. He knew that those others were conducting their tour of inspection and that Jules must have very nearly reached Belbury. He knew that he might be interrupted at any moment. He had chosen this time for this stage in Mark's initiation partly in obedience to an unexplained impulse (such impulses grew more frequent with him every day), but partly because he wished, in the uncertain situation which had now arisen, to secure Mark at once. He and Wither, and possibly (by now) Straik, were the only full initiates in the NICE. On them lay the danger of making any false step in dealing with the man who claimed to be Merlin and with his mysterious interpreter. For him who took the right steps there was a chance of ousting all the others, of becoming to them what they were to the rest of the Institute and what the Institute was to the rest of England. He knew that Wither was waiting eagerly for any slip on his own part. Hence it seemed to him of the utmost importance to bring Mark as soon as possible beyond that point after which there is no return and the disciple's allegiance both to the Macrobes and to the teacher who has initiated him becomes a matter of psychological, or even physical, necessity.

'Do you not hear what I am saying?' he asked Mark again.

Mark made no reply. He was thinking, and thinking hard because he knew, that if he stopped even for a moment, mere terror of death would take the decision out of his hands. Christianity was a fable. It would be ridiculous to die for a religion one did not believe. This Man himself, on that very cross, had discovered it to be a fable, and had died complaining that the God in whom he trusted had forsaken him – had, in fact, found the universe a cheat. But this raised a question that Mark had never thought of before. Was *that* the moment at which to turn against the Man? If the universe was a cheat, was that a good reason for joining its side? Supposing the Straight was utterly powerless, always and everywhere certain to be mocked, tortured, and finally killed by the Crooked, what then? Why not go down with the ship? He began to be frightened by the very fact that his fears seemed to have momentarily vanished. They had been a safeguard … they had prevented him, all his life, from making mad decisions like that which he was now making as he turned to Frost and said,

'It's all bloody nonsense, and I'm damned if I do any such thing.'

When he said this he had no idea what might happen next. He did not know whether Frost would ring a bell or produce a revolver or renew his demands. In fact, Frost simply went on staring at him and he stared back. Then he saw that Frost was listening, and he began to listen himself. A moment later the door opened. The room seemed suddenly to be full of people – a man in a red gown (Mark did not instantly recognise the tramp) and the huge man in the black gown, and Wither.

◆ ○ ◆

In the great drawing room at Belbury a singularly uncomfortable party was by now assembled. Horace Jules, Director of the NICE, had arrived about half an hour before. They had shown him to the Deputy Director's study, but the Deputy Director was not there. Then they had shown him to his own rooms and hoped he would take a long time settling in. He took a very short time. In five minutes he was downstairs again and on their hands, and it was still much too early for anyone to go and dress. He was now standing with his back to the fire, drinking a glass of sherry, and the principal members of the Institute were standing round him. Conversation was hanging fire.

Conversation with Mr Jules was always difficult because he insisted on regarding himself not as a figurehead but as the real director of the Institute, and even as the source of most of its ideas. And since, in fact, any science he knew was that taught him at the University of London over fifty years ago, and any philosophy he knew had been acquired from writers like Hœckel and Joseph McCabe and Winwood Reade, it was not, in fact, possible to talk to him about most of the things the Institute was really doing. One was always engaged in inventing answers to questions which were actually meaningless and expressing enthusiasm for ideas which were out of date and had been crude even in their prime. That was why the absence of the Deputy Director in such interviews was so disastrous, for Wither alone was master of a conversational style that exactly suited Jules.

Jules was a cockney. He was a very little man, whose legs were so short that he had unkindly been compared with a duck. He had a turned up nose and a face in which some original *bonhomie* had been much interfered with by years of good living and conceit. His novels had first raised him to fame and affluence; later, as editor of the weekly called *We Want To Know*, he had become such a power in the country that his name was really necessary to the NICE.

'And as I said to the Archbishop,' observed Jules, ' "you may not know, my lord," said I, "that modern research shows the temple at Jerusalem to have been about the size of an English village church." '

'God!' said Feverstone to himself where he stood silent on the fringes of the group.

'Have a little more sherry, Director,' said Miss Hardcastle.

'Well, I don't mind if I do,' said Jules. 'It's not at all bad sherry, though I think I could tell you of a place where we could get something better. And how are you getting on, Miss Hardcastle, with your reforms of our penal system?'

'Making real headway,' she replied. 'I think some modification of the Pellotoff method –'

'What I always say,' remarked Jules, interrupting her, 'is, why not treat crime like any other disease? I've no use for Punishment. What you want to do is to put the man on the right lines – give him a fresh start – give him an interest in life. It's all perfectly simple if you look at it from that point of view. I daresay you've been reading a little address on the subject I gave at Northampton.'

'I agreed with you,' said Miss Hardcastle.

'That's right,' said Jules. 'I tell you who didn't though. Old Hingest – and by the bye, that was a queer business. You never caught the murderer, did you? But though I'm sorry for the old chap, I never did quite see eye to eye with him. Very last time I met him, one or two of us were talking about juvenile offenders, and do you know what he said? He said, "The trouble with these courts for young criminals nowadays is that they're always binding them over when they ought to be bending them over." Not bad, was it? Still, as Wither said – and, by the way, where *is* Wither?'

'I think he should be here any moment now,' said Miss Hardcastle, 'I can't imagine why he's not.'

'I think,' said Filostrato, 'he have a breakdown with his car. He will be very desolated, Mr Director, not to have given you the welcome.'

'Oh, he needn't bother about that,' said Jules, 'I never was one for any formality, though I did think he'd be here when I arrived. You're looking very well, Filostrato. I'm following your work with great interest. I look upon you as one of the makers of mankind.'

'*Yes, yes,*' said Filostrato, 'that is the real business. Already we begin –'

'I try to help you all I can on the non-technical side,' said Jules. 'It's a battle I've been fighting for years. The whole question of our sex-life. What I always say is, that once you get the whole thing out into the open, you don't have any more trouble. It's all this Victorian secrecy which does the harm. Making a mystery of it. I want every boy and girl in the country –'

'God!' said Feverstone to himself.

'Forgive me,' said Filostrato who, being a foreigner, had not yet despaired of trying to enlighten Jules. 'But that is not precisely the point.'

'Now I know what you're going to say,' interrupted Jules, laying a fat forefinger on the Professor's sleeve. 'And I daresay you don't read my little paper. But believe me, if you looked up the first number of last month you'd find a modest little editorial which a chap like you might overlook because it doesn't use any technical terms. But I ask you just to read it and see if it doesn't put the whole thing in a nutshell. And in a way that the man in the street can understand.'

At this moment the clock struck a quarter.

'I say,' asked Jules, 'what time is this dinner at?' He liked banquets, and specially banquets at which he had to speak. He also disliked to be kept waiting.

'At quarter to eight,' said Miss Hardcastle.

'You know,' said Jules, 'this fellow Wither really ought to be here. I mean to say, I'm not particular, but I don't mind telling you between you and me that I'm a bit hurt. It isn't the kind of thing a chap expects, is it?'

'I hope nothing's gone wrong with him,' said Miss Hardcastle.

'You'd hardly have thought he'd have gone out anywhere, not on a day like this,' said Jules.

'*Ecco*,' said Filostrato. 'Someone come.'

It was indeed Wither who entered the room followed by a company whom Jules had not expected to see, and Wither's face had certainly good reason to look even more chaotic than usual. He had been bustled round his own Institute as if he were a kind of footman. He had not even been allowed to have supplies of blood and air turned on for the Head when they made him take them into the Head's room. And 'Merlin' (if it was Merlin) had ignored it. Worst of all, it had gradually become clear to him that this intolerable incubus and his interpreter fully intended to be present at dinner. No one could be more keenly aware than Wither of the absurdity of introducing to Jules a shabby old priest who couldn't speak English, in charge of what looked like a somnambulist chimpanzee dressed up as a Doctor of Philosophy. To tell Jules the real explanation – even if he knew which was the real explanation – was out of the question. For Jules was a simple man to whom the word 'medieval' meant only 'savage' and in whom the word 'magic' roused memories of *The Golden Bough*. It was a minor nuisance that ever since their visit to the Objective Room he had been compelled to have both Frost and Studdock in attendance. Nor did it mend matters that as they approached Jules and all eyes were fixed upon them, the pseudo-Merlin collapsed into a chair, muttering, and closed his eyes.

'My dear Director,' began Wither, a little out of breath. 'This is one of the happiest moments of my life. I hope your comfort has been in every way attended to. It has been most unfortunate that I was called away at the very moment when I was expecting your arrival. A remarkable coincidence ... another very distinguished person has joined us at the very same moment. A foreigner ...'

'Oh,' interrupted Jules in a slightly rasping voice. 'Who's he?'

'Allow me,' said Wither, stepping a little to one side.

'Do you mean *that*?' said Jules. The supposed Merlin sat with his arms hanging down on each side of the chair, his eyes closed, his head on one side, and a weak smile on his face. 'Is he drunk? Or ill? And who is he, anyway?'

'He is, as I was observing, a foreigner,' began Wither.

'Well, that doesn't make him go to sleep the moment he is introduced to me, does it?'

'Hush!' said Wither, drawing Jules a little out of the group and lowering his voice. 'There are circumstances – it would be very difficult to go into it here – I have been taken by surprise and would, if you had not been here already, have consulted you at the first possible moment. Our distinguished guest has just undertaken a very long journey and has, I admit, certain eccentricities, and ...'

'But who is he?' persisted Jules.

'His name is ... er ... Ambrosius. Dr Ambrosius, you know.'

'Never 'eard of him,' snapped Jules. At another time he might not have made this admission, but the whole evening was turning out differently from his expectations and he was losing his temper.

'Very few of us have heard of him *yet*,' said Wither. 'But everyone will have heard of him soon. That is why, without in the least ...'

'And who's *that*?' asked Jules indicating the real Merlin. 'He looks as if he were enjoying himself.'

'Oh, that is merely Dr Ambrosius's interpreter.'

'Interpreter? Can't he talk English?'

'Unfortunately not. He lives rather in a world of his own.'

'And can't you get anyone except a priest to act for him? I don't like the look of that fellow. We don't want that sort of thing here at all. Hullo! And who are *you*?'

The last question was addressed to Straik, who had at this moment, thrust his way up to the Director. 'Mr Jules,' he said fixing the latter with a prophetic eye, 'I am the bearer of a message to you which you must hear. I –'

'Shut up,' said Frost to Straik.

'Really, Mr Straik, really,' said Wither. Between them they shouldered him aside.

'Now look 'ere, Mr Wither,' said Jules, 'I tell you straight I'm very far from satisfied. Here's *another* parson. I don't remember the name of any such person coming before me and it wouldn't have got past me if it had done, see? You and I'll have to have a very serious conversation. It seems to me you've been making appointments behind my back and turning the place into a kind of seminary. And that's a thing I won't stand. Nor will the British people.'

'I know. I know,' said Wither. 'I understand your feelings exactly. You can rely on complete sympathy. I am eager and waiting to explain the situation to you. In the meantime, perhaps, as Dr Ambrosius seems slightly overcome and the dressing bell has just sounded ... oh, I beg your pardon. This *is* Dr Ambrosius.'

The tramp, to whom the real magician had recently turned, was now risen from his chair, and approaching. Jules held out his hand sulkily. The other, looking over Jules's shoulder and grinning in an inexplicable fashion, seized it and shook it, as if absent-mindedly, some ten or fifteen times. His breath, Jules noticed, was strong and his grip horny. He was not liking Dr Ambrosius. And he disliked even more the massive form of the interpreter towering over them both.

◆ 16 ◆

Banquet at Belbury

It was with great pleasure that Mark found himself once more dressing for dinner and what seemed likely to be an excellent dinner. He got a seat with Filostrato on his right and a rather inconspicuous newcomer on his left. Even Filostrato seemed human and friendly compared with the two initiates, and to the newcomer his heart positively warmed. He noticed with surprise that the tramp sat at the high table between Jules and Wither, but did not often look in that direction, for the tramp, catching his eye, had imprudently raised his glass and winked at him. The strange priest stood patiently behind the tramp's chair. For the rest, nothing of importance happened until the King's health had been drunk and Jules rose to make his speech.

For the first few minutes, anyone glancing down the long tables would have seen what we always see on such occasions. There were the placid faces of elderly *bons viveurs* whom food and wine had placed in a contentment which no amount of speeches could violate. There were the patient faces of responsible but serious diners, who had long since learned how to pursue their own thoughts, while attending to the speech just enough to respond wherever a laugh or a low rumble of serious assent was obligatory. There was the usual fidgety expression on the faces of young men unappreciative of port and hungry for tobacco. There was bright over-elaborate attention on the powdered faces of women who knew their duty to society. But if you had gone on looking down the tables you would presently have seen a change. You would have seen face after face look up and turn in the direction of the speaker. You would have seen first curiosity, then fixed attention, then incredulity. Finally you would have noticed that the room was utterly silent, without a cough or a creak, that every eye was fixed on Jules, and soon every mouth opened in something between fascination and horror.

To different members of the audience the change came differently. To Frost it began at the moment when he heard Jules end a sentence with the words 'as gross an anachronism as to trust to Calvary for salvation in modern war'. *Cavalry*, thought Frost almost aloud. Why couldn't the fool mind what he was saying? The blunder irritated him extremely. Perhaps – but hullo! what was this? Had his hearing gone wrong? For Jules seemed to be saying that the future density of mankind depended on the implosion of the horses of Nature. 'He's drunk,' thought Frost. Then, crystal clear in articulation, beyond all possibility of mistake, came, 'The madrigore of verjuice must be talthibianised.'

Wither was slower to notice what was happening. He had never expected the speech to have any meaning as a whole and for a long time the familiar catch-words rolled on in a manner which did not disturb the expectation of his ear. He thought, indeed, that Jules was sailing very near the wind, that a very small false step would deprive both the speaker and the audience of the power even to pretend that he was saying anything in particular. But as long as that border was not crossed, he rather admired the speech; it was in his own line. Then he thought, 'Come! That's going too far. Even they must see that you can't talk about accepting the challenge of the past by throwing down the gauntlet of the future.' He looked cautiously down the room. All was well. But it wouldn't be if Jules didn't sit down pretty soon. In that last sentence there were surely words he didn't know. What the deuce did he mean by *aholibate*? He looked down the room again. They were attending too much, always a bad sign. Then came the sentence 'The surrogates esemplanted in a continual of porous variations.'

Mark did not at first attend to the speech at all. He had plenty of other things to think of. The appearance of this spouting popinjay

383

at the very crisis of his own history was a mere interruption. He was too endangered and yet also, in some precarious way, too happy to bother about Jules. Once or twice some phrase caught his ear and made him want to smile. What first awoke him to the real situation was the behaviour of those who sat near him. He was aware of their increasing stillness. He noticed that everyone except himself had begun to attend. He looked up and saw their faces. And then first he really listened. 'We shall not,' Jules was saying, 'we shall not till we can secure the erebation of all prostundiary initems.' Little as he cared for Jules, a sudden shock of alarm pierced him. He looked round again. Obviously it was not he who was mad – they had all heard the gibberish. Except possibly the tramp, who looked as solemn as a judge. He had never heard a speech from one of these real toffs before and would have been disappointed if he could understand it. Nor had he ever before drunk vintage port, and though he did not much like the taste he had been working away like a man.

Wither had not forgotten for a moment that there were reporters present. That in itself did not matter much. If anything unsuitable appeared in tomorrow's paper, it would be child's play for him to say that the reporters were drunk or mad and break them. On the other hand he might let the story pass. Jules was in many respects a nuisance, and this might be as good an opportunity as any other for ending his career. But this was not the immediate question. Wither was wondering whether he should wait till Jules sat down or whether he should rise and interrupt him with a few judicious words. He did not want a scene. It would be better if Jules sat down of his own accord. At the same time, there was by now an atmosphere in that crowded room which warned Wither not to delay too long. Glancing down at the second hand of his watch he decided to wait two minutes more. Almost as he did so he knew that he had misjudged it. An intolerable falsetto laugh rang out from the bottom of the table and would not stop. Some fool of a woman had got hysterics. Immediately Wither touched Jules on the arm, signed to him with a nod, and rose.

'Eh? Blotcher bulldoo?' muttered Jules. But Wither, laying his hand on the little man's shoulder, quietly but with all his weight, forced him down into a sitting position. Then Wither cleared his throat. He knew how to do that so that every eye in the room turned immediately to look at him. The woman stopped screaming. People who had been sitting dead still in strained positions moved and relaxed. Wither looked down the room for a second or two in silence, feeling his grip on the audience. He saw that he already had them in hand. There would be no more hysterics. Then he began to speak.

They ought to have all looked more and more comfortable as he proceeded; and there ought soon to have been murmurs of grave regret for the tragedy which they had just witnessed. That was what Wither expected. What he actually saw bewildered him. The same too attentive silence which had prevailed during Jules's speech had returned. Bright unblinking eyes and open mouths greeted him in every direction. The woman began to laugh again – or no, this time it was two women. Cosser, after one frightened glance, jumped up, overturning his chair, and bolted from the room.

The Deputy Director could not understand this, for to him his own voice seemed to be uttering the speech he had resolved to make. But the audience heard him saying, 'Tidies and fugleman – I sheel foor that we all – er – most steeply rebut the defensible, though, I trust, lavatory, Aspasia which gleams to have selected our redeemed inspector this deceiving. It would – ah – be shark, very shark, from anyone's debenture ...'

The woman who had laughed rose hastily from her chair. The man seated next to her heard her murmur in his ear, 'Vood wooloo.' He took in the meaningless syllables and her unnatural expression at one moment. Both for some reason infuriated him. He rose to help her to move back her chair with one of those gestures of savage politeness which often, in modern society, serve instead of blows. He wrenched the chair, in fact, out of her hand. She screamed, tripped on a ruck in the carpet and fell. The man on the other side of her saw her fall and saw the first man's expression of fury. 'Bot are you blammit?' he roared, leaning towards him with a threatening movement. Four or five people in that part of the room were now up. They were shouting. At the same time there was movement elsewhere. Several of the younger men were making for the door. 'Bundlemen, bundlemen,' said Wither sternly in a much louder voice. He had often before, merely by raising his voice and speaking one authoritative word reduced troublesome meetings to order.

But this time he was not even heard. At least twenty people present were at that very moment attempting to do the same thing. To each of them it seemed plain that things were just at that stage when a word or so of plain sense, spoken in a new voice, would restore the whole room to sanity. One thought of a sharp word, one of a joke, one of something very quiet and telling. As a result fresh gibberish in a great variety of tones rang out from several places at once. Frost was the only one of the leaders who attempted to say nothing. Instead, he had pencilled a few words on a slip of paper, beckoned to a servant, and made him understand by signs that it was to be given to Miss Hardcastle.

By the time the message was put into her hands the clamour was universal. To Mark it sounded like the noise of a crowded restaurant in a foreign country. Miss Hardcastle smoothed out the paper and stopped her head to read. The message ran, *Blunt frippers intantly to pointed bdeluroid. Purgent. Cost.* She crumpled it up in her hand.

Miss Hardcastle had known before she got the message that she was three parts drunk. She had expected and intended to be so: she knew that later on in the evening she would go down to the cells and do things. There was a new prisoner there – a little fluffy girl of the kind the Fairy enjoyed – with whom she could pass an agreeable hour. The tumult of gibberish did not alarm her: she found it exciting. Apparently, Frost wanted her to take some action. She decided that she would. She rose and walked the whole length of the room to the door, locked it, put the key in her pocket, and then turned to survey the company. She noticed for the first time that neither the supposed Merlin nor the Basque priest were anywhere to be seen. Wither and Jules, both on their feet, were struggling with each other. She set out towards them.

So many people had now risen that it took her a long time to reach them. All semblance of a dinner party had disappeared: it was more like the scene at a London terminus on a bank holiday. Everyone was trying to restore order, but everyone was unintelligible, and everyone, in the effort to be understood, was talking louder and louder. She shouted several times herself. She even fought a good deal before she reached her goal.

There came an ear-splitting noise and after that, at last, a few seconds of dead silence. Mark noticed first that Jules had been killed: only secondly, that Miss Hardcastle had shot him. After that it was difficult to be sure what happened. The stampede and the shouting may have concealed a dozen reasonable plans for disarming the murderess, but it was impossible to concert them. Nothing came of them but kicking, struggling, leaping on tables and under tables, pressing on and pulling back, screams, breaking of glass. She fired again and again. It was the smell more than anything else which recalled the scene to Mark in later life: the smell of the shooting mixed with the sticky compound smell of blood and port and madeira.

Suddenly, the confusion of cries ran all together into one thin long-drawn noise of terror. Everyone had become *more* frightened. Something had darted very quickly across the floor between the two long tables and disappeared under one of them. Perhaps half the people present had not seen what it was – had only caught a gleam of black and tawny. Those who had seen it clearly could not tell the others: they could only point and scream meaningless syllables. But Mark had recognised it. It was a tiger.

For the first time that evening everybody realised how many hiding places the room contained. The tiger might be under any of the tables. It might be in any of the deep bay windows, behind the curtains. There was a screen across one corner of the room too.

It is not to be supposed that even now none of the company kept their heads. With loud appeals to the whole room or with urgent whispers to their immediate neighbours they tried to stem the panic, to arrange an orderly retreat from the room, to indicate how the brute could be lured or scared into the open and shot. But the doom of gibberish frustrated all their efforts. They could not arrest the two movements which were going on. The majority had not seen Miss Hardcastle lock the door: they were pressing towards it, to get out at all costs: they would fight, they would kill if they could, rather than not reach the door. A large minority, on the other hand, knew that the door was locked. There must be another door, the one used by the servants, the one whereby the tiger had got in. They were pressing to the opposite end of the room to find it. The whole centre of the room was occupied by the meeting of these two waves – a huge football scrum, at first noisy with frantic efforts at explanation, but soon, as the struggle thickened, almost silent except for the sound of labouring breath, kicking or trampling feet, and meaningless muttering.

Four or five of these combatants lurched heavily against a table, pulling off the cloth in their fall and with it all the fruit dishes, decanters, glasses, plates. Out of that confusion, with a howl of terror, broke the tiger. It happened so quickly that Mark hardly took it in. He saw the hideous head, the cat's snarl of the mouth, the flaming eyes. He heard a shot – the last. Then the tiger had disappeared again. Something fat and white and bloodied was down among the feet of the scrummers. Mark could not recognise it at first for the face, from where he stood, was upside down and the grimaces disguised it until it was quite dead. Then he recognized Miss Hardcastle.

Wither and Frost were no longer to be seen. There was a growling close at hand. Mark turned, thinking he had located the tiger. Then he caught out of the corner of his eye a glimpse of something smaller and greyer. He thought it was an Alsatian. If so, the dog was mad. It ran along the table, its tail between its legs, slavering. A woman, standing with her back to the table, turned, saw it, tried to scream, next moment went down as the creature leaped at her throat. It was a wolf. 'Ai – ai!!' squealed Filostrato and jumped on the table. Something else had darted between his feet. Mark saw it streak across the floor and enter the scrum and wake that mass of interlocked terror into new and frantic convulsions. It was some kind of snake.

Above the chaos of sounds which now awoke – there seemed to be a new animal in the room every minute – there came at last one sound in which those still capable of understanding could take comfort. *Thud – thud – thud*; the door was being battered from the outside. It was a huge folding door, a door by which a small locomotive could almost enter, for the room was made in imitation of Versailles. Already one or two of the panels were splintering. The noise maddened those who had made that door their goal. It seemed also to madden the animals. They did not stop to eat what they killed, or not more than to take one lick of the blood. There were dead and dying bodies everywhere by now, for the scrum was by this time killing as many as the beasts. And always from all sides went up the voices trying to shout to those beyond the door. 'Quick. Quick. Hurry,' but shouting only nonsense. Louder and louder grew the noise at the door. As if in imitation a great gorilla leaped on the table where Jules had sat and began drumming on its chest. Then, with a roar, it jumped down into the crowd.

At last the door gave. Both wings gave. The passage, framed in the doorway, was dark. Out of the darkness there came a grey snaky something. It swayed in the air; then began methodically to break off the splintered wood on each side and make the doorway clear. Then Mark saw distinctly how it swooped down, curled itself round a man – Steele, he thought, but everyone looked different now – and lifted him bodily high off the floor. After that, monstrous, improbable, the huge shape of the elephant thrust its way into the room: its eyes enigmatic, its ears standing stiffly out like the devil's wings on each side of its head. It stood for a second with Steele writhing in the curl of its trunk and then dashed him to the floor. It trampled him. After it raised head and trunk again and brayed horribly; then plunged straight forward into the room, trumpeting and trampling – continuously trampling like a girl treading grapes, heavily and soon wetly tramping in a pash of blood and bones, of flesh, wine, fruit, and sodden tablecloth. Something more than danger darted from the sight into Mark's brain. The pride and insolent glory of the beast, the carelessness of its killings, seemed to crush his spirit even as its flat feet were crushing women and men. Here surely came the King of the world … then everything went black and he knew no more.

◆ ○ ◆

When Mr Bultitude had come to his senses he had found himself in a dark place full of unfamiliar smells. This did not very greatly surprise or trouble him. He was inured to mystery. To poke his head into any spare bedroom at St Anne's, as he sometimes managed to do, was an adventure no less remarkable than that which had now befallen him. And the smells here were, on the whole, promising. He perceived that food was in the neighbourhood and – more exciting still – a female of his own species. There were a great many other animals about too, apparently, but that was rather irrelevant than alarming. He decided to go and find both the female bear and the food; it was then he discovered that walls met him in three directions and bars in the fourth. He could not get out. This, combined with an inarticulate want for the human companionship to which he was accustomed, gradually plunged him into depression. Sorrow such as only animals know – huge seas of disconsolate emotion with not one little raft of reason to float on – drowned him fathoms deep. In his own fashion he lifted up his voice and wept.

And yet, not very far away from him, another, and human, captive was almost equally engulfed. Mr Maggs, seated in a little white cell, chewed steadily on his great sorrow as only a simple man can chew. An educated man in his circumstances would have found misery streaked with reflection; would have been thinking how this new idea of cure instead of punishment, so humane in seeming, had in fact deprived the criminal of all rights and by taking away the *name* Punishment made the *thing* infinite. But Mr Maggs thought all the time simply of one thing: that this was the day he had counted on all through his sentence, that he had expected by this time to be having his tea at home with Ivy (she'd have got something tasty for him the first night) and that it hadn't happened. He sat quite still. About once in every two minutes a single large tear trickled down his cheek. He wouldn't have minded so much if they'd let him have a packet of fags.

It was Merlin who brought release to both. He had left the dining room as soon as the curse of Babel was well fixed upon the enemies. No one had seen him go. Wither had once heard his voice calling loud and intolerably glad above the riot of nonsense, *'Qui Verbum Dei contempserunt, eis auferetur etiam verbum hominis.'** After that he did not see him again, nor the tramp either. Merlin had gone and spoiled his house. He had liberated beasts and men. The animals that were already maimed he killed with an instantaneous motion of the powers that were in him, swift and painless as the mild shafts of Artemis. To Mr Maggs he had handed a written message. It ran as follows: 'Dearest Tom, I do hope your well and the Director here is one of the right sort and he says to come as quick as you can to the Manor at St Anne's. And don't go through Edgestow Tom whatever you do, but come any way you can I should think someone had given you a Lift. Everything is all-right no more now. Lots of love ever your own Ivy.' The other prisoners he let go where they pleased. The tramp, finding Merlin's back turned on him for a second, and having noticed that the house seemed to be empty, made his escape, first into the kitchen and thence, re-inforced with all the edibles his pockets would hold, into the wide world. I have not been able to trace him further.

The beasts, except for one donkey who disappeared about the same time as the tramp, Merlin sent to the dining room, maddened

---

* They that have despised the word of God, from them shall the word of man also be taken away.

with his voice and touch. But he retained Mr Bultitude. The latter
had recognised him at once as the same man whom he had sat
beside in the Blue Room: less sweet and sticky than on that occasion, but recognisably the same. Even without the brilliantine there
was that in Merlin which exactly suited the bear and at their meeting it 'made him all the cheer that a beast can make a man'. He laid
his hand on its head and whispered in its ear and its dark mind was
filled with excitement as though some long forbidden and forgotten pleasure were suddenly held out to it. Down the long, empty
passages of Belbury it padded behind him. Saliva dripped from its
mouth and it was beginning to growl. It was thinking of warm, salt
tastes, of the pleasant resistances of bone, of things to crunch and
lick and worry.

*   ○   *

Mark felt himself shaken; then the cold shock of water dashed in
his face. With difficulty he sat up. The room was empty except for
the bodies of the distorted dead. The unmoved electric light glared
down on hideous confusion – food and filth, spoiled luxury and
mangled men, each more hideous by reason of the other. It was the
supposed Basque priest who had roused him. '*Surge, miselle* [Get
up, wretched boy],' he said, helping Mark to his feet. Mark rose; he
had some cuts and bruises and his head ached but he was substan-
tially uninjured. The man held out to him wine in one of the great
silver cups, but Mark turned away from it with a shudder. He
looked with bewilderment on the face of the stranger and found
that a letter was being put into his hand. 'Your wife awaits you,' it
ran, 'at the Manor at St Anne's on the Hill. Come quickly by road
as best you can. Do not go near Edgestow – A. Denniston.' He
looked again at Merlin and thought his face terrible. But Merlin
met his glance with a look of unsmiling authority, laid a hand on
his shoulder, and impelled him over all the tinkling and slippery
havoc to the door. His fingers sent a prickly sensation through
Mark's skin. He was led down to the cloakroom, made to fling on
a coat and hat (neither were his own) and thence out under the

stars, bitter cold and two o'clock in the morning, Sirius bitter green, a few flakes of dry snow beginning to fall. He hesitated. The stranger stood back from him for a second, then, with his open hand, struck him on the back; Mark's bones ached at the memory as long as he lived. Next moment he found himself running as he had never run since boyhood; not in fear, but because his legs would not stop. When he became master of them again he was half a mile from Belbury and looking back he saw a light in the sky.

◆ ○ ◆

Wither was not among those killed in the dining room. He naturally knew all the possible ways out of the room, and even before the coming of the tiger he had slipped away. He understood what was happening if not perfectly, yet better than anyone else. He saw that the Basque interpreter had done the whole thing. And, by that, he knew also that powers more than human had come down to destroy Belbury; only one in the saddle of whose soul rode Mercury himself could thus have unmade language. And this again told him something worse. It meant that his own dark Masters had been completely out in their calculations. They had talked of a barrier which made it impossible that powers from Deep Heaven should reach the surface of the Earth; had assured him that nothing from outside could pass the Moon's orbit. All their polity was based on the belief that Tellus was blockaded, beyond the reach of such assistance and left (as far as that went) to their mercy and his. Therefore he knew that everything was lost.

It is incredible how little this knowledge moved him. It could not, because he had long ceased to believe in knowledge itself. What had been in his far-off youth a merely aesthetic repugnance to realities that were crude or vulgar, had deepened and darkened, year after year, into a fixed refusal of everything that was in any degree other than himself. He had passed from Hegel into Hume, thence through Pragmatism, and thence through Logical Positivism, and out at last into the complete void. The indicative mood now corresponded to no thought that his mind could entertain. He had willed with his whole heart that there should be no reality and no truth, and now even the imminence of his own ruin could not wake him. The last scene of *Dr Faustus* where the man raves and implores on the edge of Hell is, perhaps, stage fire. The last moments before damnation are not often so dramatic. Often the man knows with perfect clarity that some still possible action of his own will could yet save him. But he cannot make this knowledge real to himself. Some tiny habitual sensuality, some resentment too trivial to waste on a blue-bottle, the indulgence of some fatal lethargy, seems to him at that moment more important than the choice between total joy and total destruction. With eyes wide open, seeing that the endless terror is just about to begin and yet (for the moment) unable to feel terrified, he watches passively, not moving a finger for his own rescue, while the last links with joy and reason are severed, and drowsily sees the trap close upon his soul. So full of sleep are they at the time when they leave the right way.

Straik and Filostrato were also still alive. They met in one of the cold, lighted passages, so far away from the dining room that the noise of the carnage was but a faint murmur. Filostrato was hurt, his right arm badly mauled. They did not speak – both knew that the attempt would be useless – but walked on side by side. Filostrato was intending to get round to the garage by a back way: he thought that he might still be able to drive, in a fashion, at least as far as Sterk.

As they rounded a corner they both saw what they had often seen before but had expected never to see again – the Deputy Director, stooped, creaking, pacing, humming his tune. Filostrato did not want to go with him, but Wither, as if noticing his wounded condition, offered him an arm. Filostrato tried to decline it: nonsense syllables came from his mouth. Wither took his left arm firmly; Straik seized the other, the mauled arm. Squealing and shivering with pain, Filostrato accompanied them perforce. But worse awaited him. He was not an initiate, he knew nothing of the dark *eldila*. He believed that his skill had really kept Alcasan's brain alive. Hence, even in his pain, he cried out with horror when he found the other two drawing him through the ante-room of the Head and into the Head's presence without pausing for any of those antiseptic preparations which he had always imposed on his colleagues. He tried vainly to tell them that one moment of such carelessness might undo all his work. But this time it was in the room itself that his conductors began undressing. And this time they took off all their clothes.

They plucked off his too. When the right sleeve, stiff with blood, would not move, Wither got a knife from the ante-room and ripped it. In the end, the three men stood naked before the Head – gaunt, big-boned Straik; Filostrato, a wobbling mountain of fat; Wither, an obscene senility. Then the high ridge of terror from which Filostrato was never again to descend, was reached; for what he thought impossible began to happen. No one had read the dials, adjusted the pressures, or turned on the air and the artificial saliva. Yet words came out of the dry gaping mouth of the dead man's head. 'Adore!' it said.

Filostrato felt his companions forcing his body forwards, then up again, then forwards and downwards a second time. He was compelled to bob up and down in rhythmic obeisance, the others meanwhile doing the same. Almost the last thing he saw on earth was the skinny folds on Wither's neck shaking like the wattles of a turkey-cock. Almost the last thing he heard was Wither beginning to chant. Then Straik joined in. Then, horribly, he found he was singing himself:

Ouroborindra!
Ouroborindra!
Ouroborindra ba-ba-hee!

But not for long. 'Another,' said the voice, 'give me another head.' Filostrato knew at once why they were forcing him to a certain place in the wall. He had devised it all himself. In the wall that separated the Head's room from the ante-chamber there was a little shutter. When drawn back it revealed a window in the wall, and a sash to that window which could fall quickly and heavily. But the sash was a knife. The little guillotine had not been meant to be used like this. They were going to murder him uselessly, unscientically. If he were doing it to one of them all would have been different; everything would have been prepared weeks beforehand – the temperature of both rooms exactly right, the blade sterilised, the attachments all ready to be made almost before the head was severed. He had even calculated what changes the terror of the victim would probably make in his blood pressure; the artificial blood-stream would be arranged accordingly, so as to take over its work with the least possible breach of continuity. His last thought was that he had underestimated the terror.

The two initiates, red from top to toe, gazed at each other, breathing heavily. Almost before the fat dead legs and buttocks of the Italian had ceased quivering, they were driven to begin the ritual again:

Ouroborindra!
Ouroborindra!
Ouroborindra ba-ba-hee!

The same thought struck both of them at one moment: 'It will ask for another.' And Straik remembered that Wither had that knife. He wrenched himself free from the rhythm with a frightful effort: claws seemed to be tearing his chest from inside. Wither saw what he meant to do. As Straik bolted, Wither was already after him. Straik reached the ante-room, slipped in Filostrato's blood. Wither slashed repeatedly with his knife. He had not strength to cut through the neck, but he had killed the man. He stood up, pains gnawing at his old man's heart. Then he saw the Italian's head lying on the floor. It seemed to him good to pick it up and carry it into the inner room: show it to the original Head. He did so. Then he realised that something was moving in the ante-room. Could it be that they had not shut the outer door? He could not remember. They had come in forcing Filostrato along between them; it was possible … everything had been so abnormal. He put down his burden – carefully, almost courteously, even now – and stepped towards the door between the two rooms. Next moment he drew back. A huge bear, rising to its hind legs as he came in sight of it, had met him in the doorway – its mouth open, its eyes flaming, its fore-paws spread out as if for an embrace. Was this what Straik had become? He knew (though even now he could not attend to it) that he was on the very frontier of a world where such things could happen.

◆ ○ ◆

No one at Belbury that night had been cooler than Feverstone. He was neither an initiate like Wither nor a dupe like Filostrato. He knew about the Macrobes, but it wasn't the sort of thing he was interested in. He knew that the Belbury scheme might not work, but he knew that if it didn't he would get out in time. He had a dozen lines of retreat kept open. He had also a perfectly clear conscience and had played no tricks with his mind. He had never slandered another man except to get his job, never cheated except because he wanted money, never really disliked people unless they bored him. He saw at a very early stage that something was going wrong. One had to guess how far wrong. Was this the end of Belbury? If so, he must get back to Edgestow and work up the position he had already prepared for himself as the protector of the University against the NICE. On the other hand, if there were any chance of figuring as the man who had saved Belbury at a moment of crisis, that would be definitely the better line. He would wait as long as it was safe. And he waited a long time. He found a hatch through which hot dishes were passed from the kitchen passage into the dining room. He got through it and watched the scene. His nerves were excellent and he thought he could pull and bolt the shutter in time if any dangerous animal made for the hatch. He stood there during the whole massacre, his eyes bright, something like a smile on his face, smoking endless cigarettes and drumming with his hard fingers on the sill of the hatch. When it was all over he said to himself, 'Well, I'm damned!' It had certainly been a most extraordinary show.

The beasts had all streaked away somewhere. He knew there was a chance of meeting one or two of them in the passages, but he'd have to risk that. Danger – in moderation – acted on him like a tonic. He worked his way to the back of the house and into the garage; it looked as if he must go to Edgestow at once. He could not find his car in the garage – indeed, there were far fewer cars than he had expected. Apparently several other people had had the idea of getting away while the going was good, and his own car had been stolen. He felt no resentment, and set about finding another of the same make. It took him a longish time, and when he had found one he had considerable difficulty in starting her up. The night was cold – going to snow, he thought. He scowled, for the first time that night; he hated snow. It was after two o'clock when he got going.

Just before he started he had the odd impression that someone had got into the back of the car behind him. 'Who's that?' he asked sharply. He decided to get out and see. But to his surprise his body did not obey this decision; instead it drove the car out of the garage and round to the front and out into the road. The snow was definitely falling by now. He found he could not turn his head and could not stop driving. He was going ridiculously fast, too, in this damned snow. He had no choice. He'd often heard of cars being driven from the back seat, but now it seemed to be really happening. Then to his dismay he found he had left the road. The car, still at a reckless speed, was bumping and leaping along what was called Gypsy Lane or (by the educated) Wayland Street – the old Roman Road from Belbury to Edgestow, all grass and ruts. 'Here! What the devil am I doing?' thought Feverstone. 'Am I tight? I'll break my neck at this game if I don't look out!' But on the car went as if driven by one who regarded this track as an excellent road and the obvious route to Edgestow.

◆ ○ ◆

Frost had left the dining room a few minutes after Wither. He did not know where he was going or what he was about to do. For many years he had theoretically believed that all which appears in the mind as motive or intention is merely a by-product of what the body is doing. But for the last year or so – since he had been initiated – he had begun to taste as fact what he had long held as theory. Increasingly, his actions had been without motive. He did this and that, he said thus and thus, and did not know why. His mind was a mere spectator. He could not understand why that spectator should exist at all. He resented its existence, even while assuring himself that resentment also was merely a chemical phenomenon. The nearest thing to a human passion which still existed in him was a sort of cold fury against all who believed in the mind. There was no tolerating such an illusion. There were not, and must not be, such things as men. But never, until this evening, had he been quite so vividly aware that the body and its movements were the only reality, that the self which seemed to watch the body leaving the dining room and setting out for the chamber of the Head, was a nonentity. How infuriating that the body should have power thus to project a phantom self!

Thus the Frost whose existence Frost denied watched his body go into the ante-room, watched it pull up sharply at the sight of a naked and bloodied corpse. The chemical reaction called shock occurred. Frost stopped, turned the body over, and recognised Straik. A moment later his flashing pince-nez and pointed beard looked into the room of the Head itself. He hardly noticed that Wither and Filostrato lay there dead. His attention was fixed by something more serious. The bracket where the Head ought to have been was empty: the metal ring twisted, the rubber tubes tangled and broken. Then he noticed a head on the floor; stooped and examined it. It was Filostrato's. Of Alcasan's head he found no trace, unless some mess of broken bones beside Filostrato's were it.

Still not asking what he would do or why, Frost went to the garage. The whole place was silent and empty; the snow was thick on the ground by this. He came up with as many petrol tins as he could carry. He piled all the inflammables he could think of together in the Objective Room. Then he locked himself in by locking the outer door of the ante-room. Whatever it was that dictated his actions then compelled him to push the key into the speaking tube which communicated with the passage. When he had pushed it as far in as his fingers could reach, he took a pencil from his pocket and pushed with that. Presently he heard the clink of the key falling on the passage floor outside. That tiresome illusion, his consciousness, was screaming to protest; his body, even had he wished, had no power to attend to those screams. Like the clockwork figure he had chosen to be, his stiff body, now terribly cold, walked back into the Objective Room, poured out the petrol and threw a lighted match into the pile. Not till then did his controllers allow him to suspect that death itself might not after all cure the illusion of being a soul – nay, might prove the entry into a world where that illusion raged infinite and unchecked. Escape for the soul, if not for the body, was offered him. He became able to know (and simultaneously refused the knowledge) that he had been wrong from the beginning, that souls and personal responsibility existed. He half saw: he wholly hated. The physical torture of the burning was not fiercer than his hatred of that. With one supreme effort he flung himself back into his illusion. In that attitude eternity overtook him as sunrise in old tales overtakes and turns them into unchangeable stone.

Venus at St Anne's

Daylight came with no visible sunrise as Mark was climbing to the highest ground in his journey. The white road, still virgin of human traffic, showed the footprints of here and there a bird and here and there a rabbit, for the snow-shower was just then coming to its end in a flurry of larger and slower flakes. A big lorry, looking black and warm in that landscape, overtook him. The man put out his head. 'Going Birmingham way, mate?' he asked. 'Roughly,' said Mark. 'At least I'm going to St Anne's.' 'Where's that then?' said the driver. 'Up on the hill behind Pennington,' said Mark. 'Ah,' said the man, 'I could take you to the corner. Save you a bit.' Mark got in beside him.

It was mid-morning when the man dropped him at a corner beside a little country hotel. The snow had all lain and there was more in the sky and the day was extremely silent. Mark went into the little hotel and found a kind, elderly landlady. He had a hot bath and a capital breakfast and then went to sleep in a chair before a roaring fire. He did not wake till about four. He reckoned he was only a few miles from St Anne's, and decided to have tea before he set out. He had tea. At the landlady's suggestion he had a boiled egg with his tea. Two shelves in the little sitting-room were filled with bound volumes of *The Strand*. In one of these he found a serial children's story which he had begun to read as a child but abandoned because his tenth birthday came when he was half way through it and he was ashamed to read it after that. Now, he chased it from volume to volume till he had finished it. It was good. The grown-up stories to which, after his tenth birthday, he had turned instead of it, now seemed to him, except for *Sherlock Holmes*, to be rubbish. 'I suppose I must get on soon,' he said to himself.

His slight reluctance to do so did not proceed from weariness – he felt, indeed, perfectly rested and better than he had felt for several weeks – but from a sort of shyness. He was going to see Jane: and Denniston: and (probably) the Dimbles as well. In fact, he was going to see Jane in what he now felt to be her proper world. But not his. For he now thought that with all his life-long eagerness to reach an inner circle he had chosen the *wrong* circle. Jane was where she belonged. He was going to be admitted only out of kindness, because Jane had been fool enough to marry him. He did not resent it, but he felt shy. He saw himself as this new circle must see him – as one more little vulgarian, just like the Steeles and the Cossers, dull, inconspicuous, frightened, calculating, cold. He wondered vaguely why he was like that. How did other people – people like Denniston or Dimble – find it so easy to saunter through the world with all their muscles relaxed and a careless eye roving the horizon, bubbling over with fancy and humour, sensitive to beauty, not continually on their guard and not needing to be? What was the secret of that fine, easy laughter which he could not by any efforts imitate? Everything about them was different. They could not even fling themselves into chairs without suggesting by the very posture of their limbs a certain lordliness, a leonine indolence. There was elbow-room in their lives, as there had never been in his. They were Hearts: he was only a Spade. Still, he must be getting on ... Of course, Jane was a Heart. He must give her her freedom. It would be quite unjust to think that his love for her had been basely sensual. Love, Plato says, is the son of Want. Mark's body knew better than his mind had known till recently, and even his sensual desires were the true index of something which he lacked and Jane had to give. When she first crossed the dry and dusty world which his mind inhabited she had been like a spring shower; in opening himself to it he had not been mistaken. He had gone wrong only in assuming that marriage, by itself, gave him either power or title to appropriate that freshness. As he now saw, one might as well have thought one could buy a sunset by buying the field from which one had seen it.

He rang the bell and asked for his bill.

◆　○　◆

That same afternoon Mother Dimble and the three girls were upstairs in the big room which occupied nearly the whole top floor of one wing at the Manor, and which the Director called the Wardrobe. If you had glanced in, you would have thought for one moment that they were not in a room at all but in some kind of forest – a tropical forest glowing with bright colours. A second glance and you might have thought they were in one of those delightful upper rooms at a big shop where carpets standing on end and rich stuffs hanging from the roof make a kind of woven forest of their own. In fact, they were standing amidst a collection of robes of state – dozens of robes which hung, each separate, from its little pillar of wood.

'That would do beautifully for you, Ivy,' said Mother Dimble lifting with one hand the fold of a vividly green mantle over which thin twists and spirals of gold played in a festive pattern. 'Come, Ivy,' she continued, 'don't you like it? You're not still fretting about Tom, are you? Hasn't the Director told you he'll be here tonight or tomorrow mid-day, at the latest?'

Ivy looked at her with troubled eyes.

''Tisn't that,' she said. 'Where'll the Director himself be?'

'But you can't want him to stay, Ivy,' said Camilla, 'not in continual pain. And his work will be done – if all goes well at Edgestow.'

'He has longed to go back to Perelandra,' said Mother Dimble. 'He's – sort of home-sick. Always, always … I could see it in his eyes.'

'Will that Merlin man come back here?' asked Ivy.

'I don't think so,' said Jane. 'I don't think either he or the Director expected him to. And then my dream last night. It looked as if he was on fire … I don't mean burning, you know, but light –

all sorts of lights in the most curious colours shooting out of him and running up and down him. That was the last thing I saw: Merlin standing there like a kind of pillar and all those dreadful things happening all round him. And you could see in his face that he was a man used up to the last drop, if you know what I mean – that he'd fall to pieces the moment the powers let him go.'

'We're not getting on with choosing our dresses for tonight.'

'What is it made of?' said Camilla, fingering and then smelling the green mantle. It was a question worth asking. It was not in the least transparent yet all sorts of lights and shades dwelled in its rippling folds and it flowed through Camilla's hands like a water-fall. Ivy became interested.

'Gor!' she said. 'However much a yard would it be?'

'There,' said Mother Dimble as she draped it skilfully round Ivy. Then she said, 'Oh!' in genuine amazement. All three stood back from Ivy staring at her with delight. The commonplace had not exactly gone from her form and face, the robe had taken it up, as a great composer takes up a folk tune and tosses it like a ball through his symphony and makes of it a marvel, yet leaves it still itself. A 'pert fairy' or 'dapper elf', a small though perfect spright-liness, stood before them: but still recognisably Ivy Maggs.

'Isn't that like a man!' exclaimed Mrs Dimble. 'There's not a mirror in the room.'

'I don't believe we were meant to see ourselves,' said Jane. 'He said something about being mirrors enough to see another.'

'I would just like to see what I'm like at the back,' said Ivy.

'Now Camilla,' said Mother Dimble. 'There's no puzzle about you. This is obviously your one.'

'Oh, do you think *that* one?' said Camilla.

'Yes, of course,' said Jane.

'You'll look ever so nice in that,' said Ivy. It was a long slender thing which looked like steel in colour though it was soft as foam to the touch. It wrapped itself close about her loins and flowed out in a glancing train at her heels. 'Like a mermaid,' thought Jane; and then, 'like a Valkyrie.'

'I'm afraid,' said Mother Dimble, 'you must wear a coronet with that one.'

'Wouldn't that be rather …?'

But Mother Dimble was already setting it on her head. That reverence (it need have nothing to do with money value) which nearly all women feel for jewelry hushed three of them for a moment. There were perhaps no such diamonds in England. The splendour was fabulous, preposterous.

'What are you all staring at?' asked Camilla who had seen but one flash as the crown was raised in Mrs Dimble's hands and did not know that she stood 'like starlight, in the spoils of provinces'.

'Are they real?' said Ivy.

'Where did they come from, Mother Dimble?' asked Jane.

'Treasure of Logres, dears, treasures of Logres,' said Mrs Dimble. 'Perhaps from beyond the Moon or before the flood. Now Jane.'

Jane could see nothing specially appropriate in the robe which the others agreed in putting on her. Blue was, indeed, her colour but she had thought of something a little more austere and dignified. Left to her own judgment, she would have called this a little 'fussy'. But when she saw the others all clap their hands, she submitted. Indeed, it did not now occur to her to do otherwise and the whole matter was forgotten a moment later in the excitement of choosing a robe for Mother Dimble.

'Something quiet,' she said. 'I'm an old woman and I don't want to be made ridiculous.'

'This wouldn't do at all,' said Camilla, walking down the long row of hanging splendours, herself like a meteor as she passed against that background of purple and gold and scarlet and soft snow and elusive opal, of fur, silk, velvet, taffeta and brocade. 'That's lovely,' she said. 'But not for you. And oh! – look at that. But it wouldn't do. I don't see anything …'

'Here! Oh, do come and look! Come here,' cried Ivy as if she were afraid her discovery would run away unless the others attended to it quickly.

'Oh! Yes, yes indeed,' said Jane.

'Certainly,' said Camilla.

'Put it on, Mother Dimble,' said Ivy. 'You know you got to.' It was of that almost tyrannous flame colour which Jane had seen in her vision down in the lodge, but differently cut, with fur about the great copper brooch that clasped the throat, with long sleeves and hangings from them. And there went with it a many-cornered cap. And they had no sooner clasped the robe than all were astonished, none more than Jane, though indeed she had had best reason to foresee the result. For now this provincial wife of a rather obscure scholar, this respectable and barren woman with grey hair and double chin, stood before her, not to be mistaken, as a kind of priestess or sybil, the servant of some pre-historic goddess of fertility – an old tribal matriarch, mother of mothers, grave, formidable and august. A long staff, curiously carved as if a snake twined up it, was apparently part of the costume: they put it in her hand.

'Am I awful?' said Mother Dimble looking in turn at the three silent faces.

'You look lovely,' said Ivy.

'It is exactly right,' said Camilla.

Jane took up the old lady's hand and kissed it. 'Darling,' she said, '*aweful*, in the old sense, is just what you *do* look.'

'What are the men going to wear?' asked Camilla suddenly.

'They can't very well go in fancy dress, can they?' said Ivy. 'Not if they're cooking and bringing things in and out all the time. And I must say, if this is to be the last night and all, I do think we ought to have done the dinner anyway. Let them do as they like about the wine. And what they'll do with that goose is more than I like to think, because I don't believe that Mr MacPhee ever roasted a bird in his life, whatever he says.'

'They can't spoil the oysters anyway,' said Camilla.

'That's right,' said Ivy. 'Nor the plum pudding, not really. Still, I'd like just to go down and take a look.'

'You'd better not,' said Jane with a laugh. 'You know what he's like when he's in charge in the kitchen.'

'I'm not afraid of *him*,' said Ivy, almost, but not quite, putting out her tongue. And in her present dress the gesture was not uncomely.

'You needn't be in the least worried about the dinner, girls,' said Mother Dimble. 'He will do it very well. Always provided he and my husband don't get into a philosophical argument just when they ought to be dishing up. Let's go and enjoy ourselves. How very warm it is in here.'

''s lovely,' said Ivy.

At that moment the whole room shook from end to end.

'What on earth's that?' said Jane.

'If the war was still on I'd have said it was a bomb,' said Ivy.

'Come and look,' said Camilla who had regained her composure sooner than any of the others and was now at the window which looked west towards the valley of the Wynd. 'Oh, look!' she said again. 'No. It's not fire. And it's not searchlights. And it's not forked lightning. Ugh! … There's another shock. And there … Look at that. It's as bright as day there beyond the Church. What am I talking about, it's only three o'clock. It's brighter than day. And the heat!'

'It has begun,' said Mother Dimble.

♦ ○ ♦

At about the same time that morning when Mark had climbed into the lorry, Feverstone, not much hurt but a good deal shaken, climbed out of the stolen car. That car had ended its course upside down in a deep ditch, and Feverstone, always ready to look on the bright side, reflected as he extricated himself that things might have been worse – it might have been his own car. The snow was deep in the ditch and he was very wet. As he stood up and looked about him he saw that he was not alone. A tall, massive figure in a black cassock was before him, about five yards distant. Its back was towards him and it was already walking steadily away. 'Hi!' shouted Feverstone. The other turned and looked at him in silence for a second or two; then it resumed its walk. Feverstone felt at once that this was not the sort of man he would get on with – in fact, he had never liked the look of anyone less. Nor could he, in his broken and soaking pumps, follow the four-mile-an-hour stride of those booted feet. He did not attempt it. The black figure came to a gate, there stopped and made a whinnying noise. He was apparently talking to a horse across the gate. Next moment (Feverstone did not quite see how it happened) the man was over the gate and on the horse's back and off at a canter across a wide field that rose milk white to the sky-line.

Feverstone had no idea where he was, but clearly the first thing to do was to reach a road. It took him much longer than he expected. It was not freezing now and deep puddles lay hidden beneath the snow in many places. At the bottom of the first hill he came to such a morass that he was driven to abandon the track of the Roman road and try striking across the fields. The decision was fatal. It kept him for two hours looking for gaps in hedges, and trying to reach things that looked like roads from a distance but turned out to be nothing of the sort when one reached them. He had always hated the country and always hated weather and he was not at any time fond of walking.

Near twelve o'clock he found a road with no signposts that led him an hour later into a main road. Here, thank heavens, there was a fair amount of traffic, both cars and pedestrians, all going one way. The first three cars took no notice of his signals. The fourth stopped. 'Quick. In you get,' said the driver. 'Going to Edgestow?' asked Feverstone, his hand on the door. 'Good Lord, no!' said the other. '*There's* Edgestow!' (and he pointed behind him) – 'if you want to go *there*.' The man seemed surprised and considerably excited.

In the end there was nothing for it but walking. Every vehicle was going away from Edgestow, none going towards it. Feverstone was a little surprised. He knew all about the exodus (indeed, it had been part of his plan to clear the city as far as possible) but he had supposed it would be over by now. But all that afternoon as he splashed and slipped through the churned snow the fugitives were still passing him. We have (naturally) hardly any first-hand evidence for what happened in Edgestow that afternoon and evening. But we have plenty of stories as to how so many people came to leave it at the last moment. They filled the papers for weeks and lingered in private talks for months, and in the end became a joke. 'No, I *don't* want to hear how you got out of Edgestow,' came to be a catch-phrase. But behind all the exaggerations there remains the undoubted truth that a quite astonishing number of citizens left the town just in time. One had had a message from a dying father; another had decided quite suddenly, and he couldn't just say why, to go and take a little holiday; another went because the pipes in his house had been burst by the frost and he thought he might as well go away till they were put right. Not a few had gone because of some trivial event which seemed to them an omen – a dream, a broken looking-glass, tea-leaves in a cup. Omens of a more ancient kind had also revived during this crisis. One had heard his donkey, another her cat, say 'as clear as clear': '*Go away.*' And hundreds were still leaving for the old reason – because their houses had been taken from them, their livelihood destroyed, and their liberties threatened by the Institutional Police.

It was at about four o'clock that Feverstone found himself flung on his face. That was the first shock. They continued, increasing in frequency, during the hours that followed – horrible shudderings, and soon heavings, of the earth, and a growing murmur of widespread subterranean noise. The temperature began to rise. Snow was disappearing in every direction and at times he was knee deep in water. Haze from the melting snow filled the air. When he reached the brow of the last steep descent into Edgestow he could see nothing of the city: only fog through which extraordinary coruscations of light came up to him. Another shock sent him sprawling. He now decided not to go down: he would turn and follow the traffic – work over to the railway and try to get to London. The picture of a steaming bath at his club, of himself at the fender of the smoking room telling this whole story, rose in his mind. It would be something to have survived both Belbury and Bracton.

He had survived a good many things in his day and believed in his luck.

He was already a few paces down the hill when he made this decision, and he turned at once. But instead of going up he found he was still descending. As if he were in shale on a mountain slope, instead of on a metalled road, the ground slipped away backwards where he trod on it. When he arrested his descent he was thirty yards lower. He began again. This time he was flung off his feet, rolled head over heels, stones, earth, grass and water pouring over him and round him in riotous confusion. It was as when a great wave overtakes you while you are bathing, but this time it was an earth wave. He got to his feet once again; set his face to the hill. Behind, the valley seemed to have turned into Hell. The pit of fog had been ignited and burned with blinding violet flame, water was roaring somewhere, buildings crashing, mobs shouting. The hill in front of him was in ruins – no trace of road, hedge or field, only a cataract of loose raw earth. It was also far steeper than it had been. His mouth and hair and nostrils were full of earth. The slope was growing steeper as he looked at it. The ridge heaved up and up. Then the whole wave of earth rose, arched, trembled, and with all its weight and noise poured down on him.

◆ ○ ◆

'Why Logres, Sir?' said Camilla.

Dinner was over at St Anne's and they sat at their wine in a circle about the dining-room fire. As Mrs Dimble had prophesied, the men had cooked it very well; only after their serving was over and the board cleared had they put on their festal garments. Now all sat at their ease and all diversely splendid: Ransom crowned, at the right of the hearth; Grace Ironwood, in black and silver, opposite him. It was so warm that they had let the fire burn low, and in the candlelight the court dresses seemed to glow of themselves.

'Tell them, Dimble,' said Ransom. 'I will not talk much from now on.'

'Are you tired, Sir?' said Grace. 'Is the pain bad?'

'No, Grace,' he replied. 'It isn't that. But now that it's so very nearly time for me to go, all this begins to feel like a dream. A happy dream, you understand: all of it, even the pain. I want to taste every drop. I feel as though it would be dissolved if I talked much.'

'I suppose you *got* to go, Sir?' said Ivy.

'My dear,' said he, 'what else is there to do? I have not grown a day or an hour older since I came back from Perelandra. There is no natural death to look forward to. The wound will only be healed in the world where it was got.'

'All this has the disadvantage of being clean contrary to the observed laws of Nature,' observed MacPhee. The Director smiled without speaking, as a man who refuses to be drawn.

'It is not contrary to the laws of Nature,' said a voice from the corner where Grace Ironwood sat, almost invisible in the shadows. 'You are quite right. The laws of the universe are never broken. Your mistake is to think that the little regularities we have observed on one planet for a few hundred years are the real unbreakable laws; whereas they are only the remote results which the true laws bring about more often than not; as a kind of accident.'

'Shakespeare never breaks the real laws of poetry,' put in Dimble. 'But by following them he breaks every now and then the little regularities which critics mistake for the real laws. Then the little critics call it a "licence". But there's nothing licentious about it to Shakespeare.'

'And that,' said Denniston, 'is why nothing in Nature is *quite* regular. There are always exceptions. A good average uniformity, but not complete.'

'Not many exceptions to the law of death have come my way,' observed MacPhee.

'And *how*,' said Grace with much emphasis, 'how should *you* expect to be there on more than one such occasion? Were you a friend of Arthur's or Barbarossa's? Did you know Enoch or Elijah?'

'Do you mean,' said Jane, 'that the Director ... the Pendragon ... is going where they went?'

'He will be with Arthur, certainly,' said Dimble. 'I can't answer for the rest. There are people who have never died. We do not yet know why. We know a little more than we did about the How. There are many places in the universe – I mean, this same physical universe in which our planet moves – where an organism can last practically forever. Where Arthur is, we know.'

'Where?' said Camilla.

'In the Third Heaven, in Perelandra. In Aphallin, the distant island which the descendants of Tor and Tinidril will not find for a hundred centuries. Perhaps alone?' ... he hesitated and looked at Ransom who shook his head.

'And that is where Logres comes in, is it?' said Camilla. 'Because he will be with Arthur?'

Dimble was silent for a few minutes arranging and rearranging the fruit-knife and fruit-fork on his plate.

'It all began,' he said, 'when we discovered that the Arthurian story is mostly true history. There was a moment in the Sixth Century when something that is always trying to break through into this country nearly succeeded. Logres was our name for it – it will do as well as another. And then ... gradually we began to see all English history in a new way. We discovered the haunting.'

'What haunting?' asked Camilla.

'How something we may call Britain is always haunted by something we may call Logres. Haven't you noticed that we are two countries? After every Arthur, a Mordred; behind every Milton, a Cromwell: a nation of poets, a nation of shopkeepers; the home of Sidney – and of Cecil Rhodes. Is it any wonder they call us hypocrites? But what they mistake for hypocrisy is really the struggle between Logres and Britain.'

He paused and took a sip of wine before proceeding.

'It was long afterwards,' he said, 'after the Director had returned from the Third Heaven, that we were told a little more. This haunting turned out to be not only from the other side of the invisible wall. Ransom was summoned to the bedside of an old man then dying in Cumberland. His name would mean nothing to you if I told it. That man was the Pendragon, the successor of Arthur and Uther and Cassibelaun. Then we learned the truth. There has been a secret Logres in the very heart of Britain all these years; an unbroken succession of Pendragons. That old man was the seventy-eighth from Arthur: our Director received from him the office and the blessings; tomorrow we shall know, or tonight, who is to be the eightieth. Some of the Pendragons are well known to history, though not under that name. Others you have never heard of. But in every age they and the little Logres which gathered round them have been the fingers which gave the tiny shove or the almost imperceptible pull, to prod England out of the drunken sleep or to draw her back from the final outrage into which Britain tempted her.'

'This new history of yours,' said MacPhee, 'is a wee bit lacking in documents.'

'It has plenty,' said Dimble with a smile. 'But you do not know the language they're written in. When the history of these last few months comes to be written in *your* language, and printed, and taught in schools, there will be no mention in it of you and me, nor of Merlin and the Pendragon and the Planets. And yet in these months Britain rebelled most dangerously against Logres and was defeated only just in time.'

'Aye,' said MacPhee, 'and it could be right good history without mentioning you and me or most of those present. I'd be greatly obliged if any one would tell me what we *have* done – always apart from feeding the pigs and raising some very decent vegetables.'

'You have done what was required of you,' said the Director. 'You have obeyed and waited. It will often happen like that. As one of the modern authors has told us, the altar must often be built in one place in order that the fire from heaven may descend somewhere else. But don't jump to conclusions. You may have plenty of work to do before a month is passed. Britain has lost a battle, but she will rise again.'

'So that, meanwhile, is England,' said Mother Dimble. 'Just this swaying to and fro between Logres and Britain?'

'Yes,' said her husband. 'Don't you feel it? The very quality of England. If we've got an ass's head, it is by walking in a fairy wood. We've heard something better than we can do, but can't quite forget it … can't you see it in everything English – a kind of awkward grace, a humble, humorous incompleteness? How right Sam Weller was when he called Mr Pickwick an angel in gaiters! Everything here is either better or worse than –'

'Dimble!' said Ransom. Dimble, whose tone had become a little impassioned, stopped and looked towards him. He hesitated and (as Jane thought) almost blushed before he began again.

'You're right, Sir,' he said with a smile. 'I was forgetting what you have warned me always to remember. This haunting is no peculiarity of ours. Every people has its own haunter. There's no special privilege for England – no nonsense about a chosen nation. We speak about Logres because it is *our* haunting, the one we know about.'

'But this,' said MacPhee, 'seems a very round-about way of saying that there's good and bad men everywhere.'

'It's not a way of saying that at all,' answered Dimble. 'You see, MacPhee, if one is thinking simply of goodness in the abstract, one soon reaches the fatal idea of something standardised – some common kind of life to which all nations ought to progress. Of course, there are universal rules to which all goodness must conform. But that's only the grammar of virtue. It's not there that the sap is. He doesn't make two blades of grass the same: how much less two saints, two nations, two angels. The whole work of healing Tellus depends on nursing that little spark, on incarnating that ghost, which is still alive in every real people, and different in each. When Logres really dominates Britain, when the goddess Reason, the divine clearness, is really enthroned in France, when the order of Heaven is really followed in China – why, then it will be spring. But meantime, our concern is with Logres. We've got Britain down but who knows how long we can hold her down? Edgestow will not recover from what is happening to her tonight. But there will be other Edgestows.'

'I wanted to ask about Edgestow,' said Mother Dimble. 'Aren't Merlin and the *eldila* a trifle … well, *wholesale*. Did *all* Edgestow deserve to be wiped out?'

'Who are you lamenting?' said MacPhee. 'The jobbing town council that'd have sold their own wives and daughters to bring the NICE to Edgestow?'

'Well, I don't know much about them,' said she. 'But in the University. Even Bracton itself. We all knew it was a horrible College, of course. But did they really mean any great harm with all their fussy little intrigues? Wasn't it more *silly* than anything else?'

'Och aye,' said MacPhee. 'They were only playing themselves. Kittens letting on to be tigers. But there was a real tiger about and their play ended by letting her in. They've no call to complain if when the hunter's after her he lets them have a bit of a lead in their guts too. It'll learn them not to keep bad company.'

'Well, then, the Fellows of other colleges. What about Northumberland and Duke's?'

'I know,' said Denniston. 'One's sorry for a man like Churchwood. I knew him well; he was an old dear. All his lectures were devoted to proving the impossibility of ethics, though in private life he'd walked ten miles rather than leave a penny debt unpaid. But all the same … was there a single doctrine practised at Belbury which hadn't been preached by some lecturer at Edgestow? Oh, of course, they never thought any one would *act* on their theories! No one was more astonished than they when what they'd been talking of for years suddenly took on reality. But it was their own child coming back to them: grown up and unrecognisable, but their own.'

'I'm afraid it's all true, my dear,' said Dimble. '*Trahison des clercs*. None of us is quite innocent.'

'That's nonsense, Cecil,' said Mrs Dimble.

'You are all forgetting,' said Grace, 'that nearly everyone except the very good (who were ripe for fair dismissal) and the very bad, had already left Edgestow. But I agree with Arthur. Those who have forgotten Logres sink into Britain. Those who call for Nonsense will find that it comes.'

At that moment she was interrupted. A clawing and whining noise at the door had become audible.

'Open the door, Arthur,' said Ransom. A moment later the whole party rose to its feet with cries of welcome, for the new arrival was Mr Bultitude.

'Oh, I never *did*,' said Ivy. 'The pore thing! And all over snow too. I'll just take him down to the kitchen and get him something to eat. Wherever have you been, you bad thing? Eh? Just look at the state you're in.'

◆ ○ ◆

For the third time in ten minutes the train gave a violent lurch and came to a standstill. This time the shock put all the lights out.

'This is really getting a bit too bad,' said a voice in the darkness. The four other passengers in the first-class compartment recognised it as belonging to the well-bred, bulky man in the brown suit; the well-informed man who at earlier stages of the journey had told everyone else where they ought to change and why one now reached Sterk without going through Stratford and who it was that really controlled the line.

'It's serious for me,' said the same voice. 'I ought to be in Edgestow by now.' He got up, opened the window, and stared out into the darkness. Presently, one of the other passengers complained of the cold. He shut the window and sat down.

'We've already been here for ten minutes,' he said presently.

'Excuse me. Twelve,' said another passenger.

Still the train did not move. The noise of two men quarrelling in a neighbouring compartment became audible.

Then silence followed again.

Suddenly a shock flung them all together in the darkness. It was if the train, going at full speed, had been unskilfully pulled up.

'What the devil's that?' said one.

'Open the doors.'

'Has there been a collision?'

'It's all right,' said the well-informed man in a loud, calm voice. 'Putting on another engine. And doing it very badly. It's all these new engine drivers they've got in lately.'

'Hullo!' said someone. 'We're moving.'

Slow and grunting, the train began to go.

'It takes its time getting up speed,' said someone.

'Oh, you'll find it'll start making up for lost time in a minute,' said the well-informed man.

'I wish they'd put the lights on again,' said a woman's voice.

'We're *not* getting up speed,' said another.

'We're losing it. Damn it! Are we stopping again?'

'No. We're still moving – oh!!' – once more a violent shock hit them. It was worse than the last one. For nearly a minute everything seemed to be rocking and rattling.

'This is outrageous,' exclaimed the well-informed man, once more opening the window. This time he was more fortunate. A dark figure waving a lantern was walking past beneath him.

'Hi! Porter! Guard!' he bellowed.

'It's all right, ladies and gentlemen, it's all right, keep your seats,' shouted the dark figure, marching past and ignoring him.

'There's no good letting all that cold air in, Sir,' said the passenger next to the window.

'There's some sort of light ahead,' said the well-informed man.

'Signal against us?' asked another.

'No. Not a bit like that. The whole sky's lit up. Like a fire, or like searchlights.'

'I don't care what it's like,' said the chilly man. 'If only – oh!'

Another shock. And then, far away in the darkness, vague disastrous noise. The train began to move again, still slowly, as if it were groping its way.

'I'll make a row about this,' said the well-informed man. 'It's a scandal.'

About half an hour later the lighted platform of Sterk slowly loomed alongside.

'Station Announcer calling,' said a voice. 'Please keep your seats for an important announcement. Slight earthquake shock and floods have rendered the line to Edgestow impassable. No details available. Passengers for Edgestow are advised …'

The well-informed man, who was Curry, got out. Such a man always knows all the officials on a railway and in a few minutes he was standing by the fire in the ticket collector's office getting a further and private report of the disaster.

'Well, we don't exactly know yet, Mr Curry,' said the man. 'There's been nothing coming through for about an hour. It's very bad, you know. They're putting the best face on it they can. There's never been an earthquake like it in England from what I can hear. And there's the floods too. No, Sir, I'm afraid you'll find nothing of Bracton College. All that part of the town went almost at once. It began there, I understand. I don't know what the casualties'll be. I'm glad I got my old Dad out last week.'

Curry always in later years regarded this as one of the turning points of his life. He had not up till then been a religious man. But the word that now instantly came into his mind was 'Providential'. You couldn't really look at it any other way. He'd been within an ace of taking the earlier train; and if he had … why he'd have been a dead man by now. It made one think. The whole College wiped out! It would have to be rebuilt. There'd be a complete (or almost complete) new set of Fellows, a new Warden. It was Providential again that some responsible person should have been spared to deal with such a tremendous crisis. There couldn't be an ordinary election, of course. The College Visitor (who was the Lord Chancellor) would probably have to appoint a new Warden and then, in collaboration with him, a nucleus of new Fellows. The more he thought of it the more fully Curry realised that the whole shaping of the future College rested with the sole survivor. It was almost like being a second founder. Providential – providential. He saw already in imagination the portrait of that second founder in the new-built Hall, his statue in the new-built quadrangle, the long, long chapter consecrated to him in the College History. All this time, without the least hypocrisy, habit and instinct had given his shoulders just such a droop, his eyes such a solemn sternness, his brow such a noble gravity, as a man of good feeling might be expected to exhibit on hearing such news. The ticket-collector was greatly edified. 'You could see he felt it bad,' as he said afterwards. 'But he could take it. He's a fine old chap.'

'When is the next train to London?' asked Curry. 'I must be in town first thing tomorrow morning.'

◆ ○ ◆

Ivy Maggs, it will be remembered, had left the dining room for the purpose of attending to Mr Bultitude's comfort. It therefore surprised everyone when she returned in less than a minute with a wild expression on her face.

'Oh, come quick, someone. Come quick!' she gasped. 'There's a bear in the kitchen.'

'A bear, Ivy?' said the Director. 'But, of course –'

'Oh, I don't mean Mr Bultitude, Sir. There's a strange bear; another one.'

'Indeed!'

'And it's eaten up all what was left of the goose and half the ham and all the junket and now it's lying along the table eating everything as it goes along and wriggling from one dish to another and a breaking all the crockery. Oh, do come quick! There'll be nothing left.'

'And what line is Mr Bultitude taking about all this, Ivy?' asked Ransom.

'Well, that's what I want someone to come and see. He's carrying on something dreadful, Sir. I never seen anything like it. First of all he just stood lifting up his legs in a funny way as if he thought he could dance, which we all know he can't. But now he's got up on the dresser on his hind legs and there he's kind of bobbing up and down, making the awfullest noise – squeaking like – and he's put one foot into the plum pudding already and he's got his head all mixed up in the string of onions and I can't do *nothing* with him, really I can't.'

'This is very odd behaviour for Mr Bultitude. You don't think, my dear, that the stranger might be a *she* bear?'

'Oh, don't say that, Sir!' exclaimed Ivy with extreme dismay.

'I think that's the truth, Ivy. I strongly suspect that this is the future Mrs Bultitude.'

'It'll be the present Mrs Bultitude if we sit here talking about it much longer,' said MacPhee, rising to his feet.

'Oh, dear, what *shall* we do?' said Ivy.

'I am sure Mr Bultitude is quite equal to the situation,' replied the Director. 'At present, the lady is refreshing herself. *Sine Cerere et Baccho*, Dimble. We can trust them to manage their own affairs.'

'No doubt, no doubt,' said MacPhee. 'But not in our kitchen.'

'Ivy, my dear,' said Ransom. 'You must be very firm. Go into the kitchen and tell the strange bear I want to see her. You would-n't be afraid, would you?'

'Afraid? Not me. I'll show her who's the Director here. Not that it isn't only natural for her.'

'What's the matter with that jackdaw?' said Dr Dimble.

'I think it's trying to get out,' said Denniston. 'Shall I open the window?'

'It's warm enough to have the window open anyway,' said the Director. And as the window was opened Baron Corvo hopped out and there was a scuffle and a chattering just outside.

'Another love affair,' said Mrs Dimble. 'It sounds as if Jack had found a Jill ... What a delicious night!' she added. For as the cur-tain swelled and lifted over the open window all the freshness of a midsummer night seemed to be blowing into the room. At that moment, a little further off, came a sound of whinneying.

'Hullo!' said Denniston, 'the old mare is excited too.'

'Sh! Listen!' said Jane.

'That's a different horse,' said Denniston.

'It's a stallion,' said Camilla.

'This,' said MacPhee with great emphasis, 'is becoming indecent.'

'On the contrary,' said Ransom, 'decent, in the old sense, *decens*, fitting, is just what it is. Venus herself is over St Anne's.'

'She comes more near the Earth than she was wont,' quoted Dimble, 'to make men mad.'

'She is nearer than any astronomer knows,' said Ransom. 'The work at Edgestow is done, the other gods have withdrawn. She waits still and when she returns to her sphere I will ride with her.'

Suddenly, in the semi-darkness Mrs Dimble's voice cried sharply, 'Look out! Look out! Cecil! I'm sorry. I can't stand bats. They'll get in my hair!' *Cheep cheep* went the voices of the two bats as they flickered to and fro above the candles. Because of their shadows they seemed to be four bats instead of two.

'You'd better go, Margaret,' said the Director. 'You and Cecil had better both go. I shall be gone very soon now. There is no need of long good-byes.'

'I really think I *must* go,' said Mother Dimble. 'I can't stand bats.'

'Comfort Margaret, Cecil,' said Ransom. 'No. Do not stay. I'm not dying. Seeing people off is always folly. It's neither good mirth nor good sorrow.'

'You mean us to go, Sir?' said Dimble.

'Go, my dear friends. *Urendi Maleldil.*'

He laid his hands on their heads; Cecil gave his arm to his wife and they went.

'Here she is, Sir,' said Ivy Maggs re-entering the room a moment later, flushed and radiant. A bear waddled at her side, its muzzle white with junket and its cheeks sticky with gooseberry jam. 'And – oh, Sir' she added.

'What is it, Ivy?' said the Director.

'Please, Sir, it's poor Tom. It's my husband. And if you don't mind – '

'You've given him something to eat and drink, I hope?'

'Well, yes, I have. There wouldn't have been nothing if those bears had been there much longer.'

'What has Tom got, Ivy?'

'I gave him the cold pie and the pickles (he always was a great one for pickles) and the end of the cheese and a bottle of stout, and

I've put the kettle on so as we can make ourselves – so as he can make himself a nice cup of tea. And he's enjoying it ever so, Sir, and he said would you mind him not coming up to say how d'you do because he never was much of a one for company, if you take my meaning.'

All this time the strange bear had been standing perfectly still with its eyes fixed on the Director. Now he laid his hand on its flat head. '*Urendi Maleldil*,' he said. 'You are a good bear. Go to your mate – but here he is,' for at that moment the door which was already a little ajar was pushed further open to admit the inquiring and slightly anxious face of Mr Bultitude. 'Take her, Bultitude. But not in the house. Jane, open the other window, the French Window. It is like a night in July.' The window swung open and the two bears went blundering out into the warmth and the wetness. Everyone noticed how light it had become.

'Are those birds all daft that they're singing at quarter to twelve?' asked MacPhee.

'No,' said Ransom. 'They are sane. Now, Ivy, you want to go and talk to Tom. Mother Dimble has put you both in the little room half way up the stairs, not in the lodge after all.'

'Oh, Sir,' said Ivy and stopped. The Director leaned forward and laid his hand on her head. 'Of course, you want to go,' he said. 'Why, he's hardly had time to see you in your new dress yet. Have you no kisses to give him?' he said and kissed her. 'Then give him mine, which are not mine but by derivation. Don't cry. You are a good woman. Go and heal this man. *Urendi Maleldil* – we shall meet again.'

'What's all yon squealing and squeaking?' said MacPhee. 'I hope it's not the pigs got loose. For I tell you there's already as much carrying on about this house and garden as I can stand.'

'I think it's hedgehogs,' said Grace Ironwood.

'That last sound was somewhere in the house,' said Jane.

'Listen!' said the Director, and for a short time all were still. Then his face relaxed into a smile. 'It's my friends behind the wainscot,' he said. 'There are revels there too –

So geht es in Snützepützhäusel
Da singen und tanzen die Mäusel!

'I suppose,' said MacPhee drily, producing his snuff-box from under the ash-coloured and slightly monastic-looking robe in which, contrary to his judgment, the others had seen fit to clothe him, 'I suppose we may think ourselves lucky that no giraffes, hippopotami, elephants, or the like have seen fit to – God almighty, what's that?' For as he spoke a long grey flexible tube came in between the swaying curtains and, passing over MacPhee's shoulder, helped itself to a bunch of bananas.

'In the name of Hell where's all them beasts coming from?' he said.

'They are the liberated prisoners from Belbury,' said the Director. 'She comes more near the Earth than she was wont to – to make Earth sane. Perelandra is all about us and Man is no longer isolated. We are now as we ought to be – between the angels who are our elder brothers and the beasts who are our jesters, servants and playfellows.'

Whatever MacPhee was attempting to say in reply was drowned by an earsplitting noise from beyond the window.

'Elephants! Two of them,' said Jane weakly. 'Oh, the celery! And the rose beds!'

'By your leave, Mr Director,' said MacPhee sternly. 'I'll just draw these curtains. You seem to forget there are ladies present.'

'No,' said Grace Ironwood in a voice as strong as his. 'There will be nothing unfit for anyone to see. Draw them wider. How light it is! Brighter than moonlight: almost brighter than day. A great dome of light stands over the whole garden. Look! The elephants are dancing. How high they lift their feet. And they go round and round. And oh, look! – how they lift their trunks. And how ceremonial they are. It is like a minuet of giants. They are not like the other animals. They are a sort of good daemons.'

'They are moving away,' said Camilla.

'They will be as private as human lovers,' said the Director. 'They are not common beasts.'

'I think,' said MacPhee, 'I'll away down to my office and cast some accounts. I'd feel easier in my mind if I were inside and the door locked before any crocodiles or kangaroos start courting in the middle of all my files. There'd better be one man about the place keep his head this night for the rest of you are clean daft. Good night, ladies.'

'Good-bye, MacPhee,' said Ransom.

'No, no,' said MacPhee, standing well back, but extending his hand. 'You'll speak none of your blessings over me. If ever I take to religion, it won't be your kind. My uncle was Moderator of the General Assembly. But there's my hand. What you and I have seen together ... but no matter for that. And I'll say this, Dr Ransom, that with all your faults (and there's no man alive knows them better than myself), you are the best man, taking you by and large, that ever I knew or heard of. You are ... you and I ... but there are the ladies crying. I don't rightly know what I was going to say. I'm away this minute. Why would a man want to lengthen it? God bless you, Dr Ransom. Ladies, I'll wish you a good night.'

'Open all the windows,' said Ransom. 'The vessel in which I must ride is now almost within the air of this World.'

'It is growing brighter every minute,' said Denniston.

'Can we be with you to the very end?' said Jane.

'Child,' said the Director, 'you should not stay till then.'

'Why, Sir?'

'You are waited for.'

'Me, Sir?'

'Yes. Your husband is waiting for you in the Lodge. It was your own marriage chamber that you prepared. Should you not go to him?'

'Must I go *now*?'

'If you leave the decision with me, it is now that I would send you.'

'Then I will go, Sir. But – but – am I a bear or a hedgehog?'

'More. But not less. Go in obedience and you will find love. You will have no more dreams. Have children instead. *Urendi Maleldil.*'

Long before he reached St Anne's, Mark had come to realise that either he himself or else the world about him, was in a very strange condition. The journey took him longer than he expected, but that was perhaps fully accounted for by one or two mistakes that he made. Much harder to explain was the horror of light to the west, over Edgestow, and the throbbings and bouncings of the Earth. Then came a sudden warmth and the torrents of melted snow rolling down the hillside. Everything became a mist; and then, as the lights in the west vanished, this mist grew softly luminous in a different place – above him, as though the light rested on St Anne's. And all the time he had the curious impression that things of very diverse shapes and sizes were slipping past him in the haze – animals, he thought. Perhaps it was all a dream; or perhaps it was the end of the world; or perhaps he was dead. But in spite of all perplexities, he was conscious of extreme well-being. His mind was ill at ease, but as for his body – health and youth and pleasure and longing seemed to be blowing towards him from the cloudy light upon the hill. He never doubted that he must keep on.

His mind was not at ease. He knew that he was going to meet Jane, and something was beginning to happen to him which ought to have happened to him far earlier. That same laboratory outlook upon love which had forestalled in Jane the humility of a wife, had equally forestalled in him, during what passed for courtship, the humility of a lover. Or if there had ever arisen in him at some wiser moment the sense of 'Beauty too rich for use, for earth too dear,' he had put it away from him. False theories, at once prosaic and fanciful, had made it seem to him a mood frousty, unrealistic and outmoded. Now, belated, after all favours had been conceded, the unexpected misgiving was coming over him. He tried to shake it off. They were married, weren't they? And they were sensible, modern people? What could be more natural, more ordinary?

But then, certain moments of unforgettable failure in their short married life rose in his imagination. He had thought often enough of what he called Jane's "moods". This time at last he thought of his own clumsy importunity. And the thought would not go away. Inch by inch, all the lout and clown and clod-hopper in him was revealed to his own reluctant inspection; the coarse, male boor with horny hands and hobnailed shoes and beefsteak jaw, not rushing in – for that can be carried off – but blundering, sauntering, stumping in where great lovers, knights and poets, would have feared to tread. An image of Jane's skin, so smooth, so white (or so he now imagined it) that a child's kiss might make a mark on it, floated before him. How had he dared? Her driven snow, her music, her sacrosancitity, the very style of all her movements ... how had he dared? And dared too with no sense of daring, nonchalantly, in careless stupidity! The very thoughts that crossed her face from moment to moment, all of them beyond his reach, made (had he but had the wit to see it) a hedge about her which such as he should never have had the temerity to pass. Yes, yes – of course, it was she who had allowed him to pass it: perhaps in luckless, misunderstanding pity. And he had taken blackguardly advantage of that noble error in her judgment; had behaved as if here native to that fenced garden and even its natural possessor.

All this, which should have been uneasy joy, was torment to him, for it came too late. He was discovering the hedge after he had plucked the rose, and not only plucked it but torn it all to pieces and crumpled it with hot, thumb-like, greedy fingers. How had he dared? And who that understood could forgive him? He knew now what he must look like in the eyes of her friends and equals. Seeing that picture, he grew hot to the forehead, alone there in the mist.

The word *Lady* had made no part of his vocabulary save as a pure form or else in mockery. He had laughed too soon.

Well, he would release her. She would be glad to be rid of him. Rightly glad. It would now almost have shocked him to believe otherwise. Ladies in some noble and spacious room, discoursing in cool ladyhood together, either with exquisite gravity or with silver laughter – how should they *not* be glad when the intruder had

426

gone? – the loud-voiced or tongue-tied creature, all boots and hands, whose true place was in the stable. What should he do in such a room – where his very admiration could only be insult, his best attempts to be either grave or gay could only reveal unbridgeable misunderstanding? What he had called her coldness seemed now to be her patience. Whereof the memory scalded. For he loved her now. But it was all spoiled: too late to mend matters.

Suddenly the diffused light brightened and flushed. He looked up and perceived a great lady standing by a doorway in a wall. It was not Jane, not like Jane. It was larger, almost gigantic. It was not human, though it was like a woman divinely tall, part naked, part wrapped in a flame-coloured robe. Light came from it. The face was enigmatic, ruthless he thought, inhumanly beautiful. It was opening the door for him. He did not dare disobey ('Surely,' he thought, 'I must have died'), and he went in: found himself in some place of sweet smells and bright fires, with food and wine and a rich bed.

◆ ○ ◆

And Jane went out of the big house with the Director's kiss upon her lips and his words in her ears, into the liquid light and supernatural warmth of the garden and across the wet lawn (birds were everywhere) and past the see-saw and the greenhouse and the piggeries, going down all the time, down to the lodge, descending the ladder of humility. First she thought of the Director, then the thought of Maleldil. Then she thought of her obedience and the setting of each foot before the other became a kind of sacrificial ceremony. And she thought of children, and of pain and death. And now she was half way to the lodge, and thought of Mark and of all his sufferings. When she came to the lodge she was surprised to see it all dark and the door shut. As she stood at the door with one hand on the latch, a new thought came to her. How if Mark did not want her – not tonight, nor in that way, nor any time, nor in any way? How if Mark were not there after all? A great gap – of relief or of disappointment, no one could say – was made in her mind by this thought. Still she did not move the latch. Then she noticed that the window, the bedroom window, was open. Clothes were piled on a chair inside the room so carelessly that they lay over the sill: the sleeve of a shirt – Mark's shirt – even hung over down the outside wall. And in all this damp too. How exactly like Mark! Obviously it was high time she went in.

Voyager Classics

The Fellowship of the Ring

J R R Tolkien

The Fellowship of the Ring is the first part of J.R.R. Tolkien's epic adventure, *The Lord of the Rings*, which has been consistently acclaimed as the most popular and significant book of the twentieth century. With this work Tolkien virtually single-handedly created the fantasy genre, and no other writer has surpassed him.

When *The Fellowship of the Ring* was first published in 1954 its effect on the literary establishment was like a pebble striking still water. Attempting to find words to describe it at the time, reviewers were at a loss; the author, Richard Hughes, said: 'one can't praise the book by comparisons – there is nothing to compare it with. For width of imagination it almost beggars parallel, and it is nearly as remarkable for its vividness and for the narrative skill which carries the reader on, enthralled, for page after page.' C. S. Lewis was equally enthusiastic: 'No imaginary world has been projected which is at once so multifarious and so true to its own inner laws; none so relevant to the actual human situation yet so free from allegory.'

The ripples of its impact continue to be felt today.

0 00 711711 6

Voyager Classics

The Two Towers

J R R Tolkien

The Two Towers is the second part of J.R.R. Tolkien's epic adventure, *The Lord of the Rings*, which has been consistently acclaimed as the most popular and significant book of the twentieth century. With this work Tolkien virtually single-handedly created the fantasy genre, and no other writer has surpassed him.

'Among the greatest works of imaginative fiction in the twentieth century. If it is no more than an entertainment, we have seldom been entertained so well. The book presents us with the richest profusion of new lands and new creatures, from the beauty of Lothlórien to the horror of Mordor, adventures to hold us spell-bound, and words of beauty and evocation to bring all vividly before us.' *Sunday Telegraph*

'Tolkien's invention of strange peoples, curious incidents, miraculous doings, is poured out in this second volume of his trilogy as exuberantly and convincingly, in a dreamlike way, as ever. As the story goes on the world of the Ring grows more vast and mysterious and crowded with curious figures, horrible, delightful or comic. The story itself is superb.' *Observer*

0 00 711712 4

Voyager Classics

The Return of the King

J R R Tolkien

The Return of the King is the concluding volume of J.R.R. Tolkien's epic adventure, *The Lord of the Rings*, which has been consistently acclaimed as the most popular and significant book of the twentieth century. With this work Tolkien virtually single-handedly created the fantasy genre, and no other writer has surpassed him.

'A story magnificently told, with every kind of colour and movement and greatness' *New Statesman*

'The story moves on with a tremendous narrative rush to its climax . . . extraordinarily imaginative work, part saga, part allegory, and wholly exciting' *The Times*

'His astonishing inventiveness remains to the end and is continued in a series of appendices' *Guardian*

0 00 711956 9

Voyager Classics

The Game-Players of Titan

Philip K Dick

Philip K. Dick is one of science fiction's most outstanding and unique minds. *The Game-Players of Titan* is a brilliantly conceived vision of a future dystopia, full of wildly imaginative detail, moments of exquisite humour and mind-distorting musings on the nature of perception. The seemingly straightforward narrative quickly turns into a tumultuous nightmare of delusion, precognition and conspiracy.

Roaming the pristine landscape of Earth, cared for by machines and aliens, the few remaining humans alive since the war with Titan play Bluff. The game allows them to win or lose property, and also to form new marriages in order to maximise the remote chance that some pairings will produce a child. When Pete Garden, a particularly suicidal member of the Pretty Blue Fox game-playing group, loses his current wife and his deed to Berkeley, he stumbles upon a far bigger, more sinister version of the game. The telepathic, slug-like Vugs of Titan are the players and at stake is the Earth itself.

'The most brilliant sci-fi mind on any planet'   *Rolling Stone*

0 00 711588 1

Voyager Classics

The Martian Chronicles

Ray Bradbury

The Martian Chronicles, Ray Bradbury's second book, made his reputation and is still considered by many to be his finest work. These closely interwoven short stories, skilfully linked by recurring images and themes, evoke a beautifully nostalgic sense of loss and isolation.

The book tells the story of humanity's repeated attempts to colonize the red planet. The first men were few. Most succumbed to a disease called the Great Loneliness when they saw their home planet dwindle to the size of a fist. Those who survived found no welcome on Mars. But more rockets arrived from Earth, and more. People brought their old prejudices with them – and their desires and fantasies and tainted dreams. These strange and wonderful tales of man's experiences on Mars are filled with intense images and astonishing visions. As much a work of social criticism as of science fiction, *The Martian Chronicles* is an allegory for the tragic moral blindness of mankind, told in wonderfully evocative prose.

'Bradbury has a remarkable range and intensity of vision'
Sunday Times

0 00 711962 3

Voyager Classics

Brave New World

Aldous Huxley

Aldous Huxley's *Brave New World* is possibly the world's most famous science fiction novel. The title has become proverbial, a succinct expression of irony that progress has not led to perfection, and nor will it.

The World State has two billion standardized citizens steeped in the virtues of passive obedience, material consumption and mindless promiscuity. Hatcheries breed a mass of Epsilon-Minuses for menial labour and fewer of the castes ranked above them. Free handouts of governement-approved dope, *soma*, and mass entertainment keep all levels happy. But in the Central London Hatchery and Conditioning Centre, Alpha-Plus Bernard Marx is unhappy. Harbouring an unnatural desire for solitude, he has an ill-defined longing to break free. A visit to one of the few remaining Savage Reservations where the old, imperfect life still continues, may be the cure for his distress. Alive with invention and aphorism, *Brave New World* is a caustic satire that is utterly absorbing and gripping.

'Such ingenious wit, derisive logic and swiftness of expression, Huxley's resources of sardonic invention have never been more brilliantly displayed'   *The Times*

0 00 711589 X

Voyager Classics

The Songs of Distant Earth

Arthur C. Clarke

For many Arthur C. Clarke is the very personification of science fiction. In *The Songs of Distant Earth* he perfectly captures man's longing for the stars in a thoughtful and hauntingly evocative tale of doomsday and beyond that tells of human diversity and the meaning of loss.

Over centuries of knowing the end was at hand humanity launched probes carrying embryos to distant star-systems, relying on machines to incubate the first people of a virgin land under an alien sun. Finally, in the Last Days of Earth, the *Magellan* takes off for the stars carrying a million refugees. They witness the death of Earth as they leave: the Atlantic boils dry, the pyramids disintegrate, the ice of Antarctica melts. Then they sleep. Five hundred years later the *Magellan* must make planetfall for repairs. The voyagers awake to find themselves on the idyllic planet of Thalassa. Curious yet wary, the Thalassans offer their distant cousins a cautious welcome and alien destinies become inextricably entwined in a clash of cultures unlike any before.

'A one-man literary Big Bang, Clarke has originated his own vast and teeming futurist universe'   *Sunday Times*

0 00 711586 5

Voyager Classics

Foundation

Isaac Asimov

Foundation is the first volume in Isaac Asimov's world-famous saga. Like Gibbon's *Decline and Fall* projected onto a galactic scale, the books tell the huge story of the decay of a civilization. The fear of a new Dark Age, of a descent into barbarism, finds its best expression in this epic story, one of the great classics of science fiction.

Earth is long forgotten. A peaceful and unified galaxy is governed from the majestic city planet of Trantor. But psychohistory, the brainchild of genius Hari Seldon, predicts a galaxy-wide disaster that will bring chaos and ruin to the empire. Only the Seldon Plan, a thousand-year strategy to minimize the worst of what is to come, offers any hope. Two Foundations are established at opposite ends of the galaxy. While one is charged with responding openly and creatively to the predictions of psychohistory, the other is kept secret, and copes with the unkown.

'One of the most staggering achievements in modern SF'

The Times

0 00 711587 3